PRAI

Unique and well done. I liked it! Looking forward to Book 2 of the Space Warfare Group and commend author Charles Hack on writing an unmatched series that is sure to take off in the action thriller genre.

— HENDRICKS BOOK REVIEWS

Into the Darkness is an adventurous and exquisite beginning of a new style of military thrillers with ingenious imagination, hardcore action, and healthy mistrust of the chain of command.

— KASHIF HUSSAIN, BEST THRILLER BOOKS

Charles Hack hits it out of the park. It's like a Bourne book in space....You can tell the man cares about his craft.

— T. E. BUTCHER, AUTHOR OF THE ARMORED WARRIOR PANZERTER BOOKS

Charles Hack's debut novel 'Into the Darkness' is an excellent blend of military action, political thriller, and far-future science fiction. Colorful world- and character-building blends seamlessly with visceral, gut-punching action...If you are a fan of action, thrillers, sci-fi, or all three, then you owe it to yourself to pick up 'Into the Darkness'.

— ZACH JAMES, AUTHOR OF THE MODERN MERCENARY THRILLERS

A compelling ride filled with spec-op fun from start to finish… exciting action sequence to kick things off, followed by some intriguing world-building to suck me entirely into this futuristic universe. The intrigue and desire to learn more only grew as the story dove deeper into its lore…It all culminated in a thrilling final act that left me glued to the pages.

— BRYAN WILSON, AUTHOR OF THE FORSAKEN PLANET

This is the first sci-fi book I've read in a long time and it doesn't disappoint. Charles Hack hits you with rib-crunching action from the start. This thriller in space had me hooked from the first landing, guiding me through the many worlds and species of aliens in this universe set way in the future.

— A.C. SALTER, AUTHOR OF GALLOWS BORN

The action in this book is on nearly every few pages! Characters are well developed and believable. Enjoyed not having a five page description of the technology being explained! Easy and very entertaining story to read and enjoy!

— AMAZON REVIEWER

This book was a great read! With a wide variety of characters, species, and planets, the story was creative and engaging. It starts off quickly and continues picking up speed, keeping you eager to find out what happens next. Lots of action and political intrigue, with plenty of content to be developed further in the series. Can't wait to see what happens in the next book!

— AMAZON REVIEWER

INTO THE DARKNESS

A SPACE WARFARE GROUP BOOK 1

CHARLES HACK

ALSO BY CHARLES HACK

<u>The Space Warfare Group Books</u>

Mission Brief Book 1: The Call Back

Mission Brief Book 2: The Break In

Mission Brief Book 3: The Rendezvous

Mission Brief Book 4: The Engineers (Coming Soon)

Book 0.5: Night Terror

Book 1: Into the Darkness

Book 2: Shrouded in Darkness

Book 3: Coming Soon!

<u>The Hank Lin Mysteries</u>

Book 1: Deceitful Above All Things

Book 2: Coming Soon!

This is a work of fiction. Names, characters, organizations, places, events, and incidents are either products of the author's imagination or are used fictitiously. Any resemblance to actual persons, living or dead, or actual events is purely coincidental.

Cover Designed by: **OneGraphica** (www.onegraphica.com)

Published by **Coram Deo Books**
First Edition November 1, 2022
Revised Second Edition with new cover October 5, 2024

Paperback ISBN: 979-8833358498
Hardcover ISBN: 979-8833359792

INTO THE DARKNESS

A SPACE WARFARE GROUP BOOK 1

CHARLES HACK

For Maria

PREFACE

To the Second Edition 2024

Thank you for giving the Space Warfare Group a chance. I self-published ***Into the Darkness*** in July of 2022, as my first published book, and it needed more work. The book is the official Second Edition, rereleased in October, 2024. I didn't revise any story elements, but improved the grammar, spelling, descriptions, and removed repetition. My hope is that the book flows better and has less distractions. I want to give a special thank you to my new editor, Amber Straw, for her priceless assistance in making this book better.

I also had the opportunity to work with cover designer Onur of OneGraphica, who created new covers for the whole series. I hope you love them! Great work, Onur!

Charles Hack
October 3, 2024
Nevada

NOTE TO THE READER

From the First Edition, 2022

Thank you for giving my book a try. This book is a *Space Military Thriller*. The world you will read about in *Into the Darkness* doesn't fit comfortably into any one category. While this series is science fiction, it's heavy on the fiction and light on the science. In fact, it's as much fantasy as it is science fiction, similar to Star Wars and Star Trek. As one who grew up in the 1980s, it is impossible to avoid the deep-rooted influences of both iconic franchises. So, I'm calling this a *Space* novel, rather than traditional *Sci-fi*.

I also added the term *Military* to the description, because the story follows a team of far future tier-one operators, known as the *Space Warfare Group*. They are an amalgamation of many military influences, including the Navy SEALs and Delta Force, but entirely fictional.

Finally, this series is intended to be a *Thriller* in the traditional sense. I began reading Clive Cussler in my early teens, which quickly lead to Tom Clancy, Vince Flynn, Lee Child, and Nelson DeMille. These authors helped shape my understanding of thriller novels. More recently, I've been excited about the writing of Joel C. Rosenberg, Jack Carr, Mark Greaney, Don Bentley, Brian Andrews & Jeff Wilson, Brad Meltzer, and many others. I especially appreciate how they all weave intriguing conspiracies into their plots. I've always wanted to write a political thriller with military elements and never intended to write science fiction. In a way, this book happened by accident. But now, the characters are demanding their stories be told. So, here we are. As you crack the pages (or swipe the e-page) of this book, you enter a political conspiracy told from within a highly trained military unit. It also happens to be in space, far into the future.

I must thank a couple people: First, my wife for her years of support and help editing. Second, my daughter and son for helping create the primary aliens in this story. It brings me joy to write about the creatures they created. Finally, I want to thank Steven Day, Carol Colburn, Diane Gallian, and Sherry Bowers for their proof reading and Jacob Connell at Flipsider Productions for his awesome cover (original 2022 edition) and book trailer.

I hope you are entertained by this story and the characters. If you like it, a glowing five-star review on Amazon and Goodreads is always appreciated. Positive reviews help authors immensely.

There is a glossary at the back of the book for abbreviations and terms.

Now, on to the story!

Charles Hack
April 26, 2022
Nevada

PRINCIPAL CHARACTERS

SPACE WARFARE GROUP

Colonel Tate Miller (Officer-in-Charge of SWG)
Major Malcolm "Mac" Lambert (SWG Tactical leader)
Master Sergeant Sam Clarion
Sergeant Luis Sanchez
Sergeant Cory Allen
Master Sergeant Dan "DJ" Jameson

UNITED PLANETARY GOVERNMENT

President Carl Harrington
Prime Ambassador Harji Kumar
Aldo Sperry (Assistant to Kumar)
Corporal Kara Cooper (SWG comms specialist)
Lieutenant Louella Taylor (Interplanetary Navy Pilot)
Doctor Archibald Cornell (MedBay Doctor)
Sarina Clarion (Department of Alien Sciences)
Elite Guard Captain Tom Scott (UPG Executive Security)

OKUTAN PEOPLE

Princess Omo-Binrin Oba (Ambassador)
Jagoon Ina (Head of the Royal Guard)

BONE RATTLERS

General Sckrahhg
Chief Braeknn
Lieutenant Manstruu

PART ONE

The universe may seem benevolent. But don't be fooled. The second you let your guard down, it will eat you alive.

— CARODINE ZELEZNIK, FORMER PRESIDENT OF THE UNITED PLANETARY GOVERNMENT

CHAPTER ONE

Uninhabited Planet Tx17-k221

The Starhawk assault craft exploded through the low-hanging ice clouds, and the violent vibration ending abruptly as it entered clean air. A dull orange glow slipped through the narrow windows of the passenger cabin.

Major Malcom Lambert, strapped into the jump seat at the back of the passenger cabin, stretched his neck to look out the small window. The surface below zipped by in a blur. He recognized the orange, mountainous surface. It looked exactly as the surveillance drone video presented during the mission brief.

In front of Mac, in the dimly lit cabin, were five other Space Warfare Group operators strapped into their seats. The spacecraft was developed for the Interplanetary Army to transport up to 16 of the elite Space Warfare Group and their equipment into battle.

"Objective in sight. Ninety seconds to insertion," the pilot's voice crackled over the radio.

"Gentleman, ninety seconds. Prepare for insertion," Mac ordered his team.

Mac's fireteam for this mission included Sergeant Luis Sanchez,

Sergeant Cory Allen, Sergeant Josiah Maldonado, Sergeant Jerry Tao, and Mac's right-hand man, Master Sergeant Sam Clarion.

Mac pressed the button on the side of his helmet and the clear face shield slid down. The technology-infused helmet provided lightweight head protection, with full face shield doubling as a heads-up display. He unbuckled his harness and pulled his muscular body from the uncomfortable seat. He was relieved to stand. His forty-year-old body stiffened up much quicker these days than in his younger years.

Major Malcolm Lambert, known as *Black Team Leader* by operational command, was *Mac* to those close to him. Serving as the Interplanetary Army's tactical leader of the Space Warfare Group, he'd earned the trust and respect of Army leadership long ago. But more importantly, the operators in his charge trusted him with their lives.

As an actual Earth-born citizen, Mac was a novelty in the United Planetary Government (UPG), which now included Earth and nine other inhabited planets in varying stages of development. Someone born on Earth was quite rare. He was a big man, muscular like an elite athlete, and taller than the rest of his team. He was black, with dark brown eyes and skin the color of mahogany. His black hair and beard were both trimmed short and salted with premature gray. Some said it made him look distinguished. He thought it made him seem old, especially surrounded by men at least ten years his junior.

The others pulled themselves from their cramped seats and took up their positions to exit through the Starhawk's rear hatch. They all wore the same charcoal gray, environmentally-controlled tactical suits, known as *E-Gear*.

Mac felt the pilot slow the Starhawk and then bank to the left. He reached out and grabbed the closest seat as he lost his balance. The others did the same after bouncing against each other. He moved around the seat to peer out the window again. He could see straight down to the orange surface as the craft was making its banking turn. The objective, which was the Kraize's new communication relay station, was visible below them. Two tall antenna towers stood on a small plateau, surrounded by three equipment buildings. The Kraize species, who were hostile to the UPG and Galactic Coalition, were continually attacking the outer edges of the UPG's borders. This newly discovered relay station was a strategic target for gathering precious intel and slowing the Kraize aggressions.

The mountaintop facility looked exactly like he expected from the drone video. What he didn't expect was the steady stream of energy blasts directed at the Starhawk from the surface.

"Enemy fire!" the pilot yelled into the radio. "Taking evasive action!"

Mac and the others latched on to the closest seats and handholds as the Starhawk jerked hard and banked in the other direction. They all strained to hold on as the vessel nearly turned on its side.

"Black Leader, you're gonna have to make a hot jump," the pilot said.

"Roger," Mac said as he wrestled the g-forces.

The insertion plan was for the Starhawk to touch down, allowing the operators to step out onto the mountainside. The Starhawk would then fly a safe distance away for the short duration of the mission.

As usual, no mission plan survived contact with the enemy.

"Mac, I thought the Fish Heads didn't have security at this location. It was supposed to be an uninhabited site," Sam Clarion said, using the derogatory name for the Kraize that described their oversized catfish-like heads and mouths full of sharp teeth.

"Lead, you know military intelligence is still a long way from being dependable," Mac said.

"You'd think after centuries of practice, we'd have some improvement," Sam quipped.

The pilot steered the Starhawk in a wide sweeping circle and then leveled out near the surface of the valley below the communication relay station, which sat at the top of the rocky mountain peak. Leveling out made it easier for them to stand in the cabin. The rear exit opened, and a blast of swirling air and dust rushed in. A group of three lights mounted above the opening door flashed red.

"Listen up, Black Team, we're dropping into immediate engagement," Mac instructed his men through their team radio. "Spread out and take cover. We will assess the situation on the ground and make our move to that station."

The pilot's voice came over the radio again. "Black Leader, you are dropping onto the south side of the station, a couple hundred yards down the mountain. Twenty seconds."

"Major Mac," Sanchez's voice came over the radio speaker in Mac's helmet, "Isn't the south side the steep side of this mountain?"

"Affirmative."

"OK, Major Mac. I was just checking."

Mac recognized the sarcasm in Sanchez's voice, but before he could respond in kind, the lights changed from red to flashing yellow and the Starhawk decelerated. They stood in a single-file line, holding the handrails in the ceiling, facing the exit with Mac in the front. He shifted his feet and prepared himself by leaning back against the force. With the door open, he could see the orange surface racing by at the end of the Starhawk's exit ramp.

Suddenly, the ship tipped up and began ascending, and the lights turned green. Without hesitation, Mac launched his body forward toward the exit ramp. The Starhawk's momentum shift helped him as he sprinted several steps and leapt off the ramp, which was a couple of meters above the sloped mountain surface. He sailed farther than he'd ever experienced before, partly because of the downward slope of the mountain and partly because of the planet's weak gravitation force.

Mac landed awkwardly on his heels and then slid some distance before falling to his back on the orange mountainside. His body hit the ground hard, jarring his head and smacking his teeth together. He slid down the orange hillside in what he now realized was thick, slippery mud.

He tried to slow his descent with his heels and palms of his hands and gained a foothold near a pillar of porous orange rock. He scrambled over to the pillar, sliding on his left side, and scooting through the mud. The wide rock pillar tapered as it reached several meters toward the sky.

Up the hill, Mac saw the red energy bursts from enemy rifles being fired at the Starhawk as it ascended into the atmosphere. From his angle on the mountainside, he couldn't see the Kraize. But that also meant they didn't have a good line of fire. The huge antenna tower reached high above the plateau into the cloud filled sky.

Mac didn't let the bad intel fluster him. While this mission was supposed to be in-and-out with no combat, he'd learned to always expect the unexpected when his team received a mission assignment. He compartmentalized the intel failure to avoid an unnecessary distraction.

"Work the problem, Mac. Work the problem," he whispered to himself while calculating how they would get up the mountainside. They had to neutralize the Kraize soldiers as quickly as possible, so they could collect the coordinates of the other Kraize sites and then destroy the facility.

Sam Clarion scooted through the mud and into position next to Mac, with his rifle in his hands. Orange mud covered the left side of his charcoal gray E-Gear.

"That was interesting," Sam said, breathing heavily as he pressed in close to Mac.

They both lay flat in the mud on their chest, with the rifles pointed toward the tower. The mud-splattered group of Jerry Tao, Josiah Maldonado, and Cory Allen took cover behind a cluster of short rock pillars twenty meters above. Cory and Jo, lying on their stomachs, pulled their EP-17 energy rifles from the magnetic hold on their backs and aimed up the hill.

"Black Team, report? Any injuries?" Mac asked through the radio.

"Fine."

"We're good."

Mac looked around but couldn't see Luis Sanchez. "Black-3, report?"

No answer.

"Anyone have eyes on Black-3?" Mac asked.

Sam bumped Mac with his elbow and pointed over his shoulder

with his thumb. Mac turned to look downhill. Sanchez was fifty meters farther down, hanging onto the trunk of a sickly tree in a thin line of sickly trees growing down the mountainside. The rest of the landscape was barren and rocky, and everything was the same dull orange color.

The Kraize security force above them stopped firing at the Starhawk and started firing at them. Deadly energy blasts smashed into the surrounding mud.

"Sanchez, you alright?" Mac asked.

"Major Mac, I had a bit of a problematic landing. I think I broke my butt."

There was a muted snicker on the radio.

After a moment, Sam's voice came over the radio. "Jerry," he said to their medic, "please examine Sanchez's injury."

"Hard pass, bro," Jerry replied flatly. "He's on his own with that one."

"Don't worry, everyone," Sanchez added. "I'll get it figured out. Nobody told me I'd be falling out of a spaceship onto a peanut butter planet today."

"Get back up this hill right now," Mac ordered. "We've gotta storm this hill to get to that station. Wait for cover fire." Mac switched to the other radio channel to speak with the Starhawk pilot, making another wide, sweeping turn in the sky above. The ship's dark gray matte finish made it nearly invisible against the matching sky.

"Starhawk 01, this is Black Leader. We need cover fire right now to get up this hill," Mac said to the pilot, while energy blasts continued to smash into their surroundings with an increasing frequency.

"Roger, Black Leader. Circling back."

Mac watched the spacecraft finish its wide banking turn and dive into the valley, then pick up speed in their direction. The Starhawk shot like a bullet along the valley floor below them.

Mac glanced at Sanchez, who was dragging himself uphill

through the mud, from tree to tree. He tried to stand, but his feet slid out from under him every time.

The Starhawk reached them seconds later and unleashed a barrage of energy blasts on the Kraize's location. The Kraize concentrated their fire back on the Starhawk.

Mac and the others slogged up the hill as quickly as possible. The orange mud worked against their assault, but they made it to the next rock pillar and stopped to fire toward the station until the Starhawk could circle around and make another pass.

"Mac, we should have brought Dozer and the *Dragon*," Sam said over the radio, speaking of Owen *Dozer* Black, the Space Warfare Group's heavy gunner who carried the two-handed energy canon. "He'd level the playing field in a red hot second."

"Agreed, Black-2. Unfortunate oversight. Shall we wait here for a couple hours while he gets shuttled over?" Mac asked.

"I think we're good without him," Sam said.

In two separate groups, they scraped and scrambled their way through the mud until they could duck behind a line of boulders along the edge of the plateau. The Starhawk, and the men on the ground, repeated the shoot-and-run maneuver a third time. Mac and his men jumped over the rock wall and made it onto the small plateau.

Dark humanoid forms darted behind the equipment buildings, taking cover, as the Space Warfare Group closed in.

CHAPTER TWO

Sergeant Jo Maldonado was the first man over the rock wall onto the plateau, moving toward the relay station. The others followed him in, stepping deliberately, while each of them looked through their rifle's sight window.

"I see at least four Fish Heads taking cover behind the second building," Jo said.

"Cory and Jerry, take the left side. Sam and I will take the right. Jo, get those explosives prepped. We've gotta neutralize this defense force and access the buildings for intel before they destroy it," Mac said. "Move fast."

The elite soldiers looked ridiculous, covered in mud. Cory's face mask was covered in mud, except for the smeared area he cleared away so he could see. Mac grabbed Cory's arm before he moved off and used his own glove to clear more mud away for better visibility. Mac slapped the back of Cory's helmet before he followed Jerry to the left.

Sam followed Mac to the corner of the first small building, which was some sort of prefabricated composite structure, full of alien electronic equipment created by the Kraize. They needed to gather data on all this equipment, which would help them in this war against the Kraize.

"Black-4," Mac said, speaking to Jo Maldonado, "get those charges set on the buildings and towers as soon as possible."

"Roger. Working on it."

"Get that done and we'll clear the hostiles."

Each member of the team carried a rigid backpack containing explosive charges. They set them on the ground near where Maldonado squatted down, preparing his own explosive charge bag. Maldonado worked on securing the charge bag to the side of the first building while Mac gave the hand signal for the others to move around the side of the building.

The Kraize poked their heads and rifles around the building in front of them and fired. Mac and Sam fired back, and they could hear Cory and Jerry firing as well. Mac scooted along the side of the small building and waited at the corner. He heard three fast energy eruptions slam into the corner of the building next to him. When the firing stopped, Mac rolled around the corner and saw two Kraize soldiers kneeling by the wall. He pumped two energy blasts into each, and they fell over dead. Sam moved to Mac's left, firing at two more Kraize soldiers farther away, dropping both.

Mac paused and rolled one of the dead Kraize over onto its back. It wore a black rubber-like space suit over its muscular body. Mac had seen many Kraize over the last couple of years. They were physically built like humans, but with short, muscular limbs. This one also wore a large space helmet covering its massive pyramid-shaped head. He could see the ugly fishlike face through the glass face shield. It had a wide mouth with fat, fleshy lips and sharp teeth. Floppy whiskers poked out of its lips like a catfish.

Maldonado rushed over to Mac's location between the buildings and squatted down to prepare charges for the second building. The sounds of energy fire nearby began again as Cory and Jerry advanced toward the tower.

"We've got three more Fish Heads by the tower," Cory said.

"I'll provide cover fire," Sanchez said. Mac looked around and spotted a mud-splattered Sanchez kneeling by the line of anemic trees at the opposite edge of the plateau, firing his rifle. He was relieved to see Sanchez back with the group. Mac gave the area between the small buildings one last scan, then gave Sam the signal to move on. Mac followed Sam around to the right side of the second building, heading toward the tower structures.

As Mac was turning the corner of the second building, Sanchez shouted into the radio, "Jo, behind you!"

Sanchez was firing frantically from his position by the trees, toward the space between the buildings.

Chaos erupted. Energy bursts zipped in all directions. Mac and Sam turned back toward the space between the buildings, rifles up and at the ready. As Mac covered the short distance, he saw five Kraize soldiers coming out of a door of the first building into the space behind Jo Maldonado. One fired at Sanchez, two fired at Maldonado, who was defenseless as he squatted over the explosives by the building.

Jo tried to roll to his side and pull his rifle out, but it was too late. The Kraize fired three rapid shots into Jo's chest. Mac saw it all in slow motion. Each explosive burst of red energy with its ragged tail, like a tiny comet of death, soared across the small distance between the buildings and crashed into Jo's chest as he was trying to get his own rifle into firing position. Jo slammed against the wall of the building and crumpled to the ground. Mac watched in horror as Jo didn't move.

"No!" Mac shouted in fury, and fired as fast as his rifle would allow. He and Sam killed two Kraize at the doorway, but another exited the door and stepped over his dead comrades.

This newest Kraize soldier was the biggest Mac had ever seen. He was massive and carried a huge shoulder-mounted bazooka. The weapon was three times bigger than the typical Kraize rifle. Mac and Sam ran as the enemy turned the monstrous weapon toward them. The Kraize fired the bazooka, belching a huge flaming ball toward them. Mac tried to jump out of the way, but the energy blast hit the ground next to him. The concussive force shoved Mac several meters into the air.

The slow-motion movie reel continued as Mac flew in the air and saw the ground pass below him. He flew over the edge of the plateau and down the mountainside, where he crashed against the hillside. As his body hit the ground, the momentum caused him to roll farther down in the slippery mud until he crashed into a pile of scrap metal and garbage.

The landing knocked the air out of his chest. His head swam from the rolling. He shook his head and tried to sit up, but a sharp pain in his lower leg dropped him again.

A moment later, as his mind and vision cleared and the ringing in his ears subsided, all the noises of the combat came back into focus. He could hear the distinctive sounds of his team's frenzied rifle fire on the plateau above. He also detected Sam and Sanchez shouting over the sounds of gunfire.

Mac finally managed to sit up and check his leg. The shredded pant leg of his environmental suit revealed a sharp chunk of shrapnel sticking out of his leg above his ankle. The rip wasn't ideal in this low oxygen and low temperature atmosphere, but he would be fine. He pinched the shrapnel shard between his fingers, took a breath, and yanked hard. He clenched his teeth and groaned in pain as the shard came free. Blood oozed from the wound.

Mac rolled over onto his knees and crawled out of the junk pile and back up the slippery hillside. He stayed low, only poking his head and rifle over the plateau wall. From that position, he took out three of the remaining Kraize combatants without being seen. Across the plateau, Sam and Sanchez ran along the building, then turned toward the tower, out of sight, but he could hear them engage more enemy combatants.

"Black Leader, you copy?"

It was Sam's voice.

"Mac, you copy?"

Mac's head was still spinning and his ears still ringing even though the energy rifle fire finally stopped.

"Anyone have eyes on Black Leader?" Sam asked.

"Sam, I'm here. The explosion threw me off the mountainside," Mac said. His voice sounded weak and scratchy.

"We've neutralized the Kraize threat. But, Jo's down and Jerry just took a hit. He looks OK, though. I think he'll be fine."

Mac crawled the rest of the way onto the plateau, over the short rock wall. The corner of the building, where Mac stood when the Kraize fired the bazooka, was mangled. He stood and tried to jog towards where Jo lay a few meters away, next to the small building. After two steps unbearable pain shot up his leg. He limped the distance and fell to his knees next to Jo. He rolled Jo over onto his back, and Mac knew that he was dead. Overwhelmed by the mixture of anger and sadness, Mac punched the muddy ground three times.

Shoulda cleared that building, he scolded himself.

Sam rushed around the corner, rifle pointed toward the ground, signaling that the battle was over.

"Mac, are you alright?" Sam helped Mac to stand. Then he saw Jo's body, and he hung his head.

"We shoulda cleared that building first." Mac was furious with himself.

Sam pointed to Mac's bloody leg. "Mac, that's not good. We need to get your leg fixed up right away."

Mac looked down at his leg again and could see the bloody gash. It hurt like crazy. Blood was still oozing onto his mud-covered boots. "I'm fine. Forget about my leg, Sam."

Sanchez and Cory approached, supporting Jerry between them, helping him walk. They lowered Jerry to the ground, where he could lean against the building near Jo's fallen body.

The men were all silent for a moment as Jo's death loomed heavy.

"Major Mac, you OK?" Sanchez asked quietly, looking at Mac's leg. "That leg looks bad."

"I'm fine. Don't worry about me."

No one said anything else for several moments. Nothing could be said.

Mac said, "Cory, get the rest of these charges placed double-time. Sanchez, get into these buildings and find the relay station coordinates. Download all of it. While you are at it, get photos and scan the equipment. Grab any small equipment you can carry. Cory, once you are done, help Sanchez finish up. Sam, stabilize Jerry and get him ready to move."

Mac then limped to the small clearing in front of the buildings and gazed out into the barren valley below. He radioed the Starhawk.

"Starhawk 01, this is Black Leader."

"Go ahead, Black Leader."

"We are ready for EXFIL."

"Roger, en route."

After a couple of minutes, Sam joined Mac in the clearing. "Jerry is going to be fine. I gave him some pain blockers. Are you sure you shouldn't sit down? Maybe let me look at that leg?"

"I'm fine." Through the radio, Mac asked, "Sanchez, you find the coordinates?"

"Yessir, just finished downloading."

"Cory, make sure those charges will do the job. I don't want to come back to this hellhole."

"Roger that," Cory said.

The Starhawk flew by above them, then circled around and made a hover landing in the clearing. The rear ramp lowered, and Mac limped over to where Jo lay on the ground. Sanchez tossed Mac a small memory drive and started loading a few small devices taken from the buildings onto the Starhawk. Cory helped Jerry get to the ship. Mac lifted Jo onto his shoulders in a fireman's carry.

"Mac," Sam said, grabbing his shoulder, "come on, man, let me do that."

"I've got him."

"Ok," Sam said. Mac heard the sympathy in Sam's voice, but it gnawed at him. Tears stung his eyes, but he blinked them away.

Sam walked next to Mac as he limped to the ship and up the ramp where Sam helped steady Mac. The Starhawk engines whined and made the entire ship vibrate.

In the dim passenger compartment, Cory was securing Jerry into his jump seat and Sanchez was placing equipment in the cargo holds near the rear door. Mac took Jo's body to the small medical area near the cockpit and laid Jo on the gurney, setting the straps over his body for the rough flight. He looked at Jo, feeling the familiar sting of loss mixed with the foul odor of failure. So many questions raced through his mind.

Mac removed Jo's helmet and set it aside. "I'm sorry, Jo." Mac murmured. He felt a tear roll down his cheek. "I should have protected you. I should have been more prepared. Planned better," his voice trailed off. Continuing to look at Jo, he thought to himself, *Was it bad intel? No, fool, you can't blame anyone but yourself.* Mac always blamed himself when one of his men died, regardless of the circumstances.

He felt a hand on his shoulder and turned. It was Sam without his helmet, which had left his wavy blond hair disheveled. Sam's handsome face displayed a look of understanding and sympathy.

"Mac, come sit. We need to leave."

"Yeah, yeah, alright," Mac said in a low voice. He turned and followed Sam into the passenger compartment again. The others sat strapped into their jump seats, and the rear door closed.

"Starhawk 01, this is Black-2, we are ready for takeoff," Sam radioed as they got seated.

The Starhawk lifted vertically, turned in a flat circle, then accelerated toward the clouds.

Mac, looking out the side window, said, "Cory, blow it." Cory activated the charge detonators, and Mac watched the large fiery explosions collapse the towers and send them tumbling down the hillside as they entered the clouds.

CHAPTER THREE

Open Space Near the Regulated Zone

He sat uneasily in the oversized captain's chair, shrouded in shadows. He was having doubts of his own now. It was taking too long. His legendary anger was simmering just below the surface. A deep-throated growl emanated from his throat, lasting several seconds. He felt the urge to let his anger loose and thrash everything within reach.

The cramped control room of the spacecraft known to the crew as the *Auger* was dim and dingy. His captain's chair sat in the center of the small room where he could observe everything. The only light in the room came from the glow of the green piloting station status lights and rudimentary display screen.

He lost track of how long they'd been floating motionless in the vast open nothingness of space near the Regulated Zone border. The temperature in the ship was dropping steadily, and while he and his people reveled in the icy atmosphere, the chill was getting to him. Frost formed on the metal surfaces.

They named the *Auger*, after its appearance and purpose—built with a cylinder-shaped fuselage, with a long pointed front section ending with a gruesome auger bit. The spacecraft was quite narrow for a space flying vessel, but what it lacked in width, it made up by increasing the length. Its sole purpose was to crash into larger spacecraft and chew through the outer hull with the auger bit. It would create an access hole, allowing the *Auger's* crew to board the larger spacecraft.

This was taking too long. He stood and began pacing the cramped space. As he stood, his second-in-command, Manstruu, entered the control room.

"Manstruu, what is the status on fuel?" His voice was deep, sounding like a vicious animal. Their language was comprised of harsh words, snarls, and grunts.

"Chief Braeknn, the window of time is closing. We have a few hours at best."

Manstruu, like Chief Braeknn himself, was massive. He was tall and wide, filling the shadowy doorway. Like Braeknn, a dense and wiry golden fur covered Manstruu's body. Their face, devoid of the golden fur, were bare, leathery skin. There was no nose on their faces, only small nostril holes above thin lips that didn't full cover their sharp fangs. Above their piercing eyes were heavy, downturned brows. Long golden hair and heavy beards framed their bare face. Some decorated their beards and hair with braids and strung with beads and bones.

Braeknn snarled in disappointment, exposing his overlapping upper and lower fangs.

Atop Manstruu's golden fur, he wore only tall leather boots and thick leather pants. Hanging from his torso was a loose armor made from the bones of his victims. The bones were first dried and bleached by sunlight. Then they drilled small holes in the ends to thread leather straps through, forming the bone armor. The armor served no protective function, but was for demonstrating their battle prowess and intimidating enemies. Manstruu's beard had several thick braids with red wooden beads.

Manstruu's armor did not feature as many bones as Braeknn's own bone armor. No one on the *Auger* had as many bones in their armor as Braeknn, which is why he was the Chief. In fact, they all knew Braeknn's bone collection included some of his own kinsman who made the mistake of crossing him. He was the master warrior of the group and, therefore, their commander.

The bone armor usually included a helmet and face guard, made from the skull of larger beasts they'd killed, but they did not wear the skull helmets on the ship.

"We have been waiting too long," Braeknn growled. "Something is wrong."

"Should we contact our informant?" Manstruu asked.

"No. We can't contact him again. That was part of the deal."

"Could it be a trap?"

"No. He needs us to complete our mission." Braeknn paused for a moment, thinking through the situation. "It would be a grave mistake for him to double cross us," Braeknn said. "No one double crosses me." Braeknn said through clenched fangs.

"We must trust the intel, Chief Braeknn. They will be here. And, well, they better get here in the next hour, otherwise -"

Before Manstruu finished his statement, Braeknn took two heavy stomping steps and grabbed Manstruu by the neck with one of his powerful hands. As Braeknn moved, the bones in his armor swung and rattled menacingly. The claws on Braeknn's hand dug into Manstruu's neck. He had the strength to crush his windpipe and spine with one hand.

"Do not tell me what needs to happen!" Braeknn howled in Manstruu's face. He considered squeezing the life out of his lieutenant just to satisfy his anger, but decided against it. For now. Manstruu was still useful.

A dull beeping tone pulled Braeknn's attention to a flashing light on the control board, but he did not release his vice grip on Manstruu's neck.

The pilot turned toward Braeknn. "Chief Braeknn, they are here."

Braeknn turned back to Manstruu. "Prepare the boarding party. We will make contact immediately." He shoved Manstruu through the door, causing him to fall to his knees. Manstruu stood up straight, gasping for breath, and did as commanded. He knew better that to tempt the chief further, which is why Manstruu was still alive.

Braeknn stomped over to his observation chair, bones rattling as he moved, and sat down. "Pilot, burn the engines at full power and fire on that ship!"

CHAPTER FOUR

Open Space Near the Regulated Zone
Aboard the Okuta Royal Vessel

Omo-Binrin Oba dropped four ripe oota berries into her floral tea and watched them slowly sink to the bottom of the tall glass teacup. The aroma of bubbling berries wafted toward her. Omo-Binrin closed her eyes, breathed deeply, and smiled. She enjoyed the ritual of steeping her tea as much as she enjoyed consuming it. A male voice interrupted her pleasant ritual.

"Princess, I am going to stretch my stiff legs a bit. Can I get you anything while I'm up?" She looked up from her teacup to see her head of security, Jagoon Ina.

Jagoon adjusted his maroon warrior's robe, snapping it into place and shifting the belt. The knee-length robe was fitted closely around his thin, muscular physique and secured around his waist by a wide black belt. His tall boots matched the belt.

"Jagoon, you are aware that I'll be just fine here for a few minutes without you," she said, knowing he hated leaving her unattended for any amount of time. "Go take a walk. Check on the crew. Or go do some hand-to-hand combat exercises."

Jagoon nodded in response. She watched as he snatched his black shoulder wrap from a nearby chair, swung it around his shoulders with a flourish and clasped it in place.

Princess Omo-Binrin Oba, who was the diplomatic face of the planet Okuta, felt safe inside her personal quarters on the Okutan Royal Spacecraft, especially since they were traveling at a *faster than light* speed through the Vita System.

Jagoon Ina, who was Okuta's most formidable warrior, always remained near the princess. But, even he felt he could risk leaving her for a few minutes while they traveled at such speeds.

Still, it was difficult to leave her. As he stood staring at her, with his black shoulder wrap in place, Omo-Binrin stared back, watching him ruminate on the decision for a moment. She could tell he was contemplating changing his mind.

She waved her thin hand dismissively. "Go, Jagoon, my attendants are here. I'll be fine," she said, speaking of the two female royal servants sitting across the room on a luxurious, cushioned couch. "Besides, I'm a big girl. I can take care of myself."

"Princess, I -"

"Go on, please. You are making me crazy," she said with a friendly smile. "Let me enjoy my tea."

"Of course, Your Highness. As you wish. I'll be back soon." He gave a curt nod.

She watched him leave, then turned her attention back to her teacup. The color of the berry-infused tea now looked perfect. She lifted the glass cup by the tiny silver handle and sniffed. It smelled wonderful. She took a quick sip of the hot liquid, and relished the rich flavor.

Princess Omo-Binrin Oba was a native of her home planet, Okuta. The Okutans were a biped humanoid species with advanced space travel capabilities and technology. Culturally and societally, they shared many similarities with humans. Physically, the Okutans also shared traits with the humans. Their body's skeletal and muscular structure was consistent with humans, only shorter and leaner. The similarities, however, ended with physique.

Her Okutan face was a narrow and elongated oval shape with widely spaced almond-shaped eyes. Her nose was small and flat above her upper lip. All Okutans were completely hairless, and yet featured a unique scalp-frill, which was a cape of skin running from their forehead, over the top of their head, and to the back of their neck. Their scalp-frill normally laid flat against their skull like a mohawk, but when excited or scared, they would flare out the frill on long spines of cartilage, creating a dramatic intimidating effect.

The princess' skin, including her scalp-frill, was the classic Okutan semi-transparent with a subtle blue hue. The semi-transparent blue skin tone, like hers, was the most common skin color, but some Okutans varied between the green and purple ends of the color spectrum. Her people considered her to be one of the most beautiful Okutans. She found this frustrating because she didn't like only being known for her family lineage and beauty. She had much more to offer.

Omo-Binrin took another quick sip of the hot tea and returned to studying the translated partnership proposal dossier from the United Planetary Government on a thin handheld electronic screen. The encrypted communication from UPG officials included the details of their upcoming meeting.

The UPG was the multi-planet human government she was traveling to meet with. The official reason for the meeting centered on a discussion of Okuta's need to expand beyond their home planet because of severe overpopulation. Okuta considered the UPG a useful partner, since they had colonized nine planets beyond their home planet, Earth. The Okutan overpopulation resulted from the long Okutan lifespan, commonly over 200 Earth years. Omo-Binrin was young and in her prime, physically and mentally, at the equivalent of 117 Earth years old. Jagoon was closing in on 150.

Okuta's reputation in the galaxy was one of wealth and opulence because of an excess of diamonds on the planet, which they used as a strategic asset within the Galactic Coalition trade economy. They used diamonds liberally, in fact, including decorating and accenting everything. Princess Omo-Binrin's gold and purple dress featured gorgeous diamond lace. She also wore a diamond-studded tiara band wrapping from her brow to the back of her head on both sides of her scalp-frill.

She set her tea on the table again, with a little annoyance over the humans' vague proposal. The UPG would unveil the true details of the arrangement at the partnership summit. But it frustrated her that the terms would be seen only after she expended a lot of political capital. She anticipated being disappointed with a UPG power and resource grab, including wanting a steady flow of diamonds to sweeten the deal. Everyone always did.

Omo-Binrin was Okuta's most effective diplomat and the eldest offspring of King Binroni Oba. Her brother had died in an accident many years ago, and her younger sister was more interested in the social aspects of royal duty than diplomacy. Her father sent her to negotiate with the humans because he trusted her political instincts. She just wished she understood more about the humans' motives and strategy before entering the summit discussions. They were hard to read, and she felt underprepared.

Okuta joining the Galactic Coalition as a partner to the UPG would be a significant event in galactic history. Many member nations of the Galactic Coalition were following the progress of the UPG and Okutan relationship with eager anticipation. Several of the Coalition members stood to benefit from a formally established UPG-Okutan colonial partnership. The political posturing was so obvious to her. She was having a hard time trusting anyone right now. She didn't even know how far she could trust the humans. But she was confident they would reach a mutually beneficial arrangement.

Deep down, she was consumed by an overwhelming sense of unease, knowing that her secret mission was of utmost importance. This mission within the mission motivated the royal family to speed up the partnership summit schedule and risk trusting the humans.

She carried information that the UPG's top leaders needed to hear. The Okutans recently discovered galactic intelligence suggesting an imminent threat of great magnitude, from a distant unknown alien race known to them only as the Noct. What they'd learned about the Noct had the potential to devastate many peaceful nations within the known galaxy. It required the highest level of secrecy and urgency.

Only a few people were aware of her secret mission, which included the King and Jagoon from her side, and the UPG's President Harrington on their side. She was eager to arrive and discuss the intelligence with her soon-to-be partners. They must develop a reaction strategy as soon as possible. There was no room for failure. She couldn't return home to the king without a plan in place. There was too much at stake.

She laid the electronic dossier on the table and noticed the dark liquid in her cup was vibrating, signaling to her they were coming out of *faster than light* speed. A moment later, she felt the slight change in pressure and gravitational force as the spaceship slowed exponentially. The artificial environment reduced the effects, but nothing could eliminate it.

Jagoon returned moments later, speaking as he entered her quarters.

"Princess Omo-Binrin, we are entering the Regulated Zone and have come out of *FTL*, as required by galactic law."

She stood and met Jagoon in the center of the spacious room. As tall as Jagoon, she was just as imposing. She stood with ramrod straight posture. Her body was lean and muscular under her extravagant dress. Her bearing was not one of a pampered princess, but one of an athlete and warrior.

"Thank you, Jagoon. Please have a message sent to the United Planetary Government's President Harrington. Inform him we have arrived at the edge of the Regulated Zone, and we can now begin putting the final touches on tomorrow's arrival ceremony. We will work on preparations here on the royal vessel as we make our way to Terra Libertas."

"Yes, of course. I will make sure we send the message right away. I'll begin planning for our arriv—"

Before Jagoon could finish his sentence, the spacecraft rocked from an aggressive impact. The princess' female attendants screamed as the impact reverberated through the ship with a loud crashing sound. It shook them with great force. One attendant fell to the floor. Jagoon stumbled but stopped himself from falling. He reached out to support Omo-Binrin, who also lost her balance.

The lighting went out and five seconds later, the backup auxiliary power kicked in, bathing the room in a dim amber light. Omo-Binrin rushed over to help her attendant on the floor.

Jagoon scanned the room and joined the princess. "Princess, are you ok?"

Omo-Binrin helped her attendant back to her feet. Jagoon reached down and helped. The attendant looked distressed by the unexpected impact. Her scalp-frill extended to full width.

"Here, sit and breathe. You'll be fine," Omo-Binrin told her. She nodded and sat down on the plush sofa.

"Princess?" Jagoon asked again. "Are you ok?"

Omo-Binrin looked at Jagoon, his scalp-frill extended as well. "Yes, Jagoon, I'm fine." She gripped his forearm. "Are we being attacked?"

"I do not know, but I'm going to find out. Maybe we struck an asteroid or another ship."

Omo-Binrin felt queasy. The secrets she carried would make her a target if someone with evil intentions found out. "Jagoon," she whispered. "It could be an attack."

Jagoon nodded in agreement. He then moved over to a wall panel and touched the screen several times. A video stream opened and an Okutan with light green skin appeared. Omo-Binrin joined Jagoon in front of the screen.

"Commander Oluso, what just happened?"

The commander looked frightened. "Our information is limited at this time. We are doing everything we can to figure it out."

"Commander, did we crash into another vessel or asteroid?" Omo-Binrin asked.

"It doesn't look like it, Princess. I think a ship fired torpedoes at us."

"Fired upon?" she asked with a stern expression. "Are you sure?" Jagoon and Omo-Binrin exchanged a concerned look.

"No, Your Highness, I am not sure. It is possible something crashed into us. We saw nothing on our scanners before we were hit. We are trying to get the scanners back up and determine the cause as quickly as possible."

Behind the commander, a voice came through the video stream, "Commander, I've got something—"

Before he finished his statement, another more aggressive impact hit the ship and the screen went dark. They stumbled and fought to keep their balance. The lights flickered again, and the attendants screamed.

Jagoon was pressed several buttons and shouted into the wall panel, "Commander! Commander!" He looked at Omo-Binrin with grave concern on his face. "I can't reconnect."

"Get up to the control room and find out what is happening. I'll be fine here."

"I disagree, Princess, I need to stay—"

"No, that's an order. Get to the control room and determine what is happening."

"I'll send Akoni in to stay with you until I return."

"That will be fine. Hurry. Report back as soon as you have information." She touched his arm and whispered again. "We cannot—"

"I know, Princess. I know."

Jagoon turned and sprinted from the princess' private quarters.

CHAPTER FIVE

"Direct hit, Chief Braeknn. We knocked out primary power," the *Auger's* pilot said with a deep-throated growl. He turned triumphantly towards Braeknn who was sitting behind him. Braeknn was leaning forward, a furry elbow planted on his knee and a clawed fist under his bearded chin, watching the monitors. "It seems the information we received was accurate."

"Yes," Braeknn snarled. "So far, they've been true to their word. Now, prepare to ram the ship!" Braeknn commanded. "We must act now and catch them by surprise. We cannot give them time to prepare defenses."

Manstruu re-entered the control room. He now carried a bulky black laser rifle and was wearing his bone helmet and face mask. For a helmet, he used the skull of a sharp toothed reptilian creature he had killed. "The warriors are ready, Chief Braeknn," he announced through his skull mask. Manstruu spoke in measured tones now, knowing that he might not survive the next encounter with his superior's temper.

"Good. We will board the ship momentarily."

The pilot brought the *Auger* back to life and, after a few tense moments, increased the throttle. The small drill-like ship raced through open space as the large ship filled the pilot's view screen.

"Prepare for impact," the pilot barked into the ship wide intercom. Red lights began flashing throughout the ship, signaling to all passengers that impact was imminent.

Chief Braeknn watched the monitors with great delight as the ship filled the screen, then kept zooming in closer and closer until they crashed hard into a flat area on the top of the larger ship at a forty-five-degree angle. The *Auger*'s huge metal-eating bit mounted to its nose was the first thing to impact the outer wall of the ship.

The impact rocked the entire crew, knocking them into each other, but it disorient the Bone Rattlers. They howled and stomped there feet with increased intensity and hunger for the attack.

Braeknn, clinging to the side of his chair, recovered quickly. He pulled his huge frame back into a sitting position and saw the pilot scrambling to pull himself back into his control seat.

The pilot activated the latching mechanism by pulling a lever on the right side of his control console. The lights flickered as the power transferred.

"Are we latched on?" Braeknn asked the pilot.

This part of the procedure was essential for their success. The *Auger* must latch onto the ship so they could lower the shroud that would seal off the vacuum of space. If the shroud seal didn't engage properly, the vacuum of space would suck everything it could through the hole and make boarding the ship impossible.

"We are secure," the pilot growled. "Lowering shroud." He pulled down a second lever on his control console. Several long seconds passed while the shroud lowered down around the bit and impact zone to seal off the area. After the whirring of the shroud motors, there was a heavy thump, followed by the sound of air being evacuated from the drill site. A bank of sensor lights below the main monitor - which was displaying the front of the *Auger* latched onto the outer hull of the larger ship - all turned green.

"The shroud is in place, and we've set the seal."

"Cut the hole!" Braeknn snarled. He stood from his seat.

The pilot pounded the large round button on the control console next to the levers with his massive furry fist to activate the bit. The drill bit lowered, and the terrible screeching and grinding of metal scraping upon metal began as the bit chewed into the outer hull of the larger ship, causing strong vibrations.

Braeknn turned and left the control room, Manstruu close behind. With nothing to discuss, they strode purposefully down the corridor to the ladder leading to the entry port level. Braeknn climbed down first and dropped to the metal floor in the corridor below, skipping the last few rungs.

The cramped corridor led them to the entry port, which was a long narrow room with a thick, round metal door at the far end. When opened, they would have access to the entry tube contained within the giant drill bit. The ship continued to vibrate as the bit chewed through the hull material. The grinding and screeching sounds were even louder at the entry port, but Braeknn loved the sound.

Ten Bone Rattler warriors stood in a line with rifles in their hands and their skull masks pulled down over their faces. They were ready for battle. Braeknn growled with satisfaction. Everything was going as planned.

All of the sudden, the glorious screeching and vibrating from the drilling stopped. Manstruu handed Braeknn a smaller lightweight rifle, which he slung over his shoulder with the strap. Manstruu then handed Braeknn his own skull helmet, which he lifted and placed over his head. Braeknn's skull helmet featured eye sockets he could look through when he wore it. The skull helmet was unique among Bone Rattlers because of the two wide antlers fanning out on both sides. The antlers made Braeknn recognizable to his subordinates.

"Now, Manstruu."

Manstruu nodded and stomped past the warriors standing at attention to the access door. He pulled a lever sideways and pounded on a glowing red button beside the door, and the mechanical door opened, revealing the narrow round tube. Light shone up through the end of the tube below him from the hole in the other ship.

Manstruu was the first to enter. Braeknn watched as he squatted down to shuffle through the tube. At the end of the tube, Manstruu stood above the hole in the larger ship below. A breeze flowed between the ships, rustling Manstruu's fur and bone armor. He released a rope ladder mounted on the edge of the tube that extended down into the hole by cranking on a manual hand winch. Manstruu disappeared down the ladder, supporting himself with one hand while aiming his rifle down into the ship with the other.

Braeknn heard Manstruu land with the sounds of breaking objects, screaming, and rifle fire. Braeknn gave the signal and sent three others in before following himself.

He squeezed through the entry tube and down the ladder, into the dim room below the access hole. The room was spacious, with tall ceilings. He had to drop from the bottom rung which ended several meters above the floor. He landed on a broken table that was crushed under the weight of the Bone Rattlers dropping before him. Chaos filled the room. Small creatures with light blue skin screamed and ran in all directions. They knocked over the tables and chairs as they tried to make their escape.

Manstruu and the other Bone Rattlers fired their laser rifles, killing several of the fleeing creatures, while others escaped out the doors across the room.

Braeknn took in the scene. This is where they wanted to be. They were in the correct room. "Manstruu, that door there," he snarled, pointing across the room to a single door. "Find me the princess."

CHAPTER SIX

Jagoon ran through the princess' private quarters and into the anteroom. He nearly crashed into Akoni, who was entering the anteroom from the outer corridor. Akoni was an Okutan male, much taller than Jagoon, but wearing the same maroon warrior's robe and black wrap over his shoulders. He carried a silver Okutan energy rifle with a long skinny barrel.

"Akoni, do you know what is happening?"

"No, I do not. I think we are under attack. I ran here first to protect the princess."

"Good, I am glad you are here," Jagoon said breathlessly as he put his hand on Akoni's shoulder. "Please go stay with the princess while I go to the control room and try to gather some answers. Listen, if we are under attack, you must do everything possible to protect the princess. We must let no one get to her."

Akoni nodded, seriously, his scalp-frill fully extended. Jagoon slapped him on the shoulder and watched Akoni entered the princess' quarters. Then Jagoon ran the other direction into the corridor and sprinted its length to the elevator.

The elevator moved slower than normal, due to the auxiliary power settings. It seemed to take hours to travel up the two levels. He paced back and forth in the tiny space like a tiger looking to escape its cage. His body was rigid, and his mind raced through all the possibilities and necessary reactions they must take. Once the elevator stopped and the door started opening, he squeezed through the half-open door and stepped out of the elevator into the command center lobby, then into the small control room and piloting station.

Electronic blue light from the screens and control consoles bathed the control room. There were three consoles staffed by two technicians and the pilot. They all wore simple gray robes. Commander Oluso stood looking over the shoulder of a technician viewing a holographic image. The flickering amber hologram hovered over a flat table on the right side of the room.

Jagoon heard the technician say, "Sir, it seems to be attached to the top of our ship."

"Egba, do the sensors show any other spacecraft in this region?" the commander asked the other technician across the room.

"Nothing, Commander. We are alone," Egba answered.

Jagoon spoke up, "Commander Oluso, what is attached to our ship? Are we under attack?"

The commander, whose translucent skin and scalp-frill were in the green hue family, turned and saw Jagoon standing behind him. His scalp-frill stood rigid from stress, but the frill lowered halfway at the sight of Jagoon.

"Jagoon, let me show you," he said, pointing to the hologram in front of him. Jagoon squeezed in beside him to examine the image.

Hovering above the technician's table was a one-meter-long bright amber holographic model of the Royal Okutan Vessel. The technician moved one hand near the model, and the gesture spun the hologram.

Commander Oluso moved his fingers in a circular pattern in front of the model. The hologram zoomed in and enlarged. There was a long, skinny red cylinder flashing at the top of the Royal Vessel. It was about as long as Jagoon's hand on the holographic model and looked like a worm or leech attached to their larger vessel.

"Right here." Commander Oluso pointed at the flashing cylinder.

"Only seconds after we came out of hyper speed, our sensors picked up this small ship. I guess it is a ship. I'm not sure. It was like they came out of nowhere. There was nothing, then suddenly, before we identified or hailed them, it appears they attacked us."

"Who, or what, are they?" Jagoon asked.

"We do not know. It seems they fired on us first and we prepared to fire back, but we lost power. They hit us with a strategic shot, taking out our main power hub. Thankfully, they did not hit the auxiliary power unit."

"How would they know where to hit us? Isn't that a precise shot?"

"Yes, it is. I don't know how they could know. I suppose it could just be a lucky shot." He paused for a moment, thinking. "Or they have specific information about our ship."

"I don't like the sound of that."

"No, Jagoon, neither do I. By the time we brought up auxiliary power, they hit us a second time. They were too close to locate. Now we realize they crashed into the top of the ship and seem to be attached. That is all we have as of this moment."

"How large is this vessel?"

The technician responded, "It is 70 meters by 10 meters."

"That is an odd size for a spacecraft. Might it be a biological parasite of some kind? Space worm? Or just random space junk that crashed into us?" Jagoon asked.

"No, this is clearly mechanical and," the technician paused and pushed a few keys on his console and twisted a small dial, bringing up several bar graphs on his screen. "See, right here, it is exhibiting all the signs of electronic and radioactive activity, and it's likely containing biological life."

"And," Jagoon added, "while it is small, it is certainly large enough to carry a small army to attempt to board this ship."

"Commander," the other technician interrupted, "I don't have all my sensors back up yet because of auxiliary power limitations. However, our environmental monitors have issued an alarm."

Jagoon hurried over to look at the alarm readout on the other technician's control screen.

The technician mumbled in a shaky voice, "We have a breach in the hull-integrity."

"Commander, what is the precise location of where they are attached?" Jagoon yelled.

"Level four. Right above the dining room."

Jagoon pulled a cylinder-shaped device from his belt and flicked it hard away from his body. The cylinder telescoped out into a rigid meter-long tube. He hit the activation button, and a flickering arc of blue laser fire ignited between the hilt and the tip, radiating all around the cylinder. Wasting no time, he sprinted out of the control room and jumped into the elevator to get to level four.

CHAPTER SEVEN

Jagoon tried calling the Princess from the elevator communicator, with no success. After trying again, he called Akoni, who answered immediately.

"Jagoon, this is Akoni."

"Listen, Akoni, we are under attack. A ship latched onto ours and they've breached the hull. Whoever they are, they are coming in. You must protect the princess."

"I will. Are you coming here?"

"No, I'm going to give them a personal greeting. I'll call again as soon as the threat is neutralized."

The elevator stopped, and the door opened. Jagoon stepped out of the elevator with his laser flame sword still activated. Several screaming members of the ship's staff running through the lobby almost ran over him. In front of him, someone had propped open the translucent doors, giving him a clear view of the now empty dining room.

The elegant room was a mess. The impact had knocked over tables and chairs. In the center of the room, however, splintered tables and chairs covered the floor below a gaping black hole in the ceiling. A short ladder extended a couple meters from the hole towards the floor. Six dead Okutans lay on the floor below the hole in the ceiling. Three of the slain Okutans wore the maroon warrior's robe. From where he stood, he didn't recognize which of his warriors they were, but they were his. He ground his teeth and clenched every muscle in his body. *What is happening? Stay focused,* he chided himself.

Three slain members of the ship's staff lay nearby. He made his way toward the hole in the ceiling, pausing for a moment to check if any of the fallen staff were alive. They were not. He stared at one female lying in a contorted position on the floor close to him. An energy blast to the chest killed her. He recognized her as a nurse in the royal medical staff. It filled him with a mixture of fury and fear.

Who is doing this? Where are they?

Jagoon knew the stakes were high on this trip, and it seemed they were now in serious trouble.

After scanning the room and finding no hostiles, he made his way towards the hole in the ceiling, gripping his flame sword in his right hand. The energy arc buzzed and snapped. A moment later, he heard a hollow rattling sound like wooden wind chimes, then a grunt. His scalp frill flared out involuntarily and he froze to listen. He heard the hollow rattling sound again. It sounded like it was coming from the hole above.

As he stood at the ready, two massive figures came down the short ladder from the hole and then dropped the rest of the distance, crashing to the floor with a loud thump and lots of rattling. They landed in a kneeling position. He didn't move, but remained like a statue. When the creatures stood to their full height, he got a better view. They were tall, wide, and almost twice the size of Jagoon. They had massive thick bodies covered in a dark golden fur and white bones. Jagoon didn't understand what was before him. His mind tried to place who or what these monsters were, but had no frame of reference.

Is there a skeletal structure on the outside of their bodies?

One monster turned to the other and growled out a viscous sound, which Jagoon assumed was some type of harsh language. Its voice was deep and raspy. Jagoon saw the bones jiggle around when the monster turned.

Jagoon attacked before the monsters noticed his presence. He took three fast steps and leapt onto a chair to launch himself into a cartwheel flip through the air over the heads of the intruders. His black shoulder wrap waved in a flourish as he sailed through the air. He landed like a cat in front of the two massive monsters. He had his second energy flame sword out, telescoped, and activated before he landed in front of them.

Looking up, he saw the hairy beast's shocked expressions. Dark golden fur covered them from head to toe, except for their dark brown, bare, leathery faces. They had long beards and wore bare bone skulls from other larger alien creatures as helmets covering part of their faces. Jagoon had seen nothing like it. His blood surged with adrenaline.

Both monsters tried to get their blasters up to shoot the much smaller Jagoon, but with blinding speed he swung both swords around, rotating his wrists in a synchronized motion. The flame swords sliced through the exterior bone armor, golden fur, and then the internal bones of their arms. He sliced off the shooting arms of both at the same time. The blasters thudded hard on the floor with the hairy monster arms still attached. Jagoon spun, leapt, and brought a sword across the neck of the monster on the right, severing its head from its body.

The second monster was grabbing its severed arm and howling in pain. Jagoon dispatched it and watched the huge hairy creature tumble to the floor, crashing against another table and crumpling to the floor.

The two monsters lay in a pile on the cluttered dining room floor in front of Jagoon. He bent to look closer, letting the curiosity out now. He was unfamiliar with this alien race. Its huge fur covered hands ended in long raptor-like claws. He didn't want to be on the receiving end of a razor-sharp slash. They were, in fact, wearing bones like a makeshift chain mail armor. The bones, which Jagoon presumed were from their previous victims, had holes drilled in them and tied together with a tough rope to form the bone armor. He couldn't imagine the bones provided any protective quality beyond resisting attacks by blunt objects.

Maybe these bones are a type of trophy to intimidate their victims?

He scooted over and looked at the blasters. They were basic technology. These monsters, while looking like giant animals, were an advanced space traveling race. They were an enigma.

Jagoon heard and felt a heavy thump behind him. He turned, but he was too slow. He knew he'd made a grave mistake. As he turned his body to react, he saw the angry face of another monster and the butt of a rifle flying towards his head. The rifle connected with the side of his head before he could react, turning out the lights.

CHAPTER EIGHT

Braeknn knew time was of the essence. He and his team followed the corridors toward their target's private quarters.

At the end of one corridor, they squeezed themselves into an ornate elevator. Braeknn stood at the back. Their furry shoulders pressed up against each other, but they tried to give their leader extra space.

The elevator came to a stop, the doors opened, and Braeknn saw three of the small blue skinned aliens in the corridor. As soon as the doors opened, they all turned toward the elevator with shocked expressions on their weird oblong faces. Braeknn thought they were strange little creatures. They were too skinny and hairless. Their odd fishlike faces and fins above their head were just gross.

In the moment of inaction, as the team of monstrous Bone Rattlers stared across the short distance at the stunned fishy things, Braeknn wondered if they lived in the water half the time. They reminded him of lardlers, the two-legged aquatic species that lived in the mountain lakes on his home planet. They were one of his favorite meals. He loved the way they tasted when slow-cooked over the fire pit. He'd need to keep one of these to eat and compare the flavor to the lardlers.

The creatures in the corridor pulled their rifles up to fire, just as

Manstruu and the other Bone Rattlers at the front of the elevator stepped out, firing.

There were a couple of quick shots and two Bone Rattlers fell over dead. Manstruu stepped over his fallen comrades and shot one combatant. The Bone Rattler on his left shot another.

Braeknn stepped out of the elevator last, watching the firefight with delight. Two of his soldiers were down, but two of theirs as well. The third lardler look-alike turned and ran down the hall looking for cover. It didn't get very far; Manstruu shot it in the back and it crashed to the floor, sliding to a stop against the wall.

They left the fallen Bone Rattlers in the corridor and approached the wide double doors at the end opposite of the elevator. The wood door had intricate carvings of vines and trees.

"This is it. We should find the princess in here," Manstruu growled as they stood outside the closed doors.

"Yes," Braeknn responded. "Prepare for resistance. Do not kill or hurt the princess. We must take her alive." Braeknn pointed his clawed finger around at the group. "I will deal with anyone who screws this up."

The Bone Rattler troops shifted nervously and avoided eye contact. They knew Braeknn's anger was legendary, and none of them wanted to be *dealt with*.

"Manstruu, do you have the zapper?"

"Yes, Chief Braeknn, right here." Manstruu pulled the black box from his equipment belt and held it up.

The zapper was an electro-magnetic pulse generator designed to shut down the electronics within a small 50-meter radius. While Braeknn could have zapped the entire ship from the Auger, which they did from time-to-time, he'd learned long ago it was difficult to navigate and extricate from dead ships. So, over the years, they adapted their methods and began using small, localized zaps to handicap their prey without affecting the entire ship.

"Zap 'em, and let's get her," Braeknn said.

"Gladly," Manstruu growled as he activated the zapper.

The dim amber lighting in the corridor went out, and they stood in complete darkness. Two Bone Rattlers flicked on flashlights mounted on their weapons.

"Now," Braeknn said, and Manstruu kicked open the double doors.

Two Bone Rattlers passed through the doorway into the dark room. Someone shot at them from the back of the room. The area was lit up with blue and red staccato flashing from the ensuing fire fight.

Braeknn gave them the signal, and the remaining warriors pressed in through the double doors. The rifle fire intensified in the small room, casting flashes of distorted shadows across the walls. From the door, Braeknn heard screams and grunts amid the loud energy blasts as he stepped into the room, eager to find his prey.

CHAPTER NINE

Moments earlier…

Akoni rushed over to where Princess Omo-Binrin Oba stood. "Princess, we are under attack. Jagoon believes the attackers have attached themselves to the ship and are boarding." Omo-Binrin could see the panic on Akoni's face. "He is going now to stop them."

"Is he alone?"

"Yes."

"This is unfortunate. OK, bar the door. They are coming for me. We must resist anyone who tries to get in here. Where are the other guards?"

"I don't know where they are. I've tried calling on the communicator, and no one is answering."

"Try Jagoon again," she commanded. "Keep trying until you reach him. And keep trying the other guards."

She turned toward her attendants, who were not prepared for the terrifying experience they were facing. "You two need to go hide back there. We'll keep you safe," she told them. They got up from huddling together on the floor and ran to the corner at the back of the room, farthest from the door, and squatted down next to a table by the princess' oversized bed.

She returned to Akoni. "Anything?"

"Nothing, Princess." Akoni looked worried. His scalp-frill was extended.

She paced back and forth, considering several questions.

Were we double crossed? Is there someone on the inside who knows my secret mission but wants to stop me? Are we just the victim of being in the wrong place at the wrong time? Couldn't be. Impossible. They are after me and the information I am carrying. It doesn't matter right now. Just get ready, she told herself.

The lights flickered and then went out. Her private room went dark.

"Princess?" Akoni whispered.

"I'm here," she said through the dark. She snatched the laser sword from her belt and flicked the cylinder away from her body, and the inner rod telescoped to its full length. When she activated the trigger, the crackling laser flame illuminated the area around herself and Akoni with a haunting blue glow.

Seeing the princess' resolve emboldened Akoni, who raised his silver rifle, ready to fight to defend her.

"Get in position behind cover and shoot anything you don't recognize that comes through that door." Akoni ran to the couch in the dim blue light, and spun it around to create a cover position. He knelt behind it and rested the skinny silver barrel on the top of the couch, pointing at the door.

Omo-Binrin decided that the best place to hide to give her a chance to ambush the attackers was behind the door. Once in position, she triggered the laser sword, extinguishing the flame, and the room returned to dense blackness. She alternated between squinting and opening her eye wide, trying to adjust to the darkness. It was no use; they were in complete blackness.

She tried to control her breathing as she pressed her back against the wall and held the laser sword in her dominant hand. After what felt like an eternity, she heard noise in the anteroom beyond the door. At first, it was faint. She wished she could signal Akoni. Then, something on the other side of the door tried to open it.

Soft bumps and clanks against the door, then scratching.

The metal door was thin and lightweight, and not intended to provide impenetrable security. She knew the door wouldn't hold back someone who was determined to gain access. The Okutan Royal Vessel didn't have any enhanced security features. Omo-Binrin was experiencing something they had never expected. She vowed instruct her security team on Okuta to harden the security on all their ships when she returned home. *If she returned home.*

With the power out, the door's touchpad controller shouldn't work either.

More sounds from the door as whomever was on the other side attempted to open the door.

Where was Jagoon?

Then, something heavy slammed against the door, making a loud crashing sound. Omo-Binrin almost jumped out of her own skin. Her scalp frill stood on end. Then, a second heavy crash came against the door.

After a moment, a sound like a minor explosion made her jump again. The door cracked, and the hinges snapped.

A thin stream of yellow light pierced the blackness, and dust floated in the air. Deep growls, like that of a large predatory animal, emanated through the broken door.

Princess Omo-Binrin pressed her trembling back against the wall for stability.

Once more, the attackers slammed against the door and finally they pushed it open. Four enormous shadows moved into the room, outlined by the dim light from the anteroom. A hollow rattling sound followed the massive assailants as they moved into the room.

She knew Akoni was waiting until he had the perfect shot. Just as she was wishing he would fire, the energy rifle across the room flashed and erupted into action. The room filled with bright light from the energy bursts like a strobe. The first two shots crashed into their center mass.

Two assailants growled and collapsed to the floor. Fire erupted from both sides of the room. The attackers focused all their fire on

Akoni's position behind the couch. In return, Akoni maintained a furious volley of shot after shot toward the door.

Two more of these huge attackers collapsed in the entry way, but three more entered, firing their large, powerful rifles. Akoni gasped, then his firing stopped. Akoni was down. She wanted to run over to him and check if he was alive and help him. But she couldn't. She was on her own now.

Be strong, Omo-Binrin.

One creature crossed the room to Akoni's position behind the couch and kicked at him. Then he growled to the others in a strange, animal-like guttural language. She still couldn't quite make out who these creatures were or what they looked like in the darkness. They were huge, though. Her eyes were still adjusting from the flashes of light, and her ears were ringing from the close proximity of the rifle blasts.

No more time to waste. It was now or never. Princess Omo-Binrin pushed herself away from the wall near the door and triggered the laser sword. She stood behind one of them. When the blue laser flame formed between the hilt and tip of the rod in her hand, the flickering blue light revealed the back of the creature right in front of her.

The creature was twice her size and covered in a dense fur. Above, the fur looked like an armor of white sticks. No, she thought, not sticks, but bones.

The blue light caught the creature's attention and it turned to looked right at her. It wore a skull of a strange creature like a helmet. Its bare and brutal face snarled and growled at her through the skull mask, revealing its deadly fangs.

What was this thing?

Her heart raced as she looked up at the snarling face, frozen in fear.

"Princess Omo-Binrin Oba," the monster growled in her own language. "No move. We take you now."

Her fear turned to confusion. She was stunned. *What? How could this thing know her name? Or her native language?* She'd never even seen these creatures before.

She shook her head to clear the shock fogging her mind.

"Who are you? What do you want from me?" she shouted at the creature as she stood in a wide stance, laser sword buzzing in front of her. It took a couple of steps toward her, and she backed away from it.

"We here for you," it growled, and lunged forward.

Princess Omo-Binrin rotated her wrist with blinding speed and sliced the energy sword across the torso of the creature, slicing into its flesh four times. She could smell the singed fur. The creature howled in pain and toppled over, revealing two more monsters behind it in the dim light.

She scooted backwards even more, making room between her and the closest monster. This one didn't shoot as she feared, but suddenly sprang forward, reaching for her like the previous monster. The Princess whirled the sword around through several turns, slicing arms, and eventually planted her feet and jabbed the sword straight ahead with two hands, piercing the attacker's abdomen. It collapsed to the floor.

Six down.

The next attacker didn't move, but waited and watched her from several meters away, growling in deep, low tones. The backlit shadows of two more creatures appeared in the doorway.

How many are there?

One of the new arrivals' silhouettes included large antlers fanning out from both sides of its head and carrying a smaller rifle, which it pointed right at her. This one was going to shoot at her. She turned to run. But she heard a *poof* sound, and then felt the sting of a projectile imbedding into her shoulder.

It stopped her in her tracks. There were now five in the doorway, then ten, then five. The one with the antlers now had four antlers on the sides of its two heads. She had trouble focusing, then began losing her balance, stumbling a bit, feeling dizzy. Reaching behind her shoulder, she pulled the projectile out of her shoulder and looked at it. It was a dart. They tranquilized her. She could already feel the chemicals moving throughout her blood stream. Her vision was fading to gray. She dropped the sword and fought to stay on her feet. When she tried to turn again to run, her legs became like wet noodles and gave out. She fell flat on her face.

PART TWO

Give me soldiers willing to kill or be killed and we will make the United Planetary Government the galaxy's lone superpower.

— HENRIK STATHIS AUGUSTIN, INTERPLANETARY ARMY FIVE-STAR GENERAL

CHAPTER TEN

Interplanetary Navy Battlecruiser McDaniels
Space Warfare Group Hangar Bay

Mac was the first of the Space Warfare Group operators to walk down the ramp of the Starhawk and step onto the pristine steel floor of the launch bay hangar. The hangar was the Space Warfare Group's dedicated operational base aboard the Interplanetary Navy's colossal battlecruiser, *McDaniels.*

Mac helped support Jerry Tao, who was in serious pain, limp down the ramp. The injured soldier's weight on Mac's shoulder put extra pressure on his own injured leg. However, he would not acknowledge his own injury until he ensured his men were taken care of. They were his first priority.

Both men still wore their mud-splattered gray tactical uniforms and armored chest rig. They also still wore their helmets with the face shield in the open position, revealing their faces. Mac had his rifle mounted on the magnetic hold on his back.

"How's that feeling, Jerry? You OK, so far?" Mac asked as they limped down the ramp.

Jerry grimaced and winced as he spoke through clenched teeth, "It hurts like crazy, but I'll be alright."

As they took a few steps away from the ship, Mac waved for the waiting medical team to join them.

"You're going to be just fine. The doc will get you all fixed up," Mac said. "And you get a brief vacation for a change."

Jerry laughed a little. "Not the vacation I was hoping for."

The white-clothed medical team jogged over, leading a hovering hospital gurney that floated a meter off the floor. When they reached Mac's position, he helped Jerry sit down and lifted his legs onto the gurney so he could lie down. One medical technician removed Jerry's helmet. Another two checked his vitals and looked him over.

"He's got a gunshot wound in the shoulder, and it looks like he blew out his knee," Mac said.

"What sort of firearm was it, sir?" the technician asked as she inspected Jerry's shoulder.

Mac wiped sweat and blood from his face. "Ah, it was a Kraize energy rifle of some sort. No projectiles."

"Ok, we've seen plenty of those. We will take good care of him, sir."

"Thank you. Jerry, listen, I'll be up to MedBay to see you as soon as possible, alright?" Mac saw the relief on Jerry's face, now that he was lying on the gurney. He looked comfortable.

"Sounds good. I won't be going anywhere," Jerry said weakly.

"Sir," the medical technician said to Mac, "you need to come to MedBay and get checked over as well."

"No, I'm fine."

"Sir, I insist. That leg doesn't look fine," she pointed at his right leg, which was exposed under his shredded pants. Mac's leg was oozing blood from the large gash above his boot. "You need to get that cleaned up right away. Looks like you need stitches."

Mac said nothing more. They turned the hovering gurney away. Mac stood there in his mud-crusted uniform with hands on top of his head and watched the medical team take Jerry toward MedBay.

Mac turned and back towards the Starhawk with a heavy heart.

He had one more important task to complete. The sharp burning pain in his lower leg didn't compare to the pain in his heart from failing this mission. And failing his team. They accomplished the objective by gathering the intel and destroying the communication relay station, but losing a man always turned the mission into a failure. It made him, as their leader, a failure.

It was supposed to be a simple mission.

Simple mission? There's no such thing as a simple mission for the group, Mac thought.

He was grateful he served alongside the best trained men in the universe, but returning with the body of a brother killed in action was a crushing blow. He'd be experiencing the sting of this one for a long time. Jo Maldonado was a great young man and an excellent operator. His absence would leave a void in his team.

Steam rose from the surface of the Starhawk as he limped towards it. Large clumps of foul orange mud slid off the landing legs and splattered on the floor. He inadvertently stepped into a pile, coating his boot with a fresh layer, but he didn't care. He couldn't wait to free himself from his uniform and find the closest and hottest shower on the *McDaniels*. But first, he needed to deal with his fallen brother.

The others were exiting the Starhawk as he returned to the ramp. Cory Allen, Luis Sanchez, and Sam Clarion walked down the ramp, bedraggled, covered in orange mud, carrying their helmets, rifles and equipment cases. They all stopped at the base of the ramp.

"Mac, how's Tao?" Sam asked.

"He'll be alright. He's in a lot of pain, though."

"They'll take care of that in a hurry. "Jerry must find it challenging to be the patient rather than the team medic," Sam said with a smile.

Cory replied, "For sure. If those injuries were less severe, Jerry would still be on that planet trying to fix up his own wounds." Cory's curly black hair, which was much longer than Army regulation allowed, was a ratty mess from his helmet. The jagged scar on his left cheek enhanced his tough guy appearance. He was one of the most intimidating-looking operators in the group. His rugged face and icy-blue eyes looked downright mean most of the time. But right now, he looked softer when speaking about Jerry.

Mac perceived from their body language that the team had a similar sense of sorrow from the mission as he did. They were trying to cover up the pain, but it was there under the surface.

"Where are you going? We're all done up there. We've got all the equipment." Sam said, lifting the equipment cases he was carrying.

"Yeah, Major Mac, we've got everything," Luis Sanchez said. Sanchez was the shortest of the SWG operators, but he made up for his smaller size with his extreme aggressiveness. However, people only witnessed his legendary aggressiveness on the battlefield. The rest of the time, he was a jokester who gave anyone who came near him a hard time. Sanchez had black hair trimmed close to his scalp, and deep brown eyes that changed from a hollow mindless stare—which was part of his jokester routine—to deadly serious in battle. Mac became convinced long ago that Sanchez had some kind of internal switch he activated that instantly changed him from motor-mouth moron to elite fighting machine and back again. It was a mystery to everyone how Luis Sanchez made it past the Interplanetary Army's early screening process. But now, Mac couldn't imagine his team without Sanchez or his mouth.

"I'm going to deal with Jo. You guys get everything put away and then hit the showers."

"Mac, I already called for the medical examiner's office to come and take Jo to the morgue. I'm going to wait for them and handle it. You don't need to do it. I'll help them take care of everything."

"I appreciate that, Sam, but I need to do it. Go on, I'll catch up with you in a few minutes."

"Seriously, your leg is a mess."

"Sam. I'll take care of it. Don't make me give you an order. Besides, you need to go see that lovely wife of yours."

Sam smiled at the reference to his wife, who recently took up residence on the *McDaniels* after receiving a position in the Interplanetary Navy's Department of Alien Science. Sam was the only current

Space Warfare Group operator who was married. Most of the operators, including Mac himself, struggled to find the balance between work and personal life, let alone family life. Somehow, Sam and his wife figured it out.

"Alright, Mac. You're the boss. We'll see you in a bit." Sam put his hand on Mac's shoulder for a moment, looking him in the eyes. Mac held his gaze. Sam then followed Cory and Sanchez to the locker room.

As they walked away, Mac overheard Sanchez started digging into Sam.

"Listen, Lead, you gotta let Major Mac do what a Major Mac needs to do." Sanchez used his nickname, *Lead,* which was short for *Leading Man,* because Sam looked like the charming leading man of a romantic movie with his handsome face, winning smile, dimples, and wavy blonde hair. Sanchez was fond of the nickname because he created it.

He continued, "And what you need to focus on right now, Lead, is cleaning this smelly mud off the floor of Colonel Miller's hangar. He is going to be so mad at you."

"Sanchez," Sam said, "Shut up. This isn't the time for your mouth."

"Ok, Lead. But you know it's part of my coping mechanism to harass you. You wouldn't restrict my grieving process, would you? The Army Department of Equality is going to be disappointed to hear about this discrimination."

Mac found it impossible to not crack a small smile at Sanchez's ridiculousness as he watched them walk away, but then forced his stiff body to move up the ramp and into the Starhawk. He squeezed past the passenger seats to the small medical area where he found Jo's body still lying on the gurney. He pulled the sheet back. Maldonado lay there lifeless, eyes closed. His youthful face was peaceful.

Mac stood there for a long moment, doing nothing but thinking. He let the scene roll through his mind like a movie several times. He couldn't see any way to have saved Jo's life, besides never entering the battlefield at all. The battlefield had no rules and had no respect for life. War didn't care if Jo was one of his men or not. Mac knew when it was your time, it was your time, and there was nothing he could do about it. The hardest part was having no control.

"I'm sorry Jo." Mac tried to fight back the emotions, but a rogue tear trailed down his cheek. "I'm sorry I didn't keep you safe. We'll miss you, brother," Mac murmured.

He shook his head, fighting the emotions as he pulled the cart out to the walkway and pushed it out of the Starhawk. He struggled against the weight of the cart as he guided it down the ramp. Mac made it about 10 meters from the ramp before two technicians from the Interplanetary Navy's Medical Examiner's office arrived with another hovering gurney. This gurney, however, was more like a coffin, with an enclosed box covering the platform.

"Hello," the gray-haired woman wearing a white medical uniform said to Mac as they approached. "Thank you. We can take it from here."

Mac stopped and just nodded his head.

"What is the name of the deceased?" The medical examiner asked as she ran a handheld scanning device over the top of Jo's body.

"His name is Josiah Maldonado. Sergeant Josiah Maldonado. We called him Jo."

She looked at the screen of the scanner. "Ok. Confirmed. I'm sorry for your loss," she gave Mac a sympathetic look.

Mac set his hand on Jo's shoulder for a moment. To the medical examiner he said, "Thank you. I appreciate your help."

"Of course."

They eased Jo's body from the gurney into their floating box.

"We'll make sure this gets cleaned and put back on your ship," the woman said. She had a kind way about her.

Mac just nodded and watched as they turned and led the floating box and gurney out of the hangar into the massive ship beyond.

With nothing left to do, Mac began the walk to the locker room. It was a walk Mac made hundreds of times, but it this time it seemed unmercifully long. He limped, barely able to put his weight on the injured leg. He passed the steaming spaceship, where mud still dripped in heavy clumps onto the hangar floor. Just as he was reaching the locker room door, a voice called out to him.

"Major Lambert?" Mac recognized the voice and turned.

Colonel Tate Miller approached, looking as rigid and unfriendly as always, with two aides following at his heels. Everyone knew Colonel Miller went nowhere without his aides, leading to plenty of jokes behind his back.

Rather than the standard charcoal-colored Army fatigues, he was wearing his black formal uniform, which was covered with flags and pins for commendation. The brass buttons on his uniform coat and his meticulously polished dress shoes sparkled under the bright hangar lights. Colonel Miller's black beret sat perfectly positioned above his stony face. He looked formal, important, and intimidating. Mac looked like a disaster covered in blood, sweat, and mud.

"Major Lambert, I see you are limping," Colonel Miller said. "That leg looks bad."

"Colonel, yes, sir. I sustained an injury on that disgusting planet."

"You look and smell terrible, Major," Colonel Miller said.

"Yes, sir. I also feel terrible."

"As you should. Listen, I'm sorry about Sergeant Maldonado. He was a good young operator. We'll miss him. We will notify his family and take care of all the arrangements, as usual."

"Thank you, sir." Mac retrieved the memory drive from a pocket on his chest and handed it over to Miller. "This has the Kraize relay station coordinates. Hopefully, it will lead to fresh Kraize targets. Sanchez gathered some equipment for examination as well."

Miller took the flash drive. "Good work, Major. Listen, I want you to get to MedBay and get your leg fixed up. Then I want you in my office without delay for debrief."

"Yes, sir. I'm just going to get this uniform into the incinerator and take a quick shower." Mac said, pointing over his shoulder with his thumb. He tried to smile, but it came out as more of a squinty-eyed grimace. "Then, I'm going to go visit Jerry in MedBay. I think they were taking him to surgery right away. If possible, I'll spend a few minutes with him."

"Major, there is no time for any of that. Report to MedBay immediately and then report to my office without delay."

"Sir, can I at least check on Jerry before coming up?"

"Major, what part of I want you in my office immediately do you not understand?"

"I understand completely, sir," Mac said as he tried to stand straighter.

"That's what I thought." Colonel Miller pivoted on his heels and walked out of the Space Warfare Group hangar, his aides following close behind. Without turning back to Mac, Colonel Miller shouted, "I want you in my office for debrief without delay." He put unnecessary emphasis on the words *without delay*.

Always the professional, Mac kept his face and body language neutral, while his mind flashed through a series of possible insubordinate responses. But, instead of making his day more miserable than it already was, he pointed his sore body towards MedBay, foregoing the shower he desperately needed.

In an attempt to move *without delay*, he keyed his operational radio to call Sam. "Black-2, you copy?"

After a moment, Sam Clarion's voice came over the radio. "Roger, Black Leader, I'm here. What's up?"

"What's your position?"

"Locker room, taking these muddy boots off and about to hit the shower as ordered."

"I didn't actually give you an order, wise guy. Anyway, listen, I'm sorry to say you'll have to wait a bit for that shower. Strap those boots back on and meet me at MedBay as soon as possible. Something's up with Miller and we need to be in his office for a debrief as soon as possible."

"Debrief? Right now?" Sam asked.

"That's what he said."

"Hot wash?" Sam asked, speaking of the specialized debrief while the mission was still hot.

"Maybe, but I think something else is going on. He said there was no time for showers or delay of any kind. He ordered me to MedBay to get this leg treated first, though. Meet me up there and we'll go to his office together. We'll find out what's going on soon enough. Get moving."

"Roger that, boss. I'll be right there."

CHAPTER ELEVEN

MedBay was cold, but that suited Mac just fine since he was still in his uniform and armored chest rig. Well, he was still in *most* of his uniform, since the doctor scissored the right pant leg off at the knee. Mac did, at least, remove his helmet. Bright white light drenched MedBay's sterile white surfaces and furniture.

The doctor was rinsing Mac's leg wound when Sam entered, still wearing his mud-caked pants and boots, but without the upper layers of the suit, leaving him in a tight white t-shirt that put his lean arm and chest muscles on display.

"Hey, Mac" Sam said with a fist bump.

The gray-haired doctor looked Sam over. "You gentleman are a mess," he said, peering over a pair of medical eyeglasses like an annoyed grandma looking up from her knitting. The medical glasses provided magnification and featured several simple scanning features.

"Thanks for getting up here so quickly, Sam," Mac groaned involuntarily between words will the doctor prodded his injury. "I'm sorry, there wasn't time to see Sarina before this meeting."

"Oh, it's fine. She knows the drill. I sent her a message that we're back on the boat, but not released yet. How's that leg doing?"

"Oh, my leg's fine. No problem," Mac said. He winced, suppressing another groan.

The doctor stopped rinsing the wound and starred at Mac for a moment, then looked at Sam.

"Is he a medical professional?" the doctor asked Sam.

"No, just the galaxy's most dangerous soldier."

"Oh, OK. In that case, is he the battlefield medic?"

"Nope, that's Jerry's job," Sam said.

"That's what I thought. Disregard his uninformed medical assessment. His leg is not fine. He suffered a serious injury." He resumed rinsing the wound. Sam leaned over to catch a glimpse at his leg and grimaced when he saw the wound.

"What's that face?" Mac asked.

"Man, that's ugly," Sam said.

"So, Doc, what's the verdict?" Mac asked.

"Well, Major, I'm not a judge, I'm a doctor. I can't give you a verdict, but I can give you a diagnosis."

"Ok, Doc, what's your diagnosis?" Mac looked at Sam with wide-eyed amusement. Sam grinned in response. *Surly old dude,* Mac thought to himself.

"You have a severe 10-centimeter vertical laceration. You're lucky you didn't slice any tendons or your fibular artery. If you had, you'd have bled out and died in mere moments. It doesn't help that the wound was so dirty. Where did this mud come from?"

"It's probably best you don't ask," Mac said.

He looked at Mac. "I need to know for your wellbeing and the entire population of this battlecruiser, Major. We need to know what biological threats you could be carrying," the doctor said. "I might need to quarantine you."

"Well, Doc, that's not going to happen. My boss won't stand for any quarantine."

"It's not up to him, Major," the doctor said, emphasizing his rank with sarcasm again. "Now, tell me the origins of this mud."

"I'm sorry, Doc, but it's classified."

"Pffft! Classified. You'll be classified as patient zero of a contagious outbreak if we aren't careful." The doctor scooped mud into a vial. "I'm going to run some tests on this to make sure there are no bacterial or viral dangers. We don't need any biological contagions breaking loose on the ship. We need to be wearing hazardous protective gear."

"I'm sure we'll be fine," Mac repeated. The doctor just gave him an annoyed, squinty-eyed stare, but said nothing more.

Returning to his work, he began pressing the wound together and applied a medical grade glue along the length of the laceration. "You gentleman need to be more careful," the doctor stated flatly.

Sam began chuckling. "Good one, Doc. Do you have any idea what we do every day?"

"Let me guess," he replied in a mocking voice. "It's classified." He rolled his eyes at Sam. "I don't care how they break you. I only care about how to fix you and keeping everyone else on this ship healthy."

Sam laughed again. "Ok, we'll do our best to be more careful."

As the men watched the doctor work on Mac's leg, the ship-wide speakers announced the *McDaniels* would enter *faster than light* speed in ten minutes, and all ship personnel should prepare for the transition.

The doctor looked up at the ceiling. "Hmmmm, off and running again," he muttered to himself. "Always on the move. No one can ever sit still anymore."

"Did we have a planned *FTL* jump I missed?" Mac asked Sam. The Space Warfare Group was always privy to the flight schedules and destinations.

"Not that I'm aware of," Sam replied.

As the doctor finished wrapping Mac's bare leg, he said, "Ok, Major, I've wrapped your wound with MedTek tape, which protects against biological threats using constant immersion in UV light. The tape stores energy in this little battery power source here." He pointed to the thicker area at on the bandage. "It has plenty of charge to last you until you visit me again in three days. And, Major, please, leave the tape on."

Mac examined the thick white bandage wrapped around his leg from his ankle to just below the knee. It wasn't as cumbersome as he expected.

"And you'll need to be careful not to overdo it. I'd advise you to take several days off with your foot elevated to avoid further injury or infection."

"Well, Doc, the good news is we just finished our mission, so I'm sure we'll have a couple days doing nothing here on the *McDaniels*," Mac said.

"Make sure that you do."

Mac swung his leg around to the table's edge, and Sam handed him his mud-crusted boot, holding it between two fingers.

"I'm not sure I want to put that back on."

"I don't blame you."

Mac slipped his foot into the boot but didn't lace it up.

"You see, Jerry yet?" Sam asked.

"No time. Miller was adamant. I think he may still be in surgery. I'll come down after the debrief and check in. Let's get up to Miller's office before he sends an aide down here looking for us."

As Mac and Sam exited MedBay, the doctor shouted at Mac to rest his leg.

As they entered the wide main corridor and the hustle and bustle of foot traffic, the ship-wide speakers announced again that the *McDaniels* was entering *FTL* in one minute.

"How's that leg?" Sam asked.

"With the pain meds, it's good," Mac said, even though he still walked with a pronounced limp.

"It doesn't look good."

"It's not too bad. A little rest will make all the difference."

Sam then asked, "Mac, I'm glad your leg is patched up. But how are *you* doing?"

Mac looked at Sam. His charismatic smile was back. "You mean with Jo and Jerry?"

"Yes."

"Well, you know me better than anyone. I'm disappointed with myself."

"You couldn't have done anything different."

"I'm not sure about that, Sam. I just hate it when I can't protect the team. It never gets better. I still can't shake Crypso 5," Mac said, speaking of the battle eighteen months ago when the enemy ambushed them, causing casualties.

"Mac, I know, but you can't protect all of us all the time. We step into action, knowing the dangers we face. And I don't need to remind you. We follow you straight into the fire. We are all willing to risk life and limb for the job."

"My brain agrees. But, my heart doesn't. That's the problem. I'll give you some credit, though. That was an excellent speech," Mac said with a smile.

"Look, it's your concern for all of us that makes you the best mission leader I've ever seen. You're the best leader these guys have ever had. But sometimes bad things will happen, and I'm sorry to inform you that even you can't stop them," Sam said.

"Are you sure? It's just getting worse as the years go by. I appreciate you reminding me and keeping my head straight." Mac bumped Sam on the shoulder. "I'll fight through it. Maybe a nap and time in the sauna will help me snap out of this pattern of questioning every decision I make. I need to stop reliving the scene repeatedly."

The ship entered *FTL*. Both men stopped in the corridor, grabbed a handrail on the wall for a moment, and waited for the gravitational forces to normalize again. As experienced space travelers, both men had adapted to the momentary progression of force, energy, and balance, like most of the *McDaniels'* crew.

"Any idea why the Colonel called this immediate debrief? I wonder if this *FTL* jump has anything to do with it."

"No. It's out of character. I don't get the urgency. Miller didn't give any hints. The mission objective was a success, and we followed all protocols by the book. If it wasn't for Jo, it would have been a textbook op."

They made their way through the massive multi-level battlecruiser, dodging the busy fast-moving crowds, until they reached the Interplanetary Army offices, which was one level below the much larger Interplanetary Navy's office complex. The Space Warfare Group, spearheaded by Colonel Tate Miller, was a small direct-action group of highly-trained specialists stationed aboard the *McDaniels.* Because the Space Warfare Group was dedicated to surgical strikes and special *off the books* and *black* missions, very few people, including the McDaniels staff, knew about the group, their missions, or that they were even based on the *McDaniels.* They operated by hiding in plain sight aboard the flagship of the Navy's fleet.

Mac and Sam arrived at Colonel Miller's office suite. Mac knocked on the frame of the open door. Colonel Miller's assistant sat at a desk in the middle of the room. She looked up when Mac knocked.

"Colonel Miller and the others are waiting for you in the briefing room."

Sam mouthed *others* to Mac, who shrugged in return.

Colonel Miller's assistant stood and led them down the hall to the large briefing room. Standing outside the briefing room were two guards wearing white tactical jumpsuits and wide reflective visors over their eyes. The man was tall, bald, and white, while the woman was muscular, with dark brown skin and black hair pulled tight into a short ponytail. They both held energy rifles.

The presence of these two was unnerving. They were part of the prestigious Elite Guard. Their function was guarding government dignitaries and presidential-level executive leadership within the United Planetary Government. Their ranks consisted of former special forces, elite fighters, and other highly-trained specialists. You didn't mess with the Elite Guard. Mac assumed both guards were scanning them from head to toe with the tech in their visors and identifying them with facial recognition.

"Hold here, gentleman," the woman said, reaching her hand out.

This is not a good sign, Mac thought. Dread flowed through him, unsure what they were walking into. If the Elite Guard was present, there would be heavy brass behind the door taking part in the debrief. It made no sense. He'd never attended a mission brief with such urgency, or with anyone beyond Colonel Miller and his Interplanetary Army staff.

The woman reached out with a small scanning device attached to her glove and scanned both Mac and Sam to collect their identification from their imbedded military ID tags. "Name and rank?" she asked.

"Major Malcom Lambert."

"Master Sergeant Samuel Clarion."

The woman radioed someone with their names and waited. After a moment, "Gentleman, you can enter."

The tall bald man opened the door and gestured for them to enter.

Sitting at a large conference room table with Colonel Tate Miller, who was looking stone-faced as always, was a small man Mac recognized, but had never met. The small man was the United Planetary Government's third most senior political official, Prime Ambassador Harji Kumar. Kumar's presence explained the two Elite Guards standing in the hallway, and the two other fire breathing Elite Guards standing in the corner. Mac was sure there were more Elite Guards nearby that he couldn't see.

To say the prime ambassador's presence in a mission debrief was incongruous would be the understatement of the year. Both Kumar and Miller watched the large video screen on the wall to Mac's left, displaying the equally unexpected face of the UPG President, Carl Harrington. President Harrington was saying something when they interrupted by walking into the conference room.

Mac and Sam assessed the situation, and both men snapped to attention and shot rigid arms up and hands to the forehead in proper salutes. They stood at attention, half dressed and disheveled from battle, before two of the most powerful men in the known galaxy.

"Major Lambert and Master Sergeant Clarion are here for our

debrief of mission code name *Tranquility,* on the surface of planet Tx17-k221," Mac said.

"At ease, gentleman," Colonel Miller said.

Mac and Sam released their salutes and took up a wide leg stance, with arms behind their backs.

"Major Lambert, forget *Tranquility*. That's ancient history. We asked your here for another reason. We're here to talk about *Guardian,*" Colonel Miller said.

"Sir, I have never heard of a mission called *Guardian*."

"I wouldn't expect so, Major, because I just created it."

CHAPTER TWELVE

Mac's eyes darted from Colonel Miller, then to Prime Ambassador Kumar, and then to President Harrington on the video screen. Prime Ambassador Harji Kumar was a small bald man with brown skin and an impeccably manicured gray mustache. He shaped his goatee into a triangle on his chin. Next to Colonel Miller, who was average in build and height, made Kumar appear even smaller. Mac recognized Kumar, and had observed him on the news video streams throughout the years. However, he never fully grasped the short stature or elf-like appearance of the prime ambassador.

Colonel Miller turned his attention to the screen.

"Mr. President, Major Lambert leads our best team and has my full confidence."

"Thank you, Colonel. Your men appear a little worse for wear at the moment," President Harrington said through the video screen. "Are you sure they are fit for this mission?"

President Harrington was a handsome and distinguished black man with graying hair, due to age and the stress of leading humanity through an unpredictable galaxy. He sat alone behind his desk in his office, wearing his usual formal black executive suit. Neither of them had ever met President Harrington. He'd never joined a mission at the operator level.

"Yes, Mr. President, they are good to go," Colonel Miller replied. "I'd put my men exhausted, injured, and covered in a little toxic mud from an alien planet up against anyone, sir. There are none more qualified."

Sam snorted and choked back his laughter. Miller shot them daggers that communicated *if they embarrassed him, they'd never escape his torture.*

"In fact, sir, they just returned a few minutes ago from warding off the Kraize advancement on an unnamed planet near where we are now."

"Yes, of course. The mission focused on destroying the Kraize communication outpost?"

"Yes, Mr. President, that is correct."

"And the result?"

Colonel Miller deferred to Mac. "Major, how would you describe the results of the mission?"

"Sir, I'd classify it as a bittersweet success. We gathered the intel and destroyed the communication tower."

"I hear a *but* coming, Major," President Harrington said.

"Yes, sir. But we also walked into an ambush. One of my men is injured, lying in MedBay as we speak. He'll be out of commission for a while. We also lost a man."

"Major, I am sorry. What is the name of the soldier?" President Harrington asked. He sounded genuine.

"Josiah Maldonado. He was 28 years old, sir," Mac said. "His skills as an operator were exceptional and he was a remarkable man."

"Major, we all appreciate the sacrifice you and your men make every day. Please express my gratitude to your soldier in MedBay and the rest of the team. I will personally reach out to the Maldonado family."

"Thank you, sir. I'm sure they will appreciate the gesture."

"Major, I'm going to ask you to continue making sacrifices today.

We are dealing with an urgent issue of extreme sensitivity. It looks to me like you've suffered injuries. You both are pretty beat up. Are you sure you are up to the task?" the president asked.

Colonel Miller jumped in, "Yes, Mr. President, of course they are up to the task."

"Colonel, while I appreciate your zeal, I'd like to hear it from Major Lambert directly."

Whatever mission *Guardian* was, the presence of the president and the prime ambassador suggested how it was serious. He wished he had some advance notice about the mission or what his role would be. Being brought into mission *Guardian* in this manner concerned him. Whenever a mission was hurried, or when it became so urgent that the planning period was cut short, mistakes would inevitably occur. Mistakes often meant men dying. He couldn't have more men die on his watch.

He maintained his neutral expression, but his mind spun, trying to gain traction. A feeling of dread formed in his stomach like a rock. Mac considered the options.

How do you tell the most powerful man in the known galaxy that you are too tired to assist in his urgent and sensitive mission? Or that your team isn't ready? What are you going to do, sit on the sidelines and watch from the ship after a nap while some other team accepts the risks? Ridiculous. Mac concluded he must lead this mission with his team. He couldn't trust it to anyone else.

"Yes, sir, we are always up to the task," Mac replied.

"Alright, I am glad. Harji, can you give us the background and tell us what we know so far?" Harrington asked the prime ambassador.

Prime Ambassador Kumar brought up a galactic map with labeled planets. A photo of an unfamiliar humanoid alien species with blue skin and a lizard-like frill atop its head popped up on the screen. Mac concluded it was a female of the species, due to the elaborate jewel-studded dress.

Kumar began his monologue. "The Okutan government contacted me months ago to discuss issues vital to their future. They need our help, it seems. Now, keep in mind, we have had limited interaction in recent decades with the Okutan people. Almost none. But, during the Corning Administration," Kumar referred to the UPG President 80 years ago, "we sent emissaries to Okuta to develop relations. But nothing substantial came of these efforts. The Galactic Coalition recruited the Okutans, but they declined joining at the time."

Kumar stood and walked to the screen. Pointing at the picture of the alien, he said, "This lovely lady is Princess Omo-Binrin Oba. Her planet, Okuta, is here." Kumar pointed to the screen. "And of course, this is our own Terra Libertas here." Terra Libertas held the position as the most developed of the UPG-governed colonial planets, and the capital of the human government. Okuta existed as a faraway planet in a region of space that Mac had never visited.

"We developed a plan for a diplomatic summit to discuss overpopulation and how we could assist them into the future. This is what we told the public about the purpose of the meetings." Kumar paused for a moment to take a drink from his water glass. "You see, the Okutans live about twice as long as the average human, and as a result, they are facing serious concerns of natural resource depletion because of overpopulation. The idea is to either partner with them in developing a new grouping of planets, or to help assimilate Okutan people into our own planets and colonies. We intended this partnership summit to be the first public and formal discussion of a mutually beneficial agreement. The entire Galactic Coalition is eager for a deal, of course. All eyes are on this summit. I've prioritized closing the deal on their Coalition membership, and offering a new Okutan embassy on Terra Libertas."

Kumar paused, glancing around the room with pride and making sure everyone was following him so far.

"You said public purpose. Is there something else behind these meetings?" Mac asked.

"Great question, Major. Yes, there is. The princess contacted President Harrington directly, hinting at concerns of galactic importance. She wouldn't provide any information via normal communication channels, whether encrypted or not. She claimed her secrets were too important, and we must meet in person. So, we agreed to move up the date up several months, and we scheduled this partnership summit for two days from now on Terra Libertas. We were expecting her to arrive today."

Again, Kumar paused for effect. Mac wondered if Kumar enjoyed working the room with his story.

"The princess and her entourage travelled from Okuta to the Regulated Zone. Once they reached the Regulated Zone, they sent an encrypted S.O.S. message to President Harrington stating that someone attacked them. But since then, we haven't been able to make contact. We believe unknown assailants attacked them. Questions?"

Mac asked, "Prime Ambassador, did the Okutan government or royal family know the Princess planned this secret conversation? Was it sanctioned by her people, or kept secret from them as well?"

"Another good question, Major, but we don't have an answer for that. I expect the royal family knew. But I don't think they are aware the ship was attacked or that they've gone missing. The Okutan leaders have not contacted us yet."

Kumar gave a friendly eyebrow-raised glance to all of them and waited a moment for more questions, but hearing none, he turned the discussion over to President Harrington.

"Thank you, Harji. Colonel Miller, where are you with your planning?" President Harrington asked.

"Mr. President, the *McDaniels* is already cruising at *FTL*. We'll reach the Regulated Zone in about forty-five minutes. We have reports of an unknown and unresponsive space vessel in the region, which we are assuming is the Okutan Royal Vessel. Our team will approach this vessel first and see if we can confirm it is their ship. If it is, Major Lambert and his team will launch immediately to board the ship."

Immediately? Mac thought. He looked at Sam, whose eyes drilled into his own. He didn't like the hasty nature of this mission.

Colonel Miller continued, "They will investigate the ship for survivors and any clues to the princess' whereabouts."

"Very good, Colonel. Once we know more, we can determine our course of action," the president said. He turned his attention toward Mac. "Major Lambert, I don't need to tell you at this point that this is an extremely important and sensitive mission. We don't know what we are walking into, or what secrets the Okutan princess wanted to share with us. This kidnapping is a nightmare scenario, and puts the UPG in a compromised situation. We need to find her before everything unravels and we face a new galactic hostility."

"Understood, sir," Mac replied.

"Colonel Miller, I will instruct Admiral Vance to provide you with the full spectrum of services available on the *McDaniels* in order for you to do your work effectively."

"Thank you, sir. That would be a great help."

"Harji, I want you to remain onboard the *McDaniels* until we get this sorted out."

"Of course, Mr. President," Kumar said.

"I want updates every half hour. Get this done."

The president's screen went dark.

Colonel Miller stood and walked over to Mac and Sam, who still stood near the door. Miller's eyes softened and his voice was low and sympathetic as he leaned in to speak to him. "Major, you and your men just returned from a difficult mission and need some rest. But this is too important to trust with anyone else. I need you to lead it, and I need you to act fast."

"Understood, sir. I wouldn't want it any other way."

"There isn't time to prepare an army Stryker assault force. Besides that, President Harrington wants this mission kept totally black, so that leaves you. I am depending on you and your team, and so are the president, the prime ambassador, and the Okutan people."

"You don't need to explain it to me, sir. I understand the situation and the high stakes at play. This is what we do."

"Now, with this injury to your leg," he said, pointing to Mac's bandaged lower leg, "you should think about running the group from here on the *McDaniels* and let someone else lead the team in the field. Master Sergeant Clarion or even Master Sergeant Dan Jameson?"

"Sir, I appreciate what you are saying, and while Sam and DJ are capable, I won't put my men in danger without leading from the front. I'm going. Besides, my leg is fine. I feel fine."

"Excellent. Pick your best men. You'd better plan to go with full environmental gear and tools. We have no idea what we will find over there. There is a possibility that this ship is filled with holes and lacks environmental integrity. If it is still closed, it's likely you'll have to break into the ship to investigate."

CHAPTER THIRTEEN

The Regulated Zone
Interplanetary Navy Battlecruiser McDaniels

Mac finished locking down the seals on his environmental suit just as Colonel Miller entered the preparation room. The prep room was one of several rooms set apart for the Space Warfare Group aboard the *McDaniels.* No one else had access to this area of the ship, which included the preparation room, their private quarters, and the Starhawk launch bay.

Their environmental suits, known as E-Gear, featured black lightweight protective body panels over a gray airtight fabric. They designed the suits to handle everything from a spacewalk in the vacuum of space to protecting against biological threats. The heating and cooling functions also accounted for severe temperature swings. Mac preferred the E-Gear for most missions. The galaxy was too unpredictable, so he liked to have all his bases covered. The suits remained lightweight and agile, and provided protection against many threats, except for getting shot by the enemy.

They always had the option of the Armored Fighting Tactical

Suits (AFTS), but no one ever wanted to use them. They were too cumbersome, restricting the operator's movements. The preference in the group was always the agile E-Gear.

The E-Gear kit included a tactical vest with a chest plate over the thick airtight bodysuit, and contained grenades, medical kits, knives, and tools. A tactical belt also contained small tools and energy reloads around their waist. The most advanced part of the kit was the helmet, which included a heads-up display, multiple scanners, and visual enhancement filters. All their communications, whether radio or text, came through the helmet as well. They could also display stored data on the face shield.

Mac didn't like putting his suit and boot over the MedTek bio-inhibiting tape, which made his ankle feel more rigid than normal. He found the wound was quite sensitive. It hurt like crazy when he tightened the boot, even with the pain blockers. He considered removing the bandage for mobility, but remembered the face of the disapproving doctor and left it alone. He'd be able to work through the discomfort.

Mac summarized the mission objectives for his team while they geared up. Since he did not know what they were walking into, Mac chose the most experienced from his twenty-four-man group. This, again, included Sam Clarion, Luis Sanchez, and Cory Allen. Each was a veteran who served alongside Mac on his toughest missions. Mac gave each the ability to opt out of this one, since they'd just returned from the muddy planet debacle, but none even considered sitting out.

"Major Lambert, is your team ready?" Colonel Miller asked as he entered the preparation room and gestured toward the three other men in E-Gear.

"Yes, sir. As ready as we're going to get. The four of us will board the ship. I also have a few of the other boys prepped as QRF from the *McDaniels*."

"Good idea. Who's leading that team?"

"DJ, sir."

"Great. OK, here's the latest information, as of a couple minutes ago. We have confirmed the dead ship is in fact the Okutan Royal Vessel. We have also confirmed that the vessel is unresponsive. Scanners are showing no signs of power, environmental systems, or activity of any sort. We don't even see any residual heat from the engines. It could be empty. But if I was a betting man, I expect you'll find a giant floating coffin over there."

They all nodded and listened.

"Sir," Mac asked, "are there any other vessels in the area?"

"As of right now? No. Ops insists we're out here alone with the dead ship. And I don't need to tell you this, but I will anyway. You'd be wise to expect hostile forces aboard that ship. Be prepared to fight your way in or out."

"Yes, sir. We'll give it the standard response. Do we know anything about the floor plan or layout of the Okutan ship at this point?" Mac asked.

"Yes, Prime Ambassador Kumar got a schematic of the ship. It wasn't easy, but he got it."

"Have the schematics been uploaded to our helmets already?" Mac asked as he tapped the top of his black helmet in the crook of his elbow.

"No, we just received them. You'll have to take this." Colonel Miller handed over a thin handheld touchscreen device.

"Really? Not even a bit drive so we can upload manually?" Mac asked as he took the tablet.

"Not my department, Major," Miller said sternly. "I received this only moments ago."

Mac tapped a few icons to bring up the ship's floor plan. "Well, at least it looks like a lot of schematics are on here."

"Supposedly, you've got access codes and instructions on there as well, if needed."

"Do I want to know how the Prime Ambassador obtained this information?" Mac wondered how Kumar could gather such sensitive information that quickly from an alien race they knew little about. Nothing was ever as it seemed. There was always more than meets the eye in galactic politics.

"No, Major, I suspect that is beyond your scope. You've got what you need to do your job," Miller said. It was the exact answer Mac expected, but he couldn't help asking.

"Roger that," Mac said.

"Admiral Vance, at the president's request, has agreed to provide a Navy pilot and small crew to shuttle you guys over on a SMART Ship." The Navy's Space Maintenance, Recovery, and Transport ship, known as the SMART ship, was a simple utility vessel used for transporting people and equipment for maintenance and recovery tasks.

"Once inside, you need to assess the situation and search for any survivors. If you find any, gather them up for EXFIL. We'll be standing by. But most importantly, find the princess. The perfect situation would be that you find her unharmed, but nothing ever goes perfectly."

"My thoughts exactly, sir," Mac said.

"Gentleman, keep in mind, Prime Ambassador Kumar will sit next to me in the situation room, watching your live stream and listening in on command comms. Understand?"

"Yessir," the four operators said.

"Questions?"

No one spoke.

"Ok, then you better get moving. The SMART Ship is waiting for you in Hangar Bay 7, on Level 3."

The four operators gathered their equipment and made their way to the service lift that connected the stacked hangar bays. They carried their own helmets and equipment cases, with their energy rifles secured to the magnetic hold on their backs.

Hangar Bay 7 was an enormous, bright room with ten SMART Ships lined up, side-by-side. Interplanetary Navy crew moved around preparing the ships. The SMART ship's engine noise echoed off the hard surfaces. Each ship looked identical, except for the large painted numbers on the body. They were long, boxy vessels devoid of any style, with white painted bodies and electric blue lettering and decorative stripes. Windows, similar to those on a shuttle bus, lined the front half of the ship, with cargo doors on the back half.

"Major Lambert!" Mac turned to find a Navy crewman waving at him. He wore an orange jumpsuit and helmet with a clear face screen. Mac and the other men followed the crewman. "Your ship is ready. Right this way, sir." He had to shout over the noise as he led them to a SMART ship with the engines running. The SMART ship's exterior flood lights and flashing beacons were on. Interior lights and display screens were visible through the windows.

The crewman led them to the mobile staircase to climb into the SMART ship's passenger entrance. "Good luck, sir," he shouted and saluted.

They climbed the five steps and entered the shuttle transport ship, one at a time, with Mac as the last to enter. He tried not limp as he climbed the steps but wasn't sure it worked. Putting his full body weight on it, with the extra burden of his equipment, felt like a red-hot knife was slicing into his lower leg.

A cheerful woman with brown hair pulled into a tight bun on top of her head greeted them at the entrance. She wore a white and blue jumpsuit that matched the ship. She was tall and exuded the unique bearing of someone who was career military.

"Gentleman, welcome aboard. I'm Lieutenant Taylor, the co-pilot of this vessel today. Please find a seat, strap in, and we'll depart right away."

The main cabin included four sections of empty seats, with 20 seats per section. They sat in four jump seats near the front, where four Navy crew members and two medics were sitting.

The pilot's cabin at the front of the vessel was open to the passenger area, and they could see the control screens and blinking green and red lights on the displays. The pilot was working through pre-flight checklists and verifying systems conditions. He sat in front of a wall of windows wrapping around the front of the ship, giving them a clear view of everything in front of them. Visibility was essential for the typical SMART ship business, so they built it with more windows than Mac was used to seeing on a space vessel.

"This thing is bigger than I expected," Sanchez said. "They

always look so small when you see them from a distance. Like little flies buzzing around."

"Quite a bit more comfortable than the hawk, too," Sam said as he slouched in his seat. "Do these things lean back?"

Once Mac and the others were situated and strapped in, Lieutenant Taylor took her seat and buckled in as well. Then the lights dimmed, and the SMART ship lifted off the hangar floor.

The pilot maneuvered the ship into the hangar bay's massive airlock and waited for the interior door to close behind them. A few seconds later, they could hear the *whoosh* of air being evacuated from the airlock. The outer doors opened so the pilot could guide the flying box into the blackness of open space. Blackness splattered with trillions of tiny pinpoints of light from distant stars lay beyond the hull of the McDaniels.

"Gentleman, sit tight. It'll take us 20 minutes to reach the Okutan ship." The pilot ramped up the acceleration and the SMART ship shot forward until it reached its top speed.

Mac took the time to examine the ship schematics on the touchscreen pad with Sam. Barring some unexpected discovery, they planned to break into the ship from open space. They needed to access the ship safely while putting no potential survivors at risk. An access door would be ideal if they could find one. But if the ship's systems were dead, it was likely they wouldn't be able to open a door or hatch. Even though he didn't expect to find anyone on board, making the mistake of breaching the hull and sucking survivors into space would be unforgivable. So, Mac studied the schematics, looking for some sort of ship-to-ship access hatch or loading door.

It felt futile to study the schematics of an alien ship. They struggled to interpret the alien symbols and language. Plus, the logic of the ship made little sense. Humans arranged their ships based on a particular logic and these Okutans seemed to use different logic.

"If we were breaking into a human spaceship," Sam said, "We'd find a manual access hatch and open it from space. Do you think they have something similar?"

Sanchez, straining to see the screen from two seats away, added, "What about a hangar bay or large cargo door? See anything like that, Major Mac? A big ship like that? They've gotta load their Okutan food somehow."

"I don't know. Can't tell what's what on this schematic," Mac said. "I'm clueless about how this Okutan culture designs anything or what their basic philosophy of engineering is like."

"Yeah, I agree. Maybe when we get our eyes on the ship, we'll be able to confirm something," Sam said.

Twenty minutes later, the Okutan ship came into view, small at first, but then it quickly filled the pilot's window. The SMART ship's exterior flood lights illuminated the dull gray alien spaceship as it floated lifelessly in front of them, like a colossal arrow-shaped meteor.

CHAPTER FOURTEEN

"Well, what do you think, Mac?" Sam asked.

"I think we need to enter here, at this location," Mac said, pointing at his handheld screen at a location on the side of the Okutan ship.

Mac and Sam stood behind the pilots, looking back and forth between the ship's dimpled skin in the window and the screen on Mac's tablet. Sanchez and Allen gazed through the SMART ship's side windows, examining the surface of the Okutan Royal Vessel.

"This ship looks like a flying boulder. Are you sure it's not just a big rock? Maybe it's just a meteor," Sanchez said. "It doesn't look like any ship I've seen before."

At Mac's earlier request, the pilot guided the SMART ship around the dead vessel several times as they considered their options. The ship was much smaller than the colossal *McDaniels* - which was more of a flying city than a spaceship - but this Okutan vessel was large enough to house a substantial crew and make extended space travel comfortable.

Colonel Miller's voice came through the command channel. "Black Leader, you copy?"

"Roger, Command," Mac replied to Colonel Miller, then spoke to the pilot. "Commander, can you take us back to this area on the ship and pull up parallel so we can scope out the surface?" Mac pointed to the screen with the floor plan. "Get us in there as close as you can."

"I think so. Let's see what we can do," the pilot said as he pulled on a lever to ease the SMART ship closer.

Miller came through the radio again. "Black Leader, I've got Prime Ambassador Kumar with me. Get us up to speed. Have you found any external damage to the ship from an attack?"

"Command, there are two obvious spots that look like torpedo damage. But, more importantly, we found a smaller craft attached to the top of the Okutan vessel. Black-2 is sending you the files now."

"Attached how, Black Leader? Like with an umbilical?"

"No, more like a leech. From what we could tell, the smaller craft is latched to the top of the ship. It is too hard to tell without doing a spacewalk, but it looks like it is secure."

"Did the scanners recognize the craft or pick up anything?" Colonel Miller asked.

"No, sir. It's just as dead as the Okutan vessel."

"Ok, what is your boarding plan? Did you find an airlock entrance?"

"We are just finishing our external examination now. To be honest, we can't figure out how they board this ship. The surface looks like a giant rock with no distinguishable surface features."

"Except for the output of the propulsion engines at the rear," Sam added.

"Yeah, exactly," Mac agreed. "Command, has Navy Engineering found anything useful?"

"We've heard nothing so far, Black Leader."

"Ok, I figured. I think our best option is to enter through the outer wall of what looks like a storage tank of some sort on the Okutan schematics. It's a hollow space with no doors or access hatches inside or outside. Looks like a couple of tubes or small access points only. It is the most direct option we've found."

"Where is this on the ship?" Colonel Miller asked.

"Sir, are you looking at the schematics?

"Yes, we are."

"I'll activate the video stream and show you on the plans," Mac said. He activated the live stream of the camera on his helmet from the control screen imbedded into the underside of his left forearm. He waited a moment for the video to connect, then continued, "This area, here." He pointed to the area on the screen with his gloved finger.

"Ok, Black Leader, we see it. Walk me through it," Colonel Miller said.

"Now, keep in mind, I'm no spaceship engineer, and I know nothing about this Okuta race or their -."

"That's fine, Major. We get it. Just tell me your plan."

"If this is some sort of storage tank, it's likely to be airtight. It may store liquid or gas, therefore increasing the chances that it's airtight. We can cut our way through the outer hull and into the tank, then cover the hole from the inside before we breach the interior wall of the ship. It'll work like an airlock. If all goes as planned, we should be able to maintain the overall integrity of the ship."

"And you don't see any better options, Black Leader?"

"No, sir. This is our best bet. And the fastest way in."

"Ok, execute without delay. Keep me updated."

"Yessir."

Mac handed the tablet to Sam and turned to the pilot and Navy crew, "Ok, we have the green light to breach the ship and enter here. Get us as close as you can and secure us to the ship. We need to wire over."

Lieutenant Taylor climbed out of her piloting seat to assist the team. "Sounds like a brilliant plan, Major," she said with a friendly smile.

"Well, I'm glad you think so. Would you like to be the first one to go in?" Mac asked, teasing the Lieutenant. "We could get you a suit and rifle."

"I sure would, Major, but I doubt we can get that cleared by the top brass. Come on, let's get everything ready." She laughed, and led them toward the back of the ship.

Taylor instructed the SMART ship crew to prepare for a spacewalk as the pilot was maneuvering the small vessel into place.

Mac gathered his team to give them instructions.

"Sanchez, you are on torch duty. Cory is better at welding, so he'll handle that. Cory, confirm with the schematics that you have the right chemicals and plasma components to weld the cover to whatever metal alloy makes up that ship. Sam, once we are inside, you'll navigate. So figure out how to get us to the ship's control room from this location."

The men nodded in confirmation. Sanchez added with a wide grin, "The *Leading Man* will lead the way."

"Sanchez," Sam replied as he took a seat to study the ship floor plan. "you are an idiot."

"True story, Master Sarge," Sanchez said. "True story. I can't help it though. My momma always said to just be myself."

"I guess your momma is an idiot as well," Sam said.

"Keep that up, and I'll be cutting you open with this torch instead of that ship," Sanchez said with mock fury from across the cabin.

Mac added, "And, Sam, when you guys finish acting like teenagers, find a couple of alternate routes, since we don't know what we will find in there. We should assume interior damage."

"Roger," Sam said.

Sanchez slung the straps of the heavy laser torch over his shoulders like a backpack, glaring at Sam the entire time. Any time Sam would look his way, Sanchez would make hand signals, implying he would slit Sam's throat or break him in half. Sam grinned and went back to studying the map. Once the backpack was situated and secured by Allen, Sanchez followed Lieutenant Taylor to the SMART ship's airlock at the back of the craft.

The SMART ship jostled, and loud clanking sounds reverberated through the ship as the pilot activated a magnetic arm that gripped the side of the Okutan ship to secure and steady their position next to it.

Sanchez stood in the airlock in his gray and black E-Gear suit, tethered to the safety bar on the wall beside him. He wore the laser torch generator on his back and his helmet face screen was in the down position, ready for action. He shared the airlock with a Navy crewman in a similar white environmental suit designed for the SMART ship staff. The Navy crewman's suit featured the same electric blue found on the side of the ship, but didn't include any of the armor or weapons Sanchez had.

"Major, our docking procedure is complete. You may proceed," the pilot informed Mac while adjusting settings on the control panel in front of him.

"Sanchez, I'm going to paint the spot with an infrared target marker. Cut a hole just big enough for us to squeeze through," Mac ordered through the tactical radio channel in their helmets. "Let me know when you've got it."

Mac tapped the button to lower the helmet face shield and engaged the infrared filter. He then pulled his EP-17 rifle from his shoulder hold and pointed it out the window towards the surface of the Okutan ship. Originally designed for the Army Stryker Force and the Special Action Squad, Mac's Space Warfare Group had access to a modified version of the EP-17. They were the most reliable and effective close combat rifle available. He triggered the infrared aiming dot and saw it visible on the dimpled surface.

"Bingo, Major Mac. I see it," Sanchez said a moment later.

After confirming with Sanchez, the Navy crewman opened the outer airlock door. He fired a winch cable with a magnetic grappling head at the Okutan ship, near where Sanchez would cut his way in. The winch cable shot across the 20 meters of open vacuum between ships, slammed hard against the dimpled face of the Okutan ship, and stuck. Then the crewman tightened the winch cable and pulled on it several times to ensure it was secure. He gave Sanchez a thumbs-up sign.

Sanchez unclipped his carabiner and tether from the airlock safety bar, clipped it to the winch cable, and pushed out into space.

"Sanchez, be careful out there. Don't take any unnecessary risks," Mac said. The last thing Mac wanted was for one of his men to end up floating in space.

Once leaving the safety of the artificial gravity of the small craft, Sanchez floated weightlessly, bouncing around at the end of this short tether until he could grab hold of the winch cable to pull himself toward the ship.

"Major Mac, have I ever taken unnecessary risks?" Sanchez asked with a touch of sarcasm in his voice. He was breathing heavily after fighting to gain control of his weightless body.

"Do I need to remind you of the time we were on Zhotov 9 -"

"No, no, Major Mac. Let's not do that right now. Sam and Cory are a little young to hear that story. We should protect their innocent ears," Sanchez said, gasping.

"Or how about the time I rescued you from the bottom of that pit-"

Sanchez interrupted again, "Major Mac, if you continue to tear down my reputation in this way, I am going to report you to Colonel Miller for behavior unbecoming of an officer and harassment from a superior."

While Sanchez traversed the distance between ships, pulling himself along the winch cable, Cory Allen confirmed his welding chemical compound, gathered his equipment, and headed to the airlock where Lieutenant Taylor opened the door. He would follow Sanchez as soon as he cut the entrance hole.

Mac and Sam watched Sanchez from the window closest to where he would cut the hole. Mac kept pointing the infrared target dot on the spot. Sanchez reached the outer wall of the larger ship and secured himself to the hull by attaching his tether to the winch cable magnetic head. The laser cutting torch was on the end of a handheld wand, attached to the backpack with a flexible metal tube. The torch required two hands for accuracy, so Sanchez secured his feet to the hull and pushed out against his tether. He was standing perpendicular to the side of the hull, about 20 meters from where Mac observed through the window.

"Major Mac, you sure you like this spot right here?" Sanchez asked through the radio as he stood above the dot.

"That looks perfect," Mac said and lowered his rifle.

"Roger. I might carve your initials on the ship's side while I'm at it. *Major Mac was here* would be fitting."

Intense white light bathed the area around Sanchez as the laser stream shot from the end of the wand to the wall and began cutting. Mac radioed Command to provide an update.

After about 60 seconds, Mac checked in. "Sanchez, how is it cutting?"

Sanchez stopped the laser, and the bright light was gone.

"Cutting through like butter. Hey, wait a sec. It looks like there is some liquid beginning to spray out of the cut," Sanchez said.

Mac could see it as well, near Sanchez's foot. Liquid sprayed from the cut.

"What do you think it is?" Sanchez asked.

"No idea. We'll check the schematics again. Keep cutting," Mac said, grinning wildly. He was sure he knew what it was.

Sanchez resumed cutting. As his cut became longer, the spray showered him with a mixture of liquid and steam, as the fluid escaped and cooked in the laser beam.

"This stuff better not be toxic," Sanchez yelled through the radio over the noise of the laser torch. "I'm getting soaked."

When Sanchez's cut was nearly all the way through, he removed a wire from a compartment on his belt and unrolled another small tether with the magnetic plunger, which he placed in the center of the panel he was removing. He then clipped the other end to the winch cable. When Sanchez cut the remaining edge, the thick metal panel flew off and snapped the tether to full length, almost smacking Sanchez as it flew by. He dodged to the left. It took him a moment to regain his balance and position in the weightlessness of space.

Sanchez was unable, however, to dodge the torrent of liquid that was sucked from the interior of the ship like the water from a fire hydrant. The liquid splattered against the windows of the SMART ship as well.

Cory waited for the stream of escaping fluid to finish before he had the Navy crewman open the airlock. After the brief explosion of fluid, Cory had the airlock outer door opened. He swapped his tether from the wall to the wire and started pulling his way across the winch line to the open hole near Sanchez.

"Sanchez, you alright?" Sam asked over the radio.

"I think so. Did you figure out what that stuff was?"

"Uh, well, according to the Okutan schematics, this cavity is described as waste storage," Sam said and winked at Mac standing next to him by the window. "If we are interpreting the Okutan language correctly."

Sanchez's helmeted head jerked around towards the SMART Ship. His face mask reflecting the ship's floodlights. Cory pulled his body past Sanchez and climbed through the black hole in the ship's side.

"Waste? What kind of waste?" Sanchez asked anxiously. "You mean like radioactive waste?"

"No, I don't think so, bro."

"You mean some kind of collected condensation from the environmental system, right?" Sanchez asked.

"Not quite."

"You don't mean human waste?"

"No, no. Of course not," Sam said. "There were no humans on that ship. Only Okutans. But it is likely it was Okutan waste."

CHAPTER FIFTEEN

Mac pulled himself through the hole cut by Sanchez and entered the dark, empty interior of the ship's waste tank. Dual headlamps mounted on his helmet showed Sam and Sanchez gripping a bracket on the far wall, floating in the weightlessness of the dead ship. The waste tank was a now empty metal cavern. Mac's face shield display listed temperature and environment data.

Their helmets glowed on the inside, highlighting their faces through the face shield. Cory Allen positioned his body against the inner wall, ready to begin the welding process to seal their access hole. He grinned as Mac unclipped his carabiner from the umbilical wire connected to the SMART ship and floated by.

Sanchez complained incessantly over the radio. "Why do I always have to be the one to get drenched in alien waste?"

"Have you been drenched by alien waste often, Sanchez?" Mac asked as he floated through the dark cavernous space. "I didn't realize this about you." He could hear the other men chuckle on the radio. "Maybe I should have checked your references more thoroughly before recruiting you into the group."

"Come on, man, you know what I mean. Y'all just sat on the SMART ship, comfortable and safe as always, while I risk life and limb and experience one of the most traumatic moments of my short life. It was like that time -"

Mac cut him off, "Sanchez, you are our hero, and the most brave warrior, hands down. We appreciate you risking your life as you have." Mac pushed his floating body toward Sanchez and Sam. "I'm not sure what we would do without you."

Sanchez was the most chitty-chatty operator he'd ever met, but Mac knew he was also one of the most skilled and reliable. He was a bit of an enigma, always harassing everyone, but the second things became serious, Sanchez was who Mac wanted by his side.

"I mean, seriously, Major Mac. We don't know what is in that waste. We don't know what these things eat. What if it burns through my suit? What if it ruins all the digital circuits that keep me alive? What if I inhale it and catch some horrible bacterial infection or parasite? What if it -"

Mac interrupted, "Sanchez, what if you shut up for five minutes?"

"See that, Sam, no love from the Major Mac. No love at all."

"Hey, just do me a favor and don't touch me. I don't want any of that biohazard on my suit," Sam put his hands up. "In fact, just keep your distance, will you please? I think I can smell you from here." This caused Sanchez to launch into a new litany of complaints.

"Cory, close it up," Mac instructed, ignoring Sanchez.

Mac switched to the command channel connecting him to the situation room. "Command, Black Leader?"

Colonel Miller's voice came through the radio a moment later, "Go, Black Leader."

"We are all inside the first layer. The gravity generators are down."

"Understood, Black Leader."

"We are covering the exterior hole now. You can inform the Navy crew to standby. We'll cut the second hole in a moment and enter what we believe is a corridor on the second level."

Cory rolled out a sheet of thin, but unbreakable, hull patch material that covered the hole and held it against the inner wall. The patch material was soft enough to carry and roll out but hardened by heat once welded. The room filled with the staccato flashing of bright light as Cory began welding the edges to secure the patch material to the hull.

After a few minutes, Cory gave the all-clear sign, allowing Sanchez to cut through the inside wall.

Sanchez finished cutting, pulled the piece of the wall out, and let it float behind him. An ominous, pitch-black cavern beyond the jagged hole.

Mac switched to night vision and leaned into the hole with his rifle at the ready. The corridor was darker than night. It was a heavy, disconcerting darkness. The helmet's night vision feature, which amplified the tiniest bit of ambient light, was ineffectual. He didn't like the visibility presented, so he switched over to the infrared illuminator to enhance the night vision's capabilities. The ship's extreme darkness and low temperatures handicapped both vision enhancement filters.

Mac turned his headlamps back on and scanned around through the hole, assessing the space under the two bright cones of white light slicing through the darkness as he turned his head. It seemed they breached the corridor as he'd hoped, and it was empty. Seeing it as clear, Mac pulled his shoulders and head out of the hole and turned around in the zero gravity.

"It's too dark for night vision, guys. Pure darkness in there. We'll have to go old school with headlamps and spotlights," Mac said. "That means if any hostiles are on this ship, they'll see us coming."

The others pulled their energy rifles from the magnetic holds on their back and activated the spotlights mounted on the rifle's barrels. Light beams bounced off the waste cavern walls.

Mac gave the signal, and Sam entered first by pulling his weightless body through the sharp-edged hole, disappearing into the darkness. Mac followed a moment later, rifle leading the way.

As he pulled himself through the small hole, his injured leg bumped against the edge of the hole, sending a jolt of pain up his leg. He gasped and squeezed his eyes shut tight as the jolt of pain subsided a moment later. He had forgotten his leg injury after floating weightlessly for a while. It surprised him how sensitive the wound was, so he made a mental note to be extra careful.

Once through the hole, they were in a corridor about four meters wide. He checked both directions and found Sam on his left. Sam hand-signaled they needed to go toward the left. Their light beams flickered around the long corridor.

Mac whispered into his radio on the command channel, "Command, Black Leader. We are entering the ship now."

"Roger, Black Leader," Miller replied. "What's the situation?"

"It's pitch black. No ship lighting or environmental systems running, that I can tell. Temperatures are way below freezing. We will begin making our way toward the control room first."

"Understood," Colonel Miller said. "Proceed with caution."

"Roger," Mac said.

Sam floated against the wall in the corridor a few meters in front of Mac under the thin beam of his rifle's spotlight. Mac rotated his body in a slow arc. Sanchez crawled through the hole like some kind of demonic creature from a horror movie.

Something in Mac's periphery caught his attention. He thought it was movement, but when he scanned to his left, he saw nothing. But his heartbeat increased. He turned and glanced at Sam. Nothing. His mind raced for a moment, trying to figure out if he'd seen something. He decided it was likely just Sam's spotlight.

"Look alive, men. Head on a swivel. No telling what's waiting for us on this ship."

Thump.

"You hear that?" Sanchez asked over the radio. Sanchez was floating horizontally, face down in the middle of the corridor.

"I think so," Mac said. "Anyone see anything?"

"Negative," Sam said.

"I'm still in the tank, nothing here," Cory said.

"Mac, above you!" Sanchez screamed into the radio, causing distortion in the small speakers.

Mac's heart skipped a beat, and he tried to roll his body backwards - slower in weightlessness than he would have preferred - so that he was floating on his back looking toward the tall corridor ceiling. As his headlamps rotated along the wall to the ceiling, a figure came into view. It was above him, and he felt the instant boost of fight-or-flight adrenaline. A pale creature floated above him, its arms reaching toward him with hands opened wide.

"There's more!" Sam shouted.

Sanchez, Mac, and Sam all fired without hesitation at the same moment. A dozen energy pulses exploded from their rifles, filling the corridor with the explosive sounds and bursts of flashing light. The buzzing sensation of static electricity and echoes reverberated off the hard surfaces.

"Cease fire. Cease fire," Mac commanded. "They're already dead."

It was over as quickly as it started. The creatures, hit by the energy bursts, slammed against the walls and ceiling, which bounced them back toward the operators.

Mac aimed his light toward one body as it floated close to him. He now recognized it as a frozen Okutan corpse, dead for several hours. Its strange, contorted face with the odd scalp frill extended was enough for him to recognize that this creature died in pain from the vicious attack.

Mac scanned the length of the space above him and counted four similar corpses floating above them. The macabre scene gave him the chills. He reached out and grabbed a corpse as it floated close to him. Sanchez took up a guard position, facing down the corridor in one direction while Sam focused on the other. Cory joined Sanchez after he pulled his own body through the hole. Like Sanchez, Cory left his bulky back-mounted welding equipment in the storage tank for freedom of movement. They would sacrifice the equipment for the mission.

Mac examined the alien corpse under his headlamps. He couldn't tell if it was a male or female. He assumed the Okutan race included males and females since they were looking for a princess. But what did he know about alien cultures? It wasn't his specialty, and he didn't get the full debrief on this race of aliens.

This one wore a white robe tied tight to its thin waist with a thick leather belt. The body of the alien was small, much leaner and shorter than himself. A large and ugly energy blast wound was at the center of the Okutan's chest.

Sam leaned close to Mac and looked at the corpse as well. "What happened here?"

"I don't know, but we're dealing with something merciless," Mac replied. "No weapons in here. These guys were unarmed."

Mac keyed the command channel again. "Command, Black Leader. We've got several fatalities in the corridor. It's clear at this point there was a violent attack. This Okutan I'm looking at was shot at point blank range by a high-powered energy blast." Mac paused for a minute, shaking his head back and forth. "It's terrible."

"Ok, Black Leader. Understood. Make sure you document whatever you can as you go."

"Alright. We're going to make our way to the control room and attempt to get the ship's systems running."

"Roger," Colonel Miller said.

Then another accented voice came through the radio, "Major Lambert, this is Prime Ambassador Kumar."

"Yes, Prime Ambassador?"

"I am happy to report I just received instructions for powering up the ship's systems from my Okutan contact. I'll be able to walk you through it when you get there."

"That is excellent news. Standby as we try to find the control room," Mac said. Then, "Cory, I want you to get photos of everything you can for the Colonel as we encounter fatalities, weapons, and whatever else we come across. Start with this unfortunate one here."

Mac steadied the dead Okutan in place while Cory collected photos and a short video on his helmet camera before pushing it away.

"Alright, enough of floating around here. Let's get moving."

CHAPTER SIXTEEN

Sam led the team through the dark, cold, and shadowy ship to the control room. They encountered more victims along the way, all killed by either gunfire or blunt force. It was gut-wrenching for the men to see unarmed victims killed in cold blood. Each of them wished they could have been on the ship at the time of the attack to defend the Okutans. Sam took them on the most direct route, according to the schematics. They had to traverse one of the elevator shafts by breaking through the door and floating to the upper levels. Sanchez and Cory used their hammer crowbars to pry the doors open. Once at the top of the elevator shaft, they broke through the elevator door again to gain access to the control center of the ship.

Mac was the first to pull himself through the doors and float into the dark control room. Under the beams of his headlamps and rifle spotlight, he found five more dead Okutans. He didn't like what he was finding. These weren't soldiers on a battlefield. It infuriated him that these innocent, unarmed, and peaceful people were slaughtered. They were dealing with ruthless animals. The senseless killing, and not being able to do anything about it, burned deep within him. He committed to discover the identity of these animals, to hunt them down, and bring justice to their doorstep.

As Mac floated across the small room filled with electronic screens and control stations, he called Colonel Miller to report in. "Command, Black Leader. We've accessed the ship's main control room. We've got more fatalities in here as well. There are no weapons. They were defenseless. I think we are ready for you to walk us through the steps to get the power up and running."

"Roger, Black Leader. You need to first find the energy module, which they said was in the secondary room on the port side of the main control room."

"Ah, OK, I think I see another room over here."

Mac used the floor-mounted chairs to pull his floating body to the door at the left side of the dark room. He floated against it and had to turn his body and reorient his position to open the door. He pressed on the door, but it didn't budge. As with all the other doors on the ship, there was no latch, only a control pad beside the door on the wall.

"Command, this door won't open and there is no latch. Any other ideas?"

"Hold one, Black Leader," Colonel Miller said.

As Mac waited, floating by the door to the energy module, the others pulled themselves around the room, examining equipment and corpses.

"Black Leader." It was Kumar's voice coming through the radio this time. "It appears there is a manual override for the door. There should be a panel or hatch below the control pad big enough to put your hand in."

Mac focused his headlamps on the area below the control panel and found a square panel that was slightly raised. "Ok, I found the hatch, but it looks like it needs a key."

"Yes, Major, I believe it does."

"Hold on, I'm going to use my key," Mac said.

"You...you have a key?" Kumar's confused voice came stuttering through the radio.

Mac pressed himself off the wall. At about two meters away from the panel, he fired his rifle on the low setting. The energy explosion mangled the thin metal panel and part of the wall. He stowed his rifle and pulled out the flathead screwdriver, always tucked into his chest rig. He jammed it behind the mangled panel and popped it off the wall. It floated away. In the hole behind the panel, he could see a lever.

"Command, the key worked. I see a lever in the hand hole." Mac pulled the lever and felt the mechanical linkage break free. The door slid open a quarter of the way. "Ok, I've got access to the room now."

Mac pushed the door the rest of the way open and pulled his floating body through the doorway into the room. Mac made a full sweep of the tiny room. The scanners in his helmet reported nothing interesting. The room was small and barren, with a curved pedestal standing at the center of the room. It was about one meter tall and made of a reflective silver metal. The light from his headlamps sparkled off the shiny surface.

Sitting on top of the silver pedestal was a red translucent sphere. Mac shined his rifle spotlight at the sphere as he grasped the edge of the pedestal and pulled his body towards it. The light refracted through it dimly, casting the room in a reddish glow. The sphere was about the size of his helmet and perfectly smooth. He wondered if it was a naturally occurring material, like a gemstone, or manufactured in an Okutan laboratory.

"Command, I've got some kind of red ball on a shiny pedestal. Looks like glass or a gemstone," Mac said.

"Excellent, Major, that's what you are looking for. You need to press it down into the pedestal, which will activate the ship's power," Kumar said.

"That's it?" Mac asked. "Just flush the red ball down the tube?" That seemed ridiculous, but he reminded himself again he wasn't an expert in alien cultures and sciences.

"According to my source, that is all you need to do," Kumar said. "The red sphere is a superconductor that activates the ship's power source."

"Roger that. Flushing the red ball now."

Mac did as instructed and pushed the red sphere down with two hands. The sphere was sucked into the pedestal and disappeared with a low *floomph* sound.

To his surprise, the ship responded immediately. The small power-activation room filled with red light emanating from the top of the pedestal. An intense beam of red light shot out of the top of the pedestal. It sparkled and spun around the room, flickering.

The ship's emergency lighting system came on and the gravity generators engaged, which Mac did not expect. He floated toward the ceiling above the pedestal when the artificial gravitational force kicked in. He reached out at the pedestal as he fell, but he couldn't react quickly enough. He bounced off the pedestal and flopped to the floor.

Mac heard the *umphs* from his men through the radio as their bodies slammed against the floor in the other room.

"Command, we've got auxiliary power and gravity," Mac grunted.

"Good work, Major. Next, you need to bring up environmental controls and sensors," Prime Ambassador Kumar said with the same excited tone, as if he was enjoying himself.

"Roger, Command."

Mac struggled to get his body off the floor and back on his feet. No matter how many times he experienced it, it always took several moments for his brain to recalibrate to the effects of gravity after an extended period of weightlessness. In those few moments, his body felt heavy and sluggish.

Composing himself, he walked out into the control room, rifle in hand. His first full-weight step caused pain to shoot up his leg. He gasped and gingerly limped two more steps. Sam, who was standing at the door next to him, reached out to steady Mac.

Sam mouthed, *are you OK,* through the face shield without speaking it through the radio for the others to hear. Mac waved him off, thankful for his friend's concern, but not willing to allow the injury to affect the mission. He straightened and compartmentalized the pain so he could attempt to walk without the limp.

Sanchez and Cory were adjusting the gear on their belts and chest plates after pulling their bodies up off the floor. All the screens and monitors in the control room lit up, and small indicator lights began flashing. He heard the soft beeping of electronic alarms. The creepy darkness of the cold dead ship was now replaced with electronic activity.

"A little warning next time, Major Mac," Sanchez said as he snatched his rifle off the floor. "This desk hit me with a cheap shot to the head." He bumped the desk with his fist.

"Do I look like an Okutan ship engineer to you, Sanchez?" Mac said. "How was I supposed to know the ship was going to automatically reinstate gravity?"

"Sanchez, that is why we wear helmets. We've got to protect that valuable head of yours," Sam said.

"That's right you do, Lead. That was a close call. I can't risk damaging this handsome face of mine. Not everyone is as ugly as you," Sanchez said.

"Mac, over here. I think I've found the controls," Sam called out, now standing at a computer control console. Sam sat on the contoured floor-mounted chair in front of the screen. The chair was small by human standards. Mac walked over to where Sam was sitting and looked over his shoulder. He looked like an adult in a child's chair. "Looks like symbols, mostly. Not sure if this is an alphabet or what."

Mac keyed the command channel. "Command, we are in position at the control console. Walk us through it."

Prime Ambassador Kumar said, "Ok, the first thing you'll want to do is bring up full power and then we can work on the environmental controls like air and heat."

"Prime Ambassador, this is Master Sergeant Sam Clarion. I'm on the controls. All I see here is a symbol in the middle of this screen."

"Good. You need to touch the symbol and then it will prompt you to enter the security code," Kumar said.

Kumar painstakingly described the strange Okutan symbols and language characters over the radio to Sam, and he tried to follow the instructions by touching symbols on the screen. It wasn't easy, but they eventually entered the security password. Then in the same painstaking process, they figured out the controls and activated full power. The process was slow, and Mac felt antsy standing around.

The lights came up to full brightness. Other screens, flashing alarm lights, and notifiers were activated. While Kumar worked with Sam, Sanchez and Cory dragged the five dead bodies into a corner together, rather than leaving them scattered about where they landed.

Over to Mac's right, a table produced a floating holographic image of the Okutan Royal Vessel. The holographic image was a dark amber-yellow color and rotated in a circle. Mac slung his rifle onto his back and walked over to study it. Sanchez joined him at the edge of the table. Cory took up a position near the elevators to cover the door.

Mac noticed a small red spacecraft attached to the top of the amber-yellow Okutan Royal Vessel image.

"That must be the leech ship," Sanchez said, pointing at the smaller shape.

"For sure," Mac said. He squatted down and looked at it from a couple of different angles. "I think we breached the hull here." He was pointing at a spot on the holographic ship that was flashing. "It looks like the leech attached a couple floors above where we are now. We need to search that area first and learn what we can about that ship."

Mac stood to his full height and turned towards the others. "Alright, we've done all we can do here, boys. Let's find this princess."

"Command, we have gravity, lights, air, and heat. This ship will be flight worthy again in a little while, I suspect," Mac reported. "We will leave the ship-wide diagnostics running while we continue to search the ship. I want to investigate the location where the smaller leech-like ship is attached first and see what we can figure out."

"Roger, Black Leader. Proceed with caution."

CHAPTER SEVENTEEN

Mac was the first to step out of the elevator into the bright lobby area, rifle at the ready. He checked both directions and, seeing nothing in front of him, he moved toward the doors across the lobby from the elevator.

Maneuvering through the ship with artificial gravity and lighting was easier than floating through complete frozen darkness. He had more control over his body and weapons now. Even though he had extensive experience in weightlessness, he preferred gravity.

The ship's heating system was now working overtime to bring the overall temperature up. Mac could see the temperature increasing on the heads-up display on his face shield. The empty and deadly silent spacecraft still gave Mac a bit of the heebie-jeebies, but compared to the frozen coffin when they arrived, it felt like home.

Sam stepped in front, and when Mac gave him the head nod, Sam jerked the door open. Mac entered, rifle on his shoulder scanning the space through the rifle's small targeting sight window. Sanchez was next, fanning out to the left, Cory after him fanning out to the right. Both stared through their rifle sights, the stock pushed tight against their shoulders as they walked in a combat crouch.

The large and opulent room was some sort of dining room with tables and chairs. It was beautiful before the loss of gravity. Now, the room was a chaotic mess. Tables and chairs laid turned over and clustered in piles. Unfamiliar eating utensils and plates covered the floor.

Mac scanned the spacious room and didn't see anyone. Anyone alive, that is. "Clear," he said to his team, which was followed by confirmation statements from the others.

He lowered his rifle, stood up straight, and let out a loud exhale. In front of him were three dead Okutans, lying on the floor in awkward positions. He shook his head in disgust.

He also saw a dark, ragged hole in the ceiling near the center of the room.

"This is where they came in," Mac said, pointing toward the gaping black hole in the ceiling at the center of the room. "The attacking ship must be secured above that hole."

"We've got bodies here," Sanchez whispered.

"Same," Cory said.

"I've got three here," Mac said. "These guys were vicious. None of these fatalities appear to be soldiers or security. They slaughtered all the innocents."

Mac continued to walk toward the center of the room, taking a circuitous route to avoid the cluttered mess of furniture. As he got closer to the hole in the ceiling, his eyes darted back and forth from the hole in the ceiling to where he walked around the mess. He kept his rifled aimed at the hole.

The hole was only a couple of meters in diameter. A rope ladder with wooden rungs hung from the hole to assist the enemy combatants into the dining room. The ladder stopped several meters above the floor.

Cory and Sanchez walked the outer perimeter of the room, circling in opposite directions. Sam followed Mac's route up the middle.

Mac moved around a table laying on its side, and saw the strange sight of what looked like a large dead animal lying on the floor several meters in front of him. He wasn't expecting to see animals on the ship. He cocked his head to the left and then the right as he tried to process the strange carcass lying on the floor, never lowering his rifle. From where he stood, it looked like white bones were wrapped around the body. *Bones on the outside?* The creature was massive, and he saw more limbs than one animal should have. *Six legs? Maybe eight?* His helmet scanners suggested it was dead.

Sam joined Mac to his left.

"What in the vast unknown universe is that thing?" Sam asked.

"I don't know. It looks like a huge eight-legged cow with external bones."

Sanchez, hearing the discussion over the radio, jumped in. "Major Mac, what did you find over there?"

"Not sure what it is, but it's dead."

Mac stepped in closer, keeping his rifle trained on the massive hairy body lying on the floor, just in case. It was obvious, as he and Sam reached the dead animal, that there were two creatures, both covered in a thick golden fur with bones on the outside.

"They aren't multi-legged livestock, but furry humanoids," Sam said. "Look, it's wearing leather boots and pants." Mac could see the clothing now, as well. He could also see the deep slashing cuts and dried blood covering parts of the creatures.

Sam knelt and pushed the bones with the end of his rifle. They moved around. "The bones are hanging on them like decorations."

Mac looked up and saw the opening above him. He pointed the rifle spotlight into the hole and could see the ripped-up edge of the Okutan ship's hull. A metal access tube led up into the attacking ship.

Cory and Sanchez converged at the center of the room below the access hole, where the dead animals lay on the floor.

"Weird, what are these things?" Cory asked. "What's with the bones?"

"I have no idea. This is strange."

Mac looked at the messy carcasses and he now noticed they were headless.

"No heads," Mac said. "Someone, or something, sliced their heads off."

"Look at this," Sanchez said from a few meters away as he nudged a severed arm lying on the floor near an overturned table. "Also cut off. Looks like a clean cut. Maybe with a laser blade or something."

"Well, something strange definitely happened here," Mac said, and he stowed his rifle on his back. "I'm going to call the Colonel. See what else you can find."

Mac opened the radio channel and addressed Colonel Miller. "Command, Black Leader."

After a moment, he got the reply, "Go, Black Leader."

"Command, are you aware of any animals on the ship with the Okutans? Or maybe another race of aliens?"

"That is a strange question, Black Leader," Colonel Miller said.

"Yeah, well, we have the headless carcasses of some unknown humanoid beast."

"Standby."

"Mac, I don't think these are animals," Sam said. He picked up an unfamiliar heavy black rifle and examined it. "This rifle is nothing like I've seen before."

"Yeah, you are right," Mac said. "It's looking like these beasts may be our enemy combatants, and this is the first evidence of resistance by the Okutans."

"Command, we also have some sort of unfamiliar rifles over here."

Mac stood looking from the access hole to the carcasses to the doors, and tried to put the pieces together.

"Black Leader," Colonel Miller's voice called through the radio. "There are no records of Okutan animals aboard the ship or any evidence Okutans would ever travel with animals. There's also no information that would suggest any other race of alien was traveling with the Okutans. All indications are it was just them."

"Copy. It's likely, then, these beasts are our attackers."

"Black Leader, show us some video," Miller requested.

"Roger. One moment."

Mac tapped the video transmission app on the wrist control interface. He activated the helmet camera video stream and then moved over and stood where his helmet camera could pick up the furry body on the floor.

"Major Mac," Sanchez said, "I think I've got a head over here." Sanchez pushed a heavy, overturned table and chair out of the way.

The three other operators all joined him and looked down at the severed head. Mac's video stream transmitted to Colonel Miller in the situation room. The head was ugly and not like an animal at all. Its hairless, leathery face was more like a human than an animal. Covering the head like a helmet was a white bare bone skull.

"Man," Sanchez said, "that is one ugly beast." They all nodded in silent agreement. "I don't even think his ugly mama could love a face like that. He's so ugly he probably doesn't even have a mama. Major Mac, could you imagine how ugly this guy's beastly mama must be?"

Mac ignored Sanchez's chattering and turned back to the Colonel.

"Command, any idea what we are seeing here?" Mac asked.

"None. I'm clueless, Black Leader."

"Major," Prime Ambassador Kumar said. "Please show me the body again up close." The trepidation in his voice was obvious to Mac.

"Yessir." Mac walked back over and squatted down to allow the helmet camera to capture what he was seeing.

"Alright, Major, that is enough. I know who they are. I was afraid of this when I saw the smaller ship attached to the hull," Kumar said in a low and defeated voice. "We don't know their true name, but those who have encountered them call them Bone Rattlers."

"Prime Ambassador, did you say, Bone Rattlers?" Mac asked.

"Yes, that's right. They are called that because they wear the bones of their victims like decorative chain mail. Rumor is the bones make a hollow rattling sound when they bump together."

"Ok, that's disturbing, to say the least. Do we know anything else?" Mac asked.

"Not really, Major. We believe they operate as mercenary space pirates, attacking ships by ambush and hijacking anything they can.

They like to lie in wait and perform surprise ambush attacks. They most often take captives and demand ransoms for release. Reports suggest they are involved in the galactic slave trade industry as well."

"So, all around terrible guys, it sounds like," Mac said. "You should add to the file that they are also merciless killers."

Mac stood up straight again and allowed all the pieces to line up in his mind. *Pirates? Kidnapping and ransom?* There were still many mysteries before him. For the first time since boarding the Okutan Royal Vessel, he believed the Princess could be alive, but he didn't think he would find her on this ship.

"Command, we need to access this Bone Rattler ship and check it out before we continue to search the ship for the princess," Mac said.

Kumar responded, "Major, I agree you need to finish the search. But I don't think you'll find Princess Omo-Binrin on that ship. Most likely, the Bone Rattlers have taken her and are long gone. At this point, you need to find something to help us hunt them down."

CHAPTER EIGHTEEN

Mac killed the video stream. He stood motionless and quiet for a moment as he considered the situation. He could feel the subtle vibration of all the Okutan Royal Vessel's power and environmental systems. Otherwise, it was deadly silent. His leg injury ached, so he shifted his weight, but the pain didn't subside. It seemed likely these Bone Rattlers kidnapped the Okutan princess. Which meant their rescue mission parameters were about to expand.

Sam approached, holding his EP-17 rifle in a casual position, with it resting against his chest and the stubby barrel pointed toward the floor. His dark gray and black tactical suit stood in stark contrast to the elegant furnishings of the dining hall. The lighting above glinted off his helmet's face shield.

"Mac, what are your thoughts? What do we have happening here?"

Mac looked at Sam. Sam's face was visible through the face shield. Mac could see the signs of exhaustion, in Sam's eyes. He knew how Sam felt, after back-to-back missions, because Mac was feeling the same exhaustion. But he knew Sam and the others would press on, regardless of what happened next.

"Sam, how are you holding up? You doing alright?"

"Right as rain, Mac. Strong as on ox. I feel like I just woke up from a long nap on an island vacation."

"You, my friend, are full of it."

"Yessir. But no worries. I'm good to go."

"Well, here's what I think. The princess is not on this boat. They took her. Which is fantastic news for us, because it means our rescue mission is about to get more complicated. The scope is going to widen."

"Fine by me. Let's get some," Sam said.

"Getting some is what we do best," Mac said with a chuckle. "Listen, we need to clear both ships and gather up whatever intel we can so the science boys can pop in here and collect the evidence."

"Roger that. What's next?"

"You and I are going to get into that Bone Rattler ship," Mac said as he pointed toward the black hole above his head, "and see if we can find something useful."

"I thought you'd never ask," Sam said with a smile and swung his rifle onto the magnetic hold on his back. He began pulling a heavy round dining table toward the access hole. The legs screeched along the hard floor as he positioned the table. He was careful to avoid the Bone Rattler bodies nearby.

Once they moved the table under the hole, Cory set a heavy wooden dining chair on top of the table. Sam did the same and climbed on top of the table, then onto the chair.

Sam stood on the chair and steadied himself for a moment to gather his balance. He reached for the rope ladder, but it was still too high.

"I'm not sure how we're going to get up there from here," Sam said.

"Maybe I can boost you?" Cory asked.

Sanchez stood beside the table, looking up at the hole. "Why is it that every time we have no gravity, we need gravity? And every time we need weightlessness, we've got gravity?"

"It's because the universe hates you, Sanchez," Sam said.

Sam helped pull Cory up onto the table.

"Actually, Lead, I'm not the one trying to climb into the creepy dark hole with the Bone Monsters. Looks like the universe hates you more, my friend," Sanchez, pointed a gloved finger at Sam, followed by an annoying burst of laughter.

Cory interlaced his fingers, making a foothold for Sam to step into. Moving together, he leaped up as Cory lifted, which launched Sam's body higher than he could reach from the chair.

Sam stretched out, reaching toward the rope ladder, and snagged the lowest rung. His body weight and momentum caused him to swing out and back under the hole a few times, twisting. He strained to get control, as his body hung from the ladder. After a moment, he steadied himself and pulled himself up, hand over hand, into the access tube.

Mac watched in satisfaction for a moment as Sam's feet disappeared into the darkness of the alien ship.

"Sanchez, gather some data on these Bone Rattler creatures for the record. Scan and photograph everything you can."

"Roger, Major Mac."

"And check this rifle as well," Mac laid another of the odd Bone Rattler rifles on the table, near Cory's feet, with a heavy thud.

"Mac, I'll boost you as well," Cory said.

"Alright," Mac said, and he climbed on top of the table.

Sanchez wasted no time beginning his task. As a weapons expert, he started by examining and then disassembling the rifle.

"No need, Mac," Sam said from above. Mac looked up at Sam's head and shoulders over the access hole. "Watch out."

Sam reached across the hole and cranked on a handle, which lowered the rustic rope ladder down from the hole until it smacked against the top of the table.

Mac, standing on the tabletop with Cory, slapped him on the shoulder. "Cory, stay sharp while Sanchez gathers data. It seems like we are alone on this ship, but we can't afford to be sloppy. No surprises."

"Roger that," Cory said. He jumped off the table and pulled his rifle off his magnetic shoulder hold.

Mac grabbed the rope ladder with both hands and began climbing up through the access hole. At the top, Sam grabbed his hand and helped him into the ship. The rope ladder continued along the wall of the cylindrical metal tube, then secured to a barrel shaped winch positioned inside the threshold of the open airlock door leading into the Bone Rattler ship. Not tall enough for them to stand up straight, they knelt while looking around to get their bearings. The tube looked to be designed as a simple access portal, or umbilical, to allow movement between ships. Mac, squatting down as he walked, followed Sam through the tube and into the main ship. Mac, like Sam, turned on his headlamps and rifle spotlight again.

Before he could exit the umbilical tube, he heard Sanchez shout, "Fire in the hole!" followed by gunfire. Mac scooted back to the hole, looking down at Sanchez, who was examining the rifle again.

"What are you doing?" Mac asked.

"Just checking out the rifle. Fire in the hole," he yelled again. He put the rifle against his shoulder and fired several quick energy bursts toward the far wall. He looked up at Mac. "Hmmm. Not too bad. It's a little heavy, but fires nicely."

"Sanchez, that isn't what I meant. I said check it out, not shoot it."

"I know, Major Mac."

Mac just shook his head. "Carry on."

"Roger that," Sanchez said.

Mac joined Sam in the Bone Rattler ship.

"These guys are an enigma," Sam said. "They have this old rope ladder on this purpose-built assault ship. It makes little sense. They wear bones like some sort of pagan tribe and yet have all these technical weapons." Sam waved his open hand toward the wall in front of them.

The room was dim under their head lamps. The ship gave off an industrial, utilitarian vibe. There were no decorative materials or comfort features at all. It was all business. The wall to Mac's left contained racks of the same blaster rifles found in the dining hall below, along with handheld melee fighting weapons.

Mac grabbed one of the long spears in the rack and twisted it around in the mount. "Look at this. Spears, battle axes, swords, rifles," Mac said as he scanned the wall of weapons with his helmet camera to collect video for later analysis. "Technical modern weapons on a spaceship, but also crude handheld weapons? Enigma is right."

Sam lifted a thick rope net, "Traps and netting as well."

"This ship seems to have only one purpose. Come on, let's see what else we can find."

They moved down the weapons and staging room and found a metal ladder at the far end. Adjacent to the ladder was another airlock door, like the one they came through, but this one was closed.

"This looks like another access port," Mac said, and then he looked up into the hole in the ceiling above the ladder. "I can't tell for sure, but it looks like only two levels."

"Well, after you, Major," Sam said with a smile.

Mac climbed the ladder and stepped off to the floor above. This level was also narrow for a spacecraft. The room was longer than the staging room below and opened up in the opposite direction. The low ceilings made the space feel cramped. Built-in bunk beds ran along the entire length of the walls. He counted enough beds for a crew of thirty.

"Hey, looks like the chow hall and galley down here," Sam said from the room behind him.

Mac joined Sam at the door separating the two spaces. The room featured tables and a rudimentary kitchen preparation area. The space was a mess, with old food and bones lying around.

Sam pointed over his shoulder with his thumb. "Enigma. Chow hall looks like a bunch of wild animals have been here, rather than an advanced space traveling race. It doesn't quite fit."

"I agree. It is a strange contrast. It also seems like this ship allows for extended space travel for an assault force," Mac said. "But there are no comfort features."

They climbed the metal ladder to the third and final level. The upper floor was also devoid of all luxuries and comforts. They found the cramped captain's quarters, a door to the engine room, and the piloting station.

"You know, Mac, this ship reminds me of some of the old construction equipment my grandpa used to operate in the early days of the Terra Magna development," Sam said.

"Really? I didn't know you grandfather was involved in the colony development projects?"

"Yeah, he was. We didn't see him much. Sheesh, I hardly knew the guy. He was my dad's dad. One year, when I was thirteen, the whole family visited him and my grandmother there at Terra Magna. It is one of the strongest memories from my early teen years. I almost went into construction because of my grandpa and seeing those enormous machines."

"Well, I'm glad you decided on a rifle over a hard hat," Mac said. "That's pretty cool. Growing up on Earth, I didn't see any of the colonial planets until my second enlistment in the Army."

As they investigated the third level, Sam added, "Did you ever consider any other career paths?"

"Nope. Never. I got hooked on the idea of the Army early. At the orphanage, we'd get recruiters for the medical field, computers, and engineering all the time. We'd see the lot of them," Mac said. "We'd only seen the Army guy once. I think I was ten years old. I'd been in the orphanage for three years already. Man, when he was talking about traveling the galaxy on assault ships and fighting the enemy, I knew that was what I wanted to do."

"Did he mention special forces or anything like that at the time?"

"No, he was vague and only talked about a few aspects of typical Army life. I became a rabid researcher overnight and found some books about the Stryker Force."

"Oh, yeah, ASAF. I forgot that was what drew you in."

"Yeah, that was what I wanted to do. I thought the Strykers were the coolest."

"I mean, they are pretty cool."

"For sure. I couldn't wait until I was old enough to enlist and leave the orphanage behind for good." Mac laughed a bit. "Little did I know the Army was just a giant orphanage."

Sam laughed as well. "That's true."

Mac added, "And the Army has been my family ever since."

"One big happy family."

They poked their heads into the small captain's quarters and found no belongings from the captain. Only a pile of half-eaten meat and a few bleached bones that were broken and scattered on the floor.

The piloting station was also empty. There was a large captain's chair at the center of the cramped dark space, with two piloting chairs in front of a bank of crude flight controls. There were two video screens on the wall above the pilot controls. Below the video screens was an array of buttons, of various colors, and knobs.

"Pretty crude stuff," Mac said.

"Did you ever do flight school?" Sam asked.

"No, I wasn't on that track. I was infantry, rifles and boots, all the way."

"This cockpit is like the old GF-103 trainer ships we used at the Institute," Sam said, speaking of the Interplanetary Army Advanced Training Institute.

"You're a treasure trove of memories today," Mac said.

"What can I say? I've had a charmed life." Sam slid into one of the pilot seats and tapped the screen and a few buttons. "Let me mess around with the control panel for a minute to see if we can make heads or tails of it."

Pointing at the symbols on the buttons and control dials, Mac said, "This Bone Rattler language is nothing like I've ever seen before."

"Yeah, there isn't anything logical about the markings and symbols." Sam tapped a few more keys, but nothing changed on the screens or monitor bank. He shrugged and threw his hands up. "Nope. I'm clueless. I'm sure there is a startup procedure to follow, but it'll take too long."

"Alright, it's not important. Let's get some pictures and get moving. It's not a total waste. We've still got some good information we can process."

CHAPTER NINETEEN

Mac and Sam finished documenting the important aspects of the ship's information, then they retraced their steps and exited the Bone Rattler assault ship. When Mac climbed down the ladder to the tabletop, he saw Cory standing guard.

"How'd it go, boss?" Cory asked without looking at him.

"Not much to report. It's empty. Where's Sanchez?"

"Over there," Cory said, nodding his head toward the left across the room. Mac could see Sanchez peering through a door on the far side of the dining hall.

The men climbed off the table and made their way toward Sanchez, avoiding the tables and chairs scattered throughout.

"What'cha got, Sanchez?" Mac asked.

"Major Mac, that door is different from the others. It's wood but carved all fancy. It's not like the other doors we've seen so far. So it caught my interest. I looked behind the door and found a hallway leading to an elevator at the other end.

"Does it look like a service elevator or staff entrance?"

"No, nothing like that. It has fancy lighting and fancy artwork on the walls. Even the floor was some sort of fancy tile, all colorful and pretty-like."

"Sanchez, you've never seen anything fancy in your life," Sam said. "How are we supposed to believe you?"

"I've seen your mom, and she's pretty fancy-"

"Focus, boys." Mac shut the banter down before Sanchez warmed up. If Mac didn't shut him down now, Sanchez would go on for hours, and Sam, knowing this, loved to get him going.

"Right, right, of course, Major Mac. I'm sorry. There's also a built-in bench with a fabric seat mounted on the wall."

"OK, let's check it out. Maybe this is the private royal entrance allowing the Okutan dignitaries to come and go without mixing with their guests in the general corridors and elevators," Mac said. "It seems likely if we go that way, we'll find the princess' private quarters beyond this corridor. Sam, can you pull up the map and see if any of that makes sense?"

Sam pulled the handheld tablet from the Velcro pocket of his tactical vest. It took a few seconds before he had the corridor in question on the screen. Mac, Cory, and Sanchez all pressed in close to look over his shoulder.

"That makes some sense. I think you could be right. That corridor gets you access to this elevator." He tapped the elevator with his index finger. Four text bubbles popped up on the screen, but none of the men could read the Okutan text. Sam pressed each text bubble, and the third one led to another map screen.

"See how the elevator leads to this floor, uh, below, I think. Yeah, below, and there is a hallway that leads to these three rooms and nowhere else."

"That looks like it could be the private quarters for the dignitaries," Mac said. After a moment of contemplation, Mac said, "It's our best option at this point. Let's do it."

While he believed they were the only living beings on this floating coffin, he also knew that it was when operators became sloppy and took operational shortcuts that good men got killed.

"Are we done in here?"

"Yessir," Sanchez said.

"OK, let's move on and finish the search so we can get off this death boat. Stay frosty, boys. No time to get sloppy."

They fell into single file, with Sanchez in the lead. He led the others through the ornately carved wooden door and into the corridor, rifle at the ready.

The four operators filed into the spacious and beautifully decorated corridor. Once they reached the other end of the corridor, Sam, second in the column, began fiddling with the control pad next to the elevator door.

Sanchez whispered, "I told you guys it was fancy."

"You are right about that. This is nothing like the rest of the ship we've seen so far," Mac said, as he took in the ornate finishes and decor.

The elevator door finally zipped open, and all four blaster rifles aimed into the cab as it opened. The elevator car was empty, so they entered, and the door zipped closed again.

This elevator was larger than the others they had seen, but decorated in the same ornate style.

Mac activated his radio link to the *McDaniel's* situation room. "Command, we think we found the route to the princess' quarters. We are heading there now."

"Acknowledged, Black Leader," Colonel Miller said.

Prime Ambassador Kumar's voice came over the radio again. "Major Lambert, did you learn anything from the hostile's ship?"

"Master Sargent Clarion and I investigated the ship and found it empty and abandoned. It was a total bust. I think once we get the MIL-SIG over here to check out the ship, they might learn more. It's capable of transporting an assault force of about 30 for extended periods of time, but in a barren, comfortless fashion. It's totally industrial."

MIL-SIG was the United Planetary Army's Military Science and Investigation Group. They served as a technical data acquisition and investigation team that descended upon crime scenes or battle sites to collect anything and everything related to foreign alien culture and technology.

"Roger. MIL-SIG is already en route, along with the SMART transport ship for your return. Major, we are also sending a five-man crew to pilot the Okutan Vessel from the Regulated Zone to the spaceport at Terra Libertas. When they arrive, we'll need you to get them set up."

Mac acknowledged the message as the elevator stopped moving. The door zipped open again when they reached the first level.

Sanchez was the first out of the cab into another beautiful lobby and corridor. The lobby featured three elevators, including the one they stepped out of. They moved as a unified entity with rifles ready.

Stepping two-by-two through the lobby area into the longer corridor beyond, they again navigated around the furniture that was tossed around while the gravity generators were down. They also avoided three Okutan and two Bone Rattler corpses lying on the floor. The Okutan corpses wore burgundy robes with a thick black belt and black capes around their shoulders. They were taller and bulkier than the other Okutans they saw before, but still smaller than the average human. Near each were long, elegant silver rifles. The soft lighting in the corridor glinted off the reflective silver surface.

Mac exhaled as they stepped around the bodies.

"These Okutans look bigger and tougher than the rest," Sam said.

"Yeah, these must have been the princess' guards," Mac said. "They all had rifles and different clothing. Unfortunately, it was too little too late." Mac couldn't hide the frustration he was feeling.

The Bone Rattlers looked the same as the ones found in the dining hall. They were huge, with golden fur and wearing bone armor. The only noticeable difference was that their heads were still attached to their bodies.

Pointing toward the burn marks in the walls and floor, Mac said, "Looks like a serious fire fight happened in here. They were trying to protect the princess from the attackers."

Sanchez and Sam led the foursome to large wooden doors at the other end of the corridor. Flower and vine carvings decorated the wood. A multi-colored stained-glass panel sat in the middle of the door. The doors were half open, and they stepped over a dead Bone Rattler lying on its face, and pushed the door open all the way.

The dim room they entered was a mess. Mac could tell it had been beautiful before the battle, with heavy wooden furniture, sculptures, plants, and art—all knocked over and broken into pieces on the floor. While the styling differed from human culture, there were many similarities that would appeal to man's sensibilities. Everything left him with the impression of familiarity, but still unlike anything human.

There were two other doors in the room, one simple door that was still closed and an open, larger ornate door. The larger door suffered burn damage and gunfire. Two more Okutans in burgundy robes and three dead Bone Rattlers lay on the floor in their way.

"That has got to be the princess' room," Sam said, pointing ahead. "There's way too much carnage here."

"This place is a slaughterhouse," Sanchez added as he checked behind a desk. Each operator examined parts of the room as they moved through. One corpse was always disturbing to find, but several in a small space impacted even the most hardened warfighters.

Sanchez approached the simple door and opened it, rifle first. When the door opened, Mac could see his movement triggered motion sensors and the lighting in the room beyond.

"What do you have there, Sanchez?" Mac asked.

"I'm guessing it is servant's quarters or something. There are four beds and not much else."

"It seems like the Okutans gave a good fight, but they were overwhelmed," Sam said.

Mac replied, "I agree. It also looks like the Bone Rattlers knew where they were supposed to go. I think they came right here in search of the princess, since we didn't see any dead ones in the other places on the ship."

Sam pulled the large heavy door open further, making room for the team to pass through.

They entered the next room single-file. Each had to step on the back of a Bone Rattler lying in the room behind the doorway. As they stepped over and into the room, they fanned out in all directions, ready for any surprises.

This last room was spacious and was obviously the royal quarters. More Bone Rattler and Okutan corpses littered the floor. There were no other entrances to the large living space. Like the other rooms, destroyed furniture laid around the room. Blaster fire marks blackened the walls and ceiling. A massive built-in bed structure against the far wall looked undamaged, but several upturned cushions lay out of place on the floor. Mounted to the wall on the left side of the room was a touch screen video console.

"What is that thing?" Sam asked. Mac was thinking the same thing as they all stared at the object in the center of the room. Floating hip-high above the floor was a clear glass tube over two meters long, emanating a soft blue light. It was shaped like a translucent coffin. Lying in the glass tube was a body wearing a burgundy robe.

CHAPTER TWENTY

"You think it's dead?" Sanchez asked.

"Look alive, no surprises," Mac said. "Cory, watch the door."

Cory stayed near the door, keeping an eye on the room and corridor beyond while the others moved cautiously towards the floating tube. It was flat on the bottom, with a dark solid base hovering silently above the floor. It didn't make any noise at all. Its sides and the top curved into an oblong, oval shape that was wider than it was tall. The total length was more than the body inside, leaving hollow space on both ends. The blue light emanating from the tube spilled out, creating a pool of soft blue light on the floor around them.

Mac and the others circled the tube. They pushed overturned chairs and puffy silk pillows out of their way.

"You guys think this is the princess?" Sanchez asked. "If it is, she's not very good-looking."

Sam said, "It looks like another security guard to me. He has the same burgundy robe as those others in the corridor."

"Yeah, this is definitely not the princess, according to the pictures they gave us," Mac said.

"I think it is a male. But I don't know the difference between the males and females," Sam said. "Oh, and look, there is a head injury that looks pretty bad. Is it dead."

"Can't tell. Why would they put a dead body in this thing? And what is this tube?" Mac asked. He examined the end near the Okutan's feet. He found several blinking lights and small buttons, so he squatted down to look closer. The symbols were foreign, and he did not know what they were for, but he had a pretty good idea now what they were looking at.

"I'm thinking this is some sort of cryosleep chamber or suspended animation device," Mac said. He stood and moved closer to the head. "I think it's a he, and he is still alive, which makes him the lone survivor of this massacre."

Mac examined the Okutan's head wound. This one was different. It wasn't pale and bloated like the corpses they'd seen scattered about the ship. It looked lean and healthy. Sam and Sanchez also leaned in close. The subtle reflection of the helmeted faces looked back at them in the glass.

Mac, leaning close over the tube, pointed toward the face. "The skin is translucent. You can see the tendons and veins in the neck."

"Man, that is weird," Sanchez said.

"How do we wake it up?" Sam asked.

"No clue. We'll need to take him back to the *McDaniels* and let Engineering or Medical figure it out. We don't want to mess around with the controls and cause any damage. But we need to wake this guy up and find out what happened on this ship," Mac said.

Mac was about to trigger the radio to call Colonel Miller when the eyes of the Okutan - only centimeters away from their faces - suddenly opened to reveal menacing dark eyes. The Okutan flinched, and the wad of skin atop its head flared out like a fan. It tried to sit up and smacked its face hard against the inside of the glass tube.

Mac, Sam, and Sanchez all jumped back in fright. Sam let out a yell, and they all aimed their rifles at the face of the Okutan, who laid his head back down and closed his eyes.

Mac's heart was racing as he stepped closer to the tube, rifle still pointed at the body. After a moment of the Okutan lying still with eyes closed, they relaxed.

"Well, I guess we now know he's alive," Sam said.

Sanchez lowered his rifle and began heckling Sam. "Lead! You shoulda seen yourself. You jumped out of your own skin." He laughed, taunting Sam. "Major Mac, did you see this guy? He was like…" Sanchez imitated Sam by jumping back and letting out an emotional wail. Sanchez exaggerated and repeated the action several times. "Cory, did you see your boy, Sam?"

"No, Sanchez, I missed it."

"Oh, yeah? Lemme show you. It was like this…" Sanchez imitated Sam again, throwing his body back and wailing, arms flailing.

Sam just shook his head at Sanchez.

Mac opened the radio channel to Colonel Miller. "Command, Black Leader. How far out is that transport?"

"Major, it's at your location now. We need you to locate and activate the boarding and loading portal, and they will get in position."

"Roger. We'll do this immediately. I'm bringing back one survivor."

"A survivor? Is it the princess?" Colonel Miller's voice expressed surprise.

"No Sir. We've got a lone survivor, but it's not the Princess."

MAC and the team moved the floating suspended animation tube containing the lone surviving Okutan to the spacecraft's boarding portal. They moved the tube with ease by pushing it along the corridors as it hovered above the floor. While they were maneuvering the tube through the ship, the unconscious Okutan flinched again, causing the operators to pause and ensure the Okutan remained unconscious.

They located the boarding portal on the map and figured out how to operate the Okutan controls to extend the tunnel for the new arrivals. They waited in silence, watching the United Planetary Government MIL-SIG and Naval SMART Ship approach through the observation port window.

MIL-SIG arrived first. The small science vessel aligned itself with the boarding tunnel and made a secure connection, allowing the pilot to open the square metal door on the side of the ship so the MIL-SIG staff could enter the Royal Vessel with their equipment.

The MIL-SIG crew consisted of two men and three women in white environmental suits which protected them from any biological or chemical threats. Their helmets featured large, glass dome-like face shields. They walked down the long boarding bridge toward Mac and the others carrying several black equipment cases.

"Major Lambert?" the tall man leading the MIL-SIG crew asked as he approached Mac. His glass-domed helmet muffled his voice. The man had tan skin and short white hair that matched his trimmed white beard.

"That's right."

"Special Agent Beso Salva, with MIL-SIG," the man said and put his hand out to shake Mac's. "This is my crew. We've been briefed on the basics, but we'll need some help getting around to the pertinent locations to gather data."

"Absolutely. Sergeants Cory Allen and Luis Sanchez here will escort you as long as you need." Mac pointed to each man as he said their name.

The boarding door closed with a hiss and clunk. Then, the MIL-SIG vessel detached and moved out of the way, allowing for the SMART Ship to perform the same alignment and attachment maneuver.

"Excellent. Thank you, Major. We'll give them a ride back to the *McDaniels* when we are done."

"That will work," Mac said.

"So, what do you have here?" Special Agent Salva asked as he approached the floating tube.

"Well, to be honest, we are not sure," Mac said. "We believe it's a suspended animation chamber. This is the only survivor we found."

"You guys put him," Salva leaned closer, "or it, in there?"

"I wouldn't lean too close if I were you," Sanchez said. He then bumped Sam's shoulder with the back of his hand.

"Oh?" Salva said, surprised as he looked at Sanchez.

"No, we didn't put him in there. We found him this way," Mac said.

"Weird."

"Our thoughts exactly."

"All right, we are ready when you are. We can divide into two groups if that works for you," Special Agent Salva said.

Cory and Sanchez each took a group of MIL-SIG crew members and headed back into the depths of the ship.

The boarding port door opened again, and six more people boarded the ship.

The tall, dark-haired co-pilot from the SMART ship earlier greeted Mac again. She approached in her blue and white jumpsuit, this time with the environmental helmet on. He could see her friendly smile as she approached.

"Hello, Lieutenant…," Mac said, trailing off as he couldn't remember her name.

"Taylor, Lieutenant Luella Taylor." She extended a gloved hand, and he shook it. "But my friends call me Lou."

"Yes, of course, Lieutenant Taylor. Sorry about that, it's been a long day. Thank you for the ride."

"No problem. We're here to help. This is the piloting crew that will get this bucket of bolts to the spaceport at Terra Libertas," she said and stepped aside so Mac could greet the rest of the crew. The four men and one woman that made up the members of the piloting crew wore blue Navy flight suits with the same glass dome helmets.

"OK, great. Welcome aboard to the Okutan Royal Vessel. This is Master Sergeant Sam Clarion. He will escort you to the piloting station." Looking at Sam, Mac said, "I'll see you back on the ship. Catch a ride back with the guys and MIL-SIG. Come find me when you are back on the *McDaniels*."

Sam and Mac bumped fists and Sam led the pilot crew to the

elevator, leaving Lieutenant Taylor and Mac alone at the edge of the boarding portal.

Lieutenant Taylor pointed at the hovering suspended animation tube. "Who's your friend there, Major?" she asked smiling. Mac thought he saw a twinkle in her eye. He thought Lou Taylor was someone he'd want to be around more if he had time for such things.

Mac couldn't help but smile back. "Well, we are not sure yet. It, or probably he, is the only survivor on this ship."

"Wow, really?" she stood up straight with raised eyebrows behind the glass dome. "Is this guy one of the Akatakons?"

Mac laughed. "Okutan. They are called Okutan, not Akatakon. And, yes, he is."

"Okutan. Akatakon. It's all the same to me. If you're done here, let's get you and your pal on board and head back to the *McDaniels*. Are the others coming? Do we need to wait for them?"

"No, they will work with MIL-SIG and return to the *McDaniels* with them later."

"Perfect." Lieutenant Taylor pushed the floating tube down the long bridge towards the opening in the SMART ship. Mac followed her at the most comfortable pace he could with his aching leg wound. He tried not to limp, but it was a losing battle.

"Major, you are limping. Are you OK?"

"Ah, yeah. I'm fine. Just a leg injury from earlier today."

They crossed through the door into the SMART ship airlock, then into the bright cabin. She steered the floating tube easily. The pilot gave Mac a wave from the front of the bus-like ship.

Taylor pushed the tube to the back of the ship and positioned it in the cargo hold. Mac followed her in and helped her secure the tube against the wall.

"Major, if you'll follow me to the cabin, we'll find you a comfortable seat."

"Thank you, but I'm going to stay here with the tube, just in case. We don't know what we've got here, and he's moved multiple times already." He looked around the cargo hold and saw no chairs, but three large plastic cases along the other wall. He dragged one over closer to the tube and sat down. "This will do."

"OK, make yourself at home and let me know if you need anything. I'll be just up there," she pointed towards the front of the ship. "We'll be back on the *McDaniels* in about 30 minutes," she said as she left.

Mac, for the first time in over twelve hours, let his body and mind relax. He realized he was exhausted. Beyond exhausted. And hungry. His body hated him right now. Back-to-back missions, with a minor injury, were taking their toll. He broke the bio-safe seal on his helmet and removed it. Then he also unclipped and removed his gloves and set them in the helmet on the floor next to him. He rubbed his face and eyes with his hands.

Mac stared at the alien lying in the tube next to him. "What's your story?" he asked. The Okutan didn't respond. He didn't move at all, but was breathing. Mac figured there must be a reason these Bone Rattlers left him alive. There is no reason they should leave one alive in stasis unless they wanted him to be found. "Well, mystery alien man, we'll know your secrets soon enough," he said.

Mac rested his face in his hands with his elbows on his knees and closed his eyes.

Moments later, he felt someone shaking his shoulder. He jumped, sitting up straight in surprise. Lieutenant Taylor was shaking his shoulder and saying something. She wasn't wearing her helmet anymore, but as usual, she was smiling. She'd pulled her dark hair into a high ponytail.

"...Major Lambert? We are entering the *McDaniels* transport hangar now."

Mac shook the fog from his mind and got to his feet. His back and knees cracked, and his injured leg ached. He felt for a second like he would fall over. He gathered his bearings and prepared his mind for what would happen next.

Taylor said, "Let's get you and your Akatakon buddy to MedBay."

CHAPTER TWENTY-ONE

Earlier…
Outer Edge of the Theta District
Bone Rattler Transport Ship

Braeknn marched into the control room and removed his skull helmet. The bones he wore, along with Manstruu's behind him, rattled as they walked. He placed his skull helmet on the mount next to his captain's chair in the center of the control room. The surface of the skull helmet had worn smooth and brown now with age, but he was fond of this helmet. The prominent wide antlers were far more interesting than his previous one. He believed it was more impressive than what any other Bone Rattler wore, making it a status piece among those he commanded. As the second most powerful Bone Rattler, he was always looking for ways to maintain his position.

The soft background noises of the ship didn't cover the sounds of his rattling bones as he and Manstruu entered. A Bone Rattler was in the captain's chair when they entered.

"That'll do," Braeknn growled. The other Bone Rattler didn't hesitate, but stood and nodded reverently, almost bowing without saying a word, and moved around to a data display screen at the back of the room.

Braeknn sat down in the chair, and Manstruu remained standing at his right side.

Manstruu, snarling, demanded a status update for Braeknn from the pilots sitting in front of him. They informed him that the Bone Rattler ship was traveling at *faster than light* speed and crossing through into the Theta District.

Satisfied with the update, Braeknn said nothing. He thought about the events of the day.

It took them longer than expected to load and secure all the little blue fishy creatures from the hijacked ship. It surprised him how scrappy the ugly little things were. They'd fought back harder than expected. But they were no contest for Braeknn and his warriors. He'd caught them off guard. Surprise was a secret weapon that worked every time.

"Are we in range?" Braeknn growled at Manstruu on his right, without looking at him.

"Yes, Chief Braeknn." Manstruu answered.

"Good. Contact our client."

Manstruu marched over to the control panel against the wall and began tapping away. The large screen in front of Braeknn, and the smaller screens in front of the pilots, showed the white streaks of stars racing by. The large screen covered the entire wall from floor to ceiling. As Manstruu made the communication link, the screen turned black and then several smaller windows appeared. After a moment, groupings of numbers scrolled across the screen and Manstruu returned to his post next to Braeknn.

The screen flickered, and a human appeared. Braeknn was familiar with humans. In fact, he was far more familiar with humans than he wanted to be. He didn't like humans. Who did, really? He couldn't trust them at all. But one couldn't be picky when it came to the clientele who hired him for this sort of work. Neither the hijack and kidnap business nor the capture and kill business presented trustworthy clients.

Because of the screen size, the human displayed was oversized. The human sat in a chair with his left leg crossed over his right. He wore black pants, a black coat, and black leather boots. He sipped a light brown liquid from a clear glass mug. It was obvious the human was on a spacecraft.

The man set his mug down and looked through the screen at Braeknn and Manstruu. He leaned forward a bit. His electric blue eyes were so vibrant that Braeknn and Manstruu clearly saw the color through the video link and the uncountable miles of space between them. Above the vibrant blue eyes, his black hair was wavy with streaks of gray at the temples. He had a dense goatee, styled into a point at his chin, with a wide handlebar mustache extending beyond his cheeks.

Even with Braeknn's dislike of humans, he appreciated this one, whom he knew as Arthur Rust. He didn't mind dealing with Rust because he was as ruthless as a Bone Rattler, and he didn't cut away all his hair like other humans. Humans were normally as ugly as the hairless fish people. And they smelled funny. Except for Arthur Rust. He was as honorable-looking as a human could be.

The man's voice came through the screen before Braeknn could say anything.

"Well, well, well, if it isn't my old friend, Braeknn. Boy, it is nice to see you again. I have been awaiting your call. I assume your mission went well?" Rust was loud and animated as he spoke.

Braeknn stood from his chair and approached the screen.

"Yes, Arthur Rust. We have accomplished our mission," Braeknn growled.

"Please, call me Arthur," Rust said.

Braeknn didn't respond, but just stood there.

"So," Rust continued, not deterred by Braeknn's awkwardness, "I assume you have the package?"

"Yes, Arthur Rust, we have the little blue princess on our ship now."

"Is she alive?"

"Yes, she is alive."

"And the message?" Rust asked, one bushy eyebrow raised.

"The message has been sent."

"Well done, Braeknn. You and your bone-wearing compadres did well. So, look, I will be at your location in about four days' time—"

"Four days?" Braeknn questioned with a growl. "That is too soon."

"Nothin' is too soon when time is a wastin'," Rust said. "What? You think we've got nothing but time on our hands? You got plans to make a sight-seeing trip on your way home?"

Arthur Rust's gibberish confused Braeknn. He spoke his human language quickly without explanation for the urgency of his visit, and asked questions that didn't compute in Braeknn's mind. He looked over his shoulder at Manstruu, who confirmed his own confusion by shaking his head.

"We will not be ready," Braeknn said, "We have more—"

"Yes, you will be, you big hairy beast! Now don't go turnin' soft on me. Let's get this thing done. I will be at your location in four days. Be ready." Rust pointed his finger at the screen to emphasize his point.

Before Braeknn could say anything, the screen flickered again and returned to the view of the stars speeding by.

Braeknn felt anger surge in his body. This is why he hated humans. So impatient. So dishonorable. He turned around and he let out a guttural scream and began pounding on the captain's chair.

Mercenary Vessel Hammurabi
En Route to the Theta System

ARTHUR RUST WATCHED the screen go black, then he grabbed his mug, still half-filled with bitter ale. He took a large gulp and slammed it down on the table again.

"Stupid savages," he said to Rick Vega standing nearby, just out of view. Vega was tall and muscular, with black hair tied back in a ponytail. He also wore the same all-black outfit as Rust.

"Savages, for sure. But it seems they did their job," Vega said.

"They better have," Rust said. "We can't afford any mistakes or delays at this point. Tell Captain Foster to get this boat moving."

"Yessir," Vega said and left the room, leaving Rust alone.

Rust took another gulp from his mug and wiped the drips of ale from his oversized mustache with his sleeve. From his sitting position, he rotated a computer screen, with a touchscreen keyboard, on an articulated boom arm around in front of him. He found the application and tapped out a brief message in a communication window.

We've intercepted the mail, and the package has been acquired. Package is being rerouted to the new location.

Rust drained the last of his mug as he waited. He sat there staring at the screen while straightening his handlebar mustache with his thumb and forefinger. After a few minutes, the response came through.

Excellent news. No trouble on my end. Proceed as planned.

PART THREE

If humanity is going to be influential and have a legitimate place at the galactic table, effective diplomacy is required. The non-negotiable secret to effective galactic diplomacy is expressed by three characteristics: collaboration, collaboration, and collaboration.

— HARJI KUMAR, UPG PRIME AMBASSADOR

CHAPTER TWENTY-TWO

Interplanetary Navy Battlecruiser McDaniels
MedBay

When Mac arrived at MedBay, with two medical assistants guiding the floating tube, he found Colonel Miller and others already waiting for him outside the large double doors.

The corridors of the enormous battlecruiser *McDaniels* were spacious and decorated in pleasant colors. They designed the public areas of the ship in a way to make the staff, who spent years on the spacecraft, feel comfortable. In fact, they designed the entire battlecruiser with this goal in mind. Only the engine and maintenance rooms, storage areas, and the hangar bays kept the industrial aesthetic. The United Planetary Government studies found that prolonged confinement, even on a gigantic spacecraft, could drain the life out of even the most hardened space traveler. A ship staff with cabin fever would be detrimental to the battlecruiser's mission, but staff morale increased as the design of the spacecraft looked and felt more like home.

The *McDaniels,* which was the newest and most advanced UPG

super ship, was still relatively new at seven years old. Like its predecessors, the flying behemoth also featured a beautiful park area with living trees and plants. The park simulated stepping outside for fresh air and sunshine. The architects created temperature differentials and increased UV lighting to feel real. They even added a gentle breeze to sell the outdoor experience. Walking by the stream and listening to the running water or climbing the rocks positively influenced the mood of the staff and guest travelers.

Mac, who was in his fifth year stationed on the *McDaniels,* had little time for any of it. The Space Warfare Group command headquarters relocated to the *McDaniels* five years ago, but Mac felt like he spent more time off the battlecruiser fighting aliens than he spent on the ship. When he had extra time between missions, food and sleep were the chief priorities. Food and sleep were what was on his mind as he approached MedBay.

He strolled toward them, behind the floating tube, trying to hide his limp. He needed to acquire some pain blockers from the MedBay staff. And some food. The gnawing feeling in his stomach was becoming more distracting than the pain in his leg.

The MedBay assistants maneuvered the floating glass tube around the small crowd of people and through the double doors into the bright MedBay.

Mac, still in his charcoal gray and black E-Gear environmental suit, held his helmet with his left arm like a football. His EP-17 energy rifle hung on the magnetic holder behind his right shoulder. He had the E-gear environmental functions set to cooling to keep his body from feeling overheated.

Mac tried to appear confident as he approached Colonel Miller, but his tired face told the full story. His eyes, which were so dark they were almost black, betrayed his exhaustion. He forced a friendly grin at Colonel Miller.

"Major Lambert, you are limping," Colonel Miller remarked with a stern tone and stony face.

Miller, impeccable as always, wore his black formal Interplanetary Army uniform with shiny brass buttons and many colorful awards, medals, and badges decorating his left chest and shoulder. His black beret displayed the Interplanetary Army seal on the front.

Mac saluted Colonel Miller, who was several centimeters taller than himself. Miller was a big man in stature and reputation. Over the years, Mac heard stories of the legendary work of Miller and his team, from the early years of the Kraize insurgency almost two decades ago. Miller himself, however, wasn't one to share anything personal, let alone a story from the past.

"Yessir. I am still feeling the pain from my leg injury earlier on Tx17-k221."

"Right, Major. That seems like days ago. Every time I see you, you look even more haggard than before."

"Yessir. It's been a long day, but I'll be fine."

"Do you have any idea what we've got here, with this survivor?"

"Nothing at this point, sir. He is still alive—"

"So, you believe it is a male?"

"Yes, based on what we saw on the ship, my best guess is he was one of the princess' bodyguards."

Miller watched the medical staff guide the floating tube deeper into MedBay.

"Why do you think that, Major?"

"Because of what he is wearing. We saw similarly dressed Okutan males, killed in battle, right outside the princess' private quarters," Mac said.

"OK, not much to go on, but good work all the same," Colonel Miller said. "You said he is alive? You are sure about that?"

"Yes, for sure. He is in some sort of stasis sleep condition, but he has flinched and moved a bit. He seems restless. The first time he flinched, we just about jumped out of our suits." Mac smiled and chuckled to himself, remembering the scene.

"Something funny, Major?" Colonel Miller asked.

"Ah, no sir." Mac cleared his throat. He couldn't remember a time when anything amused Colonel Miller. "Just getting a little punchy, I guess."

Standing behind him were two of his ever-present assistants.

They both also wore Interplanetary Army formal dress uniforms and black berets. Miller turned to his right and motioned to the thin, pale man standing without a word. This man wore an expensive gray suit in the style popular with politicians.

"Major Lambert, this is Prime Ambassador Kumar's executive secretary, Aldo Sperry. He is here to observe our findings with the Okutan survivor on behalf of the Prime Ambassador, who cannot be here."

The man put his hand out in a greeting, which Mac took. The man looked sick. His skin was pale and sweaty, and his sparse gray hair was combed over the side and slicked back in an attempt to combat his baldness, but the hair was losing the battle. Mac was sure he could crush the fragile bones in the man's hand. His grip was lazy and clammy.

"Major Lambert, it is nice to meet you. I have been observing your actions all day, alongside Prime Ambassador Kumar. We are thankful for your service." He pursed his pale, thin lips when he finished speaking.

Mac disliked Mr. Aldo Sperry. *Is it too soon to hate this guy*? he thought. He disliked all politicians, but in three seconds, he knew this guy was the worst of the breed. *And this,* Mac reminded himself, *is why you are a soldier and not a politician. I'll let Colonel Miller manage these guys while I keep going downrange.*

Gathering his thoughts, Mac replied to Sperry. "Well, thank you, Mr. Sperry. It is our pleasure to serve."

"We are eager to learn what develops from the survivor you rescued," Sperry said. His voice was nasally, like he was pinching his nose when he spoke. "I'll be reporting everything back to Prime Ambassador Kumar in real time."

Mac held the friendly, respectful smile on his face while on this inside he was gagging. He wasn't sure what was worse, battling blood-thirsty alien hordes trying to rip his guts out to eat them, or having a conversation with a politician like Sperry.

"Well, gentleman," Colonel Miller jumped in authoritatively, "let's head on inside and get started."

Mac nodded in agreement. "After you, sir," he said.

As he followed the others into MedBay, he saw the same medical doctor from earlier leaning over the floating tube in the center of the room. His two medical assistants stood at both ends of the tube.

MedBay was the only medical facility on the *McDaniels*, which meant it was always full of activity. It was also brighter than seemed necessary. Every surface was glossy white and extra sterile. The bright overhead lights reflected off every surface. Mac didn't understand how the medical staff could stand working in this blinding environment.

The MedBay's main room was circular, with several corridors branching out like spokes of a wheel into other wings with private exam and recovery rooms. A busy nursing station was in the center of the main room. Medical equipment sat on carts parked along the walls. Nurses and doctors scurried around. Two frosted glass double-doors had the labels *General Practice* and *Surgery*.

Colonel Miller addressed the doctor. "Doctor, this is a sensitive situation. We need to move to a more private place as quickly as possible."

Dr. Cornell stopped examining the tube and stood up straight to look the colonel in the eye. Mac knew what was coming, having seen this same look on the doctor's face earlier in the day. Mac took a couple of steps to the side, away from Miller.

The doctor wore a traditional white physician's coat over black pants and black shirt. Several medical devices poked out of his coat pockets, and he wore a pair of medical scanning lenses, which sat low on his nose. He glared over his medical lenses at Colonel Miller with the same annoyed look of a grandmother you interrupted while she was knitting. A second set of medical scanning lenses hung around his neck and a third pair set upon his wavy gray hair.

"I'm sorry, but are you the Secretary of Medical Ethics?"

The doctor's question caught Miller off guard. "Ah, no. I'm Colonel Miller."

"That's what I thought. Why don't you back off a bit and let me do my job? You might command soldiers out there," Dr. Cornell pointed out the MedBay door, "but I command *everything* in here." He emphasized the word everything by pointing to the floor below him. He turned back to the handheld tablet displaying color-coded data.

Colonel Miller stood in shock. No one spoke to him in this way. Aldo Sperry stepped forward indignantly.

"Who do you think you are? You can't talk to the Colonel that way," Sperry said, spitting.

The doctor was unfazed. He looked over at the sickly Sperry. "Oh, I didn't know. Does the Secretary of Medical Ethics work for him?"

"Well, no, of course not. That is a ridiculous question."

"Does the Secretary of Medical Ethics work for you?"

"No, of course not." Sperry's nasal voice sounded unsure now.

The doctor stepped closer to Sperry, whose confidence was shrinking. "What's your name?"

"Aldo Sperry. I'm executive secretary to Prime Ambassador Kumar."

"Tell me, Mr. Sperry, does the Secretary of Medical Ethics work for your boss, the Prime Ambassador?"

"Well, no, of course not!" Sperry shouted, frustrated now.

"Well, neither do I, Mr. Sperry!" Dr. Cornell shouted back. "So have a seat before I have you removed from my hospital!"

Sperry's shoulders slumped. Dr. Cornell pulled his medical scanner glasses up to his eyes and scanned Sperry from head to toe. He then looked at his tablet and tapped a few symbols. Sperry's eyes darted around.

"What are you doing?" Sperry asked, but with less gusto now. "Why are you looking at me that way?"

Dr. Cornell continued to tap on the tablet and scanned him again.

"Stop it. What are you doing? Answer me! You can't do that." Sperry was losing his cool. Mac's affection for the cantankerous doctor grew. The doc had style.

Dr. Cornell made a clicking sound and removed his scanning lenses from his nose. "Mr. Sperry, you really should get that looked at." He pivoted on his heels and started walking away. "Get the patient set up in Room F5. I need to make a call."

As Dr. Cornell wandered off and disappeared into another room and the nurses pushed the tube with the Okutan down one corridor, Sperry had a look of fear on his face. His shoulders hung low, making him look small and weak. He looked back and forth between Colonel Miller and Mac, saying, "Get what looked at? What is he talking about? What is he talking about?"

CHAPTER TWENTY-THREE

Fifteen minutes later, Dr. Cornell strolled back into room F5, as stern and serious as ever. Following him was a short bald man with glasses carrying a large black briefcase. The new man wore a Naval Science and Engineering gray jumpsuit. His bald head and face were egg-like.

Mac stood just outside the room with Colonel Miller's assistants, while Miller and Sperry squeezed into the small room with the medical assistants. The floating tube containing the Okutan survivor hovered in the center of the room. It still emanated soft blue light, and the Okutan continued to flinch occasionally.

"This is Mr. Gershom from NS&E," Dr. Cornell stated to the group. Gershom nodded his egg-shaped head. "He will determine how we open this stasis chamber safely so we can access our patient—"

Aldo Sperry interrupted the doctor's monologue. "So, you think it is a suspended animation chamber of some sort?"

Dr. Cornell glared at Sperry. "Yes, we believe it is. Now, as I was saying, preliminary tests show all his vital signs seem normal for an Okutan male over a hundred years old." Mac's eyebrows raised on hearing the age of the survivor. He knew nothing of the Okutan people, and this tidbit was interesting.

Gershom sat down cross-legged on the floor at the foot of the floating tube, with his face centimeters from the tube control panel, and opened his equipment case.

"Now, who found the survivor?" Dr. Cornell asked.

Colonel Miller said, "That was Major Lambert and his men." He pointed to Mac, who stood just on the other side of the door holding his helmet.

Dr. Cornell gazed at Mac over his medical scanning glasses, still on the end of his nose for some unknown reason. Mac wondered if he slept with the glasses on the end of his nose. "Ah, yes, Mr. 10-cm vertical laceration near the fibular artery," he said, referring to Mac's leg injury. "You are supposed to be resting with your leg elevated."

"That's correct, Doc," Mac said.

"Of course it is. How does your leg feel?"

"It hurts."

"I'm not surprised, since you've been overdoing it. You don't follow directions well, do you?" Dr. Cornell asked. Mac said nothing. Looking at one of the medical assistants, he said, "Get Nurse Hoshiko to examine Major Lambert's leg." The medical assistant scooted through the crowded room to find Nurse Hoshiko.

"So," Dr. Cornell said to Mac, "when you found the patient, did you or any of your men mess with the controls or touch anything?" He held his hand up and wiggled his fingers at Mac.

"No, we examined it, but never touched the controls."

"Are you sure? You guys didn't just punch a few buttons or try a few things?" He made air quotes with his fingers.

"Positive, Dr. Cornell."

"I hope you are right. Gershom, can you open it?"

Looking up from his seated position on the floor, with tablet computer device in his lap, Gershom mumbled, "Yes, I have the instructions here in the database." Mac strained to hear what he was saying. "This suspended animation tube meets the manufacturing requirements of CWGTOS."

"Ah, what is the CWG—" Colonel Miller began to ask before being interrupted.

"The CWGTOS is the Cross Worlds Galactic Trade Organization Standards. It is the agreement between friendly alien races to manufacture products for trade and sales across species," Gershom mumbled, still sitting on the floor. "It has been in place for over 70 years."

"And how do we wake up the patient?" Dr. Cornell asked.

"This is quite simple. It operates by a mixture of gasses injected into the chamber which counteracts with—"

"We don't need a dissertation on the science, Mr. Gershom. We just need to wake the patient safely," Dr. Cornell said.

"Yes, of course, doctor. We simply open the tube, and the patient will awake when he breathes oxygen. It may help if you give him some pure oxygen at first."

Dr. Cornell snapped his fingers twice and the medical assistant scrambled to collect the oxygen mask and connect its long, clear plastic tube to the wall. The assistant then activated the oxygen flow on the wall and handed the mask to Dr. Cornell.

"Ok, everyone, let's go ahead and wake the patient now. Mr. Gershom, when you are ready."

Gershom fiddled with a few touchscreen buttons on the control panel. After a moment, the blue lights blinked off. The tube's gasses hissed as they escaped the small chamber. Then, the glass tube rotated around the Okutan patient, who was lying still with his eyes closed. The glass top rotated until it ended up below the chamber, exposing the Okutan.

Dr. Cornell placed the small oxygen mask over the Okutan's face and mouth. Colonel Miller and Aldo Sperry leaned in closer.

Just then, a short older woman of Asian descent interrupted Mac. "Excuse me, sir. I am Nurse Hoshiko. I need to examine your leg."

Mac looked from the Okutan to Nurse Hoshiko and then back again. "Ah, just a minute, please."

Mac was watching in anticipation as the Okutan's eyes popped open and darted back and forth looking around the room.

"Well, hello, there. I am Dr. Cornell. Can you understand me?

You have been in suspended animation for some time now. It would be best for you to lie—"

The Okutan, without warning, windmilled his arm in a wide circle, slapping Dr. Cornell's hand and the oxygen mask away, and catching Dr. Cornell's arm with his hand. The alien's eyes narrowed and the cape of skin running along the top of his head snapped out into a wide frill.

Mac's mind kicked into gear, and everything entered slow motion. He could hear Nurse Hoshiko's voice droning to his left as Dr. Cornell let out a wail of pain.

The Okutan appeared to defy gravity as he kicked his legs up and bicycle-pedaled in the air as he pulled hard on Dr. Cornell's arm. He rotated around and landed on his feet on the floor behind the head of the floating stasis chamber. His burgundy robe and black cape twirled in the air with a flourish. As he landed, he shoved Dr. Cornell's face into the floating stasis chamber platform where he was just lying. Cornell's medical glasses bounced off the surface and clattered to the floor. The Okutan held Cornell with his face smashed against the hard surface. Cornell kicked and screamed in resistance.

Next to the Okutan, the female medical assistant squealed and fell back against the wall. Mac watched the Okutan, with scalp frill fully extended and eyes narrowed on his blue-tinted face, assess the room. He moved with blinding speed to attack Colonel Miller.

Miller was standing in shock, like a statue. The former razor-sharp edge he'd honed as an elite fighting machine was dull and neglected now from years of administrative duties. Aldo Sperry next to him was screaming in a high-pitched wail and turning to escape the room, but he bounced off Mac's chest. Mac felt something brush against his leg and looked down to see Gershom scrambling on his hands and knees out of the exam room.

The Okutan leapt atop the floating stasis chamber surface, knocking Dr. Cornell to the floor, and took two running steps to launch himself the short distance across the room at Colonel Miller.

Mac knew he had to protect Colonel Miller and restrain the Okutan. He shoved his helmet into Nurse Hoshiko's arms and he pushed her away from the door with one hand. With his other hand, he grabbed Aldo Sperry by the shoulder. He pulled Sperry's body through the doorway with all his strength to get him out of the way. Sperry flopped hard against the floor and slid on his butt across the MedBay corridor.

The weaponless Okutan warrior slammed against the much larger Colonel Miller, snarling and grasping for his neck. Miller, rocked off balance, began stumbling back on his heels. He couldn't regain his balance and stumbled toward the doorway, falling onto his back. The small Okutan choked him with his strong, bare hands as they fell. Up close now, Mac saw the twitching and rippling muscles and tendons in his arms under the blue translucent skin. He bared his teeth in a self-protective fury.

They were within reach now. Mac swept his right arm under the Okutan's outstretched arms and threaded his open bladed hand up alongside the Okutan's neck and slapped down hard, creating an unbreakable vice-like grip on the back of his neck. This gave Mac control over the Okutan's movements and the ability to choke him out if needed. Mac then threw his body backwards, arching his back, and broke the Okutan's hold on Colonel Miller's neck.

Mac heard screaming and shouting all around him as the room and ceiling lights blurred past. With his Okutan passenger on his back, Mac smashed against a rolling medical cart, sending electronic devices clattering against the floor. He landed hard on his back, with the Okutan grappling him.

Before Mac could maneuver the Okutan in a better position of control, the Okutan unleashed a furious volley of backward elbow punches against Mac's lightweight abdominal armor. The elbow punches didn't hurt, but they were fast and disorienting. His grip on the Okutan's neck began slipping. Mac tried to get his legs wrapped around the wriggling smaller combatant but couldn't. He knew if he couldn't control the Okutan, he was going to be experiencing pain soon.

The Okutan pulled himself free from Mac's grasp and rotated his body around to face Mac. The Okutan's eyes betrayed, in that moment, the look of fear and desperation before he began pounding on Mac's face with several closed-fisted jabs. Mac kicked with his knees and tossed the Okutan over his head. He had to move fast. He tried to spin around and scramble to his feet as quickly as possible, knowing this Okutan was one of the most formidable hand-to-hand combat fighters he'd ever encountered.

As Mac spun to his knees and rose, he saw the burgundy robe fluttering as the Okutan swung his leg around in a roundhouse kick. Mac's hands came up in time, and he blocked the powerful kick intended for his head with his armored forearms. Mac tried to grab his leg and grapple him to the floor again, but couldn't hang on.

The Okutan tried a different tactic now. He took two steps and cartwheel-flipped over Mac in a graceful acrobatic maneuver. Mac watched the Okutan rotate over him and land on his feet with cat-like reflexes. He didn't waste any time attacking now. Instead, the Okutan sprinted down the corridor toward MedBay's exit doors. He stepped on the chest of Colonel Miller, who was still lying on the floor, as he ran past. The burgundy robe and black cape billowed behind him.

Sounds of panic and chaos filled the space.

Mac pulled himself to his feet. The Okutan was sprinting toward the exit, pushing his way past gawking medical staff.

Mac yelled in a booming voice, "Everyone down!"

He reached up and pulled his EP-17 pulse rifle from his magnetic shoulder hold. Everyone dropped to the ground, except for the running Okutan, who was almost to the exit doors. Mac switched the pulse rifle to the stun setting and pulled it to his shoulder, sighting in the Okutan. The rifle's sight window locked in target, and a red laser target dot flickered on the Okutan's back. It was an easy close-range shot for a career soldier like Mac. He squeezed the trigger, and a blast of energy fired from the barrel of the rifle, racing through the MedBay lobby, and crashed into the back of the fleeing target. The Okutan froze in mid-step and collapsed in a limp pile on the floor.

Dr. Cornell poked his head out of room F5 to Mac's left with a look of shock and a large red welt on his face. He held his injured arm gingerly.

Mac slung the rifle back onto his shoulder and stepped over to offer Colonel Miller a hand.

"Are you OK, sir?" Mac asked as he pulled the larger man to his feet.

"Yes, Major. A bit shook up, but I'm fine."

"I'm going to get the Okutan restrained before he wakes up."

"Yes, please do, Major."

Mac jogged over to the unconscious Okutan. Several MedBay nurses and staff came close, tentatively, unsure of what to do next.

"Can we get a wheelchair with restraints for him, please?" Mac asked the nurses. Using the wrist cuffs he and his men always carried in their tactical chest rig, he restrained the Okutan's lean muscular arms at the wrist, and used another set of cuffs to bind the alien's feet together.

A male nurse arrived with a wheelchair, and together they lifted the Okutan into the chair, positioned his body, and cinched the chair's leather restraints and chest restraints tight against his unconscious body.

Mac asked the nurse, "Can you please wheel our guest to room F5? We will wait for him to wake up."

CHAPTER TWENTY-FOUR

"When is this monster going to wake up?" Aldo Sperry asked in his whiny voice. Everything about Sperry grated on Mac's nerves. His voice, his face, his posture, even his mere existence. Sperry stood with Colonel Miller only a meter away, in front of the unconscious and restrained Okutan warrior, whose head was slumped against his chest.

"Any minute now," Mac responded from the chair next to the room F5 door. His leg rested on another chair and Nurse Hoshiko, who sat on a wheeled stool, worked to remove the bandage and MedTek bio-inhibiting tape from his wound.

Mac raised the small plastic cup to his mouth and dumped the last drops of water into his mouth. "Could I get another one of these, please?" he asked the medical assistant. "And do you have any snacks or energy drinks in here? I'm starving."

The medical assistant nodded her head with a smile and disappeared into the MedBay.

"Dr. Cornell, how is our patient doing?" Colonel Miller asked.

Dr. Cornell stood behind the Okutan, checking vital signs for the third time. His right arm was now tucked tightly against his chest in a sling. "He seems fine to me. I expect he'll be awake in moments."

As Dr. Cornell was speaking, the Okutan snorted and then

coughed. He lifted his head groggily. His eyes were only half-open, and he turned his head, looking at each face. He pulled his arms and torso, trying to break free, but couldn't.

"Well, here we are again," Dr. Cornell walk around to face the Okutan. "You've had quite the day. You should rest."

The Okutan said nothing.

"Do you understand what we are saying to you? Do you speak our language?" Colonel Miller asked in his stern voice. He pronounced every word slower and louder than normal.

The Okutan started speaking in what Mac assumed was his native language. He shouted angrily at the three men standing before him, but no one understood a word he was saying. Mac thought his tone implied threats of great harm. Mac imagined the message included something about killing them if they didn't let him go.

"Do you speak or understand GC Neutral?" Miller asked in a distinct language. He was speaking the common language of the Galactic Coalition, which was intended to be neutral and not show favoritism to any race. Many of the Galactic Coalition members, from all over the galaxy, learned the language. They promoted it for those who worked across worlds, politics, and diplomacy. As a soldier, Mac knew enough GC Neutral to get by, but languages were never his thing. He suspected Miller, Sperry, and Cornell were all fluent.

The Okutan shouted something at Colonel Miller in his own language again.

"Well, I guess not," Colonel Miller said in annoyance. "What now?"

Aldo Sperry spoke up. "Colonel Miller, I believe the prime ambassador can speak a little Okutan. I personally can't speak much, but I'm pretty sure he just said his word for princess, twice."

"Can you get the prime ambassador over here right away to talk to him?"

"I will try," Sperry said. He exited the small recovery room.

For the next fifteen minutes, Mac worked on a bland, stale sandwich and nutrient drink from the MedBay patient food supply, while Nurse Hoshiko washed and dressed his leg wound. Colonel Miller pulled a short rolling stool in front of the wheelchair-bound Okutan and sat down, staring at him. The Okutan stared back.

Nurse Hoshiko finished with Mac's leg, and he stood when Prime Ambassador Kumar arrived. Four intimidating Elite Guard in their white tactical suits and mirrored wrap-around visors accompanied him. They all carried rifles at the ready and had pistols strapped to their right thighs. One took up position at the MedBay entrance, while another took up position down the corridor, and the other two remained close to room F5.

Prime Ambassador Kumar entered the room with Aldo Sperry on his heels. His dark formal suit appeared expensive.

"Nice to see you again, Major Lambert," Kumar said. "You and your men did great work out there today."

"Thank you, sir," Mac said with a nod.

"Prime Ambassador, why don't you sit here and see if you can communicate with our new friend?" Colonel Miller asked, rose from the chair, and gestured for Kumar to sit.

Kumar slid into the seat, sitting across from the Okutan survivor, whose demeanor changed immediately. The Okutan either knew Kumar on a personal level or at least knew who he was.

Kumar spoke the Okutan language, clumsily, it seemed. Mac couldn't tell if he was stuttering or if it was part of the language.

The Okutan replied in his smooth natural delivery of his own language. They conversed back and forth several times before Kumar stood and turned to Colonel Miller, Mac, and Aldo Sperry.

"This fine Okutan gentleman is Jagoon Ina, Princess Omo-Binrin Oba's head of security and primary bodyguard. I explained to him we found him in the suspended animation chamber and brought him here to help him. He has agreed to not fight or run if we remove his restraints."

"He'll talk to us and not fight us?" Colonel Miller asked. "Are you sure? We all have injuries from the last time we let him loose."

"Yes. I told him we were trying to find Princess Omo-Binrin, and he gave me his word. He was frightened and did not know where he was when he woke up. And after being ambushed, well, you get the idea."

Jagoon Ina spoke up from behind them.

"What did he say?" Colonel Miller asked.

"Jagoon," Kumar interpreted, "is sorry for trying to kill you both and said he is grateful you rescued him."

Jagoon said more, and Kumar translated. "He also is grateful you will help find Princess Omo-Binrin."

Colonel Miller nodded his approval, while looking at Mac, silently ordering him to release Jagoon's restraints.

Mac set the remaining portion of his nutrient drink down and stepped over to work on unbuckling Jagoon's restraints. "Now, I expect you to behave like a gentleman," Mac said.

Jagoon spoke to Kumar, and they spoke back and forth until Kumar chuckled. "Major Lambert, Jagoon said he will be a perfect gentleman, especially in the presence of such a formidable warrior."

"Yeah, well, tell Mr. Jagoon here that he's no slouch either."

Mac finished releasing Jagoon and helped him stand. Jagoon bowed to each of the men. He turned to Dr. Cornell, who was standing in the back corner of the recovery room, and spoke to him.

"Jagoon expresses his deepest apology for hurting your arm and face, and says it was nothing personal. He was just protecting himself from his unknown captors."

Dr. Cornell huffed in annoyance and left the room. "Call me if you have any medical needs," he said over his shoulder.

Jagoon pointed at Mac's empty sandwich wrapper and drink bottle, rattling off something.

"Can we get our guest some food and water as well? He says he is starving after this ordeal," Kumar asked of no one in particular. The medical assistant outside the door volunteered and sped away.

"Prime Ambassador, can he tell us what happened when the ship got attacked?" Colonel Miller asked.

After the conversation in the Okutan language, Kumar summarized the conversation.

"Jagoon describes the attack as occurring upon their arrival in the Regulated Zone. He is sure they were lying in wait to ambush their vessel. He is suspicious about how the attackers knew where they would come out of hyper speed."

"Did he know the attackers? These Bone Rattlers?" Mac asked.

"No, he said he doesn't know who they were or why they wanted the princess. They attacked the ship's power systems with a strategic attack, again implying they had information about how to disable the Okutan ship. As we know already, the Bone Rattlers attached their ship atop the Royal Vessel and burrowed their way in. Jagoon and the others tried to fight back, but they were unprepared for such an attack and the Bone Rattlers moved with speed to capture the princess. They knocked Jagoon unconscious early in the attack."

"So, where are the princess and the other Okutans? And why was he left in the tube?" Mac asked.

The medical assistant returned with another sandwich and plastic bottle of nutrient drink, which they passed through to Jagoon, who dove into it.

Between bites of the sandwich, Jagoon described the situation to Kumar.

"He said the Bone Rattlers gathered up the survivors and the princess and loaded them onto a different ship before putting him in the chamber and intentionally leaving him with a message."

Jagoon added more to the story and Colonel Miller, Mac, and Aldo Sperry all leaned in closer.

Kumar, looking from Jagoon to the men, explained, "He believes they expected we, as in the United Planetary Government, would find him and deliver the message."

"And the message?" Colonel Miller asked.

Kumar asked him, and Jagoon replied with a terse statement.

Prime Ambassador Kumar's face changed.

"What did he say?" Colonel Miller asked.

Kumar rubbed his pointy goatee with his right hand and paced the small space. "Ah, I was afraid of this. This is not good."

"Prime Ambassador, sir, what is it?" Colonel Miller asked again.

Kumar stopped pacing and looked at the men. "They're offering to return the princess as a trade for the return of their leader."

Colonel Miller blurted out, "What? How are we supposed to do that? We know nothing about their people or their leader."

Aldo Sperry slowly backed out of the room.

Mac watched Sperry and then asked Kumar, who was pacing again, "Prime Ambassador, can you ask Jagoon who this Bone Rattler leader is and how we are supposed to find him?"

Kumar stopped pacing. "It's no use, Major. We don't need to ask."

"Why not, sir?"

"Because we know who he is, and we know exactly where he is."

"Ah, where is he?" Mac asked in bewilderment.

"His name is Sckrahhg, and he is right here on the *McDaniels*."

CHAPTER TWENTY-FIVE

"What?" Colonel Miller exploded. "You've known about this the whole time? What in the universe is happening around here?" He tossed his hands up in frustration. "You're kidding me, right?"

"Colonel, I know this is shocking, but there are things I can't tell you," Kumar said.

"You need to get me up to speed right now." Miller pointed toward the floor to emphasize his command.

"We didn't know this was going to happen. This is unraveling around us quickly," Kumar said. His voice remained calm and unaffected, but his body language showed.

"What is unraveling, Prime Ambassador?"

"This," he waved around the room. "This whole situation is out of control now."

"Start at the beginning and tell us what is going on."

Prime Ambassador Kumar took a deep breath, straighten his goatee and told the story. "We captured Sckrahhg three weeks ago, along with one other Bone Rattler. As I mentioned before, they operate as pirates. They focus on the Theta and Sigma Districts on the outer edge of the galaxy. They traffic in mood-altering substances, hijack and steal from any wealthy spacecraft they can attack, and they are in the slave trade business. But we've never seen them operating anywhere near our region. I'm shocked that they attacked Jagoon's people. We didn't see that coming.

"For many years, they've been harassing a species of people known as the Gaext. They have captured many and sold them as slaves to some of the less civilized races. The UPG has been trying to negotiate trade deals with the Gaext for several years without success. It is important we work out a deal with them. So when we received intelligence about the location of the Bone Rattler leader, we decided it was a way to show our loyalty and commitment to the Gaext. We found and captured Sckrahhg, attempting to gain favor from the Gaext. We thought they'd be pleased with us, but I'm wondering if they betrayed us."

"Well, that's just great," Colonel Miller said. "Now, because of your little political experiment, we have a serious issue that needs to be cleaned up."

"What special forces group did you use on the find and capture mission?" Mac asked. Normally, a mission like that would be his responsibility, or he would hear something about it. "I don't remember hearing any intel or even discussion of this mission."

Kumar waved his hand. "Oh, we just used a small assault force from the Elite Guard to find and capture him."

Mac was confused by Kumar's odd answer. He'd never heard of the Elite Guard working on direct action missions. That wasn't the function or purpose of the Elite Guard, nor were they trained for a mission of that magnitude. They were exclusively dedicated to protecting the UPG leadership. Apparently, there were many things happening in the upper echelon of the UPG that Mac was unaware of, even with his top-level security clearance. *Or,* Mac thought to himself, *Kumar isn't telling us the whole truth.*

"Does the president know?" Miller asked.

"No, no, he doesn't know, and I'd like to keep it that way if possible."

"We need to inform the president." Colonel Miller's tone was firm. "We can't do our job properly if you keep the president out of the loop."

Prime Ambassador Kumar reached out and squeezed Colonel Miller's arm, which Miller did not like. "Yes, yes. Of course, Colonel, you are right. I will take care of that right away."

"Sir," Mac broke in, "we need to talk to Sckrahhg as soon as possible and figure out where they have taken the princess. Is he in the brig?" Mac asked. The *McDaniels* routinely locked humans and aliens in the confinement facility to await transport elsewhere, or for the small judicial unit to adjudicate their cases in deep space. "I'll head down there right now."

Kumar smiled at Mac with a hint of condescension. "No, Major. You don't understand the Bone Rattlers yet. We would not want Sckrahhg in with other basic criminals. He is in a category of his own. The Bone Rattlers are a vicious race."

"Where then?"

"He is in a secure holding cell on my personal ship. I will take you there now."

"What should we do with Jagoon?" Sperry asked before Kumar could leave the MedBay recovery room.

"We need him with us," Mac said.

"Very well." Kumar said, then informed Jagoon of the situation in the Okutan language. Jagoon's countenance turned dire. Mac assumed Jagoon was feeling the same mixture of emotions as he was at hearing the leader of the princess' kidnappers were aboard their ship.

Prime Ambassador Kumar's diplomatic transport ship waited in a hangar bay Mac didn't know existed on the *McDaniels*. The small convoy of Colonel Miller, Prime Ambassador Kumar, Mac, Aldo Sperry, and Jagoon traveled through the *McDaniels,* bracketed by two rifle-carrying Elite Guards in the front and two in the back. Miller sent his assistants away to keep the circle of those knowing the Bone Rattlers were on board to a minimum.

They found the hangar entrance in a quiet part of the ship, away from the busy general staff and behind several secure doors. More Elite Guard protected the lobby. A sign above the entrance designated the hangar in elegant script as *Presidential Hangar*. The guards at the entrance door nodded and stepped aside as the convoy approached.

When they entered the bright hangar bay, the sheer size of the space surprised Mac. It was far larger than his own Space Warfare Group staging hangar.

Only one spacecraft occupied the hangar. The prime ambassador's diplomatic ship stood high on tall, spindly landing legs. Mac looked up at the unique ship standing high above him as they walked alongside. The front of the ship, closest to them, was spherical-shaped with large mirror-coated windows wrapping halfway around the sphere. A long cylindrical fuselage connected four additional windowed spheres in a line. The fuselage featured three rows of windows as well. Stubby wings jutted out of both sides of the five spheres, and a mohawk-like fin wrapped around the top. The entire ship was a dull gray color with gold highlights and gold lettering identifying the ship as *UPG Diplomatic Transport*.

"This way please, gentleman," Kumar said, leading them to an elevator tube that was lowered from the belly of the ship to the hangar bay floor. The curved doors zipped open for them. The four Elite Guards remained outside the spacecraft while the five of them rode the elevator up to an elegant room aboard the ship. Mac felt out of place when he stepped out of the lift tube and onto the plush white carpet.

There were floor-to-ceiling windows on both sides of the room, which was in the center fuselage section. Beautiful dark hardwood paneled the walls. On the left side of the room was a drink bar with a counter and bartender in a white coat, while on the right was a sitting area with white couches and short wooden tables.

Kumar walked into the center of the rectangular room. "Welcome to my home away from home, gentleman." He waved his arm, palm up, to introduce the ship to everyone. "Much of our diplomatic advancement with other races of intelligent life in the galaxy happens right here on this ship." He grinned.

Always the politician, Mac thought with growing annoyance at the prime ambassador and this whole situation.

"Very nice, sir," Colonel Miller said. "I am quite impressed. I wish the ships I traveled on were this elegant and comfortable."

"Well, let me know if you ever need a ride through the stars, Colonel. I'd be honored to escort you to your destination." Kumar then looked at Mac, who was still standing near the lift tube door. Jagoon stayed close to Mac, also unsure about everything. "What do you think of my little ship, Major?"

"I'm afraid I'll stain your clean white carpet."

Kumar laughed. "Nothing to worry about, Major. I have a full cleaning and maintenance staff for things like that. Aldo, would you be so kind as to download what we have of the Okutan language into an ALTrans and bring it to Mr. Jagoon, please?"

"Yes, of course, Prime Ambassador," Sperry said with a bow, and then disappeared down a hallway behind the elevator.

"Have you gentleman ever used one of the ALTrans?" Miller and Mac shook their heads no. "They are quite amazing. I use them all the time. They provide real time translation of foreign languages in both directions, speech and hearing. Once Aldo downloads the language matrix, we'll all be able to converse with Jagoon." Again, Kumar smiled.

Kumar turned toward Jagoon, who was standing next to Mac. He looked small, reaching only to Mac's shoulder. But he was eye-to-eye with the Prime Ambassador.

Jagoon's posture was ramrod straight and tense as a coiled spring. His scalp frill laid flat against his bald head, and his expression was one of suspicion as Kumar spoke to him in Okutan about the translator device.

I wonder if this little blue warrior dislikes politicians as much as I do?

Mac thought. Mac was also beginning to feel like Kumar was dragging his feet and delaying what needed to be done.

Waving his hand toward the bar in a welcoming fashion, Kumar said, "While we wait for the translator, can I offer any of you a liquid refreshment of your choice? We have the best selection of beverages from the far reaches of the Galactic Coalition. I recommend the fruity wine from Kalharon." Kumar smiled again. "It has a real kick to it."

"Sir, I think it would be best if we get to the prisoners first," Mac said. "We have a lot of questions to ask, and time is getting away from us."

Kumar dropped his arms in mock defeat. "We will, we will, Major Lambert. Always the soldier, aren't we? Please, let's wait just a moment longer for Aldo to provide the translator, then we will get down to business."

Mac complied, but rather than small talk with Kumar and Colonel Miller, who ask the bartender about the drinks, Mac wandered over to the other side of the room to radio Sam for an update on their progress. He re-inserted his small radio speaker earpiece.

"Black-2, you copy?"

After a moment, "Loud and clear, Black Leader," Sam's voice came through the small radio.

"How's the progress over there?"

"We're complete. On board MILSIG transport now, heading back to the ol' *Mickey D's*. The Okutan Vessel is on its way to Terra Libertas now."

"OK, great. Did you guys gather the Bone Rattler weapons and anything else helpful to bring back?"

"Yes, we did. I will deliver the weapons, all the photos, and the video we took to Sarina as soon as I arrive." Sam spoke of his wife, Sarina, who worked in the Interplanetary Navy Department of Alien Science on board the *McDaniels*. She would assist them in determining the origin and any useful information about the weapons and equipment they found.

"After you wrap that up, meet me in the staging room. I'll fill you in on the latest."

"Major Mac," Sanchez's voice came through the radio. "Did you learn anything about the Okutan survivor?"

"Yea, you could say that. We've learned more than expected."

"Really?" Sanchez's voice was full of curiosity.

Just then Aldo Sperry returned.

"Listen, meet me at the staging room and we'll regroup. I'll be there as soon as I can to fill you in. But I've gotta go now."

They cut the radio link, and Mac joined the group again. Aldo Sperry was positioning a small device around Jagoon's muscular neck.

"OK, now, watch this," Kumar said. "Hello, Mr. Jagoon. Can you understand me?"

After the device on Jagoon's neck spoke in the Okutan language for him to hear. Jagoon then replied in his language and the device translated.

"Yes, I can understand you." The voice was artificial, almost robotic sounding, but the translation worked.

"Ha! See that?" Kumar clapped his hands together. "It takes a bit to get used to the slight delay, but we are now in business."

Impressed by the little device, Mac asked, "Prime Ambassador Kumar, Sckrahhg?"

"Yes, of course. Please excuse my instinct to entertain guests aboard my ship." His voice and face turned more somber. "We have the two prisoners in a secure holding chamber on the lower deck." Kumar pointed toward the rear of the ship.

Kumar led them through the room into one of the spherical sections which featured high curved ceiling space, with windows all around the sphere and a circular window above them. A long and curvy black grand piano stood off to one side. Mac couldn't remember ever seeing an actual grand piano in person. In a technological society as they now lived, very few in the galaxy could own one. Kumar wanted his ship to impress his visitors with the extravagant furnishings.

They walked through another beautiful spherical room, passing several men and women who were either ship staff or part of Kumar's diplomatic staff, until they reached another elevator.

The elevator took them to the lower level, and they stepped off the elevator into a utilitarian room. It was dimly lit, and the ceilings were lower. The room had none of the elegance from above. This area of the ship is not for the guest's viewing, but for storage and maintenance.

Sitting in the middle of the room were two black cubes that were taller than the two Elite Guards standing next to them. The front face of each cube was a thick window with a blinking touch screen control pad on the right side. Sitting on the floor of each cube was a massive creature covered in golden fur.

As the four of them approached, one of the furry creatures unfolded its colossal frame and stood up. It couldn't stand to full height, as it was taller than the cube. It took two steps and put its hands on the glass. The creature's face was bare, dark leathery skin. His eyes were menacing. Baring his short fangs and monstrous teeth, he spoke slowly in a deep, growling voice, "Ambassador Kumar, I'll have my bones back now."

CHAPTER TWENTY-SIX

Bone Rattler Compound
Location Unknown

Princess Omo-Binrin Oba shivered as she walked down the ramp of the spacecraft. The dark night air was freezing cold. The harsh wind swirled snow around her exposed ankles. Her long purple dress did nothing to keep her warm. The bare skin on her face and head prickled in the freezing wind. This place was much colder than she'd ever experienced.

As she walked, the dark snowy night limited her visibility in all directions. The spacecraft sat on an elevated landing platform behind her. In front of her was a line of about forty of her people. She was at the very back of the line. Their captors strung them together in groups of five, hands tied in front of them, and all tied together by rope in a line. Mostly the group consisted of women and some older men, all from the ship's support staff. They walked towards a bridge leading to what looked like a dark single-story building built into the side of a craggy mountain. Glaring lights from the spacecraft and building shone toward the bridge, and shimmered off the white swirling snow.

Omo-Binrin took in the landscape, a rocky canyon separated by a deep chasm. A metal footbridge with metal handrails stretched over a dark chasm between the building protruding from the mountainside and the landing pad built on stilts on the opposite side. Small yellow lights on the handrails illuminated the surface of the bridge.

Princess Omo-Binrin looked over the edge of the handrail. All she could see was blackness. She felt uneasy, not knowing how high the bridge was or what was beneath it. It could be a bottomless pit for all she knew. The bridge's slight rocking, caused by the wind, didn't help her feel any better.

What concerned her most was that she hadn't seen Jagoon since being captured. She feared he was dead. It was the only possibility, and it broke her heart. She didn't see any of her security force either. The memory of Akoni dying trying to protect her continued to replay in her mind.

Oh, Jagoon, my dear friend. Where are you? What did we do wrong? What did I do wrong? she thought to herself, then squeezed her eyes closed in anger. *Stop it, Omo. Pull yourself together. You must be strong for your people. You must give them confidence. You will find a way out.*

Her two attendants scooted through the snow in front of her, hunched over and shivering. The Okutan people lived in a tropical climate, and this freezing snow shocked their bodies. She could hear weeping from some of her people in front of her.

One of the kidnapping monsters led the rope line of prisoners, and there was one on each side of the line growling at them and nudging them to walk faster. They were huge, nearly twice as tall as the average Okutan shuffling next to them. They wore bones over the gold fur covered bodies, like a trophy, and the bones rattled in the wind, banging against themselves, creating a hollow sound echoing over the gusts of wind. Glancing over her shoulder, Princess Omo-Binrin saw two more monsters following her at the back of the line. The lights in the distance reflected off the evil eyes glaring through the bone skull helmet.

As they approached the craggy mountainside and the dark building at the end of the bridge, there was a loud banging and clanging noise. A tall metal door opened, sliding on a track. In front of the featureless rectangular building, at the end of the bridge, was a wide section of a steel platform that merged with a dug-out part of the mountain to make an area of flat ground. The Okutan captives congregated there as the door screeched opened, revealing a gaping black hole.

The monsters pulled and prodded them through the door into the darkness of the building. They activated the power, and lights flickered on, revealing a long, empty and cold corridor. Some of the ceiling-mounted lights continued to flicker as they walked down the barren concrete corridor. A row of five pipes hung against the wall, strapped down to metal brackets.

The corridor was still cold, but a welcome relief from the freezing wind and snow flurries. After a moment, the massive heavy door clanged again and began screeching back into place.

Princess Omo-Binrin, walking at the back of the rope line, saw the dark shape appear in her periphery on her left side. She couldn't stop her scalp frill from rising halfway because of the discomfort of the monsters being so close. They gave her the creeps.

She looked to her left with her eyes only, without moving her head at all. It was the largest of the beasts, the one that appeared to be the leader, with the wide antlers fanning out from the side of his skull helmet. He was the one who shot her earlier.

Turning to the monster leader, she said with as much courage, indignation, and authority as she could muster, "You have no right to invade our ship and take us prisoner. You have committed crimes against the galactic protection of diplomats. I am the princess of the Okutan people sent to meet with leaders of the United Planetary Government. You must release us this instant." She spoke in her native Okutan language, remembering her kidnappers spoke to her earlier on the ship.

The beast responded in a deep growling voice, "We know who you are, Princess. I will not let you go. You are mine now. I'm sure we will hear from the United Planetary Government soon. They are the real criminals in this galaxy, and they will pay for their crimes."

"This is unacceptable!" she shouted as forcefully as possible, fighting through the fear coursing through her body. "You will release us right now."

The monster laughed a deep and ugly, sarcastic laugh. "Princess, it's not up to you. You are my prisoner. You will do what I say."

They reached a crossing corridor, which was identical to the one they were walking through, and the beasts forced the line of Okutan prisoners to turn right. Ahead of them was a heavy metal door being held open by one of their captors.

Several Okutans cried, and some screamed in fear as the monsters grabbed them by the rope, cut them loose, and pushed them through the door into the dark room. Princess Omo-Binrin was the last one to be cut loose and pushed through.

She didn't wander deeper into the room like the others, but turned and sprinted back out through the door. She sucker-punched the closest monster in the gut with a vicious jab, causing him to double over in pain. After only ten steps, the antler-skull helmeted leader grabbed her by the arm.

His grip was like a vice, squeezing hard on her forearm, and he dragged her kicking and fighting back to the door, which was being held closed by one of the monsters.

"You'll regret this!" she yelled as she fought against the much stronger creature.

The leader tossed her through the open door like a rag doll. She landed hard against the floor just as the metal door slammed shut. Several of the Okutans rushed over to where she lay crumpled in the dark on the hard, cold floor, and they helped her to her feet.

CHAPTER TWENTY-SEVEN

Interplanetary Navy Battlecruiser McDaniels
Presidential Hangar
Diplomatic Transport Ship

"I want my bones back," the massive creature growled again. He stood hunched over in the secure holding chamber on the other side of the glass wall.

Mac observed the Bone Rattler, known as Sckrahhg, from less than a meter away. The creature's neck muscles twitched under the thick golden fur. His size and muscular frame made it clear he was a physical threat. The thick fingers on his hands - or paws, Mac wasn't sure - ended with sharp claws that could lacerate his victims.

Seeing the dead Bone Rattler bodies on the Okutan Vessel was intimidating enough, but standing within arm's reach of a live one oozing violence and power, made it clear they were dangerous. He hoped they could negotiate an exchange for the Princess without more bloodshed. *I don't want to end up in hand-to-hand combat with these things,* Mac thought to himself.

A thin and unnatural metallic voice spoke up behind Mac. "Let me in there and I will cut off its head." As the voice spoke, Mac felt a nudge and Jagoon Ina stepped through Mac and Colonel Miller to stand close to the glass. Jagoon's scalp frill extended to full height, standing up rigid like a windsail around his head.

"Jagoon, you are not going in there," Mac said.

Jagoon whispered his own language, then the translator's awkward metallic voice said, "Then let it out and I will repay him for his crimes against my people."

"We're not going to do that, either. We need to focus on getting information from him to find your princess. He'll stay in this nice little box as long as possible," Mac said.

Sckrahhg cocked his head to one side, looking at Jagoon with curiosity. It was like a wolf trying to decide if it wanted to eat a smaller, helpless animal. He seemed amused by the smaller Jagoon threatening him.

To Jagoon, Mac asked, "Can you confirm without question he is of the same species as those who ambushed and boarded your ship?" Mac knew the answer, but confirmation was essential.

"He is," Jagoon answered through the translator, his body still rigid as he glared through the glass. "They are vicious, horrible animals. I will never forget them. They killed many of my people. They kidnapped our princess. He must pay for his crimes."

To Mac's shock and amazement, Jagoon reached his translucent, blue-tinted arm towards the control panel in the holding chamber. Mac moved quickly to wrench the smaller Jagoon by the arm away from the holding chamber.

"Listen," he said when they were several meters away. Jagoon wouldn't look at Mac, but stared around his shoulder at the beast in the box. Mac shook Jagoon by the shoulders. "Jagoon, hey. Look at me."

After another tense moment, Jagoon's large expressive eyes softened and looked up at Mac. As he did, his scalp frill lowered and laid flat against his skull.

Mac continued, "I understand how you feel. But we're not going to do it that way. I know you have no reason to trust me, but you need to right now. This is our best and only plan to rescue the princess." Jagoon said nothing. "We must talk to him and make the trade for her. We don't know where they are holding her, which means we have no other option than to speak to him and release him back to the Bone Rattlers. After that, we'll figure out how to bring justice to them. And believe me, I want to bring justice to these monsters almost as much as you do."

Mac, staring into Jagoon's enormous eyes, waited for the translator to finish translating his words into the Okutan language. Jagoon stared back. The translator's delay was annoying, but the little electronic unit's function impressed him.

After a moment, Jagoon's response came through. "I will comply."

"Good," Mac said, as he placed his hand on Jagoon's shoulder. "I have a feeling we are going to need you for this operation."

Jagoon said, "Once we have the information, they will die."

Mac just nodded his head, not sure what to say. *I'm sure they will, I'm sure they will.*

From the holding chamber, Sckrahhg asked in his thundering growl, "Who is this little insignificant one threatening me?"

Prime Ambassador Kumar, who looked tiny next to Sckrahhg, said, "He represents the Okutan people whom you attacked. That is why we are here, Sckrahhg."

"I have attacked no one. And, if I had, he would be dead."

Kumar, using a firm voice, said, "While we've kept you detained, Bone Rattlers ambushed and boarded the Okutan Royal Vessel and kidnapped the Okutan princess, who was on a diplomatic mission to the UPG. Your people have violated many Galactic Coalition laws."

The news pleased Sckrahhg. He smiled, which was more of a grimace, revealing his fangs. "Laws are for the weak. Your galactic laws have no hold on us."

"But your people left Jagoon here alive," Kumar said, pointing to Jagoon.

"Why would they do that?" he growled. "Leaving survivors is for the weak."

"Well, Sckrahhg –"

Sckrahhg interrupted prime Ambassador Kumar by correcting the pronunciation of his name. Sckrahhg boomed in response with the guttural growl pronunciation. He bared his teeth with menacing eyes.

Kumar, clearly rattled by the creature's explosive outburst, continued as if nothing happened. "They let him live and sent him with a message that we must exchange you for their princess."

Sckrahhg began laughing a horrible, ugly laugh, pleased with the actions of his people. His laugh gave Mac an uneasy feeling. This was not a race to take lightly.

The other Bone Rattler in the second holding chamber, who had been quiet and uninterested until now, unfolded his enormous frame and came to the chamber's glass wall as well. It stood there glaring at Mac and Jagoon, like a predator poised to attack. Mac was grateful for the holding cells.

Colonel Miller spoke. "The UPG does not negotiate with those who terrorize the galaxy. We are only here speaking to you because our priority is to retrieve the princess and return her to the Okutan people. You are still our prisoner, and you are going to tell us how to contact your people right now."

Sckrahhg leaned back and resumed his evil guttural laughing at Colonel Miller.

Mac could tell Colonel Miller was furious at the creature's disrespect, but he had no recourse.

"Sckrahhg, time is wasting. We need the information right now," Prime Ambassador Kumar said.

He stopped his laughing and his face turned to stone as he leaned close to the glass where Kumar stood. He hunched down, lower - clawed hands on his knees - to look Kumar in the eyes. Sckrahhg's head was twice the size of Kumar's and ten times as ugly. To Kumar's credit, he stood his ground.

"I will have my bones back now." His voice was low and quiet as he spoke.

"That's not going to happen," Kumar said. "Tell me where to find the Bone Rattlers who have the princess."

"My bones," Sckrahhg growled again.

"Listen here," Colonel Miller said with an angry, loud tone, "You won't get anything from us." Miller slapped the glass with his left hand three times to make his point. "How do we contact your people?"

"Give me my bones back, or when I get out of this box, I will make a new collection with your bones."

Sckrahhg shifted around a bit in his box and focused his attention on Mac. "Why are you so dark, human?"

"Just lucky, I guess," Mac said. "Have you seen many humans?"

"Some," he snarled. "But none like you, dark human."

"Well, you learn something new every day."

"Tell me, are your bones dark too? Maybe I will use your bones for my new armor."

"You'll never get the chance, Sckrahhg."

"We'll see, dark human. We'll see."

There was no doubt in Mac's mind, if Sckrahhg had the chance, he would kill all of them and polish their bones to wear as trophies. This creature had no conscience.

The standoff was obvious. No amount of arguing through the glass with the savage creature was going to lead to the information they needed.

Mac wondered if they should give Sckrahhg the bones, or move the interrogation to a new level of physical enhancement to motivate him to give up the details. Suddenly, Kumar reached over to the control panel with his right hand and pressed two buttons.

Four arcs of blue crackling electricity blasted out of the four upper corners of the holding chamber and intersected at Sckrahhg's body. The electricity flowed in violent streams for a moment, causing Sckrahhg to scream a bloodcurdling howl as his massive body convulsed.

Kumar said nothing, but left his finger on the control panel. His face remained placid.

When the electricity stopped, Sckrahhg collapsed to the chamber's floor with a heavy thud. He laid there for a moment and then pulled himself to his feet again.

The other Bone Rattler in the second chamber shrunk to the back of his chamber, not wanting to draw attention to himself.

Kumar pressed the button again. Sckrahhg convulsed and fell to the floor of the chamber again. This time he laid in a hairy pile, not moving, but breathing hard for several long moments, his furry chest heaving.

To Mac's even greater surprise, Kumar didn't move his hand. He was poised, ready to zap the Bone Rattler again.

Walking over next to Kumar, Mac whispered, "Prime Ambassador, sir, we need to get the information out of him. If you kill him, or cause him to lose consciousness, we'll never know how to find the princess."

"Not to worry, Major Lambert," Kumar said cheerfully. "He will give us the information we need." Raising his voice, but still in a friendly, cheerful tone, he called, "You'll tell us what we need to know, won't you, Sckrahhg?" He mispronounced the name on purpose this time.

From the floor, Sckrahhg responded in a weaker, but no less threatening voice, "Ambassador, I am going to rip your puny arms from your—"

Before he could finish, Kumar smiled gleefully as he pressed the button again. The blue arcs of electricity slammed into Sckrahhg's prone body, and he convulsed again, shaking and howling in pain. Kumar held the button down longer this time, causing the electricity to flow longer. The blue light from the electricity reflected off Kumar's diabolical face.

Mac reached out and pulled Kumar's hand away from the control screen, stopping the torture. He stepped in front of Kumar, blocking the control panel and view of Sckrahhg. Kumar's psychotic face turned to Mac and flashed in an instant back to the normal tranquil expression of a politician.

"Sir?" Mac said gently, knowing he may have overstepped his

authority. He glanced toward Colonel Miller, who was standing tense but did not reprimand him.

"Yes, of course, Major." Kumar straightened his suit coat and adjusted his sleeve cuffs. "I'm sure our friend Mr. Sckrahhg wants to assist us now with how to contact his people."

They all waited for a long moment. Mac wondered if Sckrahhg was even conscious. After a while, Sckrahhg coughed and squeaked out, "Send a request for communication link..." he coughed again and struggled to get the words out, "...send to G1562...Centurion Sat 27...portal hm.1777.k."

Colonel Miller jotted down the galactic communication link address. Mac recognized the standard Galactic Coalition addressing scheme referencing the sector and specific satellite in that sector. Each of the thousands of satellites in each sector provided millions of communication portals.

Colonel Miller read it back to Sckrahhg for confirmation.

"Yes," he said. "Send your portal link address there...and they... they will contact you."

"Sckrahhg, I don't need to tell you what will happen if you are not telling us the truth, right?" Colonel Miller said.

"Send...send there...it is true," Sckrahhg barely growled the words out before he lost consciousness.

CHAPTER TWENTY-EIGHT

Interplanetary Navy Battlecruiser McDaniels
Army Situation Room

When Mac entered the high-security Interplanetary Army Situation Room, Colonel Miller was standing behind a communication specialist who was typing into her computer. Colonel Miller introduced Mac to the specialist, Corporal Kara Cooper. Mac knew her voice from recent missions. He'd found her to be competent and professional. She looked pretty much like Mac had envisioned. Her voice over the radio was youthful and high, almost childlike, which made him wonder if they had a child prodigy working for the Army. She was young, but not a child. He guessed she was in her early twenties. Her physical appearance matched her voice, she looked tiny sitting at the communication station. Her face was round with rosy cheeks, and her orange hair pulled up into a tight bun on top of her head. Corporal Cooper had received a recent transfer to the *McDaniels* from a smaller and less critical operation because she was the best, and the best always floated to the top.

Cooper's fingers moved at lightning speed across the glass touchscreen keyboard at one of eight computer stations clustered together into an octagon-shaped workstation. Three other communication specialists sat around the octagon workstation, monitoring Army and Navy audio and video messages.

Colonel Miller stood over her, watching, while Mac took a seat in a comfortable padded chair at the end of the large conference table in the center of the room. The electronic screens on the walls bathed the entire room in a green glow. The ceiling was tall to make room for several rows of video screens. Each screen was as tall as a man and twice as wide. Some screens displayed maps of the galaxy with locations of military operations, while other screens displayed satellite information, drone video of areas under surveillance, and even around the clock UPG news feed. The largest screen in the center of the wall was black, reserved for video communication with the Bone Rattlers.

Mac watched the wall of screens in the drone section across the room. He had no way of knowing what planets these drones were monitoring. Nothing on the screen looked familiar. Two of the feeds showed cities on the surface of planets, and the other two looked like small villages. Below each screen were IA techs with radio and computer consoles. The drone section stood apart from the others on an elevated platform and was cordoned off with a handrail. Behind them stood a female officer in her formal uniform with short black hair. He could hear the murmurs from their section as they communicated with the drone pilots who hid in secure piloting cockpits on the other side of the bank of screens.

"OK, sent," Corporal Cooper said. "Now we wait. It will take a few minutes for the message packet to arrive at the specified address at the G1562 Centurion Satellite, and then they need to respond."

"Thank you, Corporal, I want to know immediately when the response comes through."

"Yessir," Cooper said.

Colonel Miller sat down at the conference table with Mac. The tabletop was a synthetic material made to look like oak and could seat twenty. "Where did you leave Jagoon?" They couldn't allow Jagoon into the top-secret situation room, even if he was a friendly.

"He's with DJ in the prep room," Mac said, speaking of Master Sergeant Dan *DJ* Jameson. "He should be fine there for a bit."

Miller just nodded. He looked as tired as Mac felt. His stony face sagged a bit, but his formal uniform and beret were still perfect. Mac had dumped his E-Gear suit in a pile on the floor of the locker room and slipped into his standard charcoal gray fatigues now.

"Colonel, can I ask you a question?" Mac asked cautiously. Colonel Miller was unpredictable. Some days he was easy to deal with and other days he was cold and prickly. "Do you think Prime Ambassador Kumar is telling us everything he knows?"

"Why do you ask that?"

"I don't know. Something just feels off about this whole situation."

"I feel that way about every politician we deal with, Major. If we ever determined the motives and actions behind someone like the Prime Ambassador, we'd be horrified by what we found." Surprisingly, Miller leaned back and chuckled. "There is nothing more untrustworthy than a galactic politician with power and influence. I'm sure he is withholding information. I just hope it doesn't come back to bite us. Just keep your head in the game and focus on the task at hand. Finding the Okutan princess and returning her home is our top priority."

Before Mac could respond, the door buzzed, signaling someone with top secret clearance was entering. The door opened and Sam entered, wearing the same charcoal fatigues. He walked over and sat down at the table next to Mac. As usual, Sam's pleasant demeanor was a comfort to Mac.

"Master Sergeant," Colonel Miller said in greeting.

"Hello, sir," Sam said to Miller, and to Mac he said, "I got your message to join you here as soon as possible. I also met our Okutan friend, Jaggle? Joogan? What was it?"

"Jagoon. Jagoon Ina. He is an interesting character, for sure."

"DJ was giving him a tour of our battle equipment. Jagoon

seemed impressed. I suggested DJ give him a tour of the Starhawk next."

"That will keep them busy for a bit while we figure out our next step," Mac said.

"What's the latest?"

"We are waiting for contact from the Bone Rattlers."

"What? Whoa, how did that come about?" Sam asked.

"Yeah, let me just say we've had an interesting couple of hours," Mac said grimly. Sam's eyes were wide with curiosity.

Mac filled Sam in on the high points of Jagoon, the hostage exchange message, Sckrahhg imprisoned on the ship, and the plan to go forward with the exchange.

From the communication workstation, Kara Cooper stood and called to Colonel Miller. "Colonel, new message coming in." Miller jumped out of his seat to get to Cooper's computer.

The primary situation room screen, positioned in the center of the wall, came to life, turning from black to a soft green color with bright green text. Mac and the others stood between the conference table and the screen, waiting. The screen, which was taller than Mac, displayed numbers and data cycling as they connected with the Bone Rattler system.

"Corporal Cooper," Colonel Miller said, "make sure to record all of this."

"Yessir, recording now."

"And I want you to trace this signal. I want to know where they are."

"Roger," Cooper said.

The communication link connection locked in, and the screen turned from the soft green glow to the image of what looked like a concrete wall. Interference polluted the signal link, causing the video stream to be distorted.

"What do we have here?" Miller asked.

Mac wasn't sure either, but the best he could tell, it was showing the wall inside a room. Then, a dark shape entered the camera view. It was a Bone Rattler for sure, even though the image was still grainy.

The dark shape of the gigantic creature was familiar to Mac now, except for the wide antlers coming off the sides of its head.

"Cooper, can you clear that up?" Miller asked.

"I'm trying sir. It seems like it is on their end."

"I don't care. Get it cleaned up!" Miller shouted angrily.

The Bone Rattler moved in close to the camera and leaned down. It looked like he smacked the side of the camera with his giant hand, which turned the video feed to static, and then cleared up. The Bone Rattler then leaned back and stood in the camera's view. Mac could now see that this Bone Rattler was wearing a skull helmet with antlers. He looked very similar to Sckrahhg in the holding chamber. This one wore his full bone armor, which hung on his shoulders and over his chest.

The Bone Rattler spoke first in his deep growling voice. "I am War Chief Braeknn. The United Planetary Government has committed crimes against our people by capturing our brave leader, General Sckrahhg."

Colonel Miller interrupted with a firm and commanding voice. "Listen here. Your people are the ones who have committed crimes against innocent people. You have hijacked the Royal Vessel of the Okutan people and kidnapped a dignitary. You will turn her over to us immediately."

The Bone Rattler laughed at Miller's command. "You are not in charge, human. We will exchange your prisoner for our prisoner. Or we will kill her and polish her bones. I need a few new bones."

"We do not negotiate with space pirates or galactic terrorists."

Braeknn laughed again, "Neither do we, human pirate. You are the terrorist. There will be no negotiations." The interference distorted the signal again. Braeknn's deep, growling voice distorted, and the video was fuzzy. "If you want this princess back, you will deliver Sckrahhg and Cruegg to the location we specify in sixteen hours. We will hand over the princess only when you return our people."

"How do we know the princess is even alive?" Miller asked.

"Trust me, human," Braeknn growled. "We will bring her to the abandoned colony on Yioturno in the Sigma District in 16 hours. Be there with our leader or your little princess will be killed." Braeknn reached toward the camera and cut the connection, and the screen turned to static before returning to the standard green screen.

Colonel Miller swore in frustration.

"Yioturno? Anyone ever heard of that planet? I'm assuming it is a planet," Sam asked.

Mac wasn't familiar with the colony, and Colonel Miller was too busy swearing up a galactic storm to respond to Sam's question.

"Corporal Cooper, were you able to trace the link to their location?" Mac asked.

"No, sir. I tried every method we have, and I couldn't get a lock. We've got nothing."

Colonel Miller shoved the chair behind him into the conference table.

"Corporal Cooper, is there anything in the system about this colony, Yioturno?" Mac asked.

"Yessir, searching for it now…hold on…OK, here you go."

Cooper sent the data to the screen in several windows. On the left side of the screen was a three-dimensional star map showing the planets and stars in the Sigma District. On the right side of the screen, she displayed a window showing pictures and text information about the colony.

The star map rotated and zoomed in toward a particular system. Cooper explained as she manipulated the map. "This is Yioturno's system." The map zoomed past stars and planets and zeroed in on a small gray planet, which rotated on the screen, showing all the features of the planet. The screen displayed atmospheric data next to the planet.

Reading the data on the screen, Mac said, "Information here says this was the second colony attempted in that system by the Tertollony race. Apparently, they aborted the colony because they didn't have the financial resources to sustain the attempt."

The pictures on the screen included wide view photos of the

rocky gray surface and a small village compound with structures of various sizes.

"Corporal Cooper," Mac asked, "How long will it take us to travel to Yioturno from our current location?"

Cooper typed several commands into the computer, and the screen zoomed out to a larger view of the galaxy with a flag marker on Yioturno and another marker on the location of the *McDaniels*. "Sir, it looks like 13.5 hours at *FTL*."

Colonel Miller swore again.

"Colonel, I'll get the men ready, and I'll start developing an approach and contingency plans," Mac said. "Cooper, can you send this data to our prep room computer?"

Cooper agreed.

"Alright Major, I'll give the president and prime ambassador an update and meet you in the preparation room. We need to leave as soon as possible."

CHAPTER TWENTY-NINE

Interplanetary Navy Battlecruiser McDaniels
Space Warfare Group Preparation Room

The preparation room was quiet when Mac and Sam strolled in. Sanchez sat on a stool at the bar with Cory. Another operator, Dominic Long, stood behind the bar to serve his teammates drinks. On the other side of the room, DJ stood with Jagoon on the sparring pads, working through hand-to-hand combat moves in slow motion.

The *preparation room* was the bland, formal name for the multi-function home base of the Space Warfare Group. And, while not luxurious, it was comfortable.

The room featured a lounge for relaxing with a bar, comfortable couches, and a variety of entertainment options, like electronic games, videos, and books. The operators spent most of their down-time in the lounge. On the left side of the prep room was the strategy and briefing area, designed for mission planning or other presentations. They set up the strategy area like a classroom, with video screens and rows of hard chairs. A small podium stood in the front near the video screens. Opposite the strategy corner was the fitness area. DJ and Jagoon sparred on the padded floor. Behind them were an array of advanced fitness and weightlifting machines. Two machines were in use. The fitness center was small but provided the group with everything they needed to maintain their elite fitness levels. Near the strategy area was the access to the group's locker room, where they stored their gear and some weapons. The operators could access the hangar from the locker room. On the far other side of the multi-function space, behind the lounge and bar, was the hallway providing access to the operator's private quarters, where each operator had their own tiny, but private, room.

The preparation room was the hub of the Space Warfare Group's day-to-day activities. All their training, planning, and recreation occurred in this small private corner of the *McDaniels*. This was for efficiency and secrecy. Everything in the preparation room was top of the line. The Army spared no expense for the group. There was no traceable budget anywhere for the Space Warfare Group, but they had the best of everything they could ever need to fulfill their mission.

As Mac and Sam entered, the others greeted them.

"Hey, Major Mac," Sanchez said as he turned around on his stool, leaning his back against the side of the bar and resting his elbows on the surface behind him. "You got an update for us?"

Cory also turned halfway around to look at Mac and Sam.

"Hey, guys. Yeah, we've got an update alright. We'll do that in a moment," Mac said.

Sam flopped onto a gray couch next to the bar and kicked his feet up onto the coffee table, as two others entered from the locker room, arguing about who was a better shot. Boone, claiming to be the best, was tall and wide, with a thick brown beard and curly hair. He wore a tight-fitting black sleeveless t-shirt, displaying his massive muscular arms and chest. He wore charcoal gray fatigue pants. His voice was deep, and it boomed through the briefing area as they walked in. Following on Boone's heels was Blake Robertson, also tall and athletic in full fatigues. Robertson was all smiles as he just shook his head at Boone. Both large men gave Sam a fist bump and sat on the couches with him.

"What's up, Lead?" Boone asked. "Tell us about that dead ship." Boone and the others in the group knew the operational details and were eager to hear about the mission.

Mac approached the bar and remained standing, leaning against it.

"Major, what will you have?" Dominic asked in a gentle tone. Dominic's skin was almost as dark as Mac's. He was also the tallest in the team by a significant amount. His frame was so wiry and lean that he was cursed with the nickname *Bones*. Mac was fond of Sergeant Dominic Long, like the younger brother he never had. They had spent many hours talking together during their downtime.

"I'm down for an energy drink, Bones," Mac said. Then he raised his voice and turned to the others in the room. "Listen up, brothers. Unfortunately, time is critical. We need to pull together for a briefing right now. I'm going to get the data ready. Meet me over there in five minutes."

Mac bumped his fist on the bar top, took his bottled drink, and gave Cory's shoulder a squeeze before heading over to the briefing area. Mac was tired, without a doubt. His leg still ached, which caused him to limp still. His aging body was stiff and sore from back-to-back missions. He just realized his neck and shoulders were sore from grappling with Jagoon. With a thirteen-hour flight ahead to Yioturno, he knew he would get enough rest to recover for the next phase. As he tapped buttons on the control screen on the podium to retrieve the data packet for the mission, *Guardian,* he rubbed his eyes and tried to clear the cobwebs from his tired head.

The others took up seats for the briefing. Sanchez, Cory, Sam, Bones, Boone, Blake Robertson, DJ, and Jagoon all piled into the uncomfortably hard seats and waited for Mac to start. The two sweaty men from the fitness area, Liang Zhou and Owen *Dozer* Black, joined them as well, sipping on water bottles with white towels around their necks.

Mac looked at the team. His tough, physically imposing men

always looked out-of-place sitting in the small classroom setting. And then there was Jagoon, sitting there looking tiny and blue in his burgundy robe and black wrap over his shoulders, managing to look even more out of place.

"As I said, we are in a serious time crunch, so I am going to move fast through his briefing. Colonel Miller is on his way here with more information," Mac said.

Mac started by introducing Jagoon to the rest of the team, and summarizing the mission to board and clear the Okutan Royal Vessel. He described the dead Bone Rattlers and finding Jagoon in the suspended animation tube. He also described the events in MedBay and discovering the purpose of the Bone Rattlers, and the shocking presence of two Bone Rattlers on the *McDaniels*.

The men had several questions, and Mac cycled through pictures on the screen as he answered them. Finally, he summarized the hostage exchange demands of the Bone Rattlers.

Colonel Miller arrived solo without his aides and joined Mac at the front of the briefing area.

"Major Mac," Sanchez said, "How far away is this Yio-whatever exchange spot?"

"It's just over thirteen hours, which means we will have plenty of time to rest once we dial in our plans. I expect the *McDaniels* will go *FTL* soon," Mac said.

Colonel Miller jumped in, "Negative, Major. That is not going to happen." Miller didn't look happy about the situation. "The *McDaniels* can't move from this location until 36 hours from now because of high-level government meetings on Terra Libertas." Miller shrugged and added, "I've done all I can to push the situation, and the president rejected my request. It seems there are priorities for the *McDaniels* that supersede our mission." Miller was obviously annoyed.

"OK, well, that's fine," Mac said. "We won't be as comfortable, but we'll just take the Starhawk. Let's get it loaded, but at least the Starhawk runs at *FTL*. We may need to double-check the timing though since the *McDaniels* is faster."

"Oh, man, Major Mac," Sanchez said. "I was looking forward to a few hours in the rack."

"Yeah, me too," Sam added.

"You do need that extra beauty sleep, Lead," Sanchez agreed with a wide grin. "I think you are getting a little ugly."

Mac was about to get them back on track when Colonel Miller spoke up again. "Sorry, men, but we aren't taking the Starhawk either. While it travels at *FTL*, Corporal Cooper did the calculations already. It can't reach Yioturno in time for the meet. We need a faster ship."

"Sir, we have no other options," Mac said.

"Yes, we do. We are being escorted by Prime Ambassador Kumar in his diplomatic vessel."

"What? No, that's not going to work, sir," Mac said.

"Well, it's going to have to work, Major. Those are the orders from way above both our pay grades."

"At least with the Starhawk, we have what we need for a mission like this. The Ambassador's ship isn't outfitted for direct action."

Colonel Miller just stared at him with an angry expression.

"Besides, how are we going to get to the surface? We can't take that diplomatic boat down there and just land on a rocky cliff. We need the Starhawk to access the site," Mac said, pleading with Miller.

"The Prime Ambassador's ship includes two ship-to-surface transports—"

"Oh, no, no, no, no. That's not going to work, Colonel. It leaves us exposed, just hanging out there. All of us will be at risk. We can't trust these Bone Rattlers."

"It will work because it is your only option."

"Sir, please ask the president to reconsider—"

"Major, I've tried, and it is out of my hands. You will make it work. And you have less than an hour to do it." Miller looked annoyed and defeated at the same time. Mac was in a corner with no options, and he could tell Miller felt the same. He'd have to make it work.

"Yessir. We will make it work." Turning back to the team, Mac said, "OK, I want Sam, Sanchez, Blake, and Boone on this one. Blake and Boone, these Bone Rattlers are massive. We need your extra size to help control these guys. Get your personal gear and Sanchez, make sure we have a standard mission kit, medical kit, and the comms kit delivered to Kumar's ship in the Presidential Hangar. I want you to set up the temporary command center. Jagoon, you of course are coming with us as well to help calm the princess and to translate. DJ, I want you, Cory, Bones, Z, and Bishop to get the Starhawk prepped, and standby for orders in case we need you as QRF. Everyone move quickly. We need to be on the Ambassador's ship and backing out of that hangar in forty-five minutes if we are going to make it to Yioturno on time. We'll regroup once we are on the way."

With no further statements or questions, the men jumped into action.

CHAPTER THIRTY

Interplanetary Navy Battlecruiser McDaniels
Presidential Hangar
Diplomatic Transport Ship

Kumar's diplomatic transport ship impressed Sergeant Luis Sanchez with its opulence. He was dumbfounded, really, having never experienced the sort of wealth and prestige that was the prime ambassador's life and persona. He stood staring out the tall window into the hanger below, waiting for the Space Warfare Group's operational package.

At Prime Ambassador Kumar recommended Sanchez use the large special events room, in the last of five spherical sections of the ship, for their makeshift operations center. The spherical room was empty and much larger than they needed, but it would work.

The window Sanchez stood before, watching for his equipment, started at the dark hardwood floor and arched up to the top of the sphere several meters above his head. Most of the dome was constructed of the thick hardened glass, while the rest of the steel arched structure was clad in the same dark hardwood as the floor.

Soft, warm light emanated from six massive crystal chandeliers hanging in a circle.

The special events room was one level above the holding area where Sckrahhg and the other Bone Rattler remained imprisoned. Sanchez felt tempted, while he had a few minutes to wait, to break protocol and sneak down and get a look at the Bone Rattler for himself. But he knew his immediate task was more important, and he'd encounter the beasts soon enough. Plus, he didn't feel the need to give Colonel Miller or Major Mac a reason to creep up his backside for freestyling his orders.

The Navy personnel appeared through the hangar doors, pushing three large crates on hover carts. The package included three unique equipment kits, with the largest of the crates containing the standard weapons, environmental suits, and miscellaneous warfighter gear. The other two smaller crates contained the enhanced medical kit and the communications equipment for the temporary operations command. All of it was designed for easy transport and set-up in ships or facilities that were not outfitted to be a special operations center. It would turn the prime ambassador's luxurious ship into a suitable temporary operations center.

The Navy crewmen disappeared from Sanchez's view as they guided the equipment crates to the ship's loading platform and made their way to the special events room.

When they arrived, Sanchez directed them to place the crates in the center of the cavernous domed space, and he jumped into action. The rest of his team would arrive soon, and they needed to be traveling at *FTL* as soon as possible, if they were going to make it to Yioturno in time for the exchange.

The largest crate was taller than Sanchez and several meters wide. Rolling up the protective doors up out of the way revealed six man-sized lockers and other cabinets. He popped his own locker door open and scanned the contents, seeing his E-Gear suit, helmet, boots, and handheld equipment that went into his tactical chest rig. He glanced through the other lockers, satisfied they contained the basics. Boone's gigantic E-Gear suit made him snicker.

Next, Sanchez inspected the massive crate's side compartment, finding a neat row of racked EP-17 rifles and pistols in form-fitted cradles. Beneath the row of pistol cradles was a roll-out tray containing a variety of grenades including energy, projectile, smoke, and flash-bang style explosive devices.

Last, he confirmed the crate also contained foldout cots and the compact packages containing food rations in the style of the ancient military's *Meal, Ready-to-Eat,* commonly known as *the MRE*. Sanchez grabbed one of the small packages labelled *SSR: Single Soldier Ration, Stew.*

Sanchez hated SSRs, and he especially hated this unknown concoction labelled as *stew*. Every soldier had a theory of what the mystery meat was floating around in the salty, dark liquid. Sanchez didn't want to know. He tossed the package back into the crate and muttered to himself, "You'd think we could make something better than this barf party." He fake gagged and dry heaved as he closed up the food compartment door.

"Well, is everything to your liking?"

The unexpected voice made Sanchez nearly jump out of his skin. Lost in his work, he didn't even consider that he wasn't alone. His heart skipped a beat, and a squeal escaped him.

After his heart restarted, Sanchez turned around to find Prime Ambassador Kumar standing behind him. Kumar was behind him, impeccably dressed in a high-collared silver executive suit. He was a small man, standing much shorter than the compact and short Sanchez. It was rare for Sanchez to look down at someone, except for children. But no one really let him be around their children. Kumar's bald head glimmered under the chandelier lighting, and a finely manicured gray mustache and pointed goatee framed his friendly smile, which was full of straight white teeth.

"Uh, Prime Ambassador," Sanchez said. "I didn't know you were behind me."

"Are you okay, Sergeant…?" His voice trailed off a bit, and he waved his hand, trying to remember Sanchez's name. "It sounded like you were getting sick for a moment. Do you need some water?

Or perhaps a doctor?" Sanchez couldn't tell if the Prime Ambassador was joking with him, or if he was serious. The politician's face remained frozen in the plastic smile.

"Uh, it's Sergeant Sanchez, sir…uh, Ambassador sir. Name's Luis Sanchez." Sanchez tried to stand up straighter and pulled his combat fatigues straight. "I'm fine, just a running joke about how terrible the SSRs are between me and the boys."

"SSRs? What is that?"

"You don't know what SSRs are?" Sanchez asked in surprise.

"No, I've never heard of it."

"They're prepackaged food rations, sir." He wanted to say, *prepackaged barf inducing gut rot,* but didn't in a momentary flash of self-control.

"That sounds dreadful."

"That, Mr. Ambassador, is the understatement of the galaxy."

"What a shame. Is everything else to your liking?"

"Yes, sir, everything seems in order."

Kumar raised his arms in a dramatic gesture. "Welcome aboard my home-away-from-home. What do you think of the ship?"

"It's very fancy, sir. Way too fancy for a bunch of warfighters like us. We'll try not to mess it up too bad," Sanchez laughed awkwardly. He didn't know how to act. He also didn't know why Kumar was standing there smiling and having this stupid conversation about his stupid ship when he had serious work to do.

Kumar stood still, hands together in front of him, smiling at Sanchez, but saying nothing. Sanchez stood, eyes darting around the room, saying nothing, wondering if he was supposed to be saying something or if he'd missed some formal social protocol.

After the excruciating moment of awkwardness, Kumar said, "I am very pleased to assist the super secret Space Warfare Group in this mission."

"Oh, yes, sir. We are also very pleased." *Was that the right thing to say?* he wondered. *Well, it is better than saying this is a stupid idea on a stupid ship and asking him what crackpot clueless idiot came up with the idea.*

"Sergeant Santini," Kumar said, getting Sanchez's name wrong, "where are you from?"

Tempted to say Kumar's name wrong as a payback, Sanchez decided against it. He also didn't need Colonel Miller or Major Mac crawling up his backside for harassing the third most powerful person in the United Planetary Government.

"Uh, sir, I'm from right here on the *McDaniels*." He laughed awkwardly again and pointed toward the team hangar and living quarters. "We're just a bit down that way."

Kumar's face didn't flinch in the slightest, and his grin remained steadfast. "No, Sergeant Santini. I mean, where were you born? Where did you grow up as a young soldier boy?"

"Oooh, I see. I was born on a housing vessel orbiting Terra Fortuna. Pretty much grew up there until we moved down to the planet when my mom got a better job."

"I see. How do you like the wood finish in this room? Isn't it beautiful?"

I guess that is the end of my personal story. "The wood is very fancy, sir." Sanchez grinned, trying to imitate Kumar's own smile.

"Do you know where it is from?"

"Uhhhh," Sanchez had no clue. *Why would I care? Wood is just wood, isn't it? As long as we don't spill any blood on it, who cares*? "Ah, my best guess would be Earth, sir?"

"No, no, Sergeant. It is much more special than that."

Sanchez looked at the floor again. It looked like regular wood to him. He didn't see the big deal.

"You see, Sergeant Santini," Kumar grabbed his arm and made him walk with him toward one wall clad in the dark wood. "This wood is no ordinary wood." Kumar stroked the palm of his hand across the wood. "This comes from the coveted Kalibachoochi tree on the Fraeklyn's planet Coorlicht." He looked up at Sanchez and opened his eyes wide.

"Wow, sir, that is amazing, Kalibachoochoo tree?" Sanchez tried to feign enthusiasm.

"Kalibachoochi tree. Go ahead, touch it," Kumar instructed.

Sanchez laughed uncomfortably again and rubbed his palm against the wood wall. "Very fancy, sir," he said trying to hold in another awkward laugh.

With his eyes still wide unnaturally wide, Kumar said, "Indeed."

Then, without warning, Kumar stepped away and clapped his hands loudly and shouted something Sanchez didn't understand. A second later, several white-coated members of the ship's staff rushed in, carrying tables and pushing carts. Over the next minute, Sanchez watched in amazement as they scurried about, setting up three long tables with gold tablecloths. They laid out a buffet of enticing food. It was far too beautiful for a bunch of soldiers.

When they finished and exited, Kumar said, "For you and the others. Please, eat and drink all that you want. I'm sure this will be far better than your pre-packaged rations." Kumar bowed at the waist and jerked upright.

"Ah, thank you, sir, this all looks very…" the words escaped Sanchez. "It all looks very…fancy."

"Indeed, it is! Enjoy!" Kumar exclaimed, and he exited the room.

Sanchez snatched up a handful of bright red bite-sized fruit and popped them into his mouth. They were tasty and sweet, with a citrus flavor. *Probably fancy Kalabachoochoo tree berries. Looks like this trip won't be so bad after all.*

Sanchez returned to the communication crate with a handful of snacks and began opening and unfolding it to set up the communication console contained within. As he was completing the setup with the fold-out chair, Colonel Miller and a tiny young woman with a round face and orange hair pulled up into a tight bun arrived at the special events room.

"Sergeant Sanchez, how is everything looking?" Colonel Miller barked. Miller was as formal and rigid as always.

"Very good, sir. We seem to have everything we need," Sanchez said. "And Prime Ambassador Kumar set up a buncha fancy food for us." Sanchez pointed toward the tables covered with food.

"Well, that will help morale."

Sanchez glanced over at the tiny young woman. He was not

familiar with her. She wore the same charcoal gray Interplanetary Army uniform as Colonel Miller and himself. Her uniform was oversized, which added to her youthful appearance. Sanchez started wondering if it was *Bring Your Daughter to War Day* for Army officers.

"Sergeant, this is our communications specialist for the mission, Corporal Kara Cooper," Colonel Miller said.

Sanchez introduced himself and shook Cooper's tiny hand. "Your station is ready."

She leaned around him and glanced at the setup. "Well, not really. But thanks anyway for getting it started."

Cooper nodded and got to work reorganizing the mobile comm console. Sanchez shrugged and thought to himself, *Kids these days. No respect for their elders.*

Just then, the room filled with noise as the other operators arrived. Mac entered first, leading Sam, Blake, Boone, and Jagoon. It was time.

CHAPTER THIRTY-ONE

Only moments after Mac and his team arrived, the Prime Ambassador's Diplomatic ship backed out of the Presidential Hangar. It moved quietly and smoothly. They watched the *McDaniels* hangar bay move past the arched dome windows as the ship exited and entered the blackness of space. The vast body of the battlecruiser *McDaniels* filled their view as they floated away until cleared to speed up into open space.

At the food table, the team talked with one another, disinterested in the familiar procedures and views of disembarking the *McDaniels* and accelerating to *FTL*. Terra Libertas floated in the distance behind the *McDaniels*. The planet hung in space, surrounded by pinpoints of light from distant stars. After a few minutes of high-speed distancing from the *McDaniels*, the diplomatic ship entered *FTL*.

"Major Lambert," Colonel Miller said, "gather the team for our briefing."

As the team gathered up, standing in a half-circle near the large equipment crate, Prime Ambassador Kumar returned with Aldo Sperry. Kumar and Sperry stood off to the side while Colonel Miller and Mac addressed the team.

Colonel Miller, standing in front of the team, began the briefing. "Gentleman, we are en route to the abandoned planet known as

Yioturno. Our objective is to rendezvous with the mercenary pirates known to us only as the Bone Rattlers. The purpose, as you know, is to exchange the two prisoners on this ship for the Okutan princess. I don't need to tell you; this is a sensitive mission. The journey will take us 13.5 hours to reach the planet at *FTL*. We will arrive with very little time remaining, which means we have no time for proper surveillance of the planet or the meeting location. I am not exaggerating when I say we are flying into this exchange blind. We have very little historical data on this planet, and there is no time for us to use a drone to scan the planet or the meeting location. If that isn't enough, we know nothing about these Bone Rattlers. This is a dangerous situation. I get it. I dislike it, but we're backed into a corner on this one with no options left. That is why you are here. You are the best. If anyone can handle these parameters, it's you.

"Now, the president and prime ambassador are behind this mission and have expressed in no uncertain terms that it is imperative we bring the princess home. I repeat, it is imperative we bring the princess home."

Mac glanced around at his men. He knew they were devoted to hard missions. Their faces were serious and somber, listening to Colonel Miller. They all knew the risks, and they could handle it. Beyond the normal pre-mission jitters, Mac had confidence in his team. Each would do what needed to be done.

Miller continued, "And, of course, I also want to thank Prime Ambassador Kumar for the use of his ship and that great buffet."

Kumar bowed to the team. Mac was a little surprised Kumar didn't have a speech prepared. Sperry stood next to Kumar, looking as gaunt and slimy as ever.

"This mission is a simple hostage exchange. If all goes well, we will turn over the two Bone Rattler thugs and bring home the Okutan princess. Major Lambert will walk us through the details of the exchange," Miller said.

Mac switched spots with Colonel Miller and addressed the team. Mac felt more exhausted than he had felt in a long time, but he hoped he didn't look as bad as he felt.

"The good news, boys, is we have a long journey to Yioturno, and we can get some proper rest. I expect each of you will take advantage of this extra time on the rack and take in as much of the Prime Ambassador's food as possible," Mac said, smiling. He knew the men could eat like champions.

Kumar bowed again.

"When we arrive, we will utilize one of Prime Ambassador Kumar's jump ships. While this diplomatic vessel can traverse most planetary atmospheres and land on the surface, we don't know if Yioturno can receive a ship of this size, where we might land and dock the ship, or if there are any other elements of concern. So, we won't risk taking this ship down there. We are going to assume the meeting location is not accessible. With the jump ship, however, we can land anywhere.

"This planet, Yioturno, is a failed colony attempted by a humanoid race of people known as the Tertollony. We know little about them, other than they are a resource-poor race and had to abandon the colony twice. The UPG doesn't even have a working relationship with the Tertollony at this time. So we have no information. All we can tell is that they gave up for good many years ago and the planet remains uninhabited.

"Now, we assume the Bone Rattlers will set up the exchange near the one and only developed area on the planet, but we'll confirm that when we arrive for sure. The developed area is an abandoned village with only a few structures in an area where we can safely land the jump ship.

"This exchange should go quick and easy. We don't have a lot of moving parts in this one. We'll make the exchange and get out as quickly as possible. Our orders do not include taking out the Bone Rattlers. Since we don't know how the Bone Rattlers will behave in this exchange, we need to be laser focused on getting the princess on board this ship and heading toward Terra Libertas at *FTL*. From what we've seen so far, the Bone Rattlers have exhibited aggression and merciless violence at every encounter. I met our two prisoners earlier, and I can tell you they are hostile. We need to stay frosty the whole time. It wouldn't surprise me if this meeting went kinetic and turned into a firefight."

"We'll be ready," Sanchez said.

"Yes, we will. Any questions so far?"

Blake Robertson asked, "Mac, what are the circumstances that led to the UPG being in possession of these Bone Rattler prisoners in the first place?"

Mac turned to Kumar. "Prime Ambassador, do you want to take that one?"

"Gentleman, that is not a topic we can discuss," Kumar said.

Everyone stood silent for a moment, and Mac knew his men were doing the political calculations in their head. As seasoned professionals, they remained quiet, even if they didn't like the answer.

Sam broke the silence. "Mac, what's the environment like on the planet?"

"Good question. I forgot to mention it. Yioturno is a friendly environment. Gravity, temperatures, and oxygen are all in Earth range. From the few images we have in the system, the planet looks mountainous and rocky, with little vegetation in the developed area. I am assuming we could encounter some difficult terrain, except where the colonial village is located. Anyone else?"

Sanchez asked, "Major Mac, are these jump ships armored or have any protective features? On board weapons? Medical gear? Anything?"

"Negative, Sanchez. The jump ships are for transporting dignitaries and not soldiers," Mac said. "I hear it will be a comfortable and luxurious ride, but we'll be at risk."

"That's not great news for us," Sanchez added. "I'd rather fly uncomfortable and safe."

"No, it's not good for us, but it is all we've got." Mac shrugged.

No one else had questions, so Mac continued. "Here is how we will do this: Colonel Miller and Corporal Cooper will remain here at the temporary command center. Sam, you will lead Blake and Boone in escorting our hostile prisoners. You three will escort them from the holding chambers in the level below us to the jump ship, and once on the surface, you will escort them from the jump ship to the Bone Rattlers. Jagoon and I will collect the princess. Jagoon needs to be there to provide a calming presence for her and do some language translation if needed. Sanchez, you will provide overwatch. The jump ship pilot will drop us and go, making a sweeping flight around the area for two reasons. First, to keep our EXFIL craft safe, and second, to scout for additional hostiles. We'll be in radio contact with the pilot and the command center the entire time. I want you three to hand over the prisoners as quickly as possible while Jagoon and I grab the princess. We will converge on the jump ship as it returns. This entire exchange could take only a couple of minutes. Everyone understand your job? If so, we need to get rest."

Sam raised his hand and spoke up. "Mac, I'd like to propose a different approach."

"OK, whatchu got?" Mac asked.

"It may make more sense to have you lead the prisoner escort in case there is any interaction with the Bone Rattlers. I should go with Jagoon to collect the princess."

"Why is that?"

"In case there are negotiations or further demands, it would be far better to have you as the lead there. Collecting the princess is much simpler. I can do that with Jagoon or even Sanchez."

Mac said, "Sam, I think I need to be on the most sensitive part of the exchange, which is the princess. There is no room for any error here—"

Before Mac could finish his statement, Colonel Miller interrupted. "Master Sergeant Clarion, can you handle Jagoon and the princess without error?"

"Yessir, no problem."

To Jagoon, Miller said, "Jagoon, will you follow our command and not go all cowboy on us?"

Jagoon's neck mounted translator spoke in Okutan so Jagoon could understand. He squinted and thought for a moment before replying, "I do not understand the question. What is meant by *all cowboy*?"

The group chuckled at Jagoon's question, yet Colonel Miller remained stone-faced.

"Jagoon, Colonel Miller is asking if you will follow orders or do your own thing and disobey our orders?" Mac said.

Jagoon stood as tall and straight as his small stature would allow and spoke in Okutan. The translator's hollow digital voice translated, "I am a sworn protector of the Okutan royal family. I will do as ordered."

"OK, good to know. Thank you, Jagoon."

Colonel Miller spoke again. "I agree with Master Sergeant Clarion's suggestion. Major Lambert, I want you running point on the prisoners and Clarion on the princess."

"Sir," Mac started, but Miller cut him off.

"Major, this is not a negotiation. You've got your orders."

"Roger that, sir."

"OK, let's hit the racks. I want everyone rested," Miller said.

The men jumped into action, pulling the folding cots out of the equipment crate and setting them up along the curved wall. Colonel Miller approached Prime Ambassador Kumar, and Cooper returned to her work at the communication console.

Mac, frustrated at the plan change, occupied his mind with inspecting the equipment crate. Checking all the gear and weapons helped clear his busy mind and helped him to focus on the mission ahead. He hated going in blind, and he was feeling an uneasy rock in his stomach.

This mission is a disaster waiting to happen, Mac thought.

Mac shook his head to clear the negative thoughts and doubts. *Focus on the task. Keep it small, keep it simple.* He pulled an energy rifle from the rack and checked its energy charge. Full load. He checked two more, also full loads.

Mac slid out the explosives drawer and as he was checking the quantity of grenades, Sam approached.

"Hey, brother. You doing OK?" Sam asked with an expression of genuine concern for Mac.

Sam put his hand on Mac's shoulder.

Mac gently bumped Sam's chest with his fist. "Thanks for asking. Yeah, I'm fine."

"You don't look fine. Why are you checking these weapons? You know Sanchez already checked all this equipment. He's the best. It's good. We're good."

"It's always wise to check again. No room for errors on this one, Sam. Gotta double check everything," Mac said, not looking at Sam. He focused on the grenades he held in both hands.

"Mac, look at me for a minute."

Mac set the grenade down and reluctantly turned to look at Sam. He leaned against the corner of the crate.

"What's really going on?" Sam asked.

"Man," Mac rubbed his tired eyes and the top of his head. "You know me too well."

"Of course, I do."

"I don't want to talk about it."

"Yeah, tough. Spill it."

With a bit of hesitation, Mac said, "Losing Jo this morning." Mac looked up at the ceiling and corrected himself. "Yesterday, I mean. Man, it's weighing on me. We're rushing the planning for this mission. It's too sloppy. I'm just not comfortable with any of it after losing Jo."

"I know. Me too. I feel the same way."

Mac remained quiet, but Sam knew what he was thinking

"Listen, Mac, it's not your job to keep us safe. You can't do that."

Mac just nodded. He was feeling the pressure, and he wasn't handling the loss of Jo very well. "I'm fine, Sam. You don't need to worry about me. I'll be mission ready."

"Of course. I'd never question that. You just need some rest. I'm sure when you wake up, you will feel like the legendary Major Lambert again." Sam smacked Mac on the shoulder. "Come on, let's grab some food. Leave these things; they're fine. You know Sanchez. He might be socially retarded, but he is so persnickety about the gear, we can trust everything is in order."

"Roger that," Mac said and stood up straight. "I know. I'm just trying to force my mind to think about things I can control."

"I know it. This is why we will all follow you into the fires of hell. We all know how much you care about us and the mission. We know how seriously you take bringing us all back home safe."

Mac smacked Sam on the shoulder this time. "Thanks, Sam. You are getting pretty good at these pep talks. Maybe you should be Black Leader."

"Do I get a raise?" Sam asked with a smile.

"Not a chance."

"I knew it. Look, we've got something you can control over here," Sam nudged Mac forward towards the food table. "Start by trying to control one of these sandwiches into your face."

CHAPTER THIRTY-TWO

Bone Rattler Compound
Location Unknown

Princess Omo-Binrin huddled close to her people, attempting to stay warm. They sat on the cold concrete floor, all touching, hoping their combined body heat would help keep them warm. Several of the Okutan women sobbed in fear. She tried to comfort as many of her people as she could, while also letting her analytical mind work on the problems they faced.

Where are we? What planet are we on? Most importantly, she thought, *is this a random unfortunate matter of being in the wrong place at the wrong time? Or,* which she suspected was the truth, *did they know the real reason she was meeting with the UPG?*

I cannot ever allow them to know the truth.

I will die before they get it out of me.

How did they know where I'd be?

Omo-Binrin's mind was spinning fast, thinking through all the possibilities for the hundredth time.

There must be a traitor. Traitor to our side or theirs? Probably both.

She tried to shake the dark thoughts from her mind, but was unsuccessful.

We are in serious trouble, but I must focus on how to escape.

The room, which she now considered her dungeon, was cold, damp, and dark. There were no windows and only the one door, which hadn't opened since their horrible captors slammed it shut many hours, maybe even a day, ago. The door was metal and cold to the touch. When she knocked on it earlier and ran her hands along the cold metal, it felt solid, and she found no handle or latch.

The room wasn't pitch black, however, because of the slightest bit of green light glowing from three tiny sources on a hulking industrial machine sitting in the middle of the room. The soft glow from the green lights, which looked like the evil eyes of a monster crouching in the dark, allowed them to see faint outlines of each other and the metal door in front of them.

The rest of the room, near the monstrous machine, was frightening to them. It was too dark around the backside of the machine. No one wanted to explore into that unknown darkness.

Omo-Binrin was unfamiliar with the machine, as it was nothing like Okutan technology. There was a strange chemical smell that filled the entire room. At least four times now, in the hours they had been in the dungeon, the machine came to life. It rumbled and made a noise so loud they couldn't hear each other talk. It would rumble with lights flashing for a long time, then it would stop and go dormant again. The first time the machine came to life, they all screamed and thought they were about to be ground to mush by the evil mechanical monster. But the machine caused no harm. *No harm yet,* Omo-Binrin thought.

She needed to build up her courage and search the rest of the room so she could develop a plan of escape. She had to lead her people from this miserable dungeon and off this miserable planet. It seemed like such a daunting task while she sat in the dark, cold dungeon behind a locked door.

Stay focused. Don't get discouraged. Be strong. You can do it.

She needed to get up and explore the rest of the room. She had to feel around on the creepy dark walls and walk around the massive machine, not knowing what she would find back there. *Maybe a nest of poisonous insects that will devour me? That would be unfortunate. Maybe a deep pit where I'd fall to my death? Maybe-*

The metal door rattled and opened with a bang, interrupting her overly active imagination. They were all startled. A blast of yellow light shot into the room, forcing them to shield their eyes.

Princess Omo-Binrin heard the hollow rattle of the horrible bones their captors wore. She squinted in the light towards the door and saw the large silhouette of one of their captors in the doorway, holding a rifle. He lumbered into the room, holding the rifle, but not pointing it at them. The small Okutan people did not threaten him at all. Omo-Binrin was a trained warrior, and she recognized this one was overly confident and sloppy with his seemingly harmless prisoners. This was the first bit of good news. *I can work with this,* she thought with hope. Another of the captors entered carrying two buckets, which he set on the floor next to the wall.

Omo-Binrin pulled her cold, hungry, and stiff body to her feet and stood ramrod straight. "You will release us," she said as firmly as possible. She had no illusions of being released, but she wanted to test them. She took bold steps toward them, exuding all the regal bearing and command she could - scalp frill extended. "You cannot detain us here. You have no right. This violates Galactic Law."

As she got within arm's reach, the beast with the rifle reached out and tried to shove her, but she grabbed his furry muscular arm. She resisted his shove for a moment, fighting hard against his considerable strength advantage, until he overpowered her, and she fell back to the ground. She landed hard on her butt with a teeth-jarring thud. The other Okutans cried out as she landed. Two attendants rushed to her side.

The one that shoved her leaned toward her and snarled in galactic common, which she could also speak, "You no give orders. You, prisoner." He stood and pointed to the buckets on the floor. "Food and water. Eat." He then backed out of the door after the other left and then slammed the heavy metal door behind him, casting the room into darkness again.

"Princess, are you hurt?" an Okutan attendant asked.

"No, no, I'm fine. Just a little bruised, but I'll be fine," Omo-Binrin said. They helped her to her feet and she and the others went to the buckets to check the food and water.

"Could it be poisoned?" someone asked.

"No, there is no reason for them to poison us. They could have killed us many times. No, they want us alive. For now, at least. Everyone, please eat. You've got to eat and stay strong."

They urged her to eat first, but she insisted she would go last. As the Okutan prisoners tried the food and water, Princess Omo-Binrin stood at the back of the group, looking at the darkness behind the machine and then back at the door, then at the darkness.

Yes, there is a way. We can do this.

CHAPTER THIRTY-THREE

Sigma District
Approaching Yioturno

Mac woke after sleeping over nine hours straight through. His eyes opened and for a moment, he couldn't remember where he was. After a moment of foggy-headed confusion, Mac's mind came back to the special events room on Prime Ambassador Kumar's diplomatic ship. His cot sat along with the others against the curved wall of the spherical room. The room was dark and quiet.

All the data and planning for the prisoner exchange mission came flooding back to the forefront of his mind. Today was an important day. This was a day that must be free of error and, he hoped, free of the unexpected. The problem with the unexpected, however, is that no one ever expected the unexpected to happen. One thing Mac learned over his career with the Space Warfare Group was that every mission was urgent and sensitive. The slightest error could cause catastrophic repercussions. All he could do was to plan and prepare the best he knew how, and adapt in the field when the unexpected happened. Unfortunately, today's mission carried the added pressure of galactic politics.

Laying there on his cot, Mac took an inventory of the various pains in his body. His cot, which was comprised of fold-out composite legs and a thin padded fabric stretched between the composite frame, wasn't horrible, but it wasn't great either. The slash on his leg was demanding the most attention. It still ached, but it was feeling better. He was sure the extra strenuous effort yesterday didn't help the wound heal. Besides the leg injury, his lower back ached. He wasn't as young and spry as the other guys on the team, and his body was reminding him of that fact. His hip was sore, and his neck was aching. *We can travel through space at speeds faster than light, but we still can't make the human body do more than it can do.*

Mac rolled over and swung his legs over so he could sit up on the edge of the cot. Some men were already awake and standing at the food table, whispering in the dark. Corporal Cooper was also working at her comm station with a small task light and display screen glowing. The arched windows still displayed the classic swirling luminescence from the millions of stars in the distance as they traveled past in *FTL*.

He stood, stretched, and joined the two men, Colonel Miller and Blake Robertson, at the buffet, which looked restocked with fresh food.

Mac learned from Colonel Miller that they were a couple of hours from reaching Yioturno, right on schedule. Mac snatched up some of the more familiar food choices and began waking the rest of the team.

It took a little while for everyone to shake out their sleepy brains and stiff muscles, but the team, including Jagoon, got the machine of mission preparation rolling into action.

A SHORT TIME LATER, the diplomatic ship dropped out of *FTL*, and the team could see out the port side windows a bluish planet with white and gray cloud swirls floating in space. A healthy star in the distance, which also shone through the starboard windows, illuminated the planet, giving the team the rare warmth and enjoyment of natural sunlight.

Before long, everyone was suited up and ready to go, each in their charcoal gray E-Gear suits with the standard black lightweight armored segments and accessories. Helmets and rifles remained in the equipment crate until they were closer to the location. Jagoon turned down the offer of a suit of his own, opting instead for his burgundy robe, black leather boots, and black shoulder wrap. He agreed to carry a rifle, however, since he lost his weapons on the Okutan Royal Vessel.

Corporal Kara Cooper spoke up loudly, summarizing the situation in her youthful, feminine voice. "OK, everyone, we have arrived. This is the planet Yioturno. We are a few minutes early, but nearly sixteen hours since the call with the Bone Rattlers, as demanded."

"Corporal, anything on the scanners?" Colonel Miller asked. He stood looking out the port side windows at the planet with Mac and the team.

Cooper sat at her comm console. "OK, checking now."

After a moment, Cooper said, "We have a single beacon signal with a repeated audio message. The beacon appears to be on the other side of the planet. Let me play the message."

Cooper tapped her touch screen, and an audio message played through the small speakers on the mobile communication station.

"Humans, you will find us at the beacon coordinates. Do not waste our time." The distorted message of the angry, growling Bone Rattler stated.

"Do you have a fix on the location?" Colonel Miller asked.

"Yes, I've got it here. It looks to be on the largest landmass and..." Cooper looked at another screen on the console displaying the archived data on Yioturno. She put her thin finger on a spot on the archive map displayed on one of her console screens. "Yup, just as we thought. That is the original colony's location."

"OK, send those coordinates to the pilots and let's get over there as soon as possible." Colonel Miller then radioed the pilot to instruct him on moving the diplomatic ship closer to the meeting point.

"Major," Colonel Miller said to Mac, as he approached the team, "Now that we have a lock on the meeting spot, you've got the green light."

"Alright, let's go, boys," Mac said.

The team passed the equipment crate, single file, to grab their rifles and helmets. Sam, Sanchez, and Jagoon stepped onto the elevator first, on their way to the jump ship. They disappeared when the reflective doors zipped shut.

A moment later, the elevator returned, and Mac, Boone, and Blake stepped in. Mac gave Colonel Miller a salute as the doors zipped closed.

The elevator opened into the storage room below with the two black prisoner containment boxes. As the men entered the room and approached the boxes, the two Bone Rattlers, who were sitting with their backs against the glass front of the box, got to their feet and turned toward the men.

"What do you want now, dark human?" Sckrahhg growled.

Boone and Blake exchanged a look, expressing surprise at seeing the creatures for the first time up close.

"It's your lucky day, Sckrahhg," Mac said, unfazed by the intimidating creature before him. "It's time to go."

"Time to go where?"

"Time to turn you over to your people. We've made a deal for a prisoner exchange."

Sckrahhg laughed in his creepy growling way, causing Boone and Blake to exchange raised eyebrows again.

"I knew you humans would fold under pressure. You are so weak."

"We are not doing this for you. As far as I'm concerned, I'd be happy to launch you and your friend here into deep space and never see your ugly mug ever again. But we made an arrangement. That's what we are going to do."

Sckrahhg laughed arrogantly again, baring his fangs.

"Here's how it's going to work," Mac said. "We are going to put these magnetic arm and leg cuffs on the two of you for everyone's safety." He pointed to Boone who was holding up a set of silver cuffs. "We are then going to escort you to the jump ship, in which we will fly to the planet's surface. We will then meet up with your people and do the exchange. If you do as you are told and don't cause any problems, this will go smoothly, and no one will get hurt."

"But I want to hurt you now, human," Sckrahhg growled. "Would you like to learn about the ways I can hurt you? I might start by ripping your arms off your body."

"There is another way we can do this," Mac replied. "I can shoot you with this tranquilizer." Mac held up the handgun containing the heavy-duty tranquilizer. "And we can drag you on your ugly face to the ship unconscious. Which will it be? I really don't care."

Sckrahhg laughed. Pointing to Boone, with the thick brown beard, he said, "That one there almost looks honorable."

"Sckrahhg, do we have a deal? You will be on your best behavior so we can transport you safely and uninjured to your people?"

"Yes, dark human, we have a deal."

"OK, good decision. I am going to take you at your word. But test me even once, and it's lights out for you." Mac pointed the tranquilizer gun at the Bone Rattler and then pushed the button on the containment box, and the glass front door opened. Mac motioned for Sckrahhg to exit the box. Sckrahhg, surprisingly, did as he was told. He stepped out and stood to his full height. He was half a meter taller than Mac and the others. The top of his head was near the ceiling of the storage room.

"Stand here, please."

Sckrahhg obeyed.

Blake and Mac kept their rifles trained on the creature.

Boone clamped the silver arm cuffs on the wrists of the furry creature and then bent down and clamped cuffs on his ankles.

"Sckrahhg, will your friend here obey as well?" Mac asked.

"He will."

Mac pressed the button, and the door of the second box opened. The second Bone Rattler stepped out obediently and Boone repeated the process of cuffing him, while he emanated a low rattling growl from deep in his chest. Mac and Blake kept their weapons pointed at the Bone Rattlers.

"Dark human, I want my bones back," Sckrahhg said in a quiet growl.

"Well, I have more good news for you. We have your bones in a box on the jump ship already. We will turn them over to you at the time of the exchange."

Sckrahhg but growled in response.

"OK, follow me," Mac said and led them out of the storage room into the narrow corridor. The Bone Rattlers had to hunch down to get through the doorway.

Mac hoped their prisoners would keep up their end of the bargain and not create a scene. A violent brawl in the narrow corridor would be a disaster. But he wasn't afraid to put them down if necessary.

Mac led them down the corridor, the Bone Rattlers in single file behind him and Boone and Blake at the rear with rifles aimed at their backs. The massive prisoners shuffled awkwardly because of the ankle cuffs.

They traversed the long corridor and turned right at an intersection, which led them to the small hangar bay entrance containing the prime ambassador's jump ship.

The hangar bay was a bright space with steel floor, white walls, and a tall ceiling. The Bone Rattlers could stand up straight again. A mezzanine level with guard rail and control room behind glass was on the left. The yellow painted handrails matched the yellow stripes painted on the floor, designating the parking position of the jump ship sitting in the middle of the hangar bay. There were two identical jump ships parked side-by-side.

The jump ships were boxy, with a sloped cockpit at the front and pontoon-style propulsion engines mounted low on each side of the ships. They were both painted reflective gold with navy blue highlights and United Planetary Government flags. The rear door of the ship closest to the entrance door was open, and the boarding ramp was down. Sam and Sanchez stood on either side of the open doors with rifles at the ready.

Mac nodded to Sam and Sanchez as he walked up the short ramp and into the small jump ship. The Bone Rattlers followed, hunching down and shuffling into the ship, followed by Boone, Blake, then Sam and Sanchez.

The jump ship interior was like nothing they'd ever used for a mission, or even basic transport. Their usual ship, the Starhawk, was purpose-built for military action. If they traveled under Army credentials, or even as private citizens, they would always be limited to basic general population transports, which were simple and functional. This ship was a whole different concept, designed for transporting dignitaries of the highest order. The surfaces included exotic woods and shiny metal and mirrored finishes. The long bench seats, which faced each other across the center aisle, were a cream-colored plush leather material. Mac noticed that everything in the small craft was designed to impress important people with comfort and luxury.

Jagoon sat at the front of the ship and looked out the front window. Mac watched him for a moment to make sure he wouldn't cause a scene. *I should have had Sanchez stay on Jagoon,* Mac thought. *Too late now.*

Jagoon seemed in control, so Mac focused on directing the massive prisoners to sit on the plush couches at the back end of the ship. The irony of seeing the huge furry beasts sitting in the luxurious environment amused Mac. His team of operators looked just as much out of place with their dark tactical gear and severe expressions. It was a study in contrasts.

Mac sat next to Sckrahhg, and the others took up seats closer to the cockpit with rifles still pointing at the prisoners. No one wanted to get into a fight, especially a gunfight, in this cramped ship.

Once everyone settled, Mac checked with the team. "We ready, boys?"

He received a round of affirmative responses.

Mac made eye contact with his men, all of whom displayed their battle faces, except for Sanchez, who mouthed the word, *fancy*, while sweeping his finger in a circle.

"Sckrahhg, you guys just keep chillin' and take it easy," Mac said.

Sckrahhg just bared his fangs and was breathing heavily.

"Pilot, we are ready when you are," Mac said.

"Roger," the pilot responded, and the rear ramp and door raised up and closed with a hiss. The ship began vibrating with a gentle hum as the pilot applied power to the propulsion system.

Out the front cockpit window, over the pilot's shoulder, Mac could see the hangar bay door opening, revealing the huge black surface of the dark side of Yioturno and the rays of the nearby star, Sigma, spilling over the curved edge of Yioturno. The star's rays were blinding, so Mac looked away. The pilot activated a dark screen to block out the intense rays.

Mac radioed the command center. "Command, Black Leader."

"Go, Black Leader," Colonel Miller's voice came through the radio.

"We are ready to jump."

"Roger, all is clear. On your command."

Mac gave the pilot the green light and the small jump ship sped through the hangar door towards the planet below.

Sckrahhg laughed to himself as they launched into the darkness.

CHAPTER THIRTY-FOUR

Yioturno

The pilot of the jump ship brought the small gold luxury craft in low near the surface of Yioturno. They were on the dark side of the planet, giving them limited visibility. Through the windows, the vague ominous outlines of mountains and trees were visible in the distance. As they passed over undisturbed fields and clusters of leafy trees in the valley, they could see under the ship's landing lights as they approached the abandoned colony.

The pilot said, "Major, I'm going to take us over the site so we can identify any hazards and find a suitable landing spot."

"Roger," Mac replied. "Alright, get ready, boys."

In the distance, Mac could see the twinkle of lights as they approached the site. The area near the colony was rocky and more dirt than fields. He soon saw the lights were coming from a large industrial spacecraft sitting on a level area, surrounded by a cluster of structures that formed a U-shape.

The pilot slowed the craft, and Mac leaned over to peer out the window at the development below. Under the two sets of lights from the spaceships, Mac could see that the site was an abandoned construction zone. They flew over large construction tractors and trucks that were not much different from the UPG's own construction equipment. They were abandoned at odd angles, as if the colony project suddenly stopped and everyone disappeared. It was a construction burial ground.

The Bone Rattler spaceship seemed to be standing in the town square or city center between the buildings. The buildings were long rectangular structures, wider at the base and tapering up at an angle to the flat-topped roof in a symmetrical trapezoid shape. They looked to be constructed of glass and wood beams. In front of the spaceship, in the pool of light, were three Bone Rattlers holding rifles, looking up at them as they flew over. The Bone Rattlers looked tiny from the air above them. The pilot directed the jump ship over the development and then, in a wide sweeping turn, came back around.

"Major, I'm going to put us down in that spot between the tractors and that fallen crane. I think you'll be about 100 meters away, but it looks like you'll have an easy walk to the meeting location," the pilot said. "I think that is about as close as I can get you safely."

"Agreed. That'll do fine."

The craft swooped in and hovered in the air for a moment, then rotated around so that the back entrance was facing the Bone Rattler ship in the distance. The craft touched down gently on the surface and the back door ramp lowered.

Sanchez and Sam were moving in an instant, along with Jagoon. They slipped through the rows of seats, jogged down the short ramp and took up a position a few meters ahead of the craft. Jagoon stayed close to Sam's side with his new EP-17 energy rifle, which was the same rifle Sam and the others carried. Sanchez, on the other hand, carried a custom sniper rifle, which was nothing like the stubby close combat EP-17. Sanchez had helped design this particular sniper rifle. It was matte black and thin with a cupped shoulder stock. The barrel was a meter long and sported a high-powered scope.

"OK, Sckrahhg, I expect complete compliance. Follow my men

without any trouble and you'll be home in time for dinner," Mac said.

Sckrahhg said, "Of course, dark human."

Blake and Boone stood, and each took a Bone Rattler by the wrist cuffs and led them with one hand out of the ship. They had to hunch over and scoot slowly. Both men kept rifles trained on the prisoners, with the other hand as they went.

Mac followed with his own rifle and stepped off the ramp, which began raising into the closed position. A moment later, the jump ship left the ground. It kicked up dust and dead leaves as it disappeared into the night, leaving the team alone in the eerie darkness.

In the distance, down the long hard-packed dirt path, three tall Bone Rattlers stood in their ship's light, waiting for them.

"Command, Black Leader," Mac said into his radio.

"Go, Black Leader," Kara Cooper said through the radio.

"We are on the surface. Making our way to the meeting now."

"Roger, Black Leader. Reminder, you are on your own down there. We don't have an eye in the sky or scanning beyond the basics up here." Mac sensed the slight distress in Cooper's voice, knowing she usually had the full array of Interplanetary Army scanning equipment and drone tech to assist the mission.

Mac stared down the path toward the Bone Rattler ship. "Acknowledged. Besides, Cooper," Mac said in a friendly tone, "It's just a simple hostage exchange, right?"

"Should be, Black Leader."

Sckrahhg turned towards Mac, pulling against Boone who held the wrist cuffs and said, "Where are my bones?"

"Who knows?" Mac said dryly, without looking at him.

"You promised to return them to me, dark human," Sckrahhg said with a threatening growl.

"I lied."

"You will pay for this," Sckrahhg said angrily.

"I don't think so," Mac said.

It was night at the abandoned colony on Yioturno. In the dark, all around the team, were construction tractors and equipment that looked like cranes, tractors, and dump trucks. It was an equipment cemetery. The path in front of them was a road wide enough for the tractors, and it led all the way to where the Bone Rattler ship stood. There were leafy trees in the distance and large boulders scattered around.

To their left was a long metal boom broken off from a fallen crane laying along the path. The faded red control cabin was still sitting on six articulated legs with flat plates for feet. It looked like a giant robotic insect.

"Man," Sanchez said, "this place is creepy."

Mac was thinking the same thing.

"Yeah, it's a ghost town," Boone added in his deep, booming voice.

Sckrahhg growled, "It will also be where you all die."

Sanchez stepped up to Sckrahhg. "You wanna go right now? We can make sure this is the place where you die, buddy. I'll drop you right here and now."

"I will rip your limbs off, eat your flesh, and pick my teeth with your bones, little human," Sckrahhg said, baring his ugly fangs at Sanchez.

"You ain't so tough," Sanchez said. "Major Mac, say the word and I'll teach this oversized fur ball a lesson."

"Alright, listen up," Mac said as he stepped over and pulled Sanchez away. "We're done with all this. Sckrahhg, shut your mouth. Your bones are gone. End of story. If you comply, we will turn you over to your people. But if not, we're going to have a real problem here today."

Sckrahhg growled but said nothing more. Mac expected more resistance, but Sckrahhg was oddly compliant.

"Sanchez, get your head in the game. I need you to pick your overwatch point. The rest of us will escort the prisoners to the ship." Mac pointed up the path. "Sam, I want you guys to hang back a bit until we know where the princess is. I don't see her up there right now. I'm hoping she is on the ship or just out of sight. Let's go. Stay razor sharp, boys. No mistakes."

"So sharp, you'd get cut just looking at us," Sanchez said in reply.

"I am going to kill you for losing my bones, dark human," Sckrahhg said. "You will be the first of my new collection."

"You're a broken record, Sckrahhg," Mac replied, unfazed. "Today, you get to go home. But I'm sure we'll pick this up later."

"I will count the days."

"Me too, Sckrahhg, me too."

Mac took the lead down the path toward the Bone Rattler ship, holding his rifle toward the ground. Boone and Blake pulled their prisoners by the wrists behind Mac, then Sam and Jagoon followed.

The team passed more equipment and large gray storage containers with red numbers painted on the side. Some containers had open doors and others were closed.

"Eyes on the shadows. We don't need to be caught in an ambush right now," Mac instructed. "Those trees out there make a good hiding place."

"It looks like the construction crew just vanished," Sanchez said, but no one replied.

When they were halfway to the Bone Rattlers, Sanchez picked a dump truck with an open bed facing the meeting spot. The dump truck's cockpit was spherical glass and sat high above the dump bed on a cylinder body. The wheels, which were as tall as Sanchez, were also spherical with finger-length spikes protruding in all directions for traction. Sanchez held his rifle with one hand and climbed the ladder on the side of the dump box. Reaching the top, he crawled over the wall into the bed where he laid on his stomach, looking through the scope down range at the Bone Rattlers.

"Major Mac, yeah, this is a prime-time spot, right here. I have a clear view of the meeting site. I don't see our princess. Just three ugly sasquatches," Sanchez said.

After a long moment, Sam's voice came through the radio. "What are you talking about, Sanchez?"

"I said, sasquatch."

"Sanchez, what is a sasquatch?" Sam said.

"You never heard of a sasquatch? You were so sheltered growing up, Lead." Sanchez chuckled a little. "It's a mythological creature from old earth days. These Bone Rattlers look just like them. People believe they live in the forests of North America on Earth."

After a moment, Sam sighed. "Sanchez..."

The rest of Black Team continued down the path and as they approached, they found a set of stone stairs leading to the town square level. The stairs were in the pool of light created by the floodlights on the Bone Rattler ship. They all climbed the ten steps and stopped at the top. Sam and Jagoon faded back toward the right, away from the others, keeping their eyes, and guns, on the three Bone Rattlers standing in front of their ship.

They were now in the u-shaped area, surrounded by the broken down and dilapidated trapezoidal buildings. The town square surface between the buildings was stone blocks fitted together. There were unrecognizable patterns made by the varying colors of the stones. Plants grew up between the cracks, disrupting the stones.

The Bone Rattler ship differed from the one Sam and Mac investigated earlier, but looked like a similar manufacturer. It was much larger than the leech-like ship but was still utilitarian, with no hint toward style or purpose beyond industrial work. It wasn't out of place with the colony's abandoned construction equipment.

The three Bone Rattlers stood side-by-side wearing their bone armor, bone helmets, and pointing black rifles toward the sky.

"I still don't see the princess," Mac said to the team over the radio. "Black-3, you see anything we can't?"

"Negative, boss," Sanchez replied.

"I don't like this," Mac said to the team. Then into the command radio channel, "Command, Black Leader. We've made contact. We don't see the princess. Standby."

"Roger, Black Leader," Cooper replied.

The three Bone Rattlers began stomping forward, and all of Black Team brought their rifles up against their shoulders, staring through the sight window at them.

"Hold it right there," Mac shouted, as he stepped forward and put his left palm out. They needed to stop. Into his radio, he said, "Black-3, drop 'em if needed."

"Gladly," Sanchez said.

The taller of the three Bone Rattlers spoke in the typical aggressive growling tone, "I am Manstruu, celebrated warrior of my people. You will turn over our honorable leader, Sckrahhg, now."

"Manstruu, I am Major Malcom Lambert of the United Planetary Government's Interplanetary Army. You have broken several intergalactic laws by ambushing the Okutan royal vessel and kidnapping an important dignitary and part of their royal family."

"You have broken laws by capturing our people!" Manstruu bellowed.

"No, Manstruu, the UPG has taken these two into custody because of galactic piracy and slave trading. But we will exchange them for Princess Omo-Binrin Oba. I will turn over your people here as soon as the princess is in our custody."

"You will let them go now," Manstruu said again, "and then I will give you the princess."

"Manstruu, you are not in a position to negotiate," Mac replied. "You will do it our way."

Sckrahhg, behind Mac, spoke in his native language to Manstruu, which sounded more like grizzly bears fighting. Whatever Sckrahhg said changed Manstruu's tune, and he calmed down right away.

"We want to see the princess now, or this exchange is over. Where is she?" Mac asked.

"She is in that building there, waiting for you," Manstruu pointed his giant furry arm toward the building to Mac's right.

"Why would you do that?" Mac asked. "That's not the agreement we had."

"We don't trust humans. You can get her after you give us our people back."

"Well, the feeling is mutual, Manstruu. We don't trust you. You will get your people after we have the princess safe and sound. We need to confirm she is alive and safe."

"Have it your way," Manstruu said.

"Sam, go check it out," Mac said. "Sanchez, anything funky going on at that front building to my right?"

"Negative, Major Mac. It's dark and quiet."

"Roger. Keep an eye on it. Sam, be careful."

Sam and Jagoon walked toward the building pointed out by the Bone Rattler and Mac radioed the update to Command.

When they arrived at the door, Sam covered Jagoon as he opened the door. Sam entered first, rifle extended and spotlights on, sweeping side-to-side as he stepped into the building. Jagoon followed behind him and Mac lost sight of them as the door closed behind them.

"Sanchez, anything?" Mac asked uneasily.

"Negative. Still quiet."

"Sam, what do you guys see?"

Sam's voice came through the radio. "The building is dark and run down. We're using spotlights, since Jagoon doesn't have night vision equipment. Searching…nothing here in the first room…"

Mac shifted his weight back and forth, fighting the urge to pace.

"Ah…wait. I think we have something. Stand by. Jagoon is saying something."

"Sam, what is it?" Mac asked.

"Mac, we have an Okutan female tied to a chair in here."

"OK, is she alive?" he asked.

"Mac, hold on…Jagoon is saying it's not the princess."

Mac started moving toward the building.

"Something's not right. It's not the princess. What the? Jagoon, watch out!" Sam yelled. Suddenly, the building erupted into a massive fiery explosion. The noise was deafening, and it filled the darkness with bright orange light.

CHAPTER THIRTY-FIVE

Moments earlier and five hundred kilometers above, in the spherical room on Prime Ambassador Kumar's ship, Colonel Miller stood behind Corporal Kara Cooper as she sat at the temporary communication station. They listened to Mac's situation report come through the radio. Prime Ambassador Kumar stood to the side, listening in.

"Where is the princess?" Colonel Miller asked angrily.

Cooper knew better than to answer Colonel Miller's rhetorical question.

Prime Ambassador Kumar asked, "Are they trying to double-cross us, Colonel? We can't trust these pirates."

A few excruciatingly slow minutes passed before they heard from the team on the ground again.

"Command, Black Leader." Mac's voice crackled over the radio.

"Go, Black Leader," Cooper replied.

"Bone Rattlers say the princess is in a building to the south and not with them. We don't see her anywhere. Black-2 and Jagoon are checking it out."

"Black Leader," Colonel Miller stepped in, "any idea what they are up to?"

"Colonel, they say they don't trust us."

"Yeah, well, we don't trust them either," Colonel Miller said.

"Nope. Not one bit. They're as crooked as a bag full of chubony vipers."

"Be careful, Major."

"Stand by, Command." Mac said.

They listened intently to the background noises and talking among the team on the ground.

"Turn it up, Corporal."

Cooper turned up the volume. A moment later, the sound of a massive explosion blasted through the speakers, creating screeching feedback. Cooper turned the sound down and looked up at Miller behind her. Her eyes were wide and terrified.

"Colonel, something has just happened," Cooper reported.

Kumar scooted in close, trying to see what was happening.

"What was that?" Miller asked.

"What's happening, Corporal?" Kumar asked as well.

"I can't tell. Scanners are picking up what looks from here like an explosion near the team."

"Are they OK?" Colonel Miller asked frantically.

"Sir, I don't know."

"Get them on the radio, right now," Kumar demanded.

"Black Leader, Command," Cooper said into the radio with no response. She tried again, "Black Leader, Command. You copy?"

No response.

Cooper tried a third time.

MAC FELL HARD against the stone surface of the town square. His body bounced, jarring his head, and smashing his teeth together. His head was spinning, but he rolled toward the stairs. The darkness gave way to flickering light from the orange and yellow flames devouring the rubble of the exploded building. Embers and debris fell all around him. He scrambled on his stomach down the stairs and glanced from the burning building to the

Bone Rattlers. He saw the gold fur of a Bone Rattler flashing past him.

It took a moment for his head to clear and vision to improve after the massive explosion. "Black-2, you copy?" No response. "Black-2! Sam! You copy?" Mac's voice cracked under the emotion of seeing his closest friend and brother-in-arms caught in such a terrible explosion.

No one could survive that, he thought.

There was no response from Sam.

Mac could hear the voice of Kara Cooper through the radio, but it was just background noise as he stared at the mangled remains of the burning building collapsing down upon itself, into the crater created by the explosion.

Mere seconds later, the night erupted again, this time from a volley of blaster rifle fire between Mac's team and the Bone Rattlers.

Mac scooted himself farther down the steps for cover and saw Boone to his left, doing the same. Mac put his rifle barrel against the top step and began firing at Manstruu and the others.

The Bone Rattler ship's engines fired up, causing smoke and steam to billow out of the bottom of the craft. The whirling scream of the ship's engines almost covered the noise of the frenzied fire fight.

Too many things were happening at the same time.

Sanchez was firing shot after shot from his overwatch position. One Bone Rattler took three explosive blasts to the chest and twisted and fell to the ground. Manstruu and the others were squatting behind a block wall far off to Mac's left, near the ramp of the spacecraft. They fired at Mac's team from behind the wall. Sanchez sent a steady flow of fire on the block wall, forcing the Bone Rattlers to stay concealed. Every time they'd try to pop their heads up to fire back, Sanchez's accurate shots would drive them back down.

Blake was wrestling with one Bone Rattler while Sckrahhg was shuffling toward the fallen Bone Rattler. He collapsed on the rifle laying on the ground. Sckrahhg used the rifle with his bound wrists to destroy the ankle cuffs, freeing his legs.

Boone jumped up from the stairs and charged toward Blake to help him wrestle with the other Bone Rattler.

At the same time, Manstruu began sprinting toward the entrance to their ship. The giant Bone Rattler was more agile and faster than Mac expected. Mac fired at the sprinting Manstruu. As Mac's energy blasts crashed into Manstruu's furry body, the other Bone Rattler hiding behind the wall stood and fired at Blake and Boone. Blake took a shot to the chest and crumpled to the ground the same way Manstruu crumpled to the surface of the ship's ramp. Their bodies hit the ground at the same time.

With Manstruu down, Mac turned to fire at Sckrahhg, who was now sprinting to the ship ramp, but was also turning and firing at Mac as he ran. Mac dove below the top of stairs again for cover as the energy blasts smashed into the ground right in front of him, kicking up dirt and chips of stone.

With a precise succession of three blasts, Sanchez took the head off the Bone Rattler at the block wall as it was shooting at Boone. The headless Bone Rattler's last shot went wide, but still hit Boone in the shoulder. Boone got knocked around and as he spun, he fell back down the stairs, rolling down several steps before stopping.

The Bone Rattler's body reacted slowly after losing its head. The arms fell, dropping the rifle, then the body fell forward over the block wall.

Mac leapt from cover and ran parallel along the stairs, dodging Sckrahhg's shots and firing back at him as he ran toward Boone's fallen location. Sckrahhg made it up the ramp and into the ship, even as Sanchez turned his focus on him. Sanchez was too late, and his shots slammed harmlessly against the side of the spaceship and the ramp.

There was one last Bone Rattler, the one broken loose from Blake and Boone, who was shuffling toward the ship as fast as his bound feet would allow him to go.

Sanchez's shots from his perch were true and three blasts slammed into the back of the Bone Rattler, who then slammed to the ground, skidding on his face, dead.

Mac dropped his rifle and grabbed Boone by the arm, and rolled him over. He groaned in pain.

"Boone, you alright?"

Boone's shoulder was a mess, bleeding through his shredded uniform. Soot and splattered blood from his shoulder covered the side of his face mask. Mac helped him into a comfortable position lying on his back on the stair step.

"Arrrgh," Boone groaned. "I'm OK, I'm OK. Shoulder hurts like hell." With his good arm, he was reaching for his rifle and craning his neck to look toward the battlefield.

"Boone, take it easy. Just rest here a bit. And stay low."

He groaned again and laid his helmeted head back on the step.

Mac turned to the radio. "Black-2, you copy? Sam?"

Still no response.

Mac lifted his head and looked toward the burning remains of the building, then toward the ship. Sckrahhg was walking down the ramp of the spacecraft, hands still cuffed. He reached down and grabbed the fallen Manstruu by the fur at the back of his neck and dragged him up the ramp, glaring at Mac the entire way.

Mac jumped up and sprinted toward the ship, firing at Sckrahhg with every step, but the ramp was already closing back up, and the shots were pointless.

Sanchez was suddenly there, near where Boone lay. He knelt and supported his sniper rifle to fire at the ship.

The ground started shaking and the Bone Rattler ship lifted off as Mac and Sanchez fired at the spacecraft, but the rifle fire did no harm as the ship accelerated into the sky and disappeared into the atmosphere.

Mac turned to Sanchez. "Go check Blake. Boone is fine for now."

Sanchez ran to Blake's prone position.

Mac turned and ran in the other direction as hard as he could, pumping his arms and legs as fast as possible toward the collapsed burning building. He came to a skidding stop in front of what used to be the building. Now, all he saw was a hole filled with burning debris and rubble.

No one could survive that explosion.

Mac frantically scanned the crater of burning rubble, looking for any sign of Sam or Jagoon. Emotion welled up inside him in a mixture of sadness and fury, like he'd never experienced before. He slammed his fists into beams next to him, several times as hard as he could, and let out a primal scream at the top of his lungs. He then climbed down into the crater.

A MINUTE EARLIER, aboard the diplomatic ship, Corporal Kara Cooper tried the radio again with no response.

"Sir, I can't get any response from them. I have no idea if any of them are alive or not."

Colonel Miller let out a frustrated barrage of profanity. He began pacing the room.

"Wait a minute, I have movement on the ship scanner. Sir, something is moving…yes, looks like a ship is taking off."

"Is it our jump ship?" Miller asked.

"No sir, the jump ship is reporting in from here," she pointed with a thin index finger at the map on the screen. "This ship seems bigger."

"It's the Bone Rattlers escaping," Prime Ambassador Kumar said in a resigned tone. He stood straight and adjusted his suit. He then walked toward the window and gazed out at Yioturno below. "They've killed our best special ops team and are escaping with the princess…if the princess was even here. We don't even know if she is alive. This is a total nightmare." He turned toward Miller, pointing his finger with a face of fury. "Your incompetent men and your incompetent leadership have ruined our chance to save the princess. This is a diplomatic disaster worse than anything we've never seen before!"

Colonel Miller took a few hard steps toward Kumar and barked, "Not so fast, Prime Ambassador!" Colonel Miller shouted, but then adjusted his attitude as he remembered he was talking to the third most powerful politician in the United Planetary Government. "Sir, I mean, we don't know that our team is dead or out of this fight. We don't know the status of the princess, either. Never count my boys out."

"Sir, the ship is leaving the atmosphere and heading straight for us," Cooper said.

"Can you get a lock on it or identify it?"

"Not yet. It will take a moment."

"What about the control room up front?" Colonel Miller asked, speaking of the diplomatic ship's control and piloting team.

"Checking now," Cooper said, and she radioed the control room. "Nothing, sir. They are trying as well."

"Call them."

"Yessir," Cooper replied.

Prime Ambassador Kumar and Colonel Miller could see, through the arched windows facing Yioturno, the distant ship coming their way. It was a pinpoint of light from the planet at first, but quickly formed into a dark shape coming straight at them.

"There they are," Kumar exclaimed.

Cooper triggered the open communication channel to hail the other ship and said, "Unidentified ship departing Yioturno, this is the United Planetary Government's Diplomatic Vessel, *UPG-3*. Identify yourself -"

Before Cooper could finish, the spaceship was already on top of them, firing several torpedoes at them as they flew past.

The ship shook violently when the torpedoes slammed into it. Kumar and Miller stumbled and steadied themselves with the wall. Cooper gripped the side of her console to keep from being flung from her seat.

Cooper adjusted her small body back into her seat and checked the ship. "Sir, the hostile ship just entered *FTL*."

"Did you get a trace on them?"

"No, sir, they're gone."

"Try the team on the ground again."

"Black Leader, this is Command. Do you copy?" Cooper said into the radio.

Finally, a voice came through in response.

"Command, this is Black-3." Sergeant Luis Sanchez's voice replied.

"Black-3, SITREP?"

"They double-crossed us," Sanchez yelled. His words came in short, choppy sentences. "It was a decoy. They blew up Sam and Jagoon. Huge explosion. All hell has broken loose."

"What is the status of Black Leader?"

Miller hurried over to stand beside Cooper and the radio.

"Not responding," Sanchez sounded like he was exerting himself, maybe running while transmitting. "Checking on him now. Black-4 is *KIA*. Black-5 is injured, but will make it."

"Roger, Black-3."

Kara dropped her face in her hands with elbows on her knees.

"Stand by, Command," Sanchez said.

On the surface of Yioturno, Mac's mind swirled. He tried to climb into the crater, but the ground was unstable and covered with burning debris. There was no way to get in or move around safely. He looked toward the center, looking for any sign of life.

He tried Sam on the radio again.

Nothing.

Behind the mental fog, he could again hear Corporal Kara Cooper's voice, but he was emotionally too far away to answer. He also heard Sanchez's voice, but he couldn't make sense of his words as tears streamed down his face.

Then, powerful hands grabbed his arm. He turned to find Sanchez. Flames reflected off his face mask.

Sanchez pulled him from the hole and began checking him over, looking for injuries, and patting him down.

"Major Mac?" Sanchez said in a gentle voice. "Major Mac, look at me. Are you OK?" Finding no obvious gunshot wounds or lacerations, Sanchez grabbed Mac by the shoulders and shook him. "Mac, listen! Are you hurt?"

"What?" Mac fought against his mind pulling him into the dark abyss and tried to focus. The mixture of sadness and fury was overwhelming.

The vision of the explosion kept running through his mind, and he could still hear Sam's voice.

"Mac, are you hurt?" Sanchez looked at the burning rubble pile and back at Mac.

Mac gathered himself, and focused on Sanchez with salty tears streaming down his face. He blinked hard to clear his vision. "He's gone," Mac said. It was all he could get out.

"I know. Sam's gone. Listen, Blake is also *KIA*. And Jagoon. They are all gone, Mac. But we gotta get out of here, right now."

Mac hunched over with his hands on his knees. He felt like he was going to be sick. It was his worst nightmare coming true. His men, the ones he was responsible for, were dead. And, even worse, his closest friend was gone. Forever.

Sanchez took a step away. Mac could hear Sanchez calling Command over the radio and calling the jump ship to pick them up.

Mac stood up straight and looked into the burning rubble pile again. Sam's wife came to Mac's mind. *Oh, poor Sarina. She will be devastated. I've failed them all.*

Something inside of Mac broke as he stared into the flames. *They will pay. They will all pay for this. They will meet fury like they've never seen before.*

In the distance, Mac heard the noise of the jump ship returning, and he turned to see the landing lights as it touched down near where Blake's body lay in the town square above the steps. Boone was standing at the top of the stairs near Blake's body, holding his injured shoulder.

Mac sniffed hard. "Let's get out of here."

"That's what I've been saying. Is there anything left to retrieve and bring home?" Sanchez said as he pointed with his thumb toward the fallen building.

"We can't get in there. It's too dangerous. Besides, there isn't anything left from the size of that explosion. Come on," Mac said, and they began jogging back toward the jump ship. Its rear door was opening.

Sanchez swung Boone's good arm around his own neck and helped support him as he walked to the ship, while Mac picked up Blake's lifeless body and fireman-carried him on his shoulder to the ship.

Mac climbed the ramp into the luxury transport ship and laid Blake's bloody body on the floor of the aisle.

Boone flopped hard onto the plush white seats with a painful groan. Fresh blood covered his shoulder, hands, and suit. Blood and dirt smeared across the seats.

The ramp and rear door closed once they were all in the vessel.

"Easy now, Boone. Just sit there while I look at this injury," Sanchez said while taking his dirty helmet off and laying it on the seat next to him.

"Aaaarrrrggh," Boone groaned again as he tried to sit up, smearing more blood on the plush white seats. "Stupid Bone Rattlers," Boone said with a grimace.

Sanchez pulled Boone's helmet off, set it to the side and checked his wound.

Mac, standing over Blake's dead body, took his own helmet off, let out an angry scream, and hurled the helmet with all his strength against the rear door. The helmet bounced back toward him, and he caught it like a ball. With two hands he smashed the helmet five times into the wood paneling along the side wall, cracking both his helmet and the wood panel.

With one eye on Mac, Sanchez pulled out bandages and blood clotting solution from the thigh pockets on Boone's suit.

"Sergeant, you ready?" the pilot asked of Sanchez, knowing better than to address Major Lambert in this moment.

"Yeah, get us out of here."

PART FOUR

Courage is now defined by coming face-to-face with the most unexpected and unknowable horrors of the galaxy and choosing to fight on for the good of humanity.

— FITO DEL BOSQUE, FOUNDER OF THE SPACE WARFARE GROUP

CHAPTER THIRTY-SIX

Sanchez cleaned and bandaged Boone's shoulder wound as they returned to Prime Ambassador Kumar's ship.

"OK, Boone, I think that is the best we can do here. Once we get you back in the TC," Sanchez said, using the abbreviation for the temporary command center established on Prime Ambassador Kumar's ship, "I'll be able to dress this wound better. You made a bloody mess outa Kumar's jumper, bro. He will not be happy."

Boone was sitting back against the plush white seat of the jump ship, eyes closed and grimacing. He was a big man, much taller and wider and heavier than both Sanchez and Mac. His shaggy brown hair and thick beard were both sweaty and disheveled.

"Alright. Thanks, Luis," Boone squeezed out through the grimace. He looked down at his own bandaged shoulder and around at the seats and floor, both covered in smeared dirt and blood. "Maybe Kumar won't notice." Boone tried to sit up straighter by pushing his body up with the heels of his boots against the floor, but just grimaced more when his feet slipped.

"Why you trying to be a tough guy?" Sanchez asked. "Let me give you the pain blocker."

"Nah, man, I'm fine," Boone said. His voice was more gravelly than usual.

Mac was sitting on the seat across from Boone with his elbows on his knees and his face in his palms, his broken helmet on the floor in the corner. He looked up at Boone. "You don't look fine," Mac added.

"I'm good. I'm good. I can handle it," Boone said.

"I'm just saying you don't get style points for fighting the pain more than you need to, bro," Sanchez said, and then smacked Boone on the leg.

"Major Lambert," the pilot said over the radio, "we will be in the hangar in three minutes."

"Roger, thank you for getting us in and out of there safely," Mac said. "Sanchez, you help Boone get back to the TC, and I'll get Blake there. I'll need your help to get him taken care of once we get there."

"Yeah, of course," Sanchez said.

Mac and Sanchez had to get Blake's body into the sealed mortuary case used for fallen soldiers. They couldn't always bring them back from the battlefield. Brothers like Sam and even Jagoon. Mac's mind replayed the explosion on repeat. Even though he had only known Jagoon for a few hours, Jagoon was a formidable warrior who'd gained his respect. He wished he had more time with both warriors.

Mac sat up straight and blinked hard a few times to clear the wetness from his eyes. *Just handle your business, Mac. Disconnect. Put it away. Just do what you must do. There will be time to mourn later. Right now, focus on finding them and make them pay. Turn the anger into vengeance.*

The jump ship slowed and maneuvered into the hangar space at the back of the diplomatic ship. Sanchez and Boone scooted down to the last seats next to the exit door, and Mac knelt by Blake's body, waiting for the ship door and ramp to open.

Once the door opened, Sanchez helped support Boone as they walked down the ramp. Mac leaned down, pulled Blake onto his shoulder and carried him down the short ramp into the bright hangar. Prime Ambassador Kumar and Colonel Miller stood in front of him. The Colonel looked stony-faced and stiff in his charcoal gray battle fatigues and black beret. Prime Ambassador Kumar, on the other hand, looked distressed. He obviously wasn't used to seeing this side of warfare. His eyes were wide and his mouth open as Sanchez and Boone passed by him. He scurried over to the jump ship ramp and surveyed the bloody mess.

"Oh, dear me," Kumar mumbled as he looked from the messy compartment to Mac carrying the fallen Blake on his shoulder.

"Sorry about your ship, Prime Ambassador," Mac said with no emotion.

"It's the least of our problems, major. We can get another jump ship, but we can't get another princess."

Mac sensed the rebuke in Kumar's words. He stopped in his tracks and glared at Kumar. Typical politician's game. Take credit for the team's success and blame them for failures. Mac's mind started building a harsh defensive response, but he caught it before it left his mouth. He'd gain nothing from giving Kumar a thrashing. He turned and kept moving.

He moved slowly, burdened by the extra weight, and he didn't stop walking when he got to Colonel Miller. "Colonel, can you arrange for our weapons and gear to be brought back to the TC?"

"Yes, I'll take care of it. Major, we've got a gurney for the body," Miller said to Mac.

"No, sir. I'll take Blake myself."

Miller, knowing the heart of the warrior brotherhood that existed in the group, said nothing. He walked alongside Mac as he entered the corridor. Miller would have done the same thing. Sanchez and Boone walked slowly a few meters in front of them as they made their way toward the elevator.

Looking over at Miller, Mac said, "So, did you get a trace on that ship? Do we know where it went?"

"Negative. By the time we knew they were moving, they were on us and attacking. They entered *FTL* immediately."

Mac's expression changed as he ground his teeth and fought back the anger. *Are you kidding me?* Mac thought, but didn't speak out loud. *How could they let them get away? Now what am I going to do?*

Mac's mind detached from his surroundings again as he considered how to find them and kill them all.

"Major, tell me what happened out there," Colonel Miller said. Miller had to repeat himself to get Mac's attention.

"Sir," Mac took a deep breath, "It was a total disaster. No other way to categorize it. We were unprepared, uninformed, and it resulted in a total mission failure. I honestly don't know what happened." He tried to control the anger and not let it leak into his voice. But he was failing. "It was a no-win situation. We trusted an enemy and good men died."

They arrived at the elevator, and Mac adjusted Blake's heavy body on his shoulder. They all squeezed into the elevator.

Mac continued angrily, "They didn't have the princess with them. It was a setup from the beginning and we fell for it like sheep to the slaughter."

"I agree, Major. Tell me what happened out there."

Mac paused for a minute, attempting to push down a mixture of emotions that were right on the surface, ready to explode. "The Bone Rattlers said the princess was in a building nearby. Sam and Jagoon went into the building to search for her. Something went wrong. The last thing I heard Sam say was they found an Okutan female, but it wasn't the princess, just some decoy. Obviously, the princess is still being held somewhere else, if she is even still alive. And now they have Sckrahhg back as well. They'll get theirs, though," Mac said, gritting his teeth.

Colonel Miller sighed deeply. "I'm going to have to inform the president and I don't know what to tell him. This thing is totally unravelling."

Mac said nothing. There was nothing left to say.

The elevator doors opened, and they entered the large spherical special events room. Corporal Kara Cooper stood near the tall equipment crate with a pained look on her face.

Sanchez got Boone situated on his cot near the back wall and then rushed over to grab the body case from the equipment crate.

Mac laid Blake on his cot and waited until Sanchez brought the case over. The body case was a hard-sided box that unfolded and sealed tightly to preserve the corpse, keeping the body fluids and odors contained. Sanchez positioned it on the floor next to Blake's cot and pulled the sides up to form the box shape. Together, they lifted Blake, Mac at the shoulders and Sanchez at the feet, and laid him in the box.

Mac and Sanchez removed the handheld firearms from Blake's thigh and removed his tactical vest, carrying grenades and tools. They then emptied his pockets and removed his helmet, setting them all aside. Finally, Mac shut his eyes and rested his hands on this stomach, then stood up straight. He walked over to the equipment crate to collect one more important item as Sanchez secured the lid and sealed the box tight.

When Mac returned to Sanchez, he unfolded the United Planetary Government Flag and handed Sanchez the corner. Together, they snapped the flag out flat and tight, then laid it over Blake's box. The UPG fabric flag was royal blue with a wide gold stripe running horizontally down the middle. In the gold band were ten embroidered stars, representing each of the developed colonial planets in the UPG Government. This flag was special, however, because it also included the Space Warfare Group stylized sword and shield emblem as a watermark in the center of the flag, behind the gold band.

Once the flag laid straight and unwrinkled over the box, Mac and Sanchez snapped to attention and saluted. Boone struggled to his feet and saluted with his good arm. Colonel Miller and Corporal Cooper joined the salute as well.

Mac spoke, but his voice was on the edge. "For Jo. For Blake. For Sam. And for Jagoon. Warriors of whom the universe knows no equal. Your lives are not given in vain, but in the pursuit of freedom and liberty throughout the galaxy and beyond." Tears streamed down Mac's cheeks. He let them go and didn't wipe them away. "You will not be forgotten, brave brothers. Rest in peace. We will see you in the next life."

THE DIPLOMATIC VESSEL hurled through space at *faster than light* speed, toward the battlecruiser *McDaniels*, still stationed in orbit at Terra Libertas. The return journey would also take thirteen hours. Thirteen hours was a long time to be confined in a small space with nothing to do other than relive the mission failures.

Mac completed the official hot wash after action review with Colonel Miller, which only took a few minutes. After that, Colonel Miller stepped, out to update Prime Ambassador Kumar and President Harrington about the situation.

For a while, Mac just stood and gazed out the curved windows at the swirling light before deciding to organize the equipment.

Sanchez and Boone sat near the fully stocked food table, eating with Corporal Cooper. They talked, passing the somber time the best they could.

Boone looked OK with his shoulder bandaged. He wore a black t-shirt with the shoulder and sleeve cut out for the bandage. He was sitting up and eating, both good signs he would recover quickly and return to action.

"Hey, Major Mac, come join us and take a break for a bit," Sanchez said from across the room.

Mac knew he should go sit and relax a bit, but he just couldn't. He wasn't up to it yet. "I will soon. I just want to clean up a bit and make sure everything is taken care of first."

Sanchez jumped up from his chair and trotted over to the equipment crate with Mac. "Here, Major Mac, let me help you get this stuff put away."

"No, it's fine. I've got it."

"Seriously, I'll help."

"Sanchez, go sit and relax. Tell some more stories. I'll handle this."

Sanchez hesitated for a moment under Mac's gaze.

"Roger that," Sanchez said, knowing not to push harder.

Rifles, helmets, and their tactical chest rigs lay on the floor next to the massive equipment crate. Mac picked up the rifles and double checked they were de-energized and in safe mode before placing them in the rifle hold. He wiped each one down with a cloth before securing it in its place. He did the same with the grenades from the tactical vests. Focusing his swirling mind on the equipment for a few minutes was a helpful distraction.

The helmets and chest rigs each had a label with the soldier's names, so he placed them in each man's lockers. He wiped down Blake's helmet, taking extra time thinking about Blake and Sam. Not having Sam's helmet or chest rig hurt. He had nothing left of Sam, except what was in his locker. As usual, Sam had a picture of him and Sarina from their wedding. It sat on the shelf, leaning against the back of the locker. Mac reached in and picked up the picture. The photograph was a digital photo reel imbedded in the thin plastic sheet. He touched the corner a few times and smiled as the photos changed, showing different scenes of Sam and Sarina together. They looked full of life in every scene. Mac placed the photo reel in his own locker to return to Sarina.

After finishing up the last of the equipment, he decided to put his weapons and equipment away and strip out of his own E-Gear suit. He put on the charcoal fatigues, which would be much more comfortable for the rest of the journey.

Colonel Miller returned and joined the others. Mac checked the time. There were many hours left before he would be back on the *McDaniels*. He'd go speak with Sarina Clarion right away. He wanted her to hear about Sam's death from him. And he knew she'd need consoling from a friend. *Horrible. How could this happen?*

He looked around the room, desperate for something to occupy his time. His eyes landed on Sam, Blake, and Jagoon's cots. They needed to be folded up and stowed away in the equipment crate. He had a little trouble folding Jagoon's, which tested his paper-thin patience. It was Blake's cot, however, which wouldn't fold closed, that pushed him over the limit.

He pushed and shoved the cot, and it wouldn't fold as intended. So he twisted it, and it fell out of his hands and landed on his foot, which was the last straw. He picked up the lightweight composite cot and hurled it across the room. The cot crashed hard against the crate, startling Kara and Boone who had their backs turned to Mac.

Mac grabbed the cot off the floor and smashed it three times against the crate until it broke in half. Colonel Miller strode across the room to where Mac was smashing the cot into the equipment crate with grunts of anger.

Everyone turned and gawked at him.

"Major Lambert!" Miller yelled. "Stand down!"

Mac stopped and dropped the broken cot on the ground, panting and looking at Colonel Miller.

"You are done, Major. You're on the bench until further—"

"No, Colonel! You're not taking me out. They're going to pay for what they've done!"

"No, you will stand down! You need to roger up right now, major. This is unacceptable behavior. You will take ten days leave and get yourself pulled together. Jameson will lead Black Team in your place until further notice."

Mac didn't respond, just paced.

Miller blocked his path. "Do you copy, Major?" Miller yelled.

Through clenched teeth, Mac said, "Loud and clear, Colonel."

Mac needed space. He needed to think. He turned and walked into the elevator, glaring at Colonel Miller as the doors closed.

Miller let him go.

CHAPTER THIRTY-SEVEN

Bone Rattler Ship
Location Unknown

The massive Bone Rattler, jammed uncomfortably into the cramped piloting console, growled, "Captain, we are approaching the compound."

The industrial ship control room was typical of Bone Rattler ships. The cabin was dim and absent of any comfort features. But, Bone Rattlers didn't do comfort. A pilot, navigator, gunner, and the captain manned the control room. Glorraak, celebrated warrior and military leader, served as ship's captain.

"Good, enter atmosphere and prepare the ship for landing," Glorraak growled.

Glorraak, the oldest of the active Bone Rattler assault teams, wore his bone armor over fur that was browner than the gold of most Bone Rattlers. He wasn't wearing his skull helmet. He rarely wore it, if ever. Instead, Glorraak preferred to show off the massive scar over his left eye and the side of his face. His left eye was missing under the mangled and disfigured wound. He was also missing his left hand and half the forearm from the same injury. An ugly, black metal claw protruded from the stump of his forearm.

Glorraak reached over with his metal claw and tapped a button on the captain's chair control board to open the intercom channel. "General Sckrahhg, we are arriving."

Glorraak was satisfied with the grunt he received in response.

As the ship approached the planet and passed through the accumulated clouds, the snowy, mountainous terrain came into view. The nearby star shined through the clouds, reflecting across the rugged snow-covered mountains set against bright blue skies. The dark gray industrial ship soared through the valleys and entered the canyon where the Bone Rattler headquarters hid deep within the mountains.

Moments before the spacecraft arrived, the heavy metal door imbedded in the mountainside screeched open. Chief Braeknn exited the compound and trudged along the bridge suspended across the deep, rocky canyon below. The metal bridge connected the main building to the landing pads built on the other side of the narrow canyon. The clear blue skies surprised him. He was more surprised, as he looked down into the deep chasm, that he could see the frozen river and boulder piles on the canyon floor. Normally, visibility was so limited, the contents of the canyon were a mystery to all. It was a rare day for sure, but a good day to welcome their leader home.

Braeknn wore his bones and his skull helmet with antlers extending proudly and stood at the end of the bridge. Several other Bone Rattlers lined up near the entrance of the mountain compound and waited.

Braeknn heard the ship coming before he could see it. The dark shape appeared over the jagged mountain peak and hovered above the closest of three landing platforms built into the rocky side of the mountain. Massive steel stilts and girders supported the platform structurally.

The ship rotated, then set down on the pad. Hissing steam billowed beneath the craft as the engines shut down. The entrance ramp lowered to the surface. Braeknn stood tall as he waited.

Sckrahhg lumbered down the ramp and toward where Braeknn

stood. Braeknn couldn't help noticing his lack of bone armor. The great warrior leader looked naked without the bone decoration.

"Ah, Chief Braeknn," Sckrahhg growled, baring his fangs.

"Welcome home, General. A feast is prepared for you," Braeknn grunted. He raised his right fist to his chest in salute to his general, which rattled the bones on his chest.

Sckrahhg came closer and placed his right hand on Braeknn's shoulder in a greeting of approval.

"You did well, Chief. I hear this was your plan?"

"Yes, General."

"Well done."

"Thank you, General. The decoy and explosion?" Braeknn asked.

"Killed two and allowed our escape."

Sckrahhg let out an ugly guttural laugh while baring his fangs. Braeknn laughed as well, satisfied with outsmarting the humans.

"What of the others?"

"Glorraak, our old friend, is fine. He is as strong as ever. Cruegg is dead. His body lies on that planet still. Manstruu is coming now. He is not doing well." Sckrahhg pointed toward the ship. Glorraak was assisting Manstruu down the ramp, with the pilot assisting on the other side.

"Seems a small price to pay to bring you home, General. I know Cruegg gave his life willingly."

"Indeed," Sckrahhg growled in agreement.

"Let's get you settled. You have been gone too long."

They turned and walked along the bridge toward the mountain compound.

Sckrahhg said, "Chief, tell me about this princess, and how your plan for the exchange developed."

"Yes, of course, General. There is much to tell you. We have one more task to accomplish before this is over. I will tell you all the details and introduce you to this little princess. She is a bit of trouble, but we won't have to deal with her much longer. Let us celebrate with the warriors first."

Sckrahhg stopped and grabbed Braeknn's arm. "Another task? What is this last task?"

"Oh, it's simple, General. We turn her over to the ones who hired us to capture her."

"And who is that?" Sckrahhg growled, a little alarmed.

"That's the best part, General. It's the stupid humans themselves."

Sckrahhg snarled and grunted, laughing at the irony. "Yes, Chief Braeknn, let us celebrate my return a bit, and then you will tell me all the details."

Together, they stepped off the metal grate bridge onto the hard rocky surface of the mountain and entered the wide compound door, to the cheering and celebration of the bone-clad warriors lining the interior walls of the compound corridor.

CHAPTER THIRTY-EIGHT

Interplanetary Navy Battlecruiser McDaniels

When Mac entered the Space Warfare Group preparation room, on his way to his tiny private quarters, Dan *DJ* Jameson and a few other somber-faced operators were waiting for him.

Some of them patted Mac on the back as he walked by, but said nothing. They knew he needed some space. He was thankful they didn't hit him with a bunch of questions or unhelpful platitudes. There was no question about it; all the men loved Sam Clarion and Blake Robertson. Devastation spread throughout the entire team.

Jameson, a wiry, shorter man with curly black hair, grabbed Mac with both hands. He gave Mac a brief, but strong, embrace. When Jameson let Mac go, he kept his left hand on Mac's shoulder and looked him straight in the eyes. Jameson was a dependable warrior and experienced team leader. Mac had great respect for him. His usually intense green eyes were soft and watery.

"Hey, DJ," Mac said, using Jameson's nickname.

"Where's your stuff?" DJ asked, since Mac wasn't carrying any equipment or bags.

"Everything is being handled over at Kumar's ship. The others are still over there."

"How's that beast Boone doing? How bad is that injury?"

Mac pointed toward the private quarters, and DJ walked with him away from the others. "Yeah, it's not too bad. He's fine. Hurting a bit, but he'll bounce back quickly."

"OK, that is good to hear, at least. And Sanchez?"

"Oh, yeah. Sanchez is uninjured like me. No physical injuries at least." Mac tried to smile, but it was too much right now.

DJ paused for a moment. "Mac, listen, I spoke with Colonel Miller earlier-"

Mac stopped walking and cut him off. "DJ, it's fine. Don't worry about me. Just focus on the job."

"I know this must be hard for you. All of it."

"It is. It's the worst thing I've ever experienced. But I'm not finished."

DJ looked at Mac, pondering his statement. "But Miller said you're on the bench until further notice."

"That's true. I am on the team's bench, but I'm going to find these…" Mac's voice trailed off.

"Mac, ah, Miller will blow a gasket if he finds out you are doing anything on the side."

"Listen, brother, don't worry about me. Focus on the team and the next mission. They need you. Just do the best job you can. I'll take care of myself."

DJ's face now showed serious concern. "I don't know, man, that sounds—"

Mac smacked DJ on the shoulder, interrupting him again. "I need to get cleaned up and go see Sarina. You see her yet?"

DJ picked up on Mac's less than subtle change of subject and went along with him. "Yeah, a couple of us checked on her about four hours ago. They told her a few hours before that."

"Who did it?"

"Couple of Army suits."

"Anyone she knew?"

"Of course not."

"I hate that. I wish I could have done it. How's she doing?"

"Devastated, of course, but you know better than anyone. She's one tough woman. She'll make it through."

"OK, thanks, DJ. I'll catch you on the flip side."

"Alright, Mac." As Mac was walking away, he added, "Hey, don't do anything stupid."

Mac turned toward DJ and shrugged with his palms up. "Stupid? Sounds like a matter of interpretation."

Mac entered the corridor leading to his private room at the end of the hall. The room was tiny. It didn't suit a political dignitary like Prime Ambassador Kumar or even an officer like Colonel Miller, but it was reasonable for a soldier. The room was about 4 meters long and 3 meters wide. While small, it felt palatial compared to the bunk rooms shared with twenty or more other smelly soldiers, like he had in the early years. Besides, he also had the benefit of sharing the prep room with his team, which made it feel like they had their own house. The Space Warfare Group had its benefits.

Mac's room was spartan, with no personal touches and few belongings. It seemed to be the way they all lived. They didn't own many belongings, and they moved around so frequently, no place ever felt enough like home to merit a personal touch. Everything always felt temporary.

The single bed hung from the wall on the right. On the left side of the room was a table with two seats, a counter with upper and lower cabinets, a small sink, and a closet. At the back of the room was a door into the private toilet and shower, which was worth its weight in gold. The entire room was one complete molded unit extruded from a tough composite plastic material. It was cheap, bland, and efficient, but it was his home for the last few years.

Mac didn't waste time after arriving in his room. He wanted to talk to Sarina as quickly as possible. If he was being honest with himself, he didn't really want to talk to Sarina, but he wanted to get it over with and get on with finding the Bone Rattlers. The idea of sitting with Sarina to talk with her about Sam being killed in action made him sick to his stomach. He'd rather be busy on a mission to keep his mind distracted.

He showered and checked his injuries. Other than numerous bruises and a collection of sore muscles, his only concern was the laceration on this leg. The doctor's bandage got ruined, and he'd removed it earlier. The cut looked to be healing, and the pain was now more manageable. He didn't have any bandages in his room to wrap it. There was no way he was going back to MedBay, so he'd just tough it out, as usual.

Mac gazed at himself in the mirror. The scars on his arms and chest were constant reminders of the tough life he'd lived. He would need a haircut and beard trim soon, as he was looking a little fluffier than he liked. It also looked like the flecks of gray in his black hair and beard were multiplying. Or maybe it was the artificial lighting. Either way, he looked terrible. He rubbed his cheeks and looked into his own brown eyes. The guy in the mirror looked sad, old, and exhausted. His eyes were bloodshot and his expression was one of pain.

"Well, you look as bad as you feel, champ," he mumbled. "And when did you get so old?"

He threw on a pair of black pants and a black long-sleeve t-shirt. Then he strapped on his black lightweight training boots.

He checked himself again in the mirror.

"Nothing to write home about, that's for sure."

SAM DIDN'T HAVE a private room with the other operators at the back of the unmarked Space Warfare Group hangar. He had been assign him a compact apartment in the family area. The *McDaniels* housed over ten thousand people, which included general staff, Navy and Army soldiers, officers, diplomats, science personnel, medical, logistics, and every other role need for the flying city to function in space for long periods of time. Many were married, and some even had children. The fourth deck, known to all as the *suburbs,* served as general and family housing. To Mac's knowledge, his covert team were the only people on board with private quarters not in the suburbs.

He knocked on the door. After a moment, the door opened, revealing a woman with long wavy blonde hair pulled up in a high ponytail. Her normally vibrant blue eyes were now red and swollen, and her small, round nose looked red and raw from crying. She tried to smile, but her lips quivered.

Mac's heart broke again. His own eyes filled with tears, and he couldn't hold back. He was a strong man, physically and emotionally, but seeing Sarina's sadness was more than he could handle.

"Hi, Sarina," was all Mac could squeak out.

"I can't believe he's gone," Sarina moaned, then began sobbing.

Mac stepped into the room and wrapped his arms around her and let her cry. He thought at first that she might collapse. After a while, he led her to the small couch along the wall.

"Here, sit down. Try to relax."

She sat, face in her hands, wiping her eyes with a soggy white handkerchief. Mac knelt on one knee, watching at her.

"Can I get you anything? Water? Tea?"

"Yes, tea." She croaked out, then sat up straight and sniffed, wiping her eyes again. With a bit more strength in her voice, she said, "Something stronger would be nice right about now."

"Do you have anything?"

"No, of course not. That stupid husband of mine was a real puritan, you know," she laughed a little, Mac couldn't help but smile with her. "Besides, we never have anything we need."

"I'll get the tea started," Mac said.

The apartment was small, but it worked for a childless married couple living on a spaceship. The sitting area, the kitchen, and bedroom were only a few steps apart, but it was a cool place. It was three times the size of Mac's room, making it feel enormous to him. *Maybe this married life has its advantages,* he thought, but then remembered an actual relationship with a woman would require him to be something he wasn't sure he could ever be. He put it out of his mind.

Mac and Sarina sat together and shared their favorite memories of Sam, telling stories and reminiscing, which led to some laughing and more crying. He shared what he could about the Okutans and Bone Rattlers, and the recent missions over the last couple of days, leading up to the explosion on Yioturno. Mac believed it was only fair for her to know what happened and why, rather than the generic *Killed in Action* classification. After all that, they also discussed the Interplanetary Army's plans for a memorial service in the following week.

After a while, Sarina asked, "Mac, will there be any follow-up on this mission?"

His body became more rigid and his face suddenly dour as he looked off into the distance. "Yeah, there will be justice for Sam and Jagoon." *I'll make sure of it,* he thought.

"What's the plan?"

Mac turned toward Sarina, lost in his thoughts for a moment. "Hmm? What did you say?"

"What do you mean, there will be justice? Are Colonel Miller and the team going to pursue them?"

"Oh, they'll try for sure, but I'm going to find them first and bring justice to their doorstep. And, hopefully, find the Okutan princess alive and bring her home."

"I thought you said the Colonel made you stand down, and DJ is leading the team right now."

"Yeah, that's true." Mac rubbed his eyes with the palms of his hands. "Let's just say I won't be making an official search."

"Don't be a fool, Mac. You can't do that. It's too dangerous." Sarina sounded rattled, speaking faster now. "You're just one man against an army. An army who, by the way, just beat the best soldiers we have to offer. And what about your career? You can't throw that away." She was sitting up straight, energized now.

"I have no choice."

"Of course you have a choice! I want these monsters dealt with more than anyone, but I can't lose you on top of losing Sam." Sarina's voice cracked, and she began sobbing again.

"Listen, Sam was more than just a friend. You know I grew up in the system. I didn't have any siblings. I mean, I didn't even have any parents either. All I had was a bunch of other homeless orphans."

She nodded, listening, tears streaming down her rosy cheeks.

"I think I joined the army because I had nothing to lose, and I hoped to gain a brotherhood or something like a family. But it wasn't until I met Sam that I finally had what I could consider family. He was my brother. All the guys in the team call each other brother, and we are. But Sam was different. He was like a real blood brother. He was really all I had."

"You've still got me," she croaked out with a smile.

Mac scooted closer and wrapped his arm around her. "I'm so thankful that you are my friend. I want you to know, I've got to do this. Trust me, I know what I'm doing." *Mac, you sound like a fool,* he thought.

Sarina cried for a few minutes, knowing that her husband's best friend would avenge her husband's death at any cost. These were the men she shared her life with, and they'd never change.

Mac gave her a few minutes to collect herself, then asked, "I hate to put pressure on you right now, but I have to ask you something."

She looked up at him.

"Did you finish the analysis of the weapons Sam brought you from the Okutan ship?" Sarina served the UPG aboard the *McDaniels* as a science officer in the Interplanetary Navy Department of Alien Science (INDAS).

"I don't know. I was too busy, so I turned it over to one of the other techs to investigate. Why, what are you thinking?"

"Those weapons are the only link we have for finding the Bone Rattlers at this point. Any information gathered could help us find them."

"I see."

"Even just information about the metal alloy and origin planet of the weapon. Or a marking in some alien language or whatever. I don't know. I'm not a scientist, but there might be something helpful."

"Yeah, we can usually trace all that information."

"Do you have any way to check on the progress?"

"Uh, yeah, I do." She sniffed to clear her sinuses and raised her eyebrows. "I don't know if I want to give you this information, Mac, and give you more reasons for this crazy plan of yours."

"Please, Sarina."

She thought for a moment, then unfolded her legs from underneath her on the couch, and disappeared into the bedroom. A moment later, she returned with a handheld computer tablet. She flopped back onto the couch next to Mac.

"OK, let's see what we've got." She tapped the screen several times and let the tablet scan her eye for security access, then tapped and swiped more. Mac leaned over to see what she was finding, but didn't understand all the codes and symbols.

"Hey, look at that," she said excitedly and turned the tablet toward him to see. "Marjatta finished the investigation already."

"Who's Marjatta?"

She waved her hand dismissively. "She's the tech assigned to the investigation."

"OK, what does it say?" he asked.

"Oh, that is interesting." She cocked her head and looked at it curiously.

"What?" Mac was getting impatient.

"She wrote only a little info. Basically, one paragraph identifying the manufacturer of the weapons and the source of the material."

"Is it the Bone Rattlers?"

"No, she says here the Trek'ets manufacture and produce the weapons, but it is a unique weapon that we didn't have in the INDAS data base. Could be a special order product."

"Seriously?" Mac stood and paced the small sitting room. "The Trek'ets?" Mac was furious. The UPG ally alien race known as the Trek'ets were doing business with the criminal space pirates. "Those double-crossing lying…," he trailed off.

"You know them?"

"A little." Mac rubbed his beard exhaled loudly.

"How far is it to their planet? Will you have to go there?" Sarina asked.

"We don't need to worry about that, because the Trek'ets have a diplomatic embassy sitting right on Embassy Row below us on Terra Libertas. One of my first missions as part of the Space Warfare Group was as a diplomatic escort posting for the Trek'et ambassador." He paused. "A guy named Bloel Uf'el. I bet that scumbag is still their ambassador."

CHAPTER THIRTY-NINE

Mac stood as casually as he could and scanned the faces streaming through the busy intersection. He stayed slightly out of view behind a column, peering around the corner.

The constant flow of people passing through the intersection was nothing new in this area of the *McDaniels*. It was the main foot traffic intersection leading to Army and Navy staff offices. This was also the route to the Army situation room. Beyond that, down several unmarked corridors, the Space Warfare Group's semi-secret hangar and preparation room could be found, if you knew what you were looking for.

He was waiting to see Colonel Miller, who he knew had spent the last few hours in the situation room. Earlier, while on Prime Ambassador Kumar's ship, Mac overheard the Colonel's plans to get an official debrief from Sanchez. When he bumped into Cory Allen a few minutes earlier, he confirmed Colonel Miller was still meeting with Sanchez. That was good news. Colonel Miller was a predictable man, and Mac was betting he'd keep his usual routine, even after returning to the *McDaniels* only a few hours ago.

Mac's less than stellar plan required speaking with Corporal Kara Cooper without Miller finding out. So he needed to get to the situation room, but avoid Miller in the process.

While watching the flow of faces in the intersection, he recognized a few, but avoided them. He didn't want anyone aware of his movements. The waiting made him impatient. He considered aborting his surveillance when he finally saw the first Elite Guard turn the corner, heading his direction.

Kumar was moving. Perfect. He'd be with Miller.

The Elite Guard stood out from the crowd in their bright white jumpsuits and silvery reflective visors. Because everyone knew who they were, the crowd parted, making room for them to pass. No one else in the UPG military system looked like the Elite Guard, and no one was stupid enough to get in their way. Mac saw a solo guard enter the intersection, and the sea of people parted. A moment later, two more came into view.

Mac tucked his body behind the column to stay out of view and peered around. He saw Prime Ambassador Kumar and Colonel Miller walking his way. Two attendants followed Miller, then several steps behind the group were the two remaining Elite Guards. The crowd made plenty of room and some stopped respectfully to let the small entourage of the high-level UPG dignitary pass. When Kumar and Miller reached the intersection, they stopped and spoke for a moment. Mac couldn't hear what they were saying. Kumar bowed, as he always did, then they went separate ways.

Mac gave them an extra moment to clear the area and let the sea of people fill the void again, then he darted down the corridor. He squeezed between people, hurrying along the wall toward the situation room. He ducked down a side corridor, which was empty, except for the high security door at the end. As he'd approached the door, Kara Cooper was exiting. She was still wearing her charcoal battle fatigues, and her normally perfect high-and-tight bun was looking messy. It was failing to constrain her wavy orange hair. She looked worn out. He knew how she felt.

Cooper looked up. Seeing Mac surprised her.

"Cooper," Mac greeted her. He smiled, attempting to be as friendly as possible.

"Hello, Major Lambert. I didn't expect to see you. Were you

supposed to be in the meeting?" she asked, pointing over her shoulder with her thumb. A strap connected to a black attaché case hung from the left shoulder.

"Ah, no. I'm not here for that. I'm sure you've heard I'm on the bench for a few days," he said.

"Yessir, I heard that." He could sense a bit of caution in her body language.

"I came down here looking for you. I'm glad I caught you."

"Yessir. What can I help you with?" Cooper's mousey voice was polite and professional, but the suspicion on her face betrayed her true feelings.

Careful, Lambert, she is no fool, he thought.

"It's just a simple thing. I need a little info from the flight manifest for when we investigated the Okutan Vessel."

"Oh?"

"Yes. Can you access that for me? It's super simple and super quick."

"Yessir, I can do that for you. But..." She was a bit hesitant, and Mac could tell she was debating in her mind if she should help Mac while he was benched. She could get in serious hot water with Colonel Miller if he found her assisting Major Lambert in something against his orders. "With all due respect, sir, that is an odd request. What is it you need from the manifest?"

"Look, Corporal, I'm sure you are worried about helping me right now, with Colonel Miller's orders and all."

She didn't respond, just watched him. Her tired eyelids blinked over her hazel eyes.

"Well, what if I told you this had nothing to do with the mission or anything else related to the group?"

"What else would you need this information for, Major? The data is classified."

"Don't forget I have top secret clearance. I could look it up myself, I'm just not good with all the techie stuff. I'm better with a blaster, if you know what I mean." He made a pistol gesture with his hand, which he immediately regretted, feeling it was too silly. "I promise you this is social. I just need the names of the pilots who flew the SMART Ship."

"Why do you need the pilot's names, Major?"

Good grief. She's no fool. I see why Miller likes her, he thought.

"Well, I'm kinda embarrassed to say." Mac looked over his shoulder, pretending to make sure no one else was around, and he leaned in closer and spoke quietly. "I want to contact the woman co-pilot. I thought she was…well, nice, you know. And she was friendly. We talked a bit during the transports." He shrugged sheepishly. "I figured while I had some time off, it would be nice to get to know her a bit. You know, see if she wants to do dinner or something." Mac smiled again.

"Why didn't you say so?" Cooper said, smiling herself now.

She's no fool, but she is a hopeless romantic.

"But," she said, "you just need the name and you'll keep this between us?"

"Yes. Absolutely."

Cooper turned and performed the retinal scan to open the situation room door. Mac followed her into the dark and quiet room glowing softly from the video screens. There were a few people working in the room. She went to her workstation, set her bag down, and slid into the seat. She tapped away for a moment and brought up several documents.

"OK, here it is…John Ster—," she stopped mid-word and giggled a bit. "Nope, you're not looking for him."

"Nope, definitely not."

"OK, here you go. The co-pilot was one, Lieutenant Louella Taylor."

"That's right. I knew I'd recognize her name. Lieutenant Taylor."

"Do you have your tab with you?" she asked, speaking of his small personal tablet to access messages and make calls.

"Of course," he said and pulled it from the pocket of his black pants.

"OK, I'll shoot you the basic personnel file, so you have her contact info. There you go. You should have it now."

Mac checked the small glass electronic screen and saw the message and file from Cooper. "Yup. I've got it. You are a lifesaver."

They left the situation room together and, in the corridor, Mac said, "Thank you, Cooper. I really appreciate it. We'll just keep this between us, right? I don't want it getting around in case…well, you know…in case it doesn't work out. The guys are merciless with stuff like this."

"Of course, Major, you can count on me. But, on just one condition."

Great, now what? He was worried about what would come next. "OK, what's that?"

"I want to hear how it goes." She with a broad smile.

Mac gave her a lazy salute. "Yes, ma'am. For sure. I won't forget this. I owe you big time." He trotted off in a slow jog.

IT DIDN'T TAKE Mac long to find where Lieutenant Louella Taylor was working, once he had her name and rank. He was pleased that he had the information he needed, but he felt a tiny twinge of guilt for manipulating Cooper. Normally, he would be unwavering in his ethical treatment of others. But not today. Today, he had no problem setting his ethical standards aside to find the monsters that killed his men and his best friend. His biggest concern now was whether Taylor was currently aboard the *McDaniels.* And, if she was, would she be willing to help him?

He knew he couldn't barge into the Navy administrative offices and start asking around for her. No one would provide information on her whereabouts without a legitimate reason. He needed to be as discreet as possible and not draw attention to himself. Cooper's accessing mission data was completely normal, but he couldn't start surfing around random personnel files and leave his electronic footprint for Miller to find.

His best bet was to try the *McDaniels'* main transport hangar complex. It was next to the SMART ship hangar, where he'd seen her last. The hangar complex included several entry and landing points for smaller spacecraft. The largest of the entry points was the Navy's own shuttle and transport multi-bay and multi-level stacked hangar complex. When traveling through the stars or stationed alone in deep space, the Navy hangar complex was a ghost town. But, with the *McDaniels* stationed at Terra Libertas, it was a beehive of activity. Tiny ships came and went at all hours, restocking the flying city, shuttling personnel, and transporting equipment. He didn't envy the logistics team responsible for all the planning and management of a workup like this.

The immense crowd of people at the Navy hangar terminal waiting area surprised Mac. Hundreds of people were coming and going, standing around, or sitting in uncomfortable chairs. There were many coalition alien races mixed in as well. He squeezed through the crowd in the terminal waiting area and was elated to find a large screen displaying flight status with additional information he couldn't quite see. He worked his way around the people to the screen so he could inspect the information closer. On the screen, with the flight status, was the flight destination, ship type, and pilot assignments.

Perfect. Exactly what I need, he thought.

His eyes darted down the column. There were many names, and a couple of Taylor's listed in the pilot assignments. It took a while, scanning the names until he found her name listed a few times for different flights. He figured out the current time and current flight information. Taylor was listed as lead pilot on a SMART ship flight expected to arrive in 30 minutes in Hangar Bay 7.

Bay 7 was the same enormous hangar he and his men had used two days earlier when being transported to the dead Okutan ship. He entered the cavernous Bay 7 and found it less crowded this time. There were only four boxy white SMART ships sitting on the shiny metal floor. The rest of them were in use and off the *McDaniels*. Painted yellow and blue stripes covered the metal floor to designate parking and movement areas. The constant hum and clatter from engines and voices filled the air. Navy crewmen were buzzing around loading SMART ships and guiding a few passengers toward their assigned vessels. Across the bay, on the other side of the ships from where he stood, the airlock doors stood open as a SMART ship was entering and preparing to depart.

To his left was a waiting area behind a glass partition. Several men, women, and alien species wearing what looked like maintenance jumpsuits sat in chairs or stood with equipment cases. Mac stood at the back of the group and leaned against the wall to wait.

Finally the airlock doors opened with a mechanical growl, allowing a SMART ship to enter. They were only a few minutes behind schedule. The little bus-like ship maneuvered toward a parking space in the center of the bay. After several long minutes, the crew stepped out and made their way toward where Mac stood.

Lieutenant Taylor was the last in the line of six people. They all wore the same white Navy flight suits with blue accents. They carried helmets and shoulder bags. As she approached, unaware that someone was watching her, she tried to adjust the somewhat messy knot of walnut brown hair atop her hair with her right hand while holding her case and helmet in the left.

Mac approached and called to her, "Excuse me, Lieutenant Taylor?"

She didn't respond. He followed a couple of steps and tried again. "Excuse me, Lieutenant Taylor?"

This time she heard him and turned around. "Yes? May I help you?" Her expression changed from curiosity to recognition. She stopped walking and Mac caught up to her.

"Hello, I don't know if you remember me—"

She interrupted with a big smile. "Of course, I remember you, Major Lambert. How could I forget such an interesting mission?"

Taylor was tall and thin. Her flight suit was baggy and loose around her lean frame. Her wide, toothy smile was a bit crooked. The twinkle in her blue eyes was still there. She seemed to always have a friendly, playful expression. Mac noticed it two days ago, and he noticed it again now. Her face was angular, with a defined jawline and chin. She was a naturally pretty woman for sure, he thought, but the beauty hid behind the practical flight suit, boots, and helmet hair.

"Oh, good. I'm glad to hear that. I wasn't sure you'd—"

She interrupted again. "Major, it was barely two days ago. Do I seem like I have a terrible memory? I even recognize you in your plain clothes, without the whole super soldier get up."

"Oh, no…no, of course not," he stammered. He thought of this woman in a conversation with Sanchez, and shuddered. *That would be a nightmare.*

"By the way, how is your Akatakon buddy? Did he ever get out of that floating tube? I've been wondering about that."

The pain and anger Mac felt at the mention of Jagoon must have registered on his face.

Taylor noticed immediately. "I'm sorry. What is it? Did I say something wrong? I can be a little overbearing at times."

He made eye contact with her again. The sarcasm and crooked smile were gone now, replaced with concern.

"No, no, it's not you. See, that's why I'm here. Jagoon and Sam." He paused for a moment, realizing she wouldn't know anything about either. "The alien in the tube you mentioned, the Okutan, well, his name was Jagoon, and he was an incredible warrior protector of the Okutan royal family."

"He was? Did something happen to him?"

"He died yesterday, along with two of my men, one of whom was my closest friend." Mac worked hard to keep his emotion out of his voice.

Taylor was shocked. "Oh, my goodness, that is terrible. I am so sorry." She stood quietly for a moment while Mac, lost in his own thoughts, stared off at one of the nearby SMART ships. "Major, I am assuming there is more to this, which is why you are here?"

Mac took a deep breath. "Yes. I need help."

"OK, name it."

"I need transport to New London City as soon as possible."

"I don't understand."

"There is a lead…a, uh…clue there that will lead to finding the ones who killed them."

"Oh, OK," she said while brushing a strand of hair from her face. "Isn't that something the Army would do, or your super soldier group? I don't see how I can help."

"Normally, yes. But see, that's the problem. I'm currently on leave. Well, benched. I don't have my group's resources at my disposal right now. So, this is an off-the-books kinda thing."

"But you have clues?"

"Yes."

"Why not give them the clues and let them sort it out?"

"It's complicated."

"Try me," she said.

"Because, if I do, they will box me out and I can't let that happen." Mac's dark face was stony and rigid.

"Is this a revenge thing? You're like a vigilante now?"

"I suppose you could say that."

"Hmmm. Major, this sounds like a bad idea."

"It may be," he said. "Bad idea or not, I need your help. I just need a lift to New London. I figured if anyone knew how to get there as soon as possible, it would be you. All I'm asking for is information on how I can get a quiet ride down to the surface. That's it. Nothing more."

She stared at him for a moment, saying nothing, but steeling her fingers in front of her lips.

"I'm sorry if I've asked for too much. If you want to say no, that's fine. I'll find another way and keep you out of it. I don't want to cause you any trouble. If you could, just give me an idea of who I can talk to about a shuttle transport to the surface. Somebody must be going down there today."

"Well, Major," she said, the smile back now, "It's your lucky day. Be in Hanger Bay 3a in three hours. I'm piloting a cargo ship to New London City. It's full of junk they want off the *McDaniels*. This plan of your sounds like a piece of junk, so you'll fit in fine. Just don't make me regret this."

CHAPTER FORTY

After sitting around, watching the clock for three hours, Mac arrived at Bay 3a a few minutes early for the flight to Terra Libertas' capital, New London City. He still wore his black pants and long sleeve black t-shirt, trying to be as invisible as possible. He didn't want to draw any attention to himself.

Bay 3a was similar to Bay 7 in every way, except for the single hulking cargo freighter standing on the metal parking surface. The cargo freighter filled the entire hangar, leaving no space for additional vessels. Mac had seen these cargo transport ships before. It was standard Interplanetary Navy, dark gray with a series of blue and white stripes and numbers painted on the hull. It was a bland, unassuming rectangular vessel. Five cargo doors on the back end were open, and robotic forklifts moved up the ramps to load the last remaining cargo onto the ship. Navy crewmen also maneuvered hover carts with crates into the cargo holds.

A mobile staircase for crew and passengers stood near the front of the ship. A small group of people stood by the stairs, including Lieutenant Taylor. She was giving the crew instructions, while the passengers, two older men with two older women, stood nearby. They looked like off-duty Navy officers with their spouses.

When Mac approached, he could barely hear Taylor's words over the echoing din of activity in the hangar. Taylor was approving the cargo manifest and instructing crewman to complete the preflight procedures. After a moment, she saw Mac and sauntered over to where he was standing.

"Hello, Major Lambert. Glad to see you found us," she said with her usual friendliness. Taylor was wearing the same baggy Navy jumpsuit, but she had freshened up. She combed out her previously messy knot of walnut hair and pulled it tight into a ponytail.

"Please, call me Mac. There is no Major Lambert here."

"OK, I can do that, but only if you call me Lou."

Mac nodded, gazing into her eyes. "Yeah, sure, Lou."

"I have just a couple things to wrap up and then we can get you and the others boarded and head down to the surface," Taylor pointed to the older couples standing nearby. She flashed another bright smile before turning and jogging up the staircase, disappearing into the spacecraft.

Mac took the hint and joined the older couples.

"Vacationing on Libertas?" one woman asked. Mac figured she was in her late sixties, maybe even in her seventies. She was petite with a shoulder-length bob haircut of black hair that was losing the battle with gray. She was of Asian descent and wore round eyeglasses with thin silver frames.

"Ah, no, not really," Mac said. "Just popping down for some last-minute family business."

"I see," the woman said.

The tall Caucasian man beside her added, "We're heading down to sample those legendary Sapphire Sea beaches. It's been two years since we had a real vacation." The man wore an odd red cloth skull cap over his bald head. Mac wondered if it was a cultural thing or a new fashion. They were all dressed in casual attire. "We're spoiled being able to catch a ride down on the cargo boat. It's not the most comfortable, but it gets us there. And we save a few credits."

The man smiled, proud of himself, and thrust his hand out toward Mac. "Captain Jamby Cahr. This is my better half, Bets." The tiny woman waved.

Mac shook the man's hand, being careful not to be too friendly. He didn't have the energy for small talk.

"This here is Commander and Mrs. Pavlina."

The other couple was younger, but dressed in similar casual clothing, minus the weird hat.

"Nice to meet you all," Mac said. "I'm Malcolm." He turned away from the group slightly.

"Navy?" Commander Pavlina asked. He was a short muscular man with dark black hair trimmed short. He had a thin, dark mustache on his craggy face.

Mac looked over at him. "Yup. Navy."

"Are you a pilot?" Bets asked.

Talkative bunch, Mac thought. *Bad idea coming over here.*

"No, no, nothing so exciting. I'm in maintenance."

Mac added nothing else, and after a moment, Bets and Mrs. Pavlina began discussing various cuisine options on Terra Libertas.

Mac withdrew into his own mind, considering again how to get to the Trek'et diplomatic building and the discussion he would have with the ambassador.

A few minutes had passed without awkward small talk when Mac felt a presence close to him, just outside his peripheral vision. He turned and couldn't believe his eyes. Standing next to him, in similar black pants, black t-shirt, and black boots, was Luis Sanchez. He also wore a black ball cap, turned backwards on his head. He had a bulky backpack on his back.

Mac glared at Sanchez.

What was he doing here?

Sanchez stood there with a crooked grin, and his eyes darting between Mac and the ship. "What's up, Major Mac?" he whispered.

Mac grabbed Sanchez by the arm and pulled him away from the others.

"What are you doing here?" Mac demanded.

"I was going to ask you the same question," Sanchez said, grinning.

"Seriously, Sanchez, why are you here?"

"I'm going to T-Lib on this cargo boat." He used the slang for Terra Libertas. "Free ticket." He raised his black eyebrows a couple of times, the stupid grin plastered on his face.

"Why?"

"To talk to an ambassador about the bone-wearing Sasquatch."

Mac couldn't believe his ears. He rubbed his tired eyes with his palms and fought back the irritation. *How was this happening? How does Sanchez know any of this?*

"How did you find me?" Mac groaned.

"It wasn't that hard. You are not as sneaky as you think. I spoke with Sarina not long after you visited her. She was worried about what you were up to. So I tracked you down and followed you."

"You've been following me?" Mac realized he was off his game. He hadn't notice Sanchez on his tail even once.

"Yup. Followed you around most of the afternoon. Pretty boring, really. I even wore the same clothes. You know, so we'd match on our mission."

"Sanchez, listen to me. There is no mission. You can't do this. You need to go back and focus on whatever the group is doing next."

"Major Mac, I'm going with you."

"You can't. Miller will end your career."

"Look who's talking. You are already on the bubble, man. Do you realize what Colonel Miller will do to you at this point if you go through with this?"

Mac was quiet for a moment before saying, "I'm resigned to that reality, Luis. I don't have a choice. I must bring justice…justice for Sam and the others. But you have a full career ahead of you still. Don't mess it up."

"I don't care about all that. Don't forget, you're not the only one who lost a brother and a great friend," Sanchez said. The smiled slipped from his face. "You can't do this on your own. It's too dangerous and you're being sloppy. You need someone you can trust."

Mac's mind was spinning. He turned and paced a few steps before turning back to Sanchez. He pointed to the cargo freighter's passenger door. "Sanchez, if you get on that ship, there is no turning back. I won't be able to protect you from the consequences."

Sanchez put his hand on Mac's shoulder and smiled, looking up into Mac's eyes. "See, that's your problem, Mac. You're the best leader I've ever known, but seriously, it's not your job to protect us. I know the risks, and I don't care. We're doing it for Sam and Sarina, Blake and Jagoon. And we're going to do it together."

Mac couldn't argue with that. He embraced Sanchez, and they moved back to where the older couples were standing and watching the exchange.

Bets asked, "Malcom, is this one of your friends from maintenance?" She sounded like a grandmother talking to her grandson.

Sanchez stood grinning with his thumbs tucked into the shoulder straps of his backpack. He glanced at Mac at the mention of maintenance. Mac winked at him.

"Yes, ma'am. My partner, Luis."

"Oh, how nice," she said and then introduced the others.

Sanchez greeted each of them.

Bets then asked, "What kind of maintenance do you guys do?"

Mac said, "Oh, you know, lots of things around-"

Sanchez interrupted, speaking over Mac, "Well, Bets, mostly toilets and sewage."

Bets' face twisted a little. "Oh, that's nice," she said with a grimace.

"This guy here," he said, slapping Mac on the back, "is probably the best toilet, or what we call 'waste swallower,' repairman in all the galaxy." Sanchez made air quotes with his fingers. "In fact, just last week, there was a serious clog in a swallower on level 4, and this guy…let me tell you what this guy did—"

"Luis, that's more than these good people need to know," Mac said while pinching the pressure point on Sanchez's upper forearm. Mac knew it hurt like crazy, but Sanchez didn't squeal.

Just then, Lieutenant Taylor poked her head out the door above the stairs. "OK, everyone, we are ready for you."

Mac and Sanchez let the others climb the stairs and enter the ship first.

"Sanchez, really? Waste swallower?"

"It just came to me. It's a gift."

"It's a gift alright. By the way—"

"Yeah, Major Mac?"

"What's in the backpack?"

Sanchez leaned down from the steps above so only Mac could hear. "Oh, you know, just some guns and stuff."

CHAPTER FORTY-ONE

Interplanetary Navy Spaceport Soriano
New London City, Terra Libertas

When the *McDaniels* was in close orbit with Terra Libertas, it mimicked the day and night hours of New London City to provide consistency for everyone traveling back and forth. Darkness shrouded New London City, the largest and most advanced city of all United Planetary Government colonial ports. Night had fallen over the city. The lights of the metropolitan coastal city that never slept passed below the cargo freighter as they approached Interplanetary Navy Spaceport Soriano, which was constructed alongside Soriano Bay.

Developed as the deep space capital of humanity, New London City was second only to the great cities of Earth. Built in a temperate weather paradise on the western shores of the Sapphire Sea, the city was surrounded by sparkling white beaches and the lush green foliage of the tropical forest. All New London City's daylight beauty was currently hidden under darkness, but the city's twinkling lights presented a different kind of beauty.

Over time, New London City matured into a town square for the galaxy. With forty-seven unique alien species represented on Embassy Row, as part of the thriving Galactic Coalition, New London City was highly influential as the center of foreign policy and diplomacy. The who's who of Galactic Coalition politics and industry not only frequented New London City, but many made it their home and base of operations. The city was enormous. Even low planetary orbit - known as docking altitude - around Terra Libertas required reservations. Everyone on the waiting list wanted a piece of the power and influence. New London City was a magical place. Spaceport Soriano was huge on its own and would rank as a major city in the UPG multi-planet system.

During the flight, Mac and Sanchez remained quiet, since they sat close to their traveling companions. Both men knew discussing the strategy for approaching a foreign embassy would invite unwanted questions from Naval officers. It would also blow their weak cover as Navy maintenance staff popping down to the surface to deal with a family issue. Mac knew he'd have heat from the Army brass the second Colonel Miller became aware of his actions. There was no need to speed that up by being sloppy.

The officers and their wives wished Mac and Sanchez luck in their venture and thanked Taylor before eagerly departing to begin their vacation. Mac waited a moment longer to talk privately with Lou Taylor, who joined them in the passenger cabin.

"I'm not sure what you guys are up to," Taylor pointed at Mac and Sanchez, "but, just so you know, I'll be here overnight and heading back to the *McDaniels* with a new load tomorrow night."

"OK, that's great," Mac said. "And, in all seriousness, it is probably best you know nothing about what we are doing."

She looked at Mac dubiously. "I don't like the sound of that, but I won't press. I'll let you keep your secrets."

"Just know it's necessary and important."

"Ha!" Taylor laughed, "I'm sure it is. Just be back here before I leave, or you'll be stuck down here, and I'm not sure how I can help after that."

"I expect we'll complete our business before then."

"OK, well, I'm literally hanging out on this rust bucket the entire time, so show up whenever." Taylor gave an exaggerated arm wave.

"Glamorous life you live," Mac said.

"We can't all run around the galaxy fighting bad guys. Some of us must suffer through a life of pampered luxury."

He realized that he was genuinely smiling for the first time in many days. Something about Lou Taylor put him at ease. "Thanks for the lift. See you in a few hours."

Mac and Sanchez exited the cargo ship's passenger door into a flexible tube bridge made of semi-translucent white tubing, which served as an umbilical cord from the cargo freighter into the Navy terminal facility.

In the tube, Sanchez asked, "So, is she your girlfriend now?"

"Sanchez, why are you the way you are?"

"I can't help it. I was born this way."

"So, I've heard."

The terminal was not crowded, but there was plenty of activity as ships were arriving and departing throughout the evening and into the night. Mac and Sanchez blended into the small crowd of others, moving toward what Mac assumed was the terminal exit.

"So, what's the big plan?" Sanchez asked.

"We need to get to Embassy Row, assess the facility, and then figure out how to get to the Trek'et ambassador."

"And then what's the big plan after that?" Sanchez asked again.

"Well, we need to extract the information about the Bone Rattler's location out of him."

"And then what's the plan after that?"

Mac looked at Sanchez, annoyed. "Then we figure out how to get to their location. We'll need a ship of some kind at that point."

"And then what's -"

Mac cut him off this time, stopped walking, and grabbed him by the shoulder. Sanchez stared directly into his eyes. "I'm going to find them and kill them, Sanchez. That's the plan. You gotta problem with that? Because if you do, you can just go back to the ship and hang out with Taylor."

"We," Sanchez said flatly, unfazed by Mac's outrage.

"What?"

"And then we find them and kill them together, Major Mac. You're not doing this alone. I just want to make sure you know what you're doing." Sanchez spoke more forcefully to Mac now than he ever would under an official mission.

"Yeah, I know what I'm doing. Come on, let's go." Mac turned and started walking again.

"So, what's the plan for getting to the Embassy?"

Mac groaned at Sanchez's incessant harassment. "Do you ever stop? I don't know. I'm making it up as I go."

"Do you want me to stop?"

Mac thought for a moment. "No, not really."

"Then, no, I never stop."

"But you are so annoying."

"I know. It's what my mother loves the most about me."

Mac shook his head and tried to suppress a laugh. After a moment, he added, "The little time I spent here with the Trek'ets as diplomatic escort, we never had to figure out how to get around. They always covered transportation, and I just went with the flow and stayed focused on keeping the ambo alive." They came to an intersection at the terminal and Mac checked the signs, looking for exiting and transportation information.

"Come on, this way, Major Mac," Sanchez said, pointing in the opposite direction. "All we gotta do is hop on the Mag-Train to the Government District. Embassy Row is an easy walk over the bridge from there," Sanchez said.

Mac looked at him. "How do you know that?"

"Oh, I spent several months here in an Army joint-training exercise with the Navy back before I joined the group."

Mac put his fist out for a fist bump from Sanchez. "Awesome, man."

Mac followed Sanchez, heading towards the Mag-Train boarding platform.

"Oh, one more thing," Sanchez said. "What's your plan for dinner?"

THEY STEPPED off the Mag-Train at the Government District Station and descended the ramp on the ground level. Scalloped pools of white light illuminated the boarding platform, and the area designated for the queueing lines, creating a stark contrast with the surrounding blackness of the night and tropical forest beyond.

Lights mounted on low planter beds framed the public walking spaces. Growing within the planters were green plants with broad tear drop leaves standing shoulder-height on thin rigid stems. Each leaf was the size of a man's outstretched hand and hung like umbrellas from curved branches. Trees of the dense forest at the edge of the public space towered over them like giant soldiers on guard. The dark bark of their trunks was visible only in the light, and vanished into the darkness of night above.

Mac followed Sanchez down the stairs and along the walkway. They moved quickly, but not so fast as to draw attention to themselves. The night air was cool, but humid. The gentle breeze coming off the sea was refreshing and brought with it several pleasant floral fragrances mixed with the musky smells of the forest. For a man who lived on a spaceship and in an environmental suit for more years than he could remember, the sights and smells of the forest were unexpected and almost overwhelming.

When they reached the Government District, the diversity of the crowd increased. As they made their way through the outer edge of the Government District, they passed more aliens than humans.

Sanchez knew where he was going. He led Mac into an expansive courtyard shaped like a wheel, with spokes heading off toward massive white buildings reaching toward the stars. The buildings were curvy; he saw no square edges. Sanchez aimed them toward the center of the wheel, where a circular fountain sat. The fountain was large enough to park Taylor's cargo freighter in it.

The fountain, known as the Fountain of the Stars, was the artistic centerpiece of the Government District. Hundreds of vertical corkscrews of water jetted out of the pool in a synchronized pattern. White, blue, purple, green, and yellow light sparkled within the twisting and leaping water streams. The flickering colors and melodious splashing water were beautiful.

Flag poles with colorful flags stood in groupings at every building, the Fountain of the Stars and the shapely buildings left Mac impressed all over again, even though he had visited the UPG Government District before. They didn't linger as they passed through the impressive center of human government.

They exited the Government District and followed the wide lighted pathway through the trees, past a cluster of skyscrapers on the shoreline.

Reaching the shoreline, the salty sea breeze was stronger. Smaller buildings housed retail businesses along with restaurants, and social clubs littered the waterfront in both directions. The sounds of laughter and unfamiliar music mingled with the sounds of the sea lapping against the shore.

A bridge extended from the shoreline, over the thin inlet feeding Soriano Bay to the peninsula on the other side, where Embassy Row was located. They wove their way through the lively melting pot crowd of professionals, wealthy socialites, and political staffers all partaking in the active New London City nightlife.

It took them several minutes at a brisk walk to traverse the bridge in the darkness with the sea breeze pressing against their bodies. A passenger train, lighted on the inside, rumbled back and forth in both directions along the outer edge of the bridge, along with a steady flow of ground vehicles passing in both directions. Above them, the sounds and blinking red lights of small hovercrafts passed overhead in both directions. Two larger spacecraft entered the atmosphere and descended to landing locations on Embassy Row, disappearing behind the trees and tall buildings.

Embassy Row was a mixture of wide, curved pathways and buildings of otherworldly architecture. They spread the forty-seven foreign embassies out along several circular arrays. The entrances were on the outer radius of the circles for public access, while the inner radius between the buildings included spacecraft landing pads for each nation's private access on and off the planet.

Some embassies were behind substantial security walls, while others seemed absent of any external security. Most of the dense forest of the peninsula had been cleared for the properties, but some allowed the natural vegetation to grow in manicured shapes for a pleasing aesthetic.

Sanchez and Mac slipped into the forest for reconnaissance when they arrived at the Trek'et Embassy.

The Trek'et embassy structure stood in the center of a cleared area, covered with some sort of gray sandy soil. It looked like a grainy decomposed stone. The building itself had a rectangular floor plan, but from the rectangular foundation, the building raised toward the sky as a series of twenty silver arrow-shaped fins with sharp edges and tips pointing into the sky. It looked like a row of huge spearheads protruding from the planet's surface. The up lighting increased the ominous appearance. The whole front face of the first arrowhead was a triangular window, glowing red from the inside. Below the window was the main entrance.

The entire spearhead structure sat upon a raised mound, causing the building to reach high into the sky. Through the gaps in the forest, they could see spacecraft parked under the yellow lights of the landing pads.

"This is the place," Mac spoke quietly, crouching on the damp ground in the darkness behind the tree line. Fern-like foliage surrounded them.

"Are you sure?" Sanchez asked.

"Yeah, certain. I spent some time here as a diplomatic escort to

Ambassador Bloel Uf'el. I'm pretty sure he is still the ambassador for the Trek'ets."

"This place is creepy," Sanchez said. "I'm not sure I want to go in there. It's probably full of blood-sucking vampires or something. I like my blood where it is."

"Well, I can tell you this then." Mac paused for a beat. "You're really going to enjoy meeting Bloel Uf'el."

CHAPTER FORTY-TWO

Trek'et Embassy
New London City, Terra Libertas

Sanchez wiggled out of the backpack straps and set the heavy pack on the ground. "I don't have much, but it's better than nothing," he said. He dropped to one knee, opened the bag, and reached in.

The first things Sanchez extracted from the pack's bulging side pocket were overhead display and vision enhancement visors for each of them. "Brought us some ODVs." Sanchez stuffed his ball cap into the bag and slipped his visor over the back of his skull and down in front of his eyes.

Mac did the same. The visors were like what the Elite Guard wore. When slipped over the eyes, they sat on the bridge of the nose like wide wraparound sunglasses. The Space Warfare Group version was solid black, rather than the Elite Guard's mirrored finish, and secured to their face with a thick elastic strap around the back of their head. On the right side of the visor was a multi-tap control pad and an earbud speaker for communication.

Mac tucked the earbud into his ear and tapped the control pad with a series of one and two finger taps to set the display features and vision setting to enhanced night vision. His view went from deep black shadows and centimeters of visible range to the light green glow of night vision enhancement. The trees remained dark shapes, but the background was now green, and the lights of the embassies and pathways beyond the tree line were bright white spots. Mac could make out Sanchez clearly now, grinning proudly at him and giving him a thumbs up.

"Brilliant, Sanchez," Mac said. He was thankful for Sanchez's involvement.

Sanchez pulled out an equipment belt with a leg holster for each of them. They each strapped the belt tightly to their waist and down the right leg and around the thigh. The belts included multiple compartments containing small hand tools and first aid items.

As Mac slowly finished securing the leg holster to his thigh, Sanchez was impatiently bumping his leg with the grip side of a standard Space Warfare Group M2-V projectile handgun. Mac grabbed it and checked the load before slipping it into his holster.

Sanchez then handed him a couple of twenty-round magazines and grenades. Mac placed the magazines and grenades in the extra compartments on his equipment belt.

Finally, Sanchez stood and tossed the empty backpack toward a tree trunk.

"OK, Major Mac, last but not least, here you go." Sanchez handed Mac a stubby black firearm that was about the length of his forearm. It was the Space Warfare Group's continuous fire energy pulse submachine gun, known as the *RAP*. The gun, like all the group's weapons, was matte black. This firearm was sleek and lightweight, with a pistol grip and extendable shoulder stock, designed for single-handed use in close combat. What it lacked in power and accuracy, as compared to their EP-17 rifle, it made up for it with the speed by which it could release energy blasts. In full continuous fire mode, the little guns seemed to spray an unbroken stream of green laser energy. They all loved the RAP.

"Excellent work, Sanchez. How'd you sneak this equipment out?" Mac asked as he secured the chest strap and tether to the RAP.

Sanchez gazed across the darkness at Mac and said nothing for a moment. Mac was wondering if he heard him, before he said, "Ah, Major Mac, let's not talk about that."

"OK. Probably a good idea. We're digging a bigger hole by the moment. As soon as we step into that embassy, there is no turning back."

"I ain't turning back, but if you are a little scared, you can wait for me here while I take care of business."

With a laugh, Mac said, "Hardly. I'm all dressed up now, with somewhere to go."

"What was your plan? I mean, by bringing no weapons or gear?"

"I was going to improvise."

"If I'm honest—" Sanchez began.

"And you are always honest," Mac interrupted.

"If I'm honest, Major Mac, this is not your best mission-planning performance."

"I know. I'm not really myself," Mac said. His voice trailed off, then he changed the subject. "By the way, I'm surprised you didn't bring us knives."

"Oh, man, I almost forgot. I'm glad you said something." Sanchez reached behind his back and pulled out a fixed blade combat knife in a sheath. He tossed it to Mac, who bobbled it and nearly dropped the catch, but got it under control.

"I guess you thought of everything," Mac said as he slipped the sheath onto his belt.

"Let's go kick some Trek'et butt," Sanchez cheered and slid around Mac toward the tree line, toward the front entrance of the Trek'et Embassy.

Mac grabbed Sanchez's arm. "No, not that way. We can't go in through the front door. The best approach is from the landing pad."

"After you, sir," Sanchez said, extending his open palm in a polite gesture and bowing at the hips.

They crept silently through the dark forest, which was much

easier now with the aid of the ODVs. Mac led them stealthily, weaving through the trees, to the edge of the landing pad on the back side of the Trek'et embassy property.

The landing pads sat behind several embassy buildings arrayed on an arc, like the outer edge of a wheel, leaving the octagonal shaped landing zone open at the center. The backs of the embassy buildings faced the landing zone. In the distance, Mac could see some of the other oddly shaped buildings. He had no idea what alien species occupied them. He was hoping they could get in, get the intel they needed, and get out with no one in the adjacent properties catching wind of their actions.

Mac stood in the shadow at the edge of the trees. The Trek'et's spearhead-shaped building was to his right, and the landing pad in front of him. Sanchez stood just behind him to the left. The pad was a hard, concrete-like surface. Mac turned off the night vision feature on his visor, since the space was well lit. Standing at the edge of the tree line, he could again feel the gentle breeze from the nearby ocean against his face.

Severa spacecraft sat under the yellow glow of the landing pad lights. Each embassy property pad, except one, included a spacecraft for deep space travel. The spacecraft all looked different, just like the embassy buildings. Behind the Trek'et embassy were three spacecraft. The first was the Trek'et transport ship, which was familiar to Mac. The ship had features like the embassy building, with sharp edges and reflective steel mixed with red and black highlights.

Leaning close to Sanchez, he whispered, "We flew on one of those when escorting the ambo."

"Never seen one of those," Sanchez whispered back. "Looks like a vampire ship."

"Yeah, it's a pretty serious vessel."

"You recognize that one?" Sanchez asked about the second spacecraft, which was more industrial looking and slightly smaller than the ambassador's transport ship. It looked like the spacecraft the Bone Rattlers used to escape from Yioturno.

"Yeah, seeing that here makes my blood boil. But it means we are on the right track."

"You think Bone Rattlers are in there?"

"I doubt it. I do think the Trek'ets are selling military hardware to the Bone Rattlers, but I don't think they would meet in such a public way. We better be ready for anything."

Mac stared at the smallest of the three spaceships on the Trek'et landing pad.

The smaller ship was too small for deep space, but was well suited to moving around the planet and jumping from the surface to moons, space stations, and the massive flying cities like the *McDaniels*. The smaller ship had a dark blue paint job on its bullet-shaped hull and pontoon landing skids. There were no symbols or markings of any kind, which probably meant it was privately owned. Clear glass made up the sloped front-end cockpit.

Mac tapped his visor to bring up his thermal sensor. Through the multi-colored view, the two larger ships were dark, nearly black, suggesting they were cold from hours or even days of sitting on the pad. The smaller ship, however, was still warm, emanating a brighter yellow color. He tapped back to regular vision.

"What do you make of that smaller craft?"

"Isn't that a Nebulite?" Sanchez, like Mac, recognized it as a human-built craft. "Is it one of ours? Or does the Trek'et ambo like to roll in style on a human-built ship?"

"I don't know. I don't think Bloel Uf'el likes human anything. They aren't the warmest of Coalition partners. I don't like seeing that ship here. It's still warm as well, so it hasn't been here long," Mac said. "Alright, let's get moving. I'm sure we will find a guard or two at the back entrance, but they never kept much of a security presence."

"R.O.E.?" Sanchez asked, speaking of what Mac believed their rules of engagement should be as they invaded the sovereign space of another government.

"I'd like to keep use stun only. I don't see any reason for killing."

"Alright, stun it is. But what if they don't feel the same, but find plenty of reasons to kill us?" Sanchez asked.

"Oh, I'm sure they won't. Let's go."

Mac rushed across the soft dirt of the forest floor to where a meter-tall wall delineated the edge of the landing zone. They leapt over the wall with ease and continued running across the hard surface of the landing pad to the backside of the blue Nebulite spacecraft. Reaching the Nebulite, Mac pressed his back against the side of the ship, keeping the craft between him and the Trek'et embassy back door. A second later, Sanchez came to a rough stop, bumping up against the side of the Nebulite.

The fuselage of the Nebulite was metal and glass. It stood on pontoon-style landing feet. The glass provided a view of the passenger cabin, which was dark. Mac could barely see in while standing on his tiptoes on top of the pontoon landing foot. Sanchez was too short to see in.

"Anything?" Sanchez whispered.

"No, it's dark. Seems empty. Try to get a look at the embassy door. I'll check the cockpit."

Sanchez gave Mac a nod and turned toward the rear of the spacecraft, which was pointed toward the forest. Mac pulled out the shoulder stock extension of his RAP firearm, tucked the stock into his shoulder, and gazed through the sights of the stubby gun.

He moved stealthily around the front of the Nebulite, business end of the RAP leading the way, and found the cockpit also dark and unmanned.

Just as he lowered his firearm, he heard a loud voice he didn't recognize. "Hey, what are you doing?" Mac spun in all directions, seeing no one. Then he heard Sanchez's voice.

"Well, hello there."

An unknown man's voice replied, "Who are you? Why are you here?" The unseen man's voice was gruff and unfriendly.

"Oh, yeah. Uhhhh, I'm with maintenance."

"What? No one called for maintenance," the voice said.

Mac couldn't see either of them, so he ran along the side of the fuselage to the corner and listened.

"Yeah, man," Sanchez said, trying to sound casual. "Told you had a capacitive problem. Your energy swallower wasn't working. We were sent by—"

"A what? What are you talking about? Wait, why do you have weapons?" The man sounded more aggressive.

A second later, he heard a heavy thud against the ship and grunting. Mac moved without delay, coming around the corner to the backside of the Nebulite. A massive, doughy man with pale skin and bushy red hair had Sanchez wrapped up in a bear hug.

Mac quickly let his RAP drop against his side and wrapped his muscular arm around the neck of the big man, locking him into a textbook choke hold. Mac squeezed the man's neck between his biceps and forearm and pulled hard, with his hand secured against his other forearm. The man finally let go of Sanchez and kicked and bucked for a moment. He was a big guy, heavy and tall. Mac had to wrestle him with all his strength. Sanchez moved in close and released a furious volley of fist punches to the man's abdomen, which caused him to quit fighting. It was over in a moment. The big guy passed out. Mac lowered him to the pavement.

Mac pulled zip ties from his belt compartment while Sanchez rolled the big man over. They wrapped the man's thick wrists and ankles together with the unbreakable cuffs. They then dragged the unconscious man to the back side of the Nebulite.

"Where'd this guy come from?" Mac asked.

"I think he is the pilot," Sanchez said, breathing heavily. "He came out of the side door as I was scoping out the embassy."

"No uniform markings. He'll wake up soon. We should tape his mouth," Mac said.

Sanchez retrieved a thin roll of utility tape and knelt next to the big man to wrap the tape around the guy's fat head and bushy red hair three times.

"That seems excessive," Mac said as Sanchez stood up straight, proud of his handy work.

"That's payback for the cheap shot to my jaw." He rubbed his jaw a bit.

"Is that why you gave him those ten blows to the solar plexus?" Mac asked.

Sanchez stood up straight. "Yes, as a matter of fact, it was."

"You're getting slow," Mac said. "How'd you let this big oaf get so close?"

Sanchez ignored his teasing and said, "There is one guard at the door. I didn't get a good look at him…or it. I guess it is an it?" Sanchez said, puzzled. "I don't know what it is."

"What did you see?"

"Tall, thin humanoid. There was some wavy yellow and blue stuff. I don't know. I'm not sure I saw a head."

"Yeah, that's a Trek'et. Did he notice you or the scuffle?"

"I don't know. I was busy trying not to be crushed by the flesh vise over there." Sanchez said, pointing to the unconscious man.

"Alright, we better move in case he saw us. I'll sprint right at him to get his attention. Since you are a better shot than me, I want you to hit him with a stun shot."

"Roger," Sanchez said, as he pulled the shoulder stock out and double checked the stun setting on his RAP.

"Oh, and Sanchez, whatever you do, don't let one of these Trek'ets touch you with their tentacles."

Sanchez's eyes grew wide. "Wait, what? They have tentacles? Why not?" he asked, but Mac was already running around the corner of the Nebulite toward the embassy.

CHAPTER FORTY-THREE

Mac pumped his legs as hard as he could, pushing his body across the open space between the landing pad and the spearhead-shaped Trek'et embassy building. The building loomed high above him, with its array of sharp points puncturing the night sky above. It glowed red from the filtered light, which was creepy and gothic. The back door was in front of him under the covered entrance., which looked like a smaller version of the embassy building, with its roofline of stacked razor-sharp peaks.

Fortunately, the Trek'et embassy was not the most secure facility in the galaxy. Mac didn't know the security protocols of the other embassies, but the Trek'ets' lack of hardened security always seemed foolish to him. The lone door guard was evidence nothing had changed. *But to be fair,* Mac thought as he sprinted toward the building, *they have no reason to suspect a human invasion force tonight.*

It seemed like forever before Sanchez released his sniper shot at the guard. He heard the sizzling of the small green laser blast zip past him and saw it smash into the wall of the embassy building. It hit the wall close to where the guard was standing, but not close enough.

The Trek'et guard was a tall, wispy humanoid creature with long thin limbs. Its body was generally humanoid with two arms and two legs, but the abdomen was small and lean, and since they wore no clothing, the vibrant blue and yellow colors of its skin were visible. The neck was long and thin, with a small head the size of a fist. Translucent jellyfish-like fins framed the Trek'ets' head and neck, and waved around constantly. The fins lining its back, arms, and legs were like blue and yellow fringe. The waving of its fins created a kaleidoscopic confusion for all who looked at them.

It didn't surprise Mac that Sanchez, the Space Warfare Group's best shooter, missed the Trek'et. Its weird liquid jellyfish movements were disorienting, and nearly impossible to zero in on from a distance.

The Trek'et, alerted now, raised a black rifle toward Mac. Sanchez quickly made the adjustments, and his second shot was true. The sizzling second blast landed square in the middle of the guard's chest. Mac was only a few meters from the guard when the stun shot connected, causing the Trek'et to flop to the ground in a squishy pile.

Mac skidded to a stop under the covered entrance, right in front of where the Trek'et lay. Under the soft red light, its fins were no longer moving. The Trek'et were not sea creatures, but they looked gooey like a fish out of water.

Sanchez ran to catch up to Mac, who was squatting down, looking at the Trek'et.

"Sorry about that first shot, Major Mac. Couldn't get a bead on him with all the squiggly-wiggly."

"We're good. It was a nice shot. He looks stable."

"He looks nasty," Sanchez said. "Squiggly McNasty."

"You think all aliens are ugly," Mac said.

"That's because they are. Look, this rifle is like what we found the Bone Rattlers using on the Okutan Royal Vessel." Sanchez nudged the fallen rifle with the tip of his boot.

"Yeah, I see it. Listen, we gotta hurry. We need to put his palm to the scanner," Mac pointed to the door. Next to the plain silver metal door was an electronic palm reader. "Don't touch those tentacles," Mac said, pointing to the long slender tendrils on the side of its abdomen.

"Uh, why?"

"They deliver a shock that messes you up. It's some kind of chemical-electrical zap. You'll pass out, you lose basic motor skills for hours, and you swell up real bad. I've seen it happen a couple of times."

"Oh, great. Why is everything always so complicated?"

"Yeah, not ideal. Come on, we've gotta hurry."

Mac grabbed the unconscious Trek'et guard by the ankles and pulled, being careful to avoid accidentally touching the tentacles. Sanchez lifted it by the neck. The Trek'et's small head featured a down-turned mouth and four small eyes. Sanchez complained the entire time, grossed out by the layer of mucus that covered the fins and skin and now his hands. He dry heaved a couple of times.

They got get him close enough for Mac to pull the Trek'et's long skinny arm up to the palm reader. Before pressing the palm against the screen, Mac looked at Sanchez and said, "Look alive. Don't hesitate. Let's put them down right away, but stun only."

"Roger that," he said and raised his RAP. "Do it."

Mac pressed the gooey palm to the reader's screen, and the door zipped open. On the other side of the door was a plain room, lit with red light, and two Trek'ets standing a few meters from the door, fins wiggling, tentacles pointing toward them, but they were caught off guard with no weapons. Sanchez put a green laser stun blast into the chest of both, and they collapsed to the floor.

Sanchez stepped over the unconscious guards and into the building. Mac followed, both with firearms at the ready. The rectangle room was devoid of any decoration or ornamentation of any sort. The walls and ceiling appeared to be metallic, like a brushed stainless steel. In front of them was another plain silver metal door that zipped open when they stepped close. Passing through the second door gave them access to a massive space where the ceiling opened to the top of the pointed roofline.

The Trek'ets had changed nothing since Mac had been there last. The barren metallic walls angled up to the pointed roof, and in the center of the space was a long rectangular pool of dark liquid with four Trek'ets submerged at the center. The liquid covered them up to their necks.

Scattered around the floor were about fifty cylinders, each a meter tall, and atop several was a Trek'et sitting hunched over and motionless in a squatting position.

After soaking it all in for three seconds, Sanchez muttered, "I hate this place."

"Yeah, it's not my favorite, either."

There where escalator ramps on both sides of the wide space. On the left side, the escalator went up to a mezzanine above the pool and, on the right side, the escalator led down from the mezzanine. The distant sounds of thunder and frequent flashing of red lightning added to the creepy atmosphere of the cavernous space.

There were multiple Trek'ets moving about on the mezzanine level, and a couple coming down the escalator.

Mac moved along the back wall toward the up escalator on the left.

Sanchez followed close behind, and whispered, "How do we know which ones are secur—"

Before Sanchez could finish his sentence, a Trek'et on the down escalator began screaming in an indecipherable language and pointing at them.

"Time to go," Mac said and took off running. He reached the escalator as heavy energy blasts smashed into the floor and walls around them.

Mac scanned the room as he ran up the escalator and detected three Trek'et guards. Two stood on the mezzanine and one on the lower surface, by the pool. "Down there!" he yelled at Sanchez, who locked his firearm's sight in on the guard by the pool and stunned him.

At the same time, Mac fired several wild shots at the two on the mezzanine before holding the trigger down and wiping across them with the RAP's constant stream of laser energy. He did finally connect with his targets, but hit two other Trek'ets on the mezzanine in the process. One guard slumped to the ground where it stood, while the other tipped over the mezzanine guardrail and fell over the side above the pool. Mac couldn't believe his eyes. He reached out with his arm, screaming, "No!" as the unconscious Trek'et and its weapon fell toward the floor below, splashing in the dark pool. Trek'ets in the pool and on the stubby cylinder columns were now screaming and wiggling toward the back of the embassy.

Mac leaned against the escalator handrail in momentary defeat as the escalator pulled him up toward the mezzanine, knowing it was unlikely the Trek'et would survive the fall.

Sanchez grabbed him and pushed him up the escalator to get him moving again. "Come on. We can't help him now."

Mac, severely disappointed with himself for a moment, compartmentalized the unfortunate accident and refocused on the mission.

They reached the mezzanine and Mac led them toward the wide featureless corridor in the middle of the mezzanine floor, which dead-ended at a pair of double metals doors. He knew they would find Bloel Uf'el, the Trek'et ambassador, behind those doors.

Just as they reached the double doors, they zipped open and four Trek'et guards poured out into the corridor. They were no match for Mac and Sanchez, who stunned them at close range. Only the one in the back got off a shot with his heavy black rifle, but it went high, as he too was stunned, and collapsed on the floor with the others.

Without slowing, Mac and Sanchez stepped over the unconscious Trek'ets and into the Ambassador's private office and living space. What Mac saw as he entered the room shocked him to his core. He didn't know what to expect, but this was beyond his imagination.

Ambassador Bloel Uf'el stood tall and regal in front of a wide picture window displaying the New London City night beyond. Bloel Uf'el wore his distinctive black and red chest ornament that covered his chest and his neck with a wide collar. He also wore black wrist and ankle cuffs. The neck and chest piece were a severe-looking accessory that set him apart from other Trek'ets. Bloel Uf'el was taller than Mac and outrageously thin by human standards.

None of this surprised him. He'd witnessed a scene like this several times before. What was shocking, however, was the small sickly-looking man with pasty skin and stringy gray hair, wearing a rumpled gray executive suit.

What is Aldo Sperry doing here? Mac asked himself repeatedly in his mind as he stepped across the room toward the two.

Sperry's body language betrayed his shock at seeing Major Malcom Lambert of the Interplanetary Army Space Warfare Group coming at him in the Trek'et Embassy with a weapon.

"Ambassador, do not move," Mac said in an authoritative voice, holding his palm out at Bloel Uf'el in a stop gesture. "Sperry, don't even think of moving."

Bloel Uf'el, said, "What is the meaning of this?" His voice was high pitched and choppy. Mac spoke the Galactic Coalition neutral language awkwardly, but well enough for the ambassador.

"You'll know soon enough, Ambassador. Sanchez, cuff Mr. Sperry here," Mac pushed the small frail man toward Sanchez, who let his RAP hang from the chest strap as he wrapped Sperry's wrists with zip-ties. He pulled them extra tight, so the ties dug sharply into Sperry's skin. He squealed and complained as Sanchez cinched them tight.

To Sperry, Sanchez said, "What are you doing here, man? You some sort of traitor? Does your boss know you are here?"

Aldo Sperry said nothing.

Mac was torn between dealing with the ambassador first or Sperry. There had to be some connection.

"I demand to know the meaning of this violation of Galactic Law. Who are you, and what do you think you are doing?" Bloel Uf'el was practically screaming now in his screeching voice. "This embassy is the sovereign land of the Trek'et people. You cannot do this." Bloel Uf'el was moving toward Mac, his dangerous tentacles pointing in his direction.

"Oh, we can, and we are, Ambassador. Consider this an invasion. And you can stay right there."

"You will not get away with this," Bloel Uf'el said.

"Probably not. But you have some information we need. And, if you move any closer, this conversation will get painful quickly."

Sanchez pushed Aldo Sperry near where the Ambassador stood, and the barrels of both RAP firearms remained pointing at them.

"You are selling military hardware to a band of raiders known as the Bone Rattlers. I need to know where to find them," Mac said. "Give us the information and we will leave without further disruption."

"Do I know you?" Bloel Uf'el asked with more curiosity than of indignation. His four tiny eyeballs in his small head darted around as his minuscule brain recognized Mac. As Bloel Uf'el spoke, his small mouth revealed sharp teeth.

"I know you. You are that human the UPG assigned to lead the protection detail years ago. Why are you violating Galactic Law? Have you gone rogue?" Uf'el extended the word rogue in an unnecessary and pompous manner.

"Answer the question, Ambassador."

"The Trek'et sells many things to many people. This is not a galactic crime," he said, "Merely good business."

"Where do I find the Bone Rattlers? They are using Trek'et weapons and spacecraft. I know you know who they are and where they are."

"Maybe they stole them from us," Bloel Uf'el said.

Mac rolled his eyes.

Mac turned to Sperry, "How about you, Sperry? Why is it that you happen to be with the people who happen to be selling hardware to the people who happened to kill my men, one of which happed to be my best friend?"

"And," Sanchez added enthusiastically, "speaking of galactic crimes, happens to have the Okutan princess held hostage somewhere?"

Sperry stuttered, "I…I…I'm simply here on diplomatic business. Totally…ah…totally unrelated to the Bone Rattlers."

Mac looked over at Sanchez. "He's really not good at this stuff, is he?"

"Nope. He's the worst," Sanchez said.

"Are you working with the Bone Rattlers, Sperry?" Mac asked.

"Ah…no," Sperry stuttered, still pulling at his tight wrist cuffs.

"Are you responsible for the kidnapping?"

"No, no, I swear."

"Where are they?"

"Ah…no…I…ah I do not know."

"Where are they?"

"I don't know."

"Sanchez, will you help Mr. Sperry remember, please?"

Sanchez reached over with his left hand and pinched Sperry's collarbone area, hitting the brachial plexus nerve cluster running from Sperry's neck, under the clavicle bone, and into his arm. His ratchet-like grip was strong enough to cause Sperry excruciating pain, but not so strong to cause him to pass out.

Sperry squirmed and screamed, and his arm went limp.

Bloel Uf'el's tiny, odd face changed from high-browed arrogance to fear as he realized these UPG army men were willing to harm them.

"Where, Sperry? Make it easy on yourself."

Sperry croaked out a weak, "I don't know."

"Sanchez."

Sanchez hit the brachial plexus nerves on the other shoulder, causing Sperry to fall to his knees in agony. The sickly little man shook and convulsed in pain.

Sanchez pulled him to his feet, but he collapsed down to his knees again.

"Sperry, be smart. Don't make it harder than it needs to be. Where do we find the Bone Rattlers?"

"I don't know."

"Sanchez, will you give Mr. Sperry more reasons to help us out?" Mac asked flatly, with no emotion.

"Gladly, Major Mac," Sanchez replied happily and reached down toward Sperry, who tried to put his bound hands up in defense, but both arms were radiating pain and mostly paralyzed.

"OK, OK," Sperry panted, spit and snot dripping from his nose and mouth. "I don't know where their base is, but I know he knows for sure. He knows where they are."

"Shut up, you stupid human," Bloel Uf'el yelled at Sperry in anger, and he tried to kick at Sperry's head with his spindly, wiggling leg.

Mac turned to the ambassador. "We can do this the easy way or the hard way. Where is their base?"

"I don't have to tell you anything."

"Sanchez, can you help the ambassador remember?"

"Yes, Major Mac, of course I can." Sanchez reached behind his back and pulled out the combat knife from its sheath. The knife, with its long, sharp, serrated blade, was intimidating to the most hardened warrior. For soft politicians like Bloel Uf'el and Aldo Sperry, it was terrifying.

Bloel Uf'el started back up, thin arms and long-fingered hands extended. In his choppy, awkward voice, loaded with fear, he said, "We sell weapons and spaceflight vehicles to the people you are talking about. They pay us well. But," he added, "I know nothing about a princess or the death of your men."

"Tell me more," Mac said.

"You call them the Bone Rattlers. They are a nearly extinct race of creatures known as the Guydrahmi. The Trek'et just manufactures and sells our products to any who pay. We are not responsible for what they do with it."

"Were you involved in the hijacking of the Okutan royal vessel?" Mac asked.

"No, I know nothing of this, but I'm sure this stupid human does, though," he screeched out and again tried to kick at Sperry's head.

Sanchez kicked Sperry gently in the side and said, "Is this true, Sperry? You helping the Bone Rattlers?"

Sperry curled up into a ball and cried, "Don't hurt me, don't hurt me."

"Ambassador, I am holding you responsible because you are selling to criminals and kidnappers," Mac said.

"Don't get self-righteous, now," Bloel Uf'el said with the sudden return of indignation. "We sell to you humans, and you have committed many galactic atrocities. In fact, you are committing the same type of crime right now of which you accuse the Guydrahmi."

Mac paused for a second. "Fair point, Ambassador. Where do I find the Guydrahmi?"

"You'll find them on Quokex."

"Quokex? Really?" Mac was surprised. "Quokex is an old failed UPG colony."

"Exactly," Bloel Uf'el said.

Mac changed the subject. "Why is he here?" Mac pointed at Sperry.

"Oh, he is negotiating a purchase of weapons, of course."

Exploding with anger at Sperry, Mac shouted, "What are you doing, Sperry?"

Sanchez reached down and pulled the whimpering Sperry to his feet.

With both fists gripping Sperry's suit, Sanchez winked at Mac and shoved Sperry into Bloel Uf'el.

Sperry stumbled and slammed into the wispy ambassador, who latched onto Sperry with hands and tentacles. Sperry got shocked with the release of electric charge and poison. He convulsed and made several strange noises with contorted facial expressions before going limp and falling flat on his face with a thud.

"Listen up, Ambassador, this will probably hurt a little, but you'll be fine." Mac shot Bloel Uf'el with a stun blast from his RAP and watched him crumple to the floor. "Grab Sperry and let's go."

"Is it OK if I touch him?" Sanchez asked hesitantly. "I won't be shocked?"

"I don't think so."

Sanchez pulled Sperry's limp body into a fireman's carry on his shoulder and followed Mac out of the ambassador's office.

They hurried across the mezzanine with no delay, down the escalator, and out into the dark cool night.

"What now?" Sanchez asked, straining under the weight of Sperry as they ran toward the landing pad.

"We're stealing the industrial ship to take us to Quokex," Mac said.

"Alright, good plan," Sanchez wheezed as they ran. After several more steps, he said, "Wait, neither of us can fly a ship like that."

"I know. But I know someone who can."

"Who?"

"Lieutenant Taylor, of course."

CHAPTER FORTY-FOUR

Interplanetary Navy Spaceport Soriano

Louella Taylor was settling down for the night in the cramped captain's quarters on the Navy cargo freighter when she received the call from Major Lambert. At first, she expected an update on his schedule, or to find out that he'd arranged a different return flight back to the *McDaniels*. Thinking about it now, she realized she felt a little something in the pit of her stomach when he called. The idea of not seeing Mac later was, she realized now, disappointing. This surprised her as she hustled around the small cabin, getting ready.

What's with the disappointment? she asked herself again as she stood in her pajamas, which consisted of tight black leggings and a white sleeveless top. On the small bed in front of her was her bright white and blue Navy transport crew uniform.

Nope, this won't do. Too bright. Too Navy.

I should be honest. I wanted to see him again.

She scrambled around to the foot of the bed and yanked the one set of personal clothes she'd packed from her small travel bag and threw them on top of the navy uniform.

Ugh. Also, not good. Too girly. Not mission worthy. But how was I supposed to know?

Her last option was the maintenance jumpsuit in the equipment cabinet at the bottom of the tiny closet. The captain's quarters were a common space, used by whomever was assigned as captain of the vessel, and she was thankful the Navy stocked it with many standard items for ship staff.

She pulled the medium-sized charcoal gray jumpsuit out of the cabinet and stepped into it. She pulled it on over her pajamas and zipped it up to her collarbones. The jumpsuit had several handy pockets for tools, padded knees and elbows, and surprisingly, it fit fairly well for a generic unisex uniform.

Not horrible. This will do.

She strapped on her boots and pulled her hair into a tight ponytail before gathering up any items she might need. She stuffed everything into her shoulder bag and jumpsuit pockets. In the equipment cabinet, she also snagged the flashlight and multi-tool. *Never know,* she thought.

Finally, she stood and looked at the smaller locked cabinet mounted on the wall. The black metal cabinet had a standard Navy label warning about firearm safety. Accessing the cabinet required Navy personnel retinal scan to unlock and open. She debated for a moment, then lined her eye up to the scanner and heard the electronic whirling sound and a soft electronic beep. She opened the cabinet, which contained two handheld firearms, sitting in a molded rack, and several energy loads. Hanging on the side of the cabinet was a holster. She slipped the holster on over her jumpsuit and clipped three pulse loads onto the belt. The handgun on the right was a bulky standard Navy duty gun, which she was familiar with. It was unloaded, but otherwise in great shape. She grabbed another pulse load and slammed it into the bottom of the weapon, and dropped it in the holster.

She left her private quarters and walked to the door of her co-pilot's room and banged on the door. A young man's face appeared in the door's crack, with an expression of surprise. He had a round face with enormous eyes and black hair trimmed high and tight.

"Lieutenant Taylor?" he asked, surprised because it was so late.

"Alcantara, follow me," she ordered and walked off without waiting for him.

"Ah, hang on, Lieutenant Taylor, I've gotta—"

"No time."

Alcantara followed her, trotting barefoot on the metal floor, in shorts and a tank top, trying to catch up as she led him through the ship.

"I've been called away on an emergency mission and you'll be on your own tomorrow."

"What?" he asked dumbly. "Ah, what mission?"

"I can't tell you. It's classified."

"Why do you have a gun?" he asked.

She looked at him with a flat expression. "It's classified, Al."

She entered the narrow corridor where she would find the entrances to the cargo freighter's three emergency escape pods. The pods were attached to the exterior of the ship and accessed through a set of airlock doors. She punched the activation buttons on the control screen at the first pod door. The lights inside the pod turned on, and the corridor door slid open.

"Why are you taking a pod?" Alcantara asked.

"I need to meet up with the mission team."

"Where are you going?"

"I can't tell you any of these things, Al," she said again. She smiled and patted him on the shoulder. "Classified, remember?"

"What if someone asks about where you are?"

"Tell them I've been called away on a special mission."

Alcantara, standing in his shorts and tank top, scratched his head and stared at her.

"Trust me. You'll be fine, Alcantara. Just do your job well. Fly this boat back to the *McDaniels*, and it will all work out fine. You're a superb pilot and can do this on your own."

"Yes, ma'am," he said apprehensively.

Taylor stepped into the airlock, and the door closed behind her. A moment later, the pod door opened, and she stepped inside. The pod seated up to ten people in its squatty bullet-shaped body, and could travel small distances in space or on a planet. It was a small and slow craft, but it was functional and met her needs perfectly.

As she sat at the pilot's seat and tapped away on the controls to disengage from the cargo ship, the increasing burden of second thoughts caused her to question whether she was making a good decision. Major Lambert's urgent request for her piloting assistance was one he described as being of *"supreme importance relating to the rescue of the Okutan princess."* She didn't understand why he was at the Trek'et embassy. And she didn't understand why he needed a pilot. When she'd pressed him hard about why she wasn't receiving orders from her commander via the normal chain of command, he didn't give satisfactory answers. Leaving her assignment to assist with another mission without proper orders was a career killer. But her career was a little stale right now, anyway.

Lambert's reasoning for requesting her help was compelling, however. He said he had found a potential mole in the highest ranks of the UPG and that he couldn't trust anyone. That was enough to motivate her to risk her career. Her loyalty to the United Planetary Government was a powerful force and her father, a former Navy pilot himself, always told her to *do what was right rather than always doing what was safe*. Choosing between doing the right thing or the safe thing were often mutually exclusive choices.

This better be the right thing, Lou, or you'll be in hot water.

Major Lambert explained he couldn't use proper channels and risk tipping off whatever treasonous forces remained hidden, which could ruin their chances of rescuing the princess. She knew little about Lambert, but she believed he was genuine in his concern. And, if he was right about treachery reaching deep into the UPG administration, she was compelled to help. Which is why she was now powering up the cargo ship's emergency escape pod.

THE LITTLE BULLET-SHAPED pod puttered quietly across the night sky towards Embassy Row. Taylor glanced down at the busy galactic city below several times as she navigated the short distance to the embassies. Embassy air control gave her clearance to land the pod at the Trek'et landing pad over the radio, with no hassle.

She made a wide sweeping turn in the pod to approach the landing pad from the north, near the spearhead-shaped embassy building. Taylor saw three spacecraft sitting below in the pool of yellow light. She knew the dark boxy utilitarian spacecraft and the severe-looking silver and red craft were both Trek'et handiwork, while the small craft she recognized as a Nebulite. She was familiar with all three spaceships from her UPG Navy pilot training program. The Trek'et were known as makers of excellent spacecraft, used by many throughout the galaxy. It seemed their sales and marketing team were the best in the industry.

As she made her slow approach in the tiny pod, Taylor also saw green and red energy blasts shooting back and forth from the embassy building and the boxy spaceship. Obviously, air control wasn't aware of the firefight, otherwise they would have never let her access the area. The bright energy blasts stood out against the dark night, even under the landing zone lighting. As she brought the little craft in closer, she could see Major Lambert and the other operator, Sanchez, taking cover behind the ship's landing legs. They sent return fire at the embassy building's security force. One of the Trek'et turned its attention to Taylor's pod, firing red energy blasts at the little craft. She could feel the energy blasts slam against the outer hull.

"Coming in hot," she said to herself as she swerved to escape their aim.

Taylor set the pod down behind the utility ship, on the edge of the landing pad. She extracted herself from the piloting seat and safety belts and snatched up her shoulder bag. With the bag's strap swung over her shoulder and neck, she darted out of the pod. As she ran hunched over toward Lambert's location, she pulled her handgun. She made it safely to the underside of the Trek'et utility ship, keeping her head low, to where Major Lambert and Sergeant Sanchez were crouched in the dark. They were both kneeling behind the ship's landing foot and the massive hydraulic ram that would pull the landing gear into the retracted position.

"Welcome to the party, Lieutenant Taylor," Sanchez greeted her as he squatted behind the landing gear. "We have refreshments available, and the live band will begin shortly." Both men were wearing dark visors and equipment belts.

"I might not have accepted the invitation if I knew what kind of party this was going to be," Taylor said. She squeezed down between them, behind the landing foot.

"Glad you could make it," Mac said with a smile. He popped up and fired off several shots from a small energy weapon before dropping low again. Then Sanchez performed the same maneuver.

Lying on the hard landing surface next to them was an older man with slimy gray hair and matching rumpled suit. He looked red and puffy, clearly not well, and likely unconscious. His hands were cuffed.

Mac saw her staring at the unconscious man. "Don't worry about him."

"Is he alive?" she asked hesitantly.

"Oh, yeah, he's alive, but he'll be out cold for a while," Mac replied, then fired toward the embassy.

"What happened?"

Sanchez said, "Got stung by the Trek'et ambassador. It wasn't pretty."

Taylor asked, "How'd that hap-" but the wide grin on Sanchez's face told her all she needed to know. "Never mind. What can I do to help? Who are we shooting at?" she asked as Sanchez released another series of green laser blasts. She felt the tingling static and heard the sizzling sounds of the laser fire, which was an odd contrast to the gentle sea breeze.

"Can you get us some punch and maybe a piece of cake? I'm feeling a bit of the munchies," Sanchez said. "Maybe you could even request my favorite song. It's called Night Life. Do you know it? That'll get this party started."

Mac ignored Sanchez and instructed Taylor, "You can put that away," nodding toward her handgun, "and get this ship running. Getting us out of here would be great."

She slipped the handgun back into her holster. "OK, I'm on it."

"You know how to fly this piece of junk?" Sanchez asked.

"Oh, yeah, of course. Nothing to it, Party Guy," she said. "Give me some cover so I can get in."

Sanchez and Mac popped up and sprayed the embassy building with green laser streams.

Taylor raced over to the control panel on the underside of the ship that would lower the access ramp from the ship's belly, allowing them into the bowels of the ship. She expected a prompt for a passcode or some security protocol, but was surprised to find none. The operators of this craft didn't fear it being stolen or even entered by anyone while it was on the embassy's landing pad. It was a logical assumption most days. But today wasn't most days.

With only a couple of finger taps on the oddly shaped buttons, the ramp detached from the hull above them with a pop and a hissing sound. The ramp descended towards the ground, but Taylor didn't wait. She jumped, grabbing the edge of the ramp, and pulled herself up onto the surface. She ran into the dark ship.

The ship's motion-activated lights came on as she searched for the cockpit. She had a pretty good idea where the cockpit would be, and after only one wrong turn, she found it. Bursting into the cockpit, she found it was not a small cockpit like the Navy ships she was used to, but more of a control room with a captain's chair and three piloting control consoles.

She slipped into the floor mounted, tall-backed swivel chair of the closest console and glanced at the controls. This was a new generation Trek'et mining and utility vessel. The ones she flew in pilot training school were a bit older. But the controls were similar. The interface was no longer buttons and dials, but a touchscreen. As she'd expected from the Trek'et design, the current system was intuitive, and she brought all systems online and waited a moment as the engine lights displayed it was in priming mode. She could hear the soft background sounds of ship systems coming up, and after a moment, the engine status lights changed to signal that priming was complete. She tapped the ignition control and felt the ship shudder as the engines fired to life. The rumble from the powerful engines gave her a rush of adrenaline.

"Oh, yeah, buddy," she said, realizing this vessel was designed with power in mind.

A little-known secret of Lieutenant Louella Taylor was her love of flying powerful spaceships. She lived for it. It's why she became a pilot in the first place. Most of the time, to her dismay, she was stuck flying the boring Naval crafts, but once in a while, she could open up the rocket engines and really fly.

Leaving the ship running and warming up, she retraced her steps toward the loading ramp and saw Sanchez at the base of the ramp firing at the Trek'et and Mac dragging the limp body of the other man, by his coat collar, up the ramp. She waited for Sanchez to run up the ramp before punching the close button.

Mac dropped the old man on his back on the metal floor of the ship. He let his firearm hang from the chest strap, and he tipped the visor up on top of his head. They were in the spacious main cargo hold, which was empty, except for a couple crates that were open, as if someone sorting deliveries walked away in the middle of their job.

"There is a lounge up here on the left. You guys could hang out there. Or you could join me up front and tell me where in the universe we are going. Oh, and, Major, next time you steal a ship," she said to Mac, "steal some crew members as well." She turned to run toward the control room again.

"We're not stealing the ship, Taylor," Mac yelled back. "We are just borrowing it."

Upon reaching the cockpit again, Taylor lifted the Trek'et utility ship off the landing pad, rotated it into the desired direction, punched the throttle to full, and the dark boxy spacecraft shot through the night sky above New London City into the stars. She ignored air control's demands for identification and clearance protocols.

CHAPTER FORTY-FIVE

Bone Rattler Compound
Quokex Compound

The hours clicked by, and the emotions of the Okutan prisoners downgraded from trembling fright to the dull resignation of caged prisoners. Hours turned into days, and dungeon life became routine and predicable. The Okutans sat huddled together for warmth and comfort. They slipped in and out of sleep, awakened when the industrial machine in the room roared back to life. They began to welcome the machine coming alive because it added some heat to the room while it ran and for a little while after.

The now predicable routine was building the skeleton of a plan in Princess Omo-Binrin's mind. She refused to be discouraged by keeping her mind active in considering the possible different conspiracies that could have led her to this place. She tried to relive everything over the last week and lock the visual images and time-line in her memory, walking through the events of the capture and transport to this dungeon. Still not knowing where she was, she at least had a decent idea of the range and distance from the Regulated

Zone, where the attack occurred. While locked away in this dark dungeon, she couldn't do anything with the information, but she was going to help her people escape, and she needed the information clear and organized in her mind for when they returned to safety.

The noisy and smelly machine continued to rumble to life every few hours, which helped her gauge the timing of the days. Her monstrous captors would arrive within a predicable time frame as well, bringing food and water. She was expecting them in the next few minutes.

After the first food drop by their captors, she pretended to be submissive and distraught, hoping they would remain sloppy and continue to underestimate her and her people. So far, the strategy seemed to work, since the guards seemed even more casual the last time they exchanged the food buckets.

Omo-Binrin stood and stretched her sore body. She moved away from the door toward the back wall where she could observe the guards when they arrived and gather more information. This might be her last opportunity to gather information. It would soon be time to act.

She didn't have to wait long before the door opened with a bang and the light from the corridor poured into the dungeon. Huge shadowy forms filled the doorway. She knew her eyes would resist the sudden brightness, so she prepared herself for the sudden shock.

The guards entered without a word and the Okutans remained sitting, dejected and submissive to their captors. The guard with the black rifle held it with one hand, as if it was more of a nuisance than a weapon he was prepared to use. As the guards picked up the old buckets and dropped the new ones in their place, sloshing the water over the top of the bucket, Omo-Binrin looked along the side of the machine as the light filled the dark corners.

She couldn't see much of anything, but that was good news. She didn't see any devilish creatures reaching clawed hands out of the shadows toward her. The floor seemed solid, with no sign of bottomless pits. The wall beyond the machine was hard to make out, other than metallic boxes and pipes mounted to the walls and ceiling closest to her. She was confident the area around the machine was harmless. In fact, it was going to be a benefit to them.

The door slammed shut again, plunging them back into darkness. The Okutans didn't move and didn't speak.

We'll use the darkness to our advantage, she thought. *And we'll use their predictability to our advantage. They should not have underestimated me. It will be their undoing.*

Omo-Binrin surveyed the area around the machine now and put the finishing touches on her plan. She moved toward the machine, and she felt the Okutans' eyes on her. She walked slowly and carefully, feeling along the rough wall, and scooting her feet along the rough surface so that she didn't trip over anything.

"Princess, no, don't go down there, it's not safe," an Okutan said, followed by the agreement of several others. They jumped to their feet but wouldn't come closer to the machine.

"I'll be fine. There is nothing to be afraid of. I've got an idea and I'll be right back."

She scooted along and found the metal boxes and pipes attached to the wall. The boxes and pipes were smooth to the touch and colder than the wall. After several more steps, she came to the back wall and turned. The wall was rough like the floor and transferred freezing temperatures from outside. She scooted along to the far wall opposite of where she started, moving behind the industrial machine. It was so much darker behind the machine. For a moment, she thought she would lose her cool. Her imagination produced images of terrifying creatures that lived in the shadows and consumed helpless fools like herself. Her skin crawled, and she shivered.

Just then, the machine rumbled to life again and the noise almost made her jump out of her skin. She was expecting it to come on again a bit later. Her calculations were off by a few minutes. She heard the cries of her people across the room, and felt the rumbling of the machine more than ever. It shook her insides and was much louder on this side of the room.

She closed her eyes while the machine shook and rattled her

whole body. She encouraged herself with words she knew her father, the King of Okuta, would say. *You can do this, Omo-Binrin. You're fine. There is no danger here. You can handle anything if you put your mind to it.* Thinking of her lovely father's face and the silly voice he would use when trying to encourage her made her smile, and her fear waned.

Keeping her eyes closed, she tried to enhance her other senses and kept scooting along, feeling the cold, rough wall. She could feel the rumbling of the machine moving the air around her and the vibration through the floor.

It was all safe, nothing to worry about. *I am safe. We can use this to our advantage.* As she scooted along the other side, she opened her eyes again and looked toward her people. She could see the crowd of scared Okutans, all on their feet now, in the soft green glow from the machine's lights. They stood some distance from the machine, gazing into the dark, waiting for her to reemerge from the shadows.

"There she is," one of her attendants said excitedly.

When she finished her trip around the machine, she approached her people, and they grabbed her and hugged her.

"Are you OK?" they asked.

"Yes, yes. I am fine. There is nothing back there to be afraid of," she told them. "I know this is scary. But, please, everyone, trust me. We need to eat some of this terrible food and rest easy. We will all need our strength. I have a plan," she said, "and I need your help."

"What kind of plan?"

"A plan to escape. When those vicious monsters come back with the next round of food, we are going to kill them and escape."

Her people didn't say anything beyond a couple of uncomfortable murmurs. But Princess Omo-Binrin was more confident than ever.

CHAPTER FORTY-SIX

Trek'et Utility Ship
En route to Quokex

"How are his vitals?" Mac asked, as Sanchez adjusted Aldo Sperry's unconscious body on the passenger lounge floor.

"He's looking OK, Major Mac," Sanchez said. He cocked his head to the side and added, "Well, the vitals are looking OK, but he looks terrible. Still super swollen and super greasy."

"I'm pretty sure Mr. Sperry here is always super greasy," Mac said. "Seriously though, how's the BP and pulse?"

"He's fine. Both are a little high and he's running a fever, but nothing to be worried about."

"He'll be out for a while still, I'd imagine. All the same, let's strap him down."

"I thought you'd never ask," Sanchez said.

"While you do that, I'll get Taylor read in on the situation so she can point this boat toward Quokex. Keep an eye on him. As soon as he is conscious, I have some important questions for Mr. Sperry."

Mac wandered down the bright metal corridors until he found the ship's control room. He let the RAP firearm hang from the chest harness, and his tactical visor remained on top of his head. When he entered the control room, Taylor was sitting at one of three piloting control consoles in a tall-backed swivel chair. She was adjusting settings on the touch screen in front of her. The screen started on the desktop, with many colorful buttons and slide controls, and curved up in front of her. The top and sides of the screen curved toward her as well, creating a colorful glass bowl-like structure, with the center of the screen displaying the star-filled galaxy ahead, while the sides displayed ship data.

"Thanks for coming. You're a lifesaver," Mac said as he entered the room.

"Yeah, well, I'm not so sure this was a good idea, Major." She tapped on the screen a couple times, then swiveled the chair toward Mac.

"Please, call me Mac. I'd be lying if I said I wasn't having any second thoughts myself. But this mission is too important, and we're hot on their trail."

"So, are you going to tell me what's really going on and where we are going?" she asked.

"Yes, I'll tell you everything, but before we get into the story, we are heading to an old, failed colony by the name of Quokex. Have you heard of it?"

"Quokex? Yeah, that sounds vaguely familiar. Wasn't that abandoned like a hundred years ago?"

"Yeah, I'm pretty sure it was."

"If I remember right, I don't think it's very far from Terra Libertas." Taylor turned her chair back to the screen and tapped a couple of icons, and the main picture displaying the galaxy switched to an interactive map of the galaxy.

"No, it's not. I think it is out there by the old Castra Fortis," Mac said about a former UPG Army space station, now turned private colony.

"Let's see what we've got in the system," she said absently while typing in the name. Mac watched over her shoulder as she worked the touch screen interface. The screen changed, and the galaxy map twisted around and zoomed in on a planet. A leader line extended from the planet to an information bubble listing Quokex data and facts. "Well, there you go," Taylor said.

"OK, how long?"

"Ah, according to the ship's computer, we are looking at seven hours and seven minutes from here."

"Is that as fast as this thing will go?"

"Yup," she said, looking back at him. "This ship moves pretty fast, but it's still seven hours at *FTL*."

Mac let out a frustrated breath. "OK. It is what it is. Can't do anything about it. Please, set the course, Lieutenant Taylor."

"Lou."

"What?"

"Call me Lou. If I'm supposed to call you by your monosyllabic first name, you must call me by mine, which is Lou."

"Yes, of course. Lou, please set the course."

She nodded in agreement and turned back to the bowl-like control interface. She entered the data and double checked before engaging. The ship took a moment to calculate the travel path, then they felt the indescribable transition to *faster than light* speed. Mac felt lightheaded for a second and leaned against Taylor's swivel chair, but the feeling passed quickly.

Taylor swiveled her chair, stood, and stepped over to the main captain's chair sitting in the center of the room. The chair was on a small, elevated platform, two steps up, which she climbed and flopped into. Mac followed, but stood on the floor in front of the captain's chair. Taylor pulled her legs up underneath herself and sat cross-legged.

"OK, Mac," she over-pronounced his name, "we're on our way now. So, let's have it. All of it. Leave nothing out."

"Technically, this is all top secret."

"Technically, I'm cleared."

"Not to this level of clearance."

"Listen, I'm probably ruining my career as a Navy pilot for this little journey of yours, so spit it out."

Mac couldn't help but like Lou Taylor. She was spunky. He knew she was taking a tremendous risk and was ruining her career, and he owed it to her to be honest.

"I know you are, and I appreciate the risk you are taking. I'll do whatever I can to shield you from the blowback. Here's what we know as of right now. A couple of days ago, President Harrington himself brought in the Space Warfare Group, along with Prime Ambassador Kumar, to investigate the dead spaceship you were involved with. The UPG, well, Kumar specifically, was in negotiations with the princess for some sort of colonial development, as I understand it."

"The Okatonakans?" she asked.

"Okutan."

"Same thing," she said.

Mac turned a piloting chair on its swivel and sat down.

"Now, according to Kumar, there was some secret purpose behind the meeting as well. Something to do with a dangerous threat to the Galactic Coalition. It was obvious, when we entered the ship, that something horrible had happened. We found evidence they of an ambush by a group of space pirates we now know are the Guydrahmi but known around the galaxy as Bone Rattlers."

"That sounds creepy," Taylor said.

"Oh, yeah, they are. You'll get to see them up close and personal in a few hours. They killed many of the Okutans on board, but the princess was missing, and presumed captured."

"Not good."

"No, not good at all," Mac agreed.

"You think they were after the princess specifically?"

"At the time, no, I thought it was a case of being in the wrong place at the wrong time. Maybe these space pirates were trying to leverage a high valued hostage for money. But now, I am convinced things are more complicated, and they were after the princess. It's gotta be about that secret message."

"What was the secret?"

"We don't know. She was waiting to share when face-to-face with Kumar and Harrington."

"So, you are missing key information on this whole thing."

"Exactly. There is a lot I can't figure out. The pieces are too scattered and confusing right now."

They sat quietly, thinking for a moment.

Lou then asked, "And what about the Okutan guy in the tube we transported? You said he died?"

"Yeah, well, this is where the story gets weirder. The Okutan, Jagoon Ina, was the head of security. We woke him from the suspended animation tube and after he calmed down, he explained how they were ambushed. It was like the Bone Rattlers knew exactly where the Okutan vessel would arrive. And this was shocking to me; they gave him a message for the UPG regarding trading the princess for their leader, who the UPG happened to have in custody."

"So, they captured her so they could do a hostage exchange?"

"Maybe." He shrugged. "I guess. But, what about the princess' secret? It's weird. How did the Bone Rattlers know where she would be? The circle of people who knew that information must be tiny."

"That is weird."

"You want to know what I really think?"

"Please, no more suspense."

"I think something dirty is happening on the inside. I think we've got double agents or traitors in the UPG. One of which may be with Sanchez right now."

"Oh, this old guy in the suit? I see what you are saying," Taylor said. "Did the UPG actually have the Bone Rattler leader?"

"Yes, they did. He's a real charmer named Sckrahhg. And guess who knew exactly who he was and where he was," Mac said flatly.

"I don't know."

"Prime Ambassador Kumar."

"Whoa," she mumbled.

"And guess where he was being held in custody."

"Terra Libertas? Maybe Spaceport Soriano?"

"Nope. Get this. This Sckrahhg character just happened to be imprisoned in a little confinement box on the Prime Ambassador's own ship, which was sitting in the *McDaniel*'s hangar."

"What? That seems way too convenient," Taylor said, and she scrunched her lips and brow, deep in thought. Mac nodded his head.

"It's all way too convenient. None of this sits well with me. Coincidences like this don't just happen. There is something going on."

"Do you suspect Kumar? Is he dirty?"

"I can't imagine. I mean, it's Harji Kumar, after all. He's humanity's number one diplomat."

"Yeah, that's crazy."

"He's the third most powerful human in the galaxy. It can't be him."

"You don't sound like you believe that," she said.

"Yeah, I don't. Because there's a lot more to the story."

"Oh, great."

"So, we set up the exchange as demanded, trying to get the princess back, and the Bone Rattlers double-cross us. We arrive with Sckrahhg and there is no princess. They were never planning to make the exchange. They set up another ambush, which is why I hate rushed missions. We didn't have our usual array of equipment and intelligence. We were forced to use Kumar's own ship and not the *McDaniels* or a military vessel."

Anger swelled up inside of him. He ground his teeth, taking a few moments to control his anger. He shook his head, trying to clear his frustration.

Taylor waited, saying nothing.

Mac continued, "We were unprepared, and it cost us big time. We got suckered into the ambush. Jagoon and Sam Clarion died in an explosion. Then, one of my other men died in the firefight that followed."

Mac went quiet again. He gazed off into the corner of the control room and couldn't look at Taylor. He could feel the toxic cocktail of anger and sadness mixed with self-condemnation. The emotions were trying to overwhelm him again. He fought, pushing it back down, compartmentalizing the thoughts and feelings. He put it in the box, closed the door, and locked it. Mac rubbed his face and eyes with his palms before continuing.

"Sam was a great warrior, but he was also my best friend. He had a way of always balancing out my weaknesses as a leader. When he died, it was the last straw for me, and I lost it."

"What happened?"

"I sorta went mental." Mac let out a little laugh, thinking of the emotional roller coaster of the last few days. He could feel the tears welling up in his eyes.

"Wow. Not much of a resume builder, eh?"

"No, definitely not."

"Is that why you they removed from duty?"

"Yeah, it was. Colonel Miller shut me down and put me on the bench. I was furious. My search for the Bone Rattlers started as a mission of pure vengeance. My plan was to find them and kill them, you know, because of Sam. It's all I could think about. But now, there is a lot more swirling around. My vengeance mission has morphed into something different. It's much, much bigger now."

"What do you mean?"

"We found Bone Rattler weapons and spacecraft information on the Okutan ship, which led us to the Trek'ets."

"Ah, right, you needed to get to the embassy."

"Yes, I did. I wanted to find out where to find the Bone Rattlers and to my shock, we find that greasy guy, the one out there with Sanchez," Mac pointed toward the lounge where Sperry lay unconscious, "standing in the Trek'et ambassador's office. That blew me away. My mind has been spinning ever since. Do you know who that guy is? His name is Aldo Sperry."

"Nope."

"He works for the Prime Ambassador. He's Kumar's right-hand man." Taylor's eyes got wide in surprise and her eyebrows raised. "Exactly. Think about this. The Prime Ambassador was supposed to meet with the Okutan princess, but the Bone Rattlers kidnapped her. The Bone Rattlers, we learned, get all their equipment, including ships like this one," Mac said while pointing around the ship, "and their weapons, from the Trek'et. And, when we show up at the Trek'et ambassador's embassy to interrogate him about the Bone Rattlers, the Prime Ambassador's right-hand man, Sperry, just happens to be there? Something is fishy."

"Ahh," Taylor saw the complete picture now. "That is why you can't contact your team? You are afraid there is a mole or a spy or something?"

"I don't know. Is it Sperry? Is he working alone? Or is he working with others? Maybe he is just working for someone else. I don't know. Who else is involved? At this point, I don't know who we can trust. Is Kumar dirty? Is someone in the Army or Navy dirty? What about my own commanding officers? I don't think I can contact the team without Kumar finding out, and I don't trust him."

"It can't be Kumar."

"It seems so unlikely, but a lot is pointing toward him."

"And what about Quokex?" she asked.

"Supposedly, it's the Bone Rattler base."

"Interesting. So, the Bone Rattler base is on an old UPG colony? That also seems a bit too convenient."

"Yup. You're getting it."

"So, what are we flying into?"

"No clue."

"There are only three of us."

"Yeah, but two of us are pretty amazing," Mac said with a grin.

"True, Sanchez and I are pretty awesome," she said. "For real, though, I don't care how amazing you are. This sounds like a suicide mission."

"You might be surprised by what we can do."

"I'm sure I would be. But we need serious back-up."

"I know. But making that call could expose us, and everything falls apart."

"There isn't anyone you can trust?" she pressed.

"Well, of course I can trust my crew. I just don't know if they can jump into action without the wrong people, whoever they are, finding out." Mac went quiet again, the whole thing running through his mind at lightning speed. "I know it's a risk we must take."

A voice came from the corridor beyond the door. "Yes, it is worth the risk," Sanchez said. Mac turned and Sanchez entered the room, RAP firearm hanging from his chest rig, visor on top of his head.

"What do you think, Sergeant?" Taylor asked.

"Mac, you need to call DJ. We can trust him, and he'll know what to do."

Mac put his face in his hands with his elbows on his knees and moaned. "You're right." His voice was muffled through his palms. He sat up straight. "How's Sperry? Maybe we can extract some information out of him first? Let's find out who he is working with."

"He's still sleeping like a puffy, greasy baby. There's no time to wait for him. He'll be out for another couple hours and who knows what condition he'll be in after that."

"How long is the trip?" Sanchez asked.

"Seven hours," Taylor said.

"Lieutenant Taylor, I mean, Lou," Mac asked, "If we make this call and the wrong people find out, can the Navy ships get to Quokex faster than we can in this one?"

"Yeah, for sure. If they bring the whole *McDaniels*, they can beat us there," Taylor said. "And if this is a high-level conspiracy, they'll bring the *McDaniels*. Somebody on high will command it."

"Yeah, that's not going to work," Mac said. "We can't allow the *McDaniels* to intercept us." He was quiet for a moment. "If the wrong people find out and beat us there, they'll arrest us before we can do anything."

"Or they may just kill us," Sanchez added. "Blow us into space dust."

Mac raised his eyebrow and nodded. Sanchez was right.

"OK, Mac. Give it enough time and then call DJ. We'll get to the planet first and they'll arrive as backup shortly after. At least that way, we will still have a shot."

"Yeah, that's our only option. We need to surprise them, which means we must arrive before any communications or speedy UPG ships can get there. And, of course, you both also know we'll likely be arrested once the cavalry arrives. Colonel Miller won't let our actions go unpunished."

"Yup," Sanchez said.

"Hearing the rest of this story, I'm all in," Taylor said. "Let's finish this."

Mac looked at Sanchez for a moment, thinking. Sanchez grinned back, confident, or insane. *Play the hand you're dealt*, Mac thought.

"Well, other than being out-planned, out-manned, and out-gunned, we've got the advantage. I'll call DJ later," Mac said.

"You guys are crazy," Taylor said.

CHAPTER FORTY-SEVEN

Aldo Sperry was finally conscious, but mumbling incoherently.

"I can't understand a word of this," Sanchez said.

Sperry sat with his back against a metal column, with tape wrapped around his chest and shoulders. Sanchez mercifully didn't wrap tape around his head, like he did the guy at the Trek'et embassy. Sperry's head bobbed up and down, and he blinked his swollen eyes.

Mac squatted in front of Sperry. Sanchez was kneeling on one knee to his left. "Sperry, make this easy on yourself. How did the Bone Rattlers know where the Okutans would be?" Mac asked.

"I...don't...know...anything," Sperry stammered.

"What did this greaseball say?" Sanchez asked angrily.

"He says he knows nothing."

"Oh, yeah, of course not. Silly me," Sanchez said.

"I guess we need to wake him up a bit," Mac said, then slapped Sperry across the side of the face. He slapped him hard enough to jolt him awake and leave red handprints on his cheek.

"Why did the Bone Rattlers capture the Okutan princess?" Mac asked.

Sperry said nothing, but looked Mac in the eyes this time with an arrogant smirk. He tried to spit on Mac, but with his swollen face, he merely drooled on himself. He tried to laugh but ended up in a coughing fit.

"Talk, Sperry," Mac said.

"I won't tell you anything," he squeaked out.

Sanchez fired a roundhouse punch that connected with Sperry's jaw. It made a crunching sound. Blood and drool splattered against the wall.

"Tell us what you know!" Sanchez yelled, but Sperry faded in and out of consciousness again.

Mac stood and paced for a minute. He watched Sperry's head bob up and down. A new flow of blood from his nose and mouth streamed down his face.

The vision of the explosion that killed Sam kept replaying in Mac's mind. *This scumbag knows. He knows why. He knows something.*

"You gonna start talking?" Sanchez yelled at Sperry again.

Sperry squeezed out, through a pained grimace, "Go to hell. I will tell you nothing."

"You think you're some kinda tough guy, Sperry?" Sanchez asked.

Mac returned and standing above him said, "Well, Sanchez, we're going to have to turn up the volume on this interrogation. Maybe this will help Mr. Sperry answer our questions." Mac reached behind his back and pulled his fixed blade knife from the belt sheath. The knife made a metallic ching sound as he pulled it out and held it in front of him. The knife was long, and the serrated blade glistened under the lights.

Mac squatted down in front of Sperry, next to Sanchez.

On cue, as if practiced, Sanchez said in a worried voice, "Oh, Major Mac, that seems like too far."

"Shut up, Sanchez," Mac said. "Sperry here is going to tell us what he knows."

"You're not going to cut him up like you did that criminal on Fortuna, are you?" Sanchez put enough emotion in his voice. Mac wondered if he was worried. Sanchez looked concerned. Mac winked at him.

Angrily, Mac said, "It made him talk, didn't it?"

"Whu...uh...what do you think you gonna do...with-wit-with that?" Sperry stuttered through swollen lips and tongue. He wasn't so arrogant now.

"Maybe I'll start by cutting off your ears. Those are easy to cut off, but it hurts like crazy. After that, hmm, maybe I'll start working on fingers until you tell us what you know."

Sanchez grabbed Mac's arm. "Come on, man. Don't lose it again."

Mac yanked his arm away and put the glistening blade in front of Sperry's good eye.

Sperry's eyes went wide. "You wouldn't. You can't." He tried to laugh again, but the fear was obvious in his face. "I'm...I'm... ahhhh...member of the diplomatic-"

Mac slapped Sperry across the face again.

"Listen up, Sperry. This is your last chance. If you don't answer my questions, I will start cutting ears off until we get the information we need. Now, how did the Bone Rattlers know where the princess would be?"

"You can't do this!" Sperry shouted, spit and blood streaming down his chin. His eyes were welling up with tears.

"What did the Bone Rattlers want with the princess?"

Sperry muttered and mumbled through tears now.

"You think he can handle the pain?" Mac asked Sanchez.

"This guy? No way."

"You...can't...do this!" Sperry was cracking. Mac could see all the signs. He tried to be the arrogant, tough guy and resist Mac, but Sperry was just a pampered politician. He couldn't hack it.

"Last chance. How did they know?"

Sperry continued muttering and shaking his head.

Mac reached over with his free hand and grabbed Sperry's ear and brought the knife up against the side of his head. The cold knife pressed against Sperry's temple, and he flinched. Mac held the knife there for a moment.

"How did the Bone Rattlers know?"

He said nothing, but he was shaking. Mac wasn't sure this guy could get any uglier, but as he sobbed, and his beat-up swollen face contorted into grotesque expressions.

Mac adjusted the knife, connecting the sharp edge of the knife to the thin skin flap attaching Sperry's ear to the side of his head. Blood poured from the shallow slice. Sperry tried to pull away. He cried out in pain.

"No, no, no, no, don't do it. Please don't do it." Sperry blubbered. "I don't know anything."

"OK, that's it," Mac yelled and reached for Sperry again.

Sanchez reached out and grabbed Mac. "Don't do it, man."

Mac pushed him away and grabbed Sperry's greasy head and brought the knife down close.

"OK, OK. Don't do it. I'll talk. I don't know anything." He sobbed and snorted bloody snot from his puffy nose.

Mac pulled back. "Talk!"

"I'm just a messenger. I don't know anything."

Mac brought the knife down again.

"OK, OK, it was Arthur Rust. Rust told them. I had nothing to do with it."

"Who is Arthur Rust?"

"He's just a guy."

"What does that mean? Who is he?"

"He's a private military contractor."

"How did he know where they would be?"

"I don't know…" Sperry's voice trailed off.

"Alright, say goodbye to your ears." Mac leaned in close and pulled on Sperry's ear with the knife a centimeter away. Blood dripped on Mac's hand, Sperry's shoulder, and the metal floor.

"How did he know?" Mac repeated as he touched the knife to his temple again. It was enough.

"I told Rust. I gave him the information." He was yelling and spitting blood with every angry word now.

"Why did you do that?"

"I was just doing what I was told. It's not my fault. I'm just a messenger."

"Who told you to do it? Was it Kumar?"

"Yes, yes, Kumar told me to do it."

"Why? Is Kumar behind the kidnapping and exchange?"

"I don't know. I was told it was for extra security. I don't know what happened. I really don't."

"Is this Rust guy the one behind the attack?"

"I don't know."

"What was the princess' secret?"

"I don't know."

Mac pulled on the ear again, knowing it hurt. "Sanchez, the other ear."

"Ah, no, man."

"Do it."

Sanchez pulled his matching knife from his belt and grabbed the other ear.

"Fine. Stop, stop, stop. All I know is she had information about a powerful alien race searching for some sort of resource in this region. The Okutans believe there is a conspiracy to harm the UPG and Coalition planets if these aliens get their hands on whatever they are looking for. It'll be devastating. She wanted our help."

"What are they looking for?"

"I don't know."

"Sperry, do you know anything? Who are these aliens?"

"I don't know. All I've heard is they are powerful and from deep space, far beyond the galaxy, farther than humanity has ever gone before. They are called the Noct."

"Who did you hear this from?"

"Prime Ambassador."

Sanchez, backing his knife off, said, "So, Kumar knows about these Noct aliens and their intentions?"

"Yes."

"Who does Rust work for? Does he work for you? Kumar?" Mac asked.

"Nobody works for me. I'm just a lowly messenger."

"So, we've heard. Who does Rust work for?"

"I don't know. Rust is in the shadows. No one knows. He's a ghost. But he is a dangerous and powerful ghost."

"Listen, Sperry, we need more info. Keep it up and you won't get hurt."

He just nodded his head. Blood and snot still oozing onto his suit and dress shirt.

"Why were you at the Trek'et embassy?"

"Kumar told me to deliver a message."

"What was the message, Sperry?"

"It was a secret. Kumar doesn't give me any details. He is very secretive."

"So, how did you deliver the message?"

"He gave me a data card. It was password protected. I don't know what the content of the message was. I gave Bloel Uf'el the card and transferred a large sum of UPG credits to his private account. And then you barged in and now I'm here. I don't know what the message was." After a moment, he said, "I was just doing what I was told."

"One last thing, Sperry. Was Sckrahhg's arrest legitimate? Why was he on Kumar's ship?"

Sperry looked and sounded broken, and he was fighting for consciousness. "Leverage. Nothing is ever what it seems, Major," he said weakly. His eyes closed and chin rested on his chest.

Sanchez pushed on his forehead and then let go. Sperry's head flopped down again. "Did you scare him to death?"

"I don't think so." Mac checked Sperry's pulse. "It's weak, but he's still alive."

"You want me to wake him up again?"

Mac stood, and Sanchez joined him. They looked down at the unconscious Sperry. "You think he has more information?"

"I doubt it."

"I'm still confused. Kumar is dirty. We can't trust that guy. But how deep does it go?"

"Who's this Rust guy?" Sanchez asked as he wiped his knife blade on Sperry's suit sleeve and stowed it in the sheath on his belt.

"No clue, but we need to find out. I think we've got all we're going to get for now. Let's go." Mac and Sanchez left the lounge. "Oh, and that was some pretty good acting on the fly you did there."

"Well, Major Mac, I wasn't quite acting at first."

CHAPTER FORTY-EIGHT

Mercenary Vessel Hammurabi
Quokex

Arthur Rust secured his hip holster and adjusted it into a comfortable position. He then took two blaster pistols from the weapons cabinet and set them on the counter in his private quarters on the Hammurabi. His private room wasn't just a room, but more like a suite of rooms. Rust wasn't into frivolous decoration, but preferred his space to be clean, functional, and spacious. He enjoyed the largest private living quarters on the Hammurabi, which carried over one hundred people.

Rust didn't own the Hammurabi, nor did he own the private company, Babylon Security Services, that owned the mercenary spaceship. Babylon Security Services was one of the United Planetary Government's most lucrative contractors. They built equipment, machinery, and weapons, as well as staffing nearly a million UPG workers. Babylon was also a principal developer of UPG colonial ventures. Their greedy fingers were in every sector of UPG business.

Untold sums of UPG credits flowed into Babylon Security

Services, under public contracts and through the deep black contracts hidden in the shadows of government few people knew about. They were not exclusive to the UPG and human business either, but profited from secret dealings with alien nations. No one outside the accounting department and secret board of directors knew for sure, but rumors suggested Babylon Security Services' business with other nations was even more lucrative than their UPG contracts. There was no limit to the reach or influence Babylon Security Services had in the galaxy.

Rust took each pistol, checking the charge and sliding it into the holster. Babylon's weapons development branch designed and manufactured the pistols. He gazed at the row of energy pulse rifles, standing in their molded rack, deciding if he'd take one or not. He hummed to himself for a moment as he tapped out a drum solo on the countertop with his index fingers.

Why not? Never hurts to be extra prepared, he thought.

He snatched one of the stubby black energy rifles with the shoulder strap and checked the charge before slinging the rifle over his shoulder. His employer manufactured the rifles as well. Before closing the weapons cabinet door, Rust added a couple of extra energy charges to the empty compartments in his holster.

As usual, Rust wore black combat boots, black tactical pants, his double pistol holster, and a black tight-fitting long sleeve t-shirt that accentuated his muscular physique. He was a tall, athletic man, fit and strong for his age. Several years ago, he crested the summit of fifty years of age, but it wasn't slowing him down at all. Rust was making it his mission to remain an example of human physical excellence, even if very few people knew who he was.

There was a soft buzz from his communicator, and he answered it with a terse greeting.

"The shuttle is ready when you are," the deep voice said. It was Rick Vega, Rust's right-hand man.

"Understood. I'll be there in a jiffy. Make sure my seat warmer is on."

"Already is, boss," Vega said, and the line went dead.

Rust took a moment to stand in front of the mirror, and adjusted the holster one last time. He also twirled both ends of his bushy handlebar mustache with both hands and straightened his triangular shaped goatee. His wavy black hair, which was streaked with gray like his facial hair, he combed to one side. It looked perfect today. He swept his hand through the right side for good measure and left his suite.

Within the deep, dark, shadowy bowels of Babylon's secret business dealings around the galaxy was a group managed by Arthur Rust that no one knew about. In the world of *off the books* secret contracts, Arthur Rust operated in the shadows of the shadows' shadows. No one even whispered about his work. His group didn't even have a name. He was a ghost, and because he was excellent at what he did, his shady benefactors paid him an obscenely excessive salary. Not only did he have full control of the Hammurabi and staff, but he also had unchecked access to all the resources of Babylon Security Services at his fingertips.

He strutted through the corridors of the ship to the small shuttle bay where the little armored and weaponized jump ship was running and ready to go. He gave a lazy salute to the shuttle bay crew sitting behind the thick airtight glass. The crew were ready to operate the airlocks for the jump ship to exit the Hammurabi on its way to mountainous planet Quokex.

Rust ducked down into the small craft. Rick Vega sat behind the piloting controls. He was a massive man, about twenty years Rust's junior. Vega wore the same black tactical outfit and looked uncomfortable, squeezed into the pilot's seat. Vega was head and shoulders taller than anyone else, at over two meters tall. His bulging arm and chest muscles were obvious through his black t-shirt, and his black hair was pulled into a ponytail.

Rust pulled the rifle off his shoulder and slid into the co-pilot's seat next to Vega.

"Ready to go, boss?" Vega asked. His gravely baritone voice fit his appearance.

"Let's light this candle," Rust said enthusiastically. Rust did everything with an excess of enthusiasm. It was as if he was always having the time of his life.

Vega nodded toward Rust's rifle and said, "Decided on some extra firepower, I see."

"Yes, I did."

"Me too."

"Well, Rick, I wouldn't expect anything less. These hairy beasts are so unpredictable and uncivilized, we don't know what they might do."

"So, if they don't cooperate, you'll just put them down?" Vega asked matter-of-factly.

"Ab-so-lutely. I call that Co-lat-eral Dam-age, my friend," Rust said, emphasizing each syllable. "These creatures are as dumb as a box of rocks. Dumb as a fence post. They might try to double-cross us, and they'll learn quickly I'm no one to mess with. Can't double-cross a double-crosser."

"Well, actually, they won't learn anything because they'll be dead," Vega said dryly.

"Ha! Indeed!" Rust shouted and slapped Vega on the shoulder. "You can't out-evil the devil, can ya, Rick?"

"Not a chance."

When the jump ship departed the Hammurabi, Quokex's lone moon glowing against the vast black curtain of space filled their window. It was an impressive, picturesque view. Vega piloted the little jump ship away from the Hammurabi, and a dull gray planet came into view. He traversed the short distance of open space and entered Quokex's upper atmosphere. The rough vibration from the upper atmosphere smoothed out as they approached the planet's surface, which was covered by a dense layer of ominous storm clouds. Lightning flashed in the distance, highlighting the endless layers of gloomy clouds. The jump ship's lights looked like rigid beams of yellow glass piercing the clouds as they zipped through the storm.

"Lovely as always here on Quokex," Arthur Rust said. He

glanced at the navigation screen. "Stay on this course and follow the beacon in."

Vega grunted in response while flying against the storm winds that shoved the tiny vessel around. His attention bounced between the sensor displays, control buttons, and the unsettling lightning strikes flashing outside the small ship.

"When we get down there, we'll find the landing zone built along the side of the mountaintop. It's precarious on a clear day."

Vega grunted again, and the ship suddenly dropped about twenty meters before he resumed control. Rust felt his stomach flip from the sudden drop. Both stopped breathing for a moment.

"Whoa there," Rust said with a laugh. "It's like a buckin' bronco out here."

Vega ignored Rust's comments and concentrated on keeping the ship on track as he exited the cloud layer and slowed the ship to approach speed. The overcast sky was a depressing gray, and snowflakes, heavy with water, swirled around them in the wind. Flying by instruments and sensors, Vega entered the wide canyon between two rocky mountain ridges leading to the Bone Rattler compound.

Vega, more relaxed now, spoke for the first time since leaving the Hammurabi. "This visibility is horrible."

"It gets much worse here. There it is." Rust pointed out the sloped front window at the blinking red lights in the distance.

The landing zone included six circular landing pads built on the side of the mountain in the narrowest part of the canyon. The canyon between the mountains narrowed into a deep and severe gash between solid rock cliff faces. It looked like the strain of tectonic plates shifting caused a giant quake, ripping the rocky mountain in half. The resulting crevasse between the protruding cliff faces descended into an ominous darkness below. Through the poor visibility, they could see the shadowy shapes of the landing pads supported by massive metal stilts and girders, suspending them above the unseen depths of the crevasse below. Steel bridges interconnected the pads.

"Is it always like this?" Vega asked. The small ship was being pushed around by the winds gusting out of the crevasse.

"Always. This is actually a nice day for Quokex," Rust said.

"How many times have you been here?"

"This would be my third time. This is the first since these stupid two-legged cows moved in. The first two trips were scouting the potential of this old base."

"How'd that go?"

"The scouting? Not great. This place is a total dump. What idiot builds a base in a mountain on a cliff face? It's just an old loser outpost with ancient equipment. It's uninhabitable for civilized people. But these gangly, fur-brained retards seem to love it. I think they are too stupid to know anything different."

Vega's amused dark eyes glanced at Rust. He grunted in agreement.

Three sets of the landing pads contained larger ships, so Vega set his little jump ship down on an empty pad and started the shutdown sequence.

A moment later, Rust and Vega stepped out onto the thick metal grate landing pad. Snow covered all surfaces except the landing pads, where the snow fell through the grating. Vega looked around at the menacing mountainside and rock cliff face, admiring the severe landscape. For a better view, he walked to the edge of the landing pad to gaze down into the crevasse below.

"No welcoming party?" Rust said loudly from the ship. "How rude."

"What's down there?" Vega asked.

"Who knows," Rust said, "I don't want to find out."

They trudged through the swirling snowstorm, careful to not slip and fall on the icy metal. The temperature was below freezing, and the cold was biting at the exposed skin on Rust's face and hands. His whole body shivered after only a minute.

Wide metal bridges interconnected the landing pads' grating material, with handrails on the edges. Lights mounted to the railing emitted a soft yellow glow in the snowy gloom. In the distance, the large bridge crossed over the crevasse from the landing zone to the old compound building. As they walked across the bridge, they couldn't resist gazing over the handrails into the pitch blackness of the seemingly bottomless crevasse. As they neared the end of the bridge, the massive metal door of the compound building jutting out from the side of the mountain in front of them clanged loudly and screeched open.

When the door stopped moving, and the unbearable screeching noise stopped, Rust saw the Bone Rattler greeting party standing in the lighted corridor, but they didn't step into the storm. *How rude,* he thought. There were three Bone Rattlers, all wearing their bone armor, and two carried rifles. The one standing in the middle wore his skull helmet with wide antlers.

"Well, Braeknn," Rust said with an irritated tone once he stepped through the enormous doorway into the barren corridor with the Bone Rattlers. Looking up at Braeknn's fierce eyes, Rust said, "You couldn't be bothered to greet us at the ship? I thought y'all liked the cold snow? Didn't your momma teach you any manners?"

Behind the skull helmet, Braeknn bared his fangs and growled, "We do like the cold. We only come out for important visitors."

"Well, now, Braeknn, it's not very polite to treat your business partners like that," Rust chided. "And just a little tip for you." He pointed to the big metal door. "Why don't you put some lubricating oil on that door? How can you stand listening to that screeching noise?"

"Come, Arthur Rust," Braeknn said, and he turned and started down the corridor as the door began its noisy closing procedure.

Rust and Vega, happy to be out of the freezing snow, followed Braeknn with Bone Rattlers on either side of them. Rust pointed to the rifles they carried.

"Braeknn, when you are guys going to give up on those terrible Trek'et rifles and buy some of ours? You know ours are so much better than that Trek'et garbage."

Lumbering down the barren corridor in front of them, Braeknn said, "Trek'et give us a good deal, unlike you greedy humans."

Rust exploded in laughter. "Humans, greedy?" he asked with surprise. "You have no room to talk. Have you seen your fees?"

"Our work is very specialized," Braeknn growled with irritation.

"Your work is thuggery. Y'all are just a bunch of hairy space pirates. Nothing specialized about that. I could teach a couple of Coorlitchian monkeys to do this job. I'm surprised you don't beat your chests like a bunch of gorillas." Rust laid the insults on heavy to get a rise out of Braeknn. "We could have hired any number of stupid criminal mercenaries. You should be thankful we used you. Next time, I'll pay you with a pile of bananas and you'll be in paradise."

Braeknn growled but said nothing. The other two Bone Rattlers tightened their grip on their rifles with their clawed hands.

They led Rust and Vega down a couple of side corridors, and Rust noticed the occasional Bone Rattler sentry standing guard.

"Now, time's a wasting. Take me straight to the princess. We need to interrogate her right now."

"Settle down, little angry human," Braeknn said, which got a good laugh out of Rust. "You just arrived. General Sckrahhg says talk first."

"Oh, yes, of course, the infamous general is here. See how we follow through with our end of the agreement? Now, you need to follow through with your part."

They turned again, and the corridor ended in a set of double metal doors. An armed Bone Rattler stood on each side of the door. Braeknn opened the door and said, "This way, Arthur Rust."

Rust glared at Braeknn through squinty eyes and entered the room. He scanned the space to assess risks. Rust was confident he and Vega could fight off several Bone Rattlers, but he didn't like the idea of being stuck in a room full of them. He didn't trust these space pirates and wouldn't put it past them to try some sort of double-cross at the last minute.

He remembered being in the room on a previous scouting trip. It was a cavernous space with tall ceilings, plain gray concrete walls, and a few dim lights that flickered. He counted twenty total Bone

Rattlers standing around the front of the room near the door. To the right, a few more sat at computer and communication equipment. Others sat around a table eating meat and sloshing drinks of some kind. The smell of the rotting meat nearly made Rust gag. He fought the urge to dry heave. The left side of the room was full of crates of Trek'et rifles and other gear. He recognized the Trek'et language on the side of the crates.

The centerpiece of the cavernous room, however, was the Bone Rattler sitting on the oversized throne, made of massive bones. Four Bone Rattlers stood beside the throne holding rifles.

Rust leaned toward Vega and quietly said, "What a pompous bunch of cows. All the same, stay sharp."

The Bone Rattler on the throne stood dramatically and snarled, "Arthur Rust, welcome to our outpost."

"Hello, again, General Sckrahhg, I'm glad we could orchestrate your safe return to your people. Now, where is my princess?"

CHAPTER FORTY-NINE

Bone Rattler Compound
Quokex Colony

It took Omo-Binrin longer to convince the other Okutans they could do it than it took describing the plan itself. The plan was simple, but required courage and desperate action. The Okutans were a meek and quiet people. They were gentle and elegant. They knew how to work hard, but they weren't comfortable in an adventure like this, let alone the violence. These particular Okutans were from the Okutan high society. They were members of the social bubble around the royal family. They were more at home at an elegant ball than executing an escape plan.

Huddled together on the hard, damp floor, Omo-Binrin looked at her people. In the darkness of their prison cell, she saw her own personal attendants, renowned chefs, artists, musicians, some of her administrative support team, and general staff from the royal vessel. As she considered her plan, she recognized the disadvantage of having so many females, and none of her security force.

She remembered the faces of her beloved people who were

viciously killed just days ago and felt deep sadness and regret. Then, the face of Jagoon. Jagoon was so good to her and her family for so many years. He was a legend in the Okutan security force. She assumed he died in the ambush, and it gave her the resolve she needed to execute her plan. *Do it for dear Jagoon. Make him proud.*

After encouraging her people they could accomplish their part of the plan, they agreed and everyone took their places when the time came. Omo-Binrin knew the monsters would be back with the next food drop on schedule. Their timing was consistent and predictable now. The Okutans stood in the darkness without moving or making a sound, staying alert.

The anticipation of what was to come ate away at her insides. Omo-Binrin felt the anxiety and adrenaline surging through her veins and knew her people were frightened. She just hoped they were ready.

Oh, I wish I had my swords, she thought. *Even a staff or a tool. Anything would be better than nothing. Ugh. Be tough. Be resolute. Be strong. Jagoon, I wish you were here. But he's not, Omo-Binrin. You've got to do this. You are the weapon now. Attack fast. Attack with extreme violence.*

Sounds beyond the door interrupted her personal pep talk. Their ugly growling voices on the other side of the door filtered into the room. Her scalp frill raised as her mind zeroed in on the task at hand. She closed her eyes.

Princess Omo-Binrin stood alone near the door, against the chilly wall. She would be behind the heavy metal door when they opened it. The other Okutans stood in the shadows behind the noisy and smelly industrial machine. From where she stood, she couldn't see any of them in the dark, and she felt alone.

The door rattled and banged open. Yellow light sliced through, illuminating the center of the room where they usually sat. But now, the floor was empty. There was not a soul in sight.

The two Bone Rattler guards entered the room in their usual lazy fashion, and it took them a moment to figure out that the room was empty.

The first growled, "Hey, where are they?"

"What happened?" the other shouted. "Were the prisoners moved?"

"I don't know."

The two massive Bone Rattlers stepped deeper into the room. The one with the food and water buckets just stood there dumbfounded, and the other with the rifle turned around several times in the yellow pool of light, confused. He was growling out many words that Omo-Binrin didn't understand. As they moved, their bone armor rattled against each other, creating the hollow rattling sound.

Her people timed their move perfectly. As the Bone Rattlers were caught off guard and confused, the Okutans broke into two groups and came running out of the shadows on both sides of the machine. The first group closest to the door ran as quickly as their cold and tired bodies would go toward the open door and the corridor beyond, while the other group ran at the Bone Rattlers.

The Bone Rattlers responded just as she predicted. First, they were startled at the movement from the dark, but then they tried to react to the two groups of small blue bodies moving in different directions. The Bone Rattler with the buckets tried to set the buckets down and pursue the Okutans who were already at the door, and the other also moved that direction and they bumped into each other.

The second group of Okutans crashed into the Bone Rattler without the rifle. There were ten of them, and while they were lightweight and not strong alone, ten of them overwhelmed the surprised Bone Rattler.

Princess Omo-Binrin now made her move as planned. Ten of the youngest and strongest Okutans wrapped up a Bone Rattler. Fifteen of the others poured into the bright corridor, and the Bone Rattler with the rifle tried to pull the rabid Okutans off his partner.

Omo-Binrin took the few steps from behind the door, moving toward the Bone Rattler with the rifle and rolled into a smooth cartwheel that launched her body with extra momentum into the air and a blindingly fast helicopter kick. Her elegant dress, with its diamond decorations, flowed like a cape and sparkled under the light from the corridor. She aimed perfectly, and her right foot swung around and connected full force in the throat of the distracted beast. Her foot smashed into the soft squishy part of the Bone Rattler's neck above the collarbone and below the bone mask.

As she landed softly in a squat, on her feet, she heard her victim gargle and choke. He released the small Okutan he was pulling on and reached up to his throat in agony. Omo-Binrin was sure she smashed his trachea. She didn't delay even a second, but sprung up from her squat and put the heel of her foot into the abdomen of the beast. She aimed for just below the rib cage, above the stomach, and about six inches behind the target. Her heel connected with the brutal force of a hammer. She felt the exterior bones of his armor snap and she felt something inside snap as well.

The Bone Rattler stumbled backwards on his heels now, gasping and choking. Omo-Binrin was in complete control now. She followed the flailing giant toward the back wall, away from the others. She threw her body into a flip by dipping her head and rotating her legs over her head in a forward rotation, completed with her right leg hammering into the extended rifle carrying arm of the Bone Rattler.

By throwing her body into acrobatic maneuvers, she enhanced the power of each attack, and this last one was no different. Her leg impacted the dazed Bone Rattler with enough force to cause him to drop the rifle. The heavy black metal weapon clanged against the hard floor as she was raising herself back up. She straightened her dress and reached down to pick up the heavy weapon. She held it in two hands with the butt of the rifle tucked against her stomach. The rifle's warm metal felt smooth. Her finger found the trigger and she fired. The room filled with flashing red energy erupting from the mouth of the weapon. It smashed into the Bone Rattler's chest, and he crumpled to the floor. She shot him again as he lay on the floor, and his body convulsed as the second blast smashed into his body.

The Okutans screamed at the shots, and she turned toward the group. She saw the first group of Okutans huddle together in the corridor, waiting. A couple of Okutans were on the floor, knocked down by the other Bone Rattler, frantically fighting off the mass of bodies hanging on his legs, arms, and around his neck. They saw the princess with the rifle now, and as planned, they all let go of the Bone Rattler.

Princess Omo-Binrin put two close range blasts into the chest of the final Bone Rattler. The red flashes from the energy blasts cast warped shadows on the walls, and the static in the air was palpable. The Bone Rattler's dead body flopped to the floor on his face, and the foul odor of singed fur wafted toward her.

"Let's go," she said matter-of-factly, and shooed the remaining Okutans out into the bright corridor. "Is everyone here?" They did a quick count and confirmed everyone was accounted for.

She pulled the metal door closed and began down the corridor in a light jog, rifle leading the way. Looking back to her people, she said, "We must hurry. Follow me and stay close together."

PART FIVE

We're fighting a war we can't predict against an enemy we don't understand

— COLONEL TATE MILLER, SPACE WARFARE GROUP COMMANDER

CHAPTER FIFTY

Interplanetary Navy Battlecruiser McDaniels
Near Terra Libertas
Hours Earlier…

When the communication screen went black and Mac's distressed face disappeared, Dan *DJ* Jameson slumped in his seat and rubbed his forehead with the palm of his hand.

"This is not good," he said to himself, alone in his personal quarters.

In the tray, on the table next to him, was a long, thin, smoldering cigar. It was black in color, and a wisp of smoke snaked toward the ceiling. He snatched it up and jammed it between his teeth. He loved the aroma of this Coorlichtian tobacco, but its usual calming effect was absent in the face of Mac's recklessness.

Mac contacted him outside of normal channels, choosing to talk with DJ privately, which only added to his trepidation about this entire situation. *Why was Mac being so reckless? Has he lost his mind?*

DJ stood. He knew he had no time to waste. Mac left him with little time to react. He made his way down the corridor and into the preparation room where Bones, Cory, and the injured but recently released Jerry Tao sat laughing and playing a virtual reality video game. Despite being bandaged, Tao appeared strong.

"DJ, you gotta get in here," the lanky Bones said.

"Yeah, come on," Cory added.

"Can't right now, guys," he replied through cigar-clenching teeth. "Cory, a quick minute?"

"Sure thing." Cory handed the visor and controller to Jerry. "Be careful now, Tao, Bones is pretty good at this, and we don't need you suffering any more injuries."

Cory joined DJ near the door. "What's up?"

DJ pulled him through the door into the hallway for privacy. They were about the same height. Both were taller than the average and extremely fit. While a lot of the Space Warfare Group operators focused on muscle bulk, DJ and Cory built muscle like endurance athletes with ropey lean muscles. They both had wavy black hair and dark stubble on their rugged faces.

"We've got a serious problem." DJ puffed on the cigar twice, releasing a plume of aromatic smoke.

"I don't like the sound of that."

DJ pulled the cigar from his mouth. "Well, it gets worse. I just heard from Mac."

"Oh, really?"

"Yup, it's not good."

"I don't like the sound of that."

"He and Sanchez are on a stolen Trek'et spacecraft traveling at *FTL* to the Bone Rattler secret base."

Cory's jaw dropped. "What? How'd they find them?" He shook his head. "Wait, why are they going alone? Have they lost their minds?"

"Apparently. And, to make it worse, Mac knows he needs us and, of course, he knows he has to report locating the Bone Rattler base, but he waited to notify us so he could get there first."

"Why would he do that?" Cory threw his arms up.

"Partly, because he's hell-bent on revenge."

"Because of Sam?"

"Yeah. You know, Sam was like a brother to him. But there is more to it. This part makes me think Mac hasn't lost his mind. I need you to keep this quiet. Not only from the other guys, but from Miller, from everyone. You got that? Just you and I know."

Cory nodded, but his icy blue eyes betraying his skepticism. Cory knew Mac better than most, but the puzzle pieces were not connecting.

"Are you with me on this?" DJ asked after Cory only nodded.

"Yes, of course. Anything for Mac," Cory said.

"Mac is suggesting there's some sort of conspiracy within the UPG, and maybe the Army. He's worried if the word gets out, they'll try to stop him, and maybe kill him, before he can get to the Bone Rattlers."

Cory exhaled and rubbed the scar on his cheek. "I don't know, DJ. I mean, that sounds crazy."

"Yeah, I don't know what to think. I do know I'd trust Mac in any situation over anyone."

"Even over Miller?" Cory asked.

It was a good question. DJ held his cigar up to look at the smoldering tip as he pondered for a moment.

"I don't think Miller is dirty, but he could be unaware and inadvertently provide information to the mole or conspirators." DJ shrugged and stuck the cigar between his teeth.

"Did Mac give any more information?"

"No, that's the meat of it. So, listen, I've gotta go inform Miller." DJ looked around. "I'm not sure I'll make it back alive. I'm sure Miller is going to blow a gasket."

"You think he'll shoot the messenger?"

"Oh, for sure. I think Miller is going to shoot anyone he sees after he hears what Mac is doing. And, Sanchez? Can you believe that guy? I get Mac going off the reservation, but why would Sanchez risk his career?"

"Well, he looks up to Mac. We all do."

"Would you risk your career for him?" DJ asked.

"Yeah, I would."

"Me too," DJ said. "We may still face that decision."

"This is an unbelievable situation. Where'd they get the ship?"

"Get this, he didn't tell me much, but it sounds like they interrogated the Trek'et Ambassador on Terra Libertas and stole his ship. That's where they learned of the Bone Rattlers' location."

Cory groaned. "They are in real trouble, then."

"They've put all of us in a bind. While I go get my head ripped off by Miller, I need you to work up some information on an old, failed colony called Quokex," he spelled it for Cory. "And work up some options for a Starhawk assault. I'm pretty sure we'll *FTL* the *McDaniels* and jump the Starhawk near the planet."

Cory raised an eyebrow.

"Plan for a full fire team. Quietly figure out who is available and get the load-out list prepped. We'll have to move fast." DJ put the cigar between his teeth again. "Keep it quiet for now and everything will be last minute."

Cory raised his fist, and DJ bumped it with his own.

Colonel Miller was, according to his office staff, in the situation room. As DJ approached the secure access-controlled door, he realized he still had his Coorlichtian cigar. He wasn't supposed to have the cigar on the ship at all, but he got away with it in the Space Warfare Group's area with no comment. He knew their special status afforded some luxuries other soldiers couldn't enjoy. But he was smart enough to not to press his limits by strolling into the situation room, puffing away like he owned the place.

He looked around the corridor. There was nothing but the heavy metal door and the retina scanner next to it. No garbage chutes, no shelves, no artwork, nothing. So he snuffed out the burning tip of the cigar on the sole of his boot. He then slipped the cigar in the small accessory pocket on the sleeve of his gray fatigues.

After a quick scan of his retina, the door clicked, and he entered the nerve center of the *McDaniels'* military operations. The room was dark and cold, illuminated by the green and blue light of screens and communication equipment. Several oversized screens hung on the walls, and the large conference table sat at the center of a raised platform with a view of all the screens. In the back corner were several communication specialists sitting in front of screens with keyboards and headsets, juggling the incoming and outgoing information.

To DJ's right and left, on either side of the door, were two beefy men wearing white uniforms and reflective visors. He grimaced. *If the Elite Guard were here, then…yup, there he was.* Standing at a smaller screen across the room was the diminutive form of Prime Ambassador Kumar with Colonel Miller, two staffers, and two additional Elite Guards.

DJ approached Colonel Miller and Prime Ambassador Kumar. Miller saw him right away.

"Master Sergeant Jameson, what is it?" Miller asked with his usual irritation. He didn't look at DJ, but read from a tablet screen, too busy to make eye contact. Kumar turned toward him, though. While his suit and appearance were as immaculate as ever, he looked tense. DJ just walked into a pressure cooker.

"Colonel. Prime Ambassador," DJ saluted. I just had a conversation with Major Lambert."

Miller's head spun toward him, and his eyes bored into DJ like the laser drills his dad used to mine minerals on Terra Placidus' Mount Pax. DJ stood a little more rigid, staring straight ahead, legs spread, hands behind his back.

"Major Lambert contacted you?"

"Yes, sir. Just a couple minutes ago, on my personal line. I came to find you right away, sir."

Miller handed the tablet to a staffer and approached DJ. Kumar approached as well.

"What did he say?"

"Well, sir, he told me he and Sanchez have found the Bone Rattler base and they will arrive in a couple of hours, and he needs reinforcements. We need to organize an assault force."

"Reinforcements!" Miller exploded. "Reinforcements! Who does he think he is?"

DJ said nothing.

"Where is the Bone Rattler base?"

"He said it is on an old colony called Quokex."

"Did he happen to tell you how he came by this information?"

"He said he got it from the Trek'et Ambassador on Terra Libertas."

"Well, he obviously left out the part where he and that idiot Sanchez broke into the Trek'et embassy and assaulted the Ambassador. Did he tell you that?" Miller was fuming, shouting every word.

"No, sir, he did not."

"Well, isn't that convenient? Did he tell you he also assaulted and kidnapped Prime Ambassador Kumar's associate, Aldo Sperry?"

"No, sir, he did not."

"Of course not. He's completely lost control. He's a criminal on the run. I should have locked him up when we returned from Yioturno. He's gone totally mad. Did he tell you that at least one Trek'et died in their assault on the embassy?"

"No, sir, he did not."

"Do you know how much trouble he has caused for us, Master Sergeant?"

"I can't imagine, sir."

Miller's face was red, and DJ could see veins popping out on his forehead. "That is right. You couldn't possibly know the difficulty he has caused us."

Kumar spoke up. "This is a diplomatic catastrophe the likes we haven't seen in a generation. Major Lambert is single-handedly ruining our position in the galaxy. We'll be cleaning up this mess for years! Decades!"

"Sir, with all due respect, I believe Major Lambert is still trying to rescue the Okutan princess-"

Miller cut him off before he could complete his sentence. "He better hope by some supernatural miracle he finds that princess alive, or we'll throw him into a hole so dark and so deep, he'll wish he was never born!"

DJ said nothing, just stared straight ahead. This was thin ice for sure. And he could hear that thin ice cracking under his feet. He needed to tread carefully and not get himself or the others caught in the crossfire. *Way to go, Mac.*

Miller ordered, "Organize your team and present me with your plan in thirty minutes. I want you to plan to assault this old colony with two objectives. First, to search for the princess and eliminate these Bone Rattler monsters. And second, to apprehend Major Lambert and Sergeant Sanchez. You will bring them back here, under arrest. Do I make myself clear?"

"Crystal, sir."

"And," Kumar added, "you will take Captain Scott and his team with you to ensure you handle everything appropriately." Kumar pointed to the short muscular man with wavy black hair standing a few meters off. Captain Scott tipped his head. DJ couldn't see his eyes, but knew Scott by reputation. He was former Army Stryker Force and as tough as they come.

This mission is shaping up to be a royal pain in my buttocks. Mac is going to owe me big time. If he survives.

"Master Sergeant, do you understand your orders?" Miller asked.

"Yessir."

"The clock is ticking. Get it done."

DJ saluted, turned, and exited. A dense rock of dread was settling in his gut. After a few steps toward the exit, Miller called out to him.

"And, Master Sergeant." DJ stopped and turned back. "Don't even think about ignoring my orders by helping Lambert."

"Would never think of it, sir," he responded and left the situation room.

When he reached the corridor outside the situation room, he paused for a moment to let his nerves settle. *Mac, what have you done?* DJ unzipped the small pocket on this sleeve and retrieved his cigar.

He took a moment - probably the last moment of peace he'd have for a while - with the cigar between his teeth, raised the lighter and inhaled. The small fire at the tip of the cigar glowed as he inhaled. He puffed out a thick cloud, shook his head and jogged down the hall.

CHAPTER FIFTY-ONE

General Sckrahhg sauntered toward Rust, who stood as tall and firm as possible. The Bone Rattler towered over Arthur Rust. He'd woven colorful beads and small bones into the beard of golden fur around his face and neck. The bone armor he was wearing rattled menacingly.

Sckrahhg bared his fangs in an ugly expression. Rust couldn't tell if he was attempting to smile or intimidate him. Either way, it wasn't pretty, and it didn't work. Rust was neither put at ease nor intimidated. In his mind, Sckrahhg was an imbecile he could barely tolerate.

"Arthur Rust, you are so impatient," Sckrahhg growled. "First, let's talk about the terms of our agreement."

Rust jabbed a rigid gloved finger toward Sckrahhg. "Listen here, General. We are not discussing the terms of our agreement again. We had an agreement and we're sticking to it."

The other Bone Rattlers moved closer, sensing Rust's negative energy. Rick Vega also stepped closer, bringing his rifle up a bit.

In a calm but threatening voice, Rust said, "Sckrahhg, you have two simple choices. One," he pointed his finger toward the ceiling, "you can choose to double-cross us, and you know you'll never escape our reach. We will hunt you down and pull your intestines out through your nostrils. None of you animals will survive. We'll make you extinct. You'll be a distant memory that no one cares about." He dramatically lifted a second finger. "Or, two, you can take me to the princess right now, and you'll remain a valued asset and we'll make you rich beyond your wildest harebrained imagination. So, what's it going to be?"

Sckrahhg looked around the room at his troops, and then back to Rust, and began laughing. His beastly laugh disgusted Rust. The noises escaping his ugly scrunched face were somewhere between a snarl and gagging to death. Rust grimaced. He couldn't help himself.

"Arthur Rust, you are a funny human. We are good friends. Good partners. I make…what you call it? Ah, yes…I make joke."

"Sckrahhg, the only joke around here is you."

"Yes, I am funny joke," Sckrahhg snarled with more laughing.

Rust looked at Vega and rolled his eyes.

"Now that we have that unpleasant business out of the way, time is wasting. Where is my princess?" He overemphasized every word.

"She is close. They should be feeding them now. Will you take all of them?"

"What do you mean, all of them?"

"We have many of the little blue creatures with the princess."

"You captured more than just the princess?" Rust shrugged. "Well, they're your problem now. I don't care what you do with them. Consider them a bonus. Do what you want with them. Sell them into slavery, for all I care."

"That is a good deal," Sckrahhg nodded. "Now, Arthur Rust, let's go get the princess."

Sckrahhg left the cavernous, rank room first, followed by Braeknn and four other Bone Rattlers wearing bone armor and carrying their hefty black rifles. Rust and Vega trailed behind. Sckrahhg led them down the cold barren corridors, under the flickering yellow lights, to a heavy metal door.

"They are here," Sckrahhg said and motioned for one of his warriors to open the door.

The Bone Rattler stepped in front of the group, used one of several keys to unlock the metal door, and he pulled it open.

"Grab the princess for Arthur Rust and leave the others," Sckrahhg commanded one of his warriors. This Bone Rattler entered the room and spun around in the slash of yellow light spilling into the room. He growled something in his native language and all the other Bone Rattlers, including Sckrahhg, stormed through the door into the small room.

Rust knew immediately he had a problem. He couldn't depend on these beasts to do a man's job. He and Vega followed through the door into the dark room, both pulling flashlights from their belt and scanning the room. It was a small industrial room containing an antique power generator system. The room smelled terrible. Rust hated the stink of animal waste mixed with blood and death. The room was empty. He saw no Okutans. Laying on the floor in a puddle of spilt water and food slop were two dead Bone Rattlers. Sckrahhg and the others stood over the bodies.

"What is happening here?" Rust asked. "Where is the princess?"

Sckrahhg let out a guttural scream; fury exploding out of him. "They have escaped. Find them!"

"You better find her, Sckrahhg. This cannot happen!" Rust yelled.

Just as Sckrahhg was snarling orders to his warriors, another Bone Rattler approached, running down the corridor. "General Sckrahhg," he growled as he reached the door. Sckrahhg followed him into the corridor with Rust right on his heels.

"What is it?" Sckrahhg boomed.

"General, an unidentified spacecraft is approaching the outpost."

"United Planetary Government ship?"

"No, General. Trek'et," he snarled.

"What? That cannot be."

Rust tried to calculate in his own mind why a Trek'et vessel was approaching. He had to find the princess and get off Quokex as soon as possible. Just as he was considering his next move, his communicator pad buzzed in his pocket. He pulled it out, reading the simple text statement: *You've got company. Trek'et freighter en route. Assume hostile intent.*

Sckrahhg shook his fists at his Bone Rattlers. "Horrk, take warriors and find the princess, now!" He grabbed Braeknn by the arm and pulled him away from the door. "Braeknn, take your team and confront that ship!"

PRINCESS OMO-BINRIN OBA heard the guttural scream of fury from the monster echoing through the hard surfaces of the compound. The others flinched in fear. *Well, they now know we've escaped,* she thought. *Or trying to escape.* She wasn't sure how to get out of this building. It was like a maze of corridors. Every turn made her more confused. She'd found their way back to their prison cell when she heard the scream. They hid in the shadows of a darkened portion of the facility. While the others remained pressed together against the cold rough wall, Princess Omo-Binrin poked her head around the corner and looked down the long corridor toward the scream, hoping to remain concealed in the shadows as she watched.

She saw one of their monstrous captors run toward their prison room. A moment later, she saw several of the monsters come out of the room. As she watched the scene, her heart skipped a beat when she saw two humans emerge from the direction of the prison room. At first, she had the urge to shout out and move their way, thinking they were there to rescue them. But something wasn't right. *Why are these humans with the monsters?*

Several of the monsters charged off in the other direction, stomping and growling in anger. Thankfully, they moved away from her, rather than toward their hiding place.

One of the humans had long black hair and was tall, almost as tall as the monsters. He wore all black and carried a rifle. The other looked normal human height, with wavy dark hair on his head and on his face. He also wore the same black clothes and seemed like the leader. They were speaking with the angry monster. It sounded like they were arguing, and angry.

Are they here for us? Are they safe? Omo-Binrin didn't know. *I've got to get our people out of this compound to safety.*

She listened as she peered cautiously around the corner. She could hear words, now that the furious screaming stopped. The two men stood face-to-face with two monsters, talking.

It surprised her these monsters could speak several languages, including her own. She heard the word *princess* used several times. They *were* talking about her.

The human said, "You'd better find her right now, General, or things are going to go badly for you." The hairy-faced human was jabbing his finger at the large furry monsters, and looked like he was about to explode in violence. "We paid you good money to capture her, and we got you returned to your people. You owe me! Now, find her!"

Omo-Binrin's scalp frill involuntarily became rigid as she panicked. *What am I going to do?*

She stood, frozen in place, unsure what to do next or where to go. The last of the monsters turned and stomped in the direction away from her while the hairy-faced human and the other stayed where they were. He turned in her direction and ran his hand through his wavy, dark hair in frustration. He said nothing, but just gazed down the hallway toward her.

Oh, no. She pulled back behind the wall. She closed her eyes tightly for a moment. *Go away, go away, go away.*

She peeked around the corner again and he was closer, about halfway from where he was before, stilling coming her way. Her eyes locked onto his, and she heard him whisper in a voice that made her skin crawl, "Ah, there you are, Princess Omo-Binrin."

An immediate surge of fear raced through her body and her scalp frill snapped into its full extended width. They were in big trouble. She didn't hesitate; she wasn't one to hesitate in protecting herself or her people. Jagoon had trained her well. Lifting the heavy rifle chest high, she pulled the trigger multiple times and sent three energy blasts toward the humans. The first two shots went wild, crashing into the floor and wall in front of them. Moving the barrel across her field of view, the third shot hit the man who spoke her name in the lower leg. He grimaced and stumbled to the floor, causing the bigger human to reach down to help him.

Princess Omo-Binrin didn't wait to see what happened, but turned and pushed her people farther into the darkness of the building, spitting out a fear-infused whisper, "Run!"

CHAPTER FIFTY-TWO

Trek'et Utility Ship
Quokex
5 Minutes Earlier...

"Coming out of *FTL*...right...now," Luella Taylor said, while she worked multiple ship controls at the same time to pull the spacecraft out of hyper speed. Her concentration impressed Mac. Her eyes were darting back and forth between the alarms and data displays, juggling multiple variables and controls in her mind. "OK, this should drop us right on top of Quokex," she said.

Mac assumed Taylor would have at least a co-pilot to assist with these control maneuvers. This ship, like many others, was intended for a piloting team, but in a pinch, could be flown by a single pilot.

Mac stood behind Taylor's swivel chair, looking at the same monitors and view screen, feeling frustrated he couldn't help. Luella Taylor was a superb pilot, and she was making do with what she had. He wasn't a pilot and received no cross-training, like some of the other men. *Like Sam,* he thought. *He was a decent pilot.* Sam's face came into his mind.

He shook the emotional thoughts from his head and looked over at Sanchez, who stood to his right with a helpless expression on his face. Mac knew Sanchez wasn't cross-trained either. Spaceships weren't in either of their specialty toolboxes. They were both trained in the Space Warfare Group's primary purpose of killing bad guys.

He gripped the side of the chair as he felt the dizzying effects of coming out of *FTL*. The view screen suddenly filled with the dark form of the planet Quokex and the nearby star sparkling behind, with light rays spreading brilliantly into the upper left corner of the screen.

"There she is. Quokex," Taylor said. "Scanners on."

She tapped various buttons and turned a dial. Then she took manual control of the craft, pointing the utility ship tangentially to the planet, beginning to travel the circumference. The screen now displayed the planet along the bottom, with pinpoint white stars filling most of the screen.

"What's that?" Sanchez asked, while pointing at a flashing light.

"Ahh, that, oddly enough, looks like a signal beacon," Taylor said.

She tapped more buttons, and the screen changed to a diagram of Quokex that zoomed around and positioned with a red flashing beacon in the center. "I guess this is the place. It's just a low energy locator beacon."

"Like a distress call or something?" Mac asked.

"No, this is an old style, like a coordinates beacon used for location and direction. It's so low energy, only those in orbit can detect it."

"That ain't too smart," Sanchez quipped. "Not very secret if your secret base has a signal beacon to help you find it."

"Oh, and look at that," Taylor added. "It still has UPG credentials. Old though. That's where we'll find the old colony."

"That's where we'll find the Bone Rattlers," Mac said. "Set course for those coordinates."

Just then, another alarm sounded, this one with a larger flashing light and a muted horn.

Before anyone could ask, Taylor explained, "Oh, no. Ah, there's another ship in the vicinity." Her voice had the unmistakable wobble of unease. "And it's close."

"Lou, can you tell what it is? Or who it is?" Mac asked, feeling concern as well.

"Is it one of those Bone Rattler leech ships?" Sanchez asked. "Where are they going to latch on? I'll fight them to the death." Sanchez stepped back, raised his rifle, ready to greet any incoming marauders.

"No, nothing like that. It looks way too big for that," Luella answered. "I don't know who it is or what it is. It's a big ship. Really big. It appears to be of the deep space variety."

"Can you put it on the screen?" Mac asked.

"Yes, hold on a sec. I gotta come around and line up. There, there it is." She pointed to the screen.

They all stared at the screen and the tiny speck grew as they approached.

"Do we want to hail them?" she asked. "Find out who they are?"

"I don't know," Mac mumbled. "This doesn't feel right." He thought for a moment. "Let's wait. We don't know what we've walked into here."

The ship continued to grow, and they could see the shape and some features now.

"Major Mac, you see that? That is a human spaceship," Sanchez said.

"I've never seen a ship like that," Taylor said. "It must be some sort of private vessel."

"Any D-BICs on the scanner?" Mac asked, using the common acronym of the Galactic Coalition *Digital Broadcast Identifiers and Credentials*.

"None. They aren't broadcastings D-BICs at all." Taylor looked up at Mac. "That violates Galactic Coalition spaceflight law."

"Hinky-jinky," Sanchez said.

As they gazed at the screen in silence for a moment, the lights switched from soft white to flashing red, and an obnoxious claxon alarm erupted.

"Dah!" Taylor yelled. "Incoming fire!"

A bright red dot appeared on the screen as Mac watched, paralyzed. It became larger and larger, then slammed into their ship, rocking them violently. The screen went blurry for a moment. Mac kept his eyes on the screen and saw several more red dots on the screen now.

"Incoming!" Mac yelled.

"Hold on!" Taylor yelled.

It was too late for Mac and Sanchez to secure themselves, however, as Taylor was already dipping the ship into a forward dive to evade the laser torpedo fire. Mac and Sanchez both bumped against the piloting station and Sanchez tumbled to the floor, letting out a grunt, followed by several curses.

Mac bounced off Taylor's chair and fell into the chair next to her. He gripped the arms of the seat.

The alarms continued to scream, and lights continued flashing red.

Taylor tipped the ship up now and rammed the power lever against the full-power stops, maxing out the powerful rocket engines. She then swirled the boxy ship into a corkscrew spin. The Trek'et utility ship wasn't designed for these evasive maneuvers and aerobatics, but Taylor didn't seem to care. She was pushing the ship to its farthest extremes.

The unknown enemy ship remained stationary and continued to fire at them.

"Still firing!"

She straightened the ship for a moment, rocketing under the other spaceship. Another laser torpedo slammed against the roof of the ship. The lights blinked out for a second and flickered back on.

As the ship was momentarily level, Sanchez tried to get back to his feet, but Taylor yanked the power acceleration lever to low and pulled up on the stick, sending the Trek'et ship into a huge flat roll over the top of the enemy ship. Sanchez bounced off the captain's platform and rolled against the back wall.

Mac couldn't understand the words Sanchez was shouting over the screaming rocket engines, but he had a pretty good idea what he was trying to communicate.

"What are our options?" Mac asked, while straining against his seat.

"We have two options," Luella said. "*FTL* the heck out of here or go atmospheric."

"We can't leave," Mac said sternly. "Not after all this. We must get down there."

"Atmospheric it is, then," Taylor said.

"Any weapons on this ship?"

"None!" she yelled back. "It's a stupid freighter."

She continued the flat roll, zooming past the firing enemy ship, until pointing perpendicular to the planet's surface.

"Hold on!" Taylor yelled again. "It's about to get rough!"

Sanchez, dragging himself on the floor toward Mac, said, "It's about to get rough? What has this been?"

The Trek'et ship sailed through the black vacuum of space at max acceleration for several moments as a couple of laser torpedoes crashed into the back end of the ship, rocking them violently each time. Finally, they slammed into Quokex's stormy atmosphere at an angle Taylor's flight school trainers would have never advised.

The vibration started as the flat-fronted ship pushed through the upper atmosphere, but as the atmosphere thickened, the entire ship was rattling and vibrating so hard, Mac wasn't sure they would make it through alive.

"Come on…hold…together…girl!" Taylor shouted to the ship, her voice vibrating so much she sound like a robot. She held on with all her strength, keeping the control and power levers pinned against the case.

They all groaned in unison in the last moments, Mac feeling like his brain was being squished into the back of his skull. Then, suddenly, the vibration stopped, and the ship broke into smooth air.

"Yes!" Taylor yelled and pulled herself up straight in her chair. Her hair was a frizzy mess, walnut brown strands going in all directions. She slowed the ship, pulled into a gentle cruise, and wiped the loose strands of hair from her face. "Yes, we made it. That was crazy!" She beamed at Mac next to her with wide-eyed excitement. She looked like she was having the time of her life. They both looked down at Sanchez, who was rolling onto his back. He looked exhausted. The flashing lights and horn alarms were all silenced now.

"Lou, you are one crazy pilot," Sanchez squeaked out, "but I like it."

CHAPTER FIFTY-THREE

Bone Rattler Compound
Quokex Colony

"This canyon looks a little tight. Are we going to make it?" Mac asked from behind Taylor as she expertly piloted the Trek'et ship.

"Oh, yeah. No problem," she replied sarcastically.

Mac was waiting for the side of the ship to bounce off one of the rocky canyon sides. Under the ship's lights, a thick blanket of snow covered the planet's surface, and the sheets of ice on the cliff faces glistened.

"We'll be right on top of them in about five minutes," Taylor stated.

Several minutes earlier, Mac sent Sanchez to double-check that Aldo Sperry was secure, and to search the ship for any weapons. They geared up with what little equipment they had. Mac's visor still rested on top of his head. Other than his fixed blade fighting knife, he had the pistol in his thigh holster and the RAP Sanchez took from the *McDaniels*. He was feeling naked and unprepared. He'd never assaulted a location with so little information, men, or equipment. Sanchez had the same load as Mac, and Taylor's only weapon was her Navy handgun.

Sanchez returned, visor on top of his head and RAP hanging from the shoulder sling. He was carrying a small black case.

"Anything?" Mac asked.

Sanchez checked the viewscreen, which displayed the dark canyon and falling snow.

"Three minutes," Taylor stated.

"Greaseball is locked up tight and barely conscious. I slapped his face, just for looking greasy. No actual weapons on the ship, but I found these." Sanchez laid the case on one of the piloting chairs and opened it. He pulled out two handheld tools shaped like a pistol, but not quite a pistol.

Mac raised an eyebrow.

"These," Sanchez explained, "Are power riveters. You know, right? Rivets to keep the ship held together. Look at these things." He pulled out the magazine on the back end to reveal about ten fat metal rivets. "These will do some damage in a pinch." Sanchez handed one to Mac.

"Better than nothing, I guess," Mac said. "Especially, if we need to make emergency ship repairs." Mac rolled his eyes, disappointed Sanchez couldn't find anything more lethal.

"Well, I wouldn't want to be shot by one of these," Sanchez said.

"Two minutes," Taylor said. "You got one for me?" she asked Sanchez.

"Ah, no. I only found two."

"Lou, it doesn't matter, because you are staying on the ship. This is too—"

"Listen, Mac, I'm here to help and I'm not staying on the ship. It doesn't matter how dangerous this is. I'm in enough trouble as it is."

"I can't put you in any more—"

Taylor interrupted again, "Negatory, buddy. I'm going."

Mac, knowing he wouldn't win this argument, gave in. "Just promise me you'll do what I say out there."

She saluted. "Understood, Major." A moment later, "We're one minute out."

Braeknn and six other Bone Rattlers stood at the massive metal door, waiting for it to move. The princess escaping had stoked the raging fire within him. Having the untrustworthy human, Arthur Rust, inside the compound, threw additional fuel on his fury fire. Now, some unknown ship, likely hostile, was approaching. Braeknn was going to slaughter them all. Whoever they were. It didn't matter, they were about to meet a tornado of fury.

"Open this door!" he screamed impatiently, pointing his rifle at the Bone Rattler manning the door controls nearby. After what felt like forever, the locking mechanism released with a heavy clank and the usual earsplitting screeching of metal on metal began.

Braeknn waited only long enough to fit his body and antler-adorned skull helmet through the opening before stomping out into the snowy frozen night.

The compound building lights reflected off the blanket of snow, which covered everything. Heavy snowflakes fell silently. If it wasn't for the screeching metal door, it would have been a serene and beautiful scene. Braeknn, however, didn't appreciate the beauty of the peaceful snowy night, but shuffled into the ankle-high snow toward the chasm bridge, followed by his warriors.

He could hear the ship before he could see it. He stopped in the middle of the bridge and waited, listening. The others stopped as well. As the noise from the ship's engines got louder, he turned around. They were coming in along the canyon, heading straight for him.

Braeknn waited and pulled his rifle up, and the others imitated him. Then, out of the darkness, several yellow spots of light emerged, followed by a huge dark shape, slicing through the falling snow, engines screaming and vibrating the bridge.

"Fire!" he commanded and let loose with the blaster rifle, firing as the ship came straight toward him.

"WATCH OUT, BRIDGE!" Mac warned, looking at the viewscreen.

"Got it," Taylor responded and tilted the ship up. "This is the compound." She slowed the ship as they approached.

"Are those people?" Sanchez asked. "Nope, bone dudes. Lots of bone dudes."

Standing on the bridge in the dark, under the lights, were a handful of Bone Rattlers looking their way. They began firing blasters at them.

"Whoa!" Taylor exclaimed when the blaster fire started. "I guess they knew we were coming."

"Yup, they knew we were coming," Mac said. "I bet that ship that tried to destroy us notified them."

"Those blasters can't hurt the ship," Sanchez said. "But this isn't my idea of a welcoming party."

"We'll give them a welcome of our own," Mac said grimly. "Lou, come around again close and see if we can land near that bridge." He pointed at the viewscreen. "Looks like landing pads there. But there are several ships taking up all the space. I want to land close to that bridge."

"Roger."

Taylor put the ship into a vertical climb and rolled back toward the bridge. Everyone was ready for the maneuver this time and hung on tight.

"There is a spot between those pads. It'll be tight, but I'll get it in there."

Taylor pointed the ship at the bridge and zoomed by again, closer this time.

"Kill that ship," Braeknn yelled at his warriors. He watched as the ship flew past them and then made a big sweeping turn in the dark sky before coming back their way. "Get ready," he growled.

They were ready for the timing, but not ready for the full force of the spaceship's rocket engines as it passed overhead, almost close enough to touch. They fired relentlessly, with no effect, until the rocket blast hit them as the ship passed. The snow on the bridge melted away, and the force of the engines knocked them over. Braeknn and three others fell to the bridge floor, pushed up against the side rails like leaves in the wind. He watched two of his warriors get pushed up against the side rails, then toppled over the side of the bridge into the dark, bottomless chasm. Their screams trailed off to silence as they fell.

Braeknn, unfazed by the loss, climbed to his feet again and watched the ship turn in the sky again to make a third approach.

"Ha!" Sanchez exclaimed. "Knocked two over the side. Just leveled the playing field a bit."

"I'm guessing there are a lot more of them inside that building," Mac said.

Taylor turned the ship, made the slow approach toward the end of the bridge, and lowered the ship into the small opening.

"Nope, not going to fit," she said.

"It's fine. We gotta go now. Element of surprise is gone."

"Mac, its—"

"Just set it down."

"You got it," she said.

Taylor set the ship down. The landing feet didn't sit level. The surface of the plateau along the cliff face wasn't as level as it looked from the sky. One of the four massive landing feet set down on the edge of a landing pad and another set down on a boulder pile, leaving the two other landing feet hanging in the air. As she shut down the power to the lift engines, the ship rocked back and forth, then slammed down to the ground, leaving them parked in an inclined position.

"Well, we are here," she said. "Welcome to Quokex."

"Leave it running, and let's go," Mac said. He pulled his visor down and hurried out of the piloting room, Sanchez and Taylor close on his heels.

As the boarding ramp lowered, a gust of cold snowy wind blew into the ship, causing them to shiver a bit.

"Whew, that's cold," Sanchez's whole body quivered. When the ramp lowered enough to give them a visual of the bridge area, the first thing they saw were the red energy blasts from Bone Rattler rifles. The energy blasts began crashing into the ramp and the wall inside the ship.

Mac and Sanchez returned fire with their RAPs.

"Find cover! Move!" Mac shouted as he ran down the lowering ramp.

CHAPTER FIFTY-FOUR

All Mac could see through the Trek'et ship's boarding ramp were the bridge's yellow lights glistening against the falling snow and red energy blasts coming in at a frantic pace. He zig-zagged down the ramp, scanning for a place to find cover. The enemy fire seemed to materialize out of nothing, as the Bone Rattler combatants hid in the darkness. As he ran, he fired his RAP toward the hidden source of those energy blasts.

The heat and thrust from the rocket engines had cleared a large area of snow on the ground, but Mac found the surface to be icy as he darted into the darkness toward a boulder pile on the right side of the chasm bridge.

He slid into position, slamming against the hard cold stone. On the other side of the bridge entrance, near a short parapet wall at the edge of the chasm, Sanchez was sliding on his hip, like he was stealing second base. He ended up concealed behind an old forklift tractor parked near the wall. Mac hadn't noticed the old tractor until he saw Sanchez sliding toward it.

Good job, Sanchez. Now, where is Lou? He thought, searching for Luella Taylor in the dark. He found her by her muzzle blast from the pistol they'd given her. She was hiding behind the landing legs, under the ship. *That will do fine,* he thought.

Mac rolled out from behind the rocks, on his back at first, then onto his chest. There were Bone Rattlers running down the last few meters of the bridge. He fired a sustained burst of green laser fire from ground level up at the closest charging monster. His target was caught off guard by Mac's low position. His shot was true, slamming into the chest of the Bone Rattler, stopping his forward momentum and causing him to stumble backwards onto his back, dead.

Two other Bone Rattlers charged in Sanchez's direction, concentrating fire on his location behind the tractor. Taylor's pistol fire on a moving target wasn't accurate enough from her distance. Mac saw bullets smashing into the ground near them, kicking up snow. He got to his feet, careful to keep his balance, and fired at the Bone Rattlers charging toward Sanchez. He connected with the closest one, laying a barrage of laser blasts into his back, causing him to collapse to the ground face first and slide on the slippery surface for several meters.

Before Mac could rotate around and lock in on the other target, a shadow crossed his periphery for a fraction of a second. There were four Bone Rattlers, and he lost track of number four in his haste.

Careless rookie move, Mac.

As the thought entered his mind, he got hit on the right side by what felt like an elephant. The impact knocked the breath out of him and snapped his neck, creating painful whiplash. The massive beast took him to the ground, crushing him beneath his body weight.

Mac held onto his weapon but couldn't move his arms under the crushing weight of his attacker, pressing him like a vice between the frozen rocky ground and his hard bone armor. The Bone Rattler was spitting and snarling through his bone helmet with the antlers, which Mac recognized.

He couldn't comprehend anything the Bone Rattler was growling, and he tried to wriggle free, but it was no good. He was severely over-matched in the strength category. The Bone Rattler shifted his weight by sitting up and pressing Mac down with one hand while he began pounding on him with a giant meaty fist. Mac dodged two blows, but the next three jack hammer blows connected, and he saw stars. He felt his tactical visor snap under the pressure of the blows.

He struggled to stay conscious, when suddenly Mac heard a mechanical *pop-pop* sound, and the Bone Rattler tumbled over sideways onto the frozen ground. Mac squirmed loose and found Taylor standing over him, aiming a weapon at the dead beast.

"The rivet gun works," she said with a wide grin.

Breathlessly, Mac replied, "I sure am grateful for that." He rubbed his sore jaw.

"What did they call the women in the ancient world wars? Was it Lucy Riveter? Riveter Rachel?" She offered a hand and Mac took it. She helped him to his feet. "No, it was Rosie the Riveter."

She posed, standing proudly, riveter in hand.

"OK, Rosie. I owe you one."

"If we are keeping track, Mac, you owe me two or three now."

"Good point," he said.

Mac pulled the visor off his face and rubbed the back of his neck. He was fortunate Taylor was close enough to kill the Bone Rattler. He was two punches from blacking out and failing his mission. That was a sloppy move. He had to refocus.

He held up the visor. It was cracked in several places. Broken and destroyed.

"That doesn't look so good," Taylor said.

"Nope, it's toast." Mac tossed it over his shoulder. He stood straight to stretch his body, and said, "Where did you get that riveter?"

"Oh, I found another case in the cargo hold. On the shelf there… about eye level?" She held her hand up to her eyes.

"Well, I sure am glad you did."

"Yeah, me too. My pistol is out of ammo."

Mac pulled his own M2-V pistol from his holster and handed it to her. "Here, use this." He also handed her several full magazines.

Sanchez joined them, RAP resting against his chest. "You good, there, Major Mac? That looked rough."

"Yeah, yeah…fine. Just a couple of bruises. What about you?"

"Good," Sanchez said.

Taylor scooted over to the dead Bone Rattler near the bridge entrance and bent down to pick up the bulky energy rifle laying on the ground. "I think I'll use this," she said.

"Even better," Mac agreed.

Just then, they heard the guttural roar of several Bone Rattlers in the distance, from across the bridge. They all turned and stared down the bridge at the same time. A group of Bone Rattlers emerged from the dark interior of the building on the other side of the chasm, charging toward the bridge two-by-two.

"Here we go," Taylor said as she raised the rifle.

Mac raised his RAP to eye level and checked the charges. The three small lights were dark orange, signaling low charge. He dumped the dying energy cartridge and slammed a new one into the bottom of the firearm. The three lights on the RAP turned green. Sanchez did the same.

"Last charge," Sanchez said.

"Me too," Mac replied and lifted his RAP toward the Bone Rattlers in the distance. "Let's make it count."

"Hey, hang on," Sanchez said. "I've got an idea. Let's level the playing field a bit." He ran back toward the tractor.

Arthur Rust and Rick Vega turned the corner into the dark corridor, following the direction the princess had fled. Rust limped from the gunshot wound on his leg. Pain radiated though his leg with each step, causing him to grimace and swear under his breath.

This corridor was pitch black. He and Vega both snatched their flashlights from their belts and illuminated the space. It was identical to all the other cold barren corridors and, after about twenty meters, the corridor dead-ended into a crossing corridor.

"Of course," Rust said with irritation. "We end up in a stupid maze."

They reached the crossing corridor and stood for a moment, shining their flashlights in both directions. There were a couple of closed metal doors along each corridor and ninety degree turns at the end.

"Well, I guess we split up," Rust said, signaling Vega to go right, while he headed left.

Rust limped down the hallway behind his flashlight beam and checked the two closed doors as he reached them. Both doors were unlocked, and he found the small, dark rooms empty.

The corridor turned ninety degrees to his left again, making him wonder if the designer of this concrete maze was an idiot or lunatic. *Who would do such a thing?* As he turned left, he glanced down the direction he came from and saw Vega checking the doors at his end of the corridor.

No surprise, as he turned the corner, he found under his flashlight beam that the corridor dead-ended with another metal door. In front of the metal door, huddled on the floor, were the Okutans. They whimpered and cried, flinching as the light beam passed over them. Standing in front of the whimpering Okutans was a non-whimpering and resolute-looking Princess Omo-Binrin Oba.

"Don't come any closer," she ordered Rust. Her accent was thick, but he understood her. She held the black rifle with both hands, and it looked huge compared to her tiny body.

Rust put up one hand, attempting to look unthreatening. "It's OK, Princess. Just take it easy," he said in his friendliest voice. He added a smile to put her at ease. "You already shot me once with that thing. I don't want to get shot again."

"What do you want with me?" Her voice was firm.

"We are here to rescue you," Rust said. He doubted she'd believe it, but he thought it was worth a try.

"You are a liar. What do you want with me?"

"True, true…I see I can't fool you." He kept his voice measured, calm. *How do I get that weapon out of her hands?* he wondered. He doubted she'd miss if she fired again, especially at close range.

"I just want to talk. You have some very important information that I need."

"I have no information."

"Princess, please. Neither of us is that stupid. We both know the publicity about your supposed diplomatic meeting with the President Harrington is a total farce. I need the information you were bringing to him."

"How do you know about that?" Her confidence was waning a bit. He saw the rifle muzzle dip toward the floor a bit.

"Yes. It is true. I know it's true. Let's just say my employer has friends in high places. Nothing escapes our notice." Rust's leg was throbbing, and he ground his teeth against the pain, trying to hide it from the princess. He didn't need her emboldened.

"I won't tell you anything," she spat back at him with a surprising amount of rage. "You and your treasonous partners will get nothing from me." She was so small and dainty, even though her scalp frill was standing at full height, giving the illusion of being taller.

"Princess, let me make this as simple as possible. You will give me the information, or I'll start killing your people."

"No!" she screamed and turned the rifle toward him and started firing with no warning.

Rust, surprised by her willingness to fight back, dove out of the way. One shot skidded across his right shoulder as he dove into the crossing corridor. It burned through his thin shirt to the skin. It hurt, but it wasn't bad. He hit the floor hard and rolled his body out of view. He scrambled around behind the corner.

Vega came to a skidding stop right next to him and squatted down as Rust pushed himself up into a kneeling position.

"I found the princess," Rust said with a crooked grin.

"I see that."

"I'm getting a little sick and tired of her shooting me though," he said as he shined the flashlight on his shoulder. It was bleeding, but the injury wasn't deep.

The princess continued to fire the rifle in their direction, energy blasts slamming against the concrete walls, throwing up dust and debris.

"Give me the stun gun. I'm done playing around with this one. I'll put her out and we'll deal with this on the ship."

Vega retrieved a pistol-sized weapon from his belt and handed it to Rust.

Rust peeked around the corner, and the princess fired right at him. He barely retreated behind the corner in time. Closing his eyes for a second, he took a few deep breaths, then threw his body around the corner, spinning as he fell toward the floor, firing three quick shots with the stun gun at Princess Omo-Binrin.

He successfully surprised her and his third shot hit her right in the chest, just after his first two shots hit other Okutans in the huddle. All three slumped to the floor, unconscious. Her heavy rifle clattered to the floor.

Rust got to his feet with a grimace and tossed the stun gun to Vega. He straightened his holsters and then brushed his mustache with his fingers and twirled the ends back to perfection. It didn't matter where he was or what he was doing, it was unacceptable for his mustache to get out of place.

He limped over to where the princess was lying on the floor, grabbed her by the arm, and dragged her back toward Vega. She was very light, and it was easy, like dragging a child.

"What about the others?" Vega asked.

"Who cares?" Rust said. "Not my problem."

"They'll die down here."

Rust leaned toward Vega's face and gave him a squinty-eyed look. "Yeah, well, like I said, Vega, not my problem. What do I look like to you, the galactic peace corps?" Rust felt super annoyed at the whole situation. "Listen, forget them. That barbarian, Sckrahhg, and his hairy friends will eat them for breakfast. Just carry this one, and let's get out of here." He handed Vega the princess' limp arm, and Vega lifted her unconscious body onto his shoulder.

As Rust limped down the corridor, heading toward the exit, he pulled his digital communicator out and sent a message to his crew on the orbiting Hammurabi.

Package in hand. Send jump ship to pick us up at the chasm bridge.

After a moment, a reply came through. "*Roger. En route. Be aware, hostile assault force on the ground.*"

Rust rolled his eyes in annoyance, then tapped out a response. *Well, then you'd better hurry.*

CHAPTER FIFTY-FIVE

Space Warfare Group Starhawk
Quokex

The massive battlecruiser *McDaniels* dropped out of extreme *FTL* near the planet Quokex. Capable of traveling at humanity's fastest hyper speeds, the *McDaniels* arrived on the heels of Mac's Trek'et vessel. They came to rest close enough for DJ's team to assault the planet. The Space Warfare Group Starhawk sat pre-positioned in the hangar airlock, and DJ's team waited, suited up and ready to go. As soon as the *McDaniels* dropped out of FTL, the outer hangar doors opened, and the Starhawk shot into space.

"Master Sergeant," the pilot's voice came through the radio, "I'm estimating twenty minutes to the surface." His voice was dull and a bit robotic.

"Roger. We'll be ready to go," he replied and climbed out of the seat he'd been sitting in while they waited to exit the *McDaniels*.

He and his men sat scattered about the cramped cabin. The cabin was a dull silver metal and all business. Most of the space was filled with passenger seats, which were designed larger than commercial transport seats in anticipation of larger and more muscular operators wearing tactical gear or space suits sitting in them. They still felt cramped, though. Display screens near the cockpit provided access to mission data and maps. Cabinets and drawers containing extra weapons and gear hung on the port side of the cabin. There was a small medical bay, the size of a closet, at the front. At the back of the cabin, near the ramp, was an additional open space for storing larger equipment. They could even squeeze in a small surface buggy or a couple of speeders if needed.

DJ stood and announced through the cigar in his mouth, "Alright, troops, we'll be on the surface in about twenty mikes. Check your gear again. Be ready because we're likely dropping immediately into action."

He received a series of confirmation grunts from the team.

He stretched and twisted his back a bit to loosen up the tight muscles, and rolled his shoulders and stiff neck. The cigar, pinched between his teeth, was nearing the end of its life, so he grabbed it with thumb and forefinger and snuffed it out against his gloved palm. He looked around and found nowhere to discard it, so he tucked into a small pocket on his chest plate. He'd yet to figure out how to smoke his cigar while wearing his E-Gear helmet.

The other operators also got out of their seats and gathered their gear. The lanky Dominic Long was the tallest of the whole Space Warfare Group's roster. They called him Bones. He gave him a nod and smiled. His white eyes and teeth stood out against his dark brown skin. Next to Bones, the youngest team member, Dozer, pulled his helmet down over his curly brown hair. Owen *Dozer* Black was the opposite of Bones in every category. He was short with pale white skin, almost pink at times when he exerted himself. They called him Dozer because he was almost as wide as he was tall, constructed of dense, bulging muscles. He could blow through almost any obstacle with his body or with his massive weapon. Dozer's permanent assignment was carrying the heavy X560 energy weapon the team called *the Dragon*. The Dragon was line-fed by a backpack energy module and required two hands to hold and fire. Dozer was the perfect man for the job.

DJ tightened the straps on his armored chest rig, cinching it down against his body so that it wouldn't slip or wiggle at all, and before he could grab his helmet from the seat next to him, Cory Allen approached.

Cory, kitted up and ready to go, had his helmet face shield up. His stern, craggy face and icy blue eyes screamed concern. Quietly, he said, "DJ, I don't know about our traveling companions." Cory was referencing the three Elite Guard soldiers in the back corner of the Starhawk cabin. They showed up only moments before the team climbed aboard the Starhawk, leaving no time for discussion amongst the team. DJ looked over Cory's shoulder at the three of them. They stood in a huddle behind DJ's fourth team member, the wiry Liang Zhou. Prime Ambassador Kumar's Elite Guard soldiers wore similar E-gear tactical suits, which were white as opposed to the Space Warfare Group's charcoal gray. Captain Tom Scott, whom he'd seen earlier, led the team, but they didn't know the man or the woman he'd brought with him.

"I don't disagree," DJ whispered.

"Can we trust them?"

"I doubt it. I don't even know why they are on this mission other than because the prime ambo said so."

"Since when does the prime ambo direct our ops?"

"Since today, apparently," DJ said with a shrug.

"I don't know what their motives are, but I can tell you this," Cory looked over his shoulder at the three soldiers in white. "I know Mac is off the reservation right now and gone native, but he's still Mac. There is no way I'm treating him like a criminal. He's our major and as far as I'm concerned, I'm coming in here to help him."

"I get it. I really do. Just don't let any of them hear you talk like that."

"And don't forget about Sanchez. The guy is a total idiot, and ninety percent of the time I hate him. But I love him." Cory paused for a second. "These are our brothers we're talking about."

"I'm trying to forget about Sanchez. Maybe we can leave him here," DJ said with a wink, which cracked Cory's intense mood, causing him to smile.

"What an idiot."

"Totally. So, Cory, here's the deal. We have orders to bring Mac and Sanchez back to base. We've gotta follow those orders. But I assure you, I won't do anything to harm either of these brothers. Mac is my mentor."

"And what about them?" he asked with a subtle nod toward the Elite Guard.

"Well, it's our responsibility to bring them back, so I won't be letting them touch Mac or Sanchez. They are simply in an observation role."

"Good."

DJ put his gloved hand on Cory's shoulder. "But we are following our orders, roger?"

"Roger that," Cory replied.

DJ slapped the top of his shoulder hard several times, followed by an affectionate side slap against Cory's helmet.

DJ checked his watch. *Getting close.* "Hey, Bones, you geared up?"

"Five by five, Boss."

"Get the fast rope ready."

"Roger," Bones replied and made his way to the drop hatch on the floor of the cabin. Above it was a winch in the ceiling with a spool of fat synthetic rope.

A small, hollow voice crackled through his comm earpiece again. "Master Sergeant, we've got company out here."

"Great," he said sarcastically. "What are we dealing with?"

"Looks like some kind of military cruiser. They are signaling hostility. They won't respond to our open channel request to identify. A moment ago, they lit up their weapons."

"What about credentials?"

"None. Unregistered and unaffiliated."

"Does the type of vessel tell us anything?"

"Negative. The vessel appears to be custom, no known matches in our system."

"Copy. We need to get to the surface of that planet. Do whatever it takes to get us there ASAP."

"Roger," the pilot responded.

A moment later, the pilot yelled over the ship wide speakers for everyone to hear, "Incoming fire, brace yourself!"

DJ's body lurched backward as Starhawk sped up. He reached for the handrail in the ceiling as the pilot threw the Starhawk into a roll.

CHAPTER FIFTY-SIX

Bone Rattler Compound Bridge
Quokex Colony

On the surface of Quokex, in the darkness of the snowy night, Mac glanced at the hoard of angry Bone Rattlers. They were howling furiously and storming the bridge. He turned back to Sanchez running toward the old tractor. He glanced back and forth several times. *No time, Sanchez. Hurry up.* There were only a few short few seconds before he and Lou would have to dive behind cover and open fire at the rampaging beasts coming their way.

SANCHEZ SLID to a stop between the two vehicles parked against the short stone wall separating him from the dark and seemingly bottomless chasm. He could hear the howls of the Bone Rattlers charging their way.

The tractor rested next to a smaller cart, with three flatbed trailers attached. Of the two vehicles, the smaller one was flat and provided no protection. The larger one, however, was perfect. The tractor part forklift and part transport vehicle, designed for loading a unloading cargo from the spacecraft on the landing pad. A flatbe platform extended from the back of the tractor, for carrying cargo, and the enclosed operator's cockpit sat in the middle, with two thick metal forks extending forward to lift heavy cargo at the front.

Sanchez ripped the cockpit door open and climbed up into the machine, pausing for a second to look at the bridge, which was swarmed by rampaging Bone Rattlers. He flopped into the single seat behind a steering wheel and scanned the controls. He laughed.

"Booyah, baby! It's one of ours," he blurted out to himself, realizing the tractor was human made. It was an obvious leftover from the UPG development of Quokex.

He rammed the gear lever into place and pressed the engine start button. The machine controls and cockpit light flickered for a moment and then failed. He did the steps again and felt the vibration of the engine trying to start, running rough for a second, and then failing again.

"Come on, you old run-down piece of junk," he muttered and performed the steps again. This time the engine started, coughed, and burped, then smoothed out.

"Oh, yeah! I'm coming for you, 'squatches!"

Without wasting a second, he backed out and turned the tractor toward the bridge. The wheels slipped a few times on the slick stone surface as he approached Mac and Lou. He tapped the brakes, and the tractor slid a couple meters past where he intended to stop. Mac and Lou jumped onto the flatbed, and Mac slapped the roof twice. Sanchez pressed the accelerator forward. The tires slipped and the tail end spun out to the right, but by spinning the steering wheel, Sanchez recentered the machine and pointed it down the chasm bridge.

"Hold on!" Sanchez yelled to the others. "Things are about to get ugly and really hairy!"

Mac grasped the frame of the tractor with all his strength as Sanchez stomped on the accelerator. The machine's engine made a dull rattling sound, and the tires slipped and fishtailed on the snowy ground. He heard Sanchez yell something indecipherable while shaking his fist at the incoming Bone Rattlers. Taylor was holding on tightly to the frame as well, in a crouch by Mac's knees. Her jumpsuit looked wet, and she was shivering in the cold. Mac's own long sleeve t-shirt was doing very little to keep his body heat in.

Sanchez pointed the tractor down the bridge and drove straight without sliding all over the place, which gave Mac the opportunity to let go and aim over the top of the tractor cab. Standing with a wide stance for balance and leaning against the back of the driver's cab, he rested his arms on the top of the cab and aimed the RAP down the bridge. Once balanced, he began spraying down the hoard of attackers as they approached.

Mac's laser fire cut down several Bone Rattlers running at the front of the pack. As they collapsed dead, the next layer of attackers stopped and fired back. Energy blasts smashed into the tractor repeatedly, causing Mac to drop into a cover position. Taylor gave him a wide-eyed look. The Bone Rattlers shot out the windows and a front tire. The tractor lurched to the left, bumping against the handrail before Sanchez jerked it back in the other direction. Mac and Taylor held on tightly, their bodies tossed back and forth as Sanchez drove like a wild man.

The tractor bounced over something like a speed bump, which lifted Mac and Taylor's bodies off the surface of the flatbed. When they crashed down hard, Mac landed painfully on his hip. A moment later, the tractor slammed to a stop, smashing into something in front of them. The momentum tossed them against the back of the cab, where Mac smacked his head. He felt disoriented for a moment, he realized they were not moving anymore. They were still on the bridge, a little more than halfway to the compound building.

After a quick mental assessment of his body for injuries, and finding nothing more than bruising and soreness, he checked on Taylor. She was pulling herself up to her knees. "Lou, you good?"

"Yes, fine," she said.

"Injuries?"

"None. Does being frozen count?"

Mac laughed, then saw movement. Multiple Bone Rattlers poured around, between the tractor and the bridge wall, on both sides. He fired, and Bone Rattler energy blasts crashed into the cab of the tractor near his head. He felt the static buzz from the energy sizzling around him. Taylor fired in the other direction.

Mac could hear Sanchez screaming, and feared he'd been injured. He concentrated on Sanchez's voice and realized Sanchez was cursing and insulting the enemy.

Good, Sanchez is fine.

Taylor and Mac dropped at least six Bone Rattlers trying to surge around the tractor. There was a brief pause in the action, and Mac looked over at Taylor again to make sure she was doing well. It shocked him to find her jumping off the side of the flatbed and running forward into the battle, with the rifle against her shoulder.

Hmmm, she's a tough one.

Before he could turn back around, huge powerful hands clamped down on his shoulders and jerked him sideways. He was tossed like a rag doll off the back end of the flatbed and onto the bridge surface, rattling his already bruised body. He rolled to a stop in the cold snow, looking up at the snowflakes gently falling on this face. If he hadn't been in a violent firefight against an enemy trying to kill him, the snowflakes would have been beautiful.

Get up and move, he told his freezing body.

The Bone Rattler charged and tried to stomp on Mac, but he rolled out of the way. Mac scrambled to his feet, slipping in the snow. The vicious and snarling Bone Rattler grabbed him again. He lifted Mac off the ground and tossed him toward the tractor, where he bounced off the flatbed and slumped to the bridge again.

Mac's head was spinning. Using the flatbed, he pulled himself to his feet and pushed off toward the handrail just in time. The Bone Rattler was swinging his two hands over his head together like a meaty sledgehammer, just missing Mac, pounding into the flatbed with a grunt.

There was a brief opening, and Mac took it. He gave the beast five fast body blows, hoping he'd hit a kidney or any internal organ. The Bone Rattler flinched and turned around. Mac danced away from him, more in control now.

This Bone Rattler was almost twice his size, and it was not as agile as he was. He took a couple of steps and jumped onto the flatbed, ending up behind his attacker as he was turning around, looking for his prey. Mac jumped onto his back and put a vice-like choke hold around the neck of the beast. The bone helmet got knocked off his head as Mac latched onto the beast's neck with all his strength. Grinding his teeth and wrapping his legs around the enormous monster's abdomen, Mac squeezed and squeezed with his arm. The smell of his dirty, wet fur was disgusting.

The Bone Rattler turned frantically, reaching behind, but he couldn't get a hold on Mac. He tried to smash Mac into the back of the tractor, which didn't work since the flatbed was too low, and they crashed down together against the surface of the bed.

The Bone Rattler rolled off the flatbed and back to his feet, with Mac going for a ride, hanging on as if his life depended on it, which it did.

Mac, realizing he wasn't going to be able to choke out this larger creature, gambled by keeping one arm tight around his neck, used his other hand to slip his combat knife from the sheath on the back of his belt. As the Bone Rattler twirled wildly trying to break Mac free, Mac brought the large glinting blade up and jammed it into the back of the neck at the base of his skull. It was like he'd hit the power switch, as all brain functions ceased immediately. The dead creature collapsed forward, with Mac still riding on its back, and crashed face first against the bridge surface with a puff of snow.

Mac first yanked his arm free and then pulled his knife from the dead skull. He wiped the blood off on the furry shoulder and slipped it back into the sheath. He was safe for a moment, but could see the staccato green and red flashes from the firefight on the other side of the tractor. Sanchez and Taylor were giving it all they had. His RAP was gone, lost in the snow. He scanned around and saw a blaster rifle on the flatbed. Farther away, he spotted the RAP laying in the snow several yards down the bridge.

Mac jogged down and grabbed his RAP and did a quick function check. It was fine, but running low on charges. As he began jogging back toward the tractor and the firefight, a massive black form, shadowed against the dark night, climbed to the top of the tractor cab, and then jumped down onto the flatbed with a heavy thud. Roaring like a banshee, the Bone Rattler took two steps and leapt off the flatbed, landing on the bridge with a heavy thud, and began charging at Mac.

"This is getting old," he said.

He raised the RAP and placed the laser stream into the chest of the charging bone-covered beast. The RAP fire stopped him in his tracks and knocked him backward onto his back, dead. Steam from the laser blast rose from the wet fur. It wasn't a pleasant smell.

He stepped over the dead Bone Rattler he'd just shot, then several others that were dead on the bridge. Some had been driven over by Sanchez. He crept around the right side of the tractor and fired at every Bone Rattler he saw. He took a quick glance over the bridge's rail into the chasm and shivered. It was an amazing sight. The huge snowy mountain peak in front of him, with the building jutting out of the sloped surface above the deep dark, and super creepy chasm, was impressive.

As he rounded the front of the tractor, firing at Bone Rattlers in his view, he saw the tractor's forks hovered about a meter from the ground. Hanging from each of the forks was a dead Bone Rattler, slumped over, blood oozing out onto the forks, and dripping into a dark pool below them. It was a grizzly sight. Sanchez impaled two Bone Rattlers in the gut, killing both.

Taylor was crouched behind the hanging Bone Rattler corpses, firing her rifle. With no cover, many of the hoard retreated to the building, and hid behind the chasm wall near the building entrance. Mac could see into the building since the door was still open, and lights were on inside. The light spilled out onto the snowy surface in front of the entrance where the bridge attached to the mountainside.

The battlefield was total chaos. He added fire to the chaos, then checked Sanchez's status on the other side of the tractor. He was standing in the open, wrestling with a Bone Rattler, but finally fired several shots into the gut of the beast and it dropped to the ground. Sanchez moved on, all business, combat crouch, RAP firearm extended, taking out enemy combatants with precision.

Mac moved toward the building, then glimpsed out of the corner of his eye, the Bone Rattler he thought Sanchez had just killed climb to his feet again. He was behind Sanchez, and Sanchez was unaware. Mac took off running at the Bone Rattler behind Sanchez and, as he got close, launched his body, feet first, at the large furry target. The soles of his boots connected with the monster at mid-body, and the force of Mac's unexpected blow caused him to stumble sideways, crashing into the bridge guardrail. The Bone Rattler, who was much taller than the guardrail, tried to catch his balance. He spun his arms, trying to change the momentum for a second, then tipped over the guardrail and fell into the chasm with a guttural scream that faded with the body as it fell.

Mac looked up to see Sanchez running in his direction shouting, "Pull back, pull back!" He paused to help Mac to his feet, and Mac saw the reinforcements pouring out of the compound door. He followed Sanchez, and they met up with Taylor on the back of the tractor flatbed again.

They took turns popping up and firing downrange at the surging enemy. Their shots were effective, dropping many. At Mac's third turn to pop up and fire, they all heard an incoming spacecraft. It was loud, engines screeching as it raced up the canyon toward them. Mac knew what it was just from the sounds of the rocket engines.

Starhawk.

The team is here.

His heart was torn in that moment. He needed his brothers right now, but he knew trouble was coming.

The Starhawk slowed to a hover over the bridge and opened fire, spraying the Bone Rattlers with an inescapable barrage of energy fire. Red light from the energy blast lit up the area with a deafening sound. The sheer force of the Starhawk's relentless assault ripped apart some Bone Rattlers and knocked several over the side of the bridge. A lucky few escaped to the building.

The Starhawk rotated around behind the tractor and hovered about twenty meters above. The engines were blowing snow all around, and the ship's lights were glaring in Mac's eyes. Mac knew what was coming next. The hatch opened on the bottom of the spaceship and the heavy rope to drop to the surface. He recognized his men as they slid down the rope. Zhou followed by Bones, then Dozer, Cory, and DJ. One after another, they slid down the rope and crouched on the bridge surface before running in Mac's direction, rifles at the ready. Mac was jealous that they wore E-Gear suits because he knew they'd be comfortable in the inhospitable environment, unlike himself, Sanchez, and Taylor, who were soggy and shivering.

Consequences. There are always consequences.

What Mac was not prepared for was the Starhawk to remain hovering and for three more soldiers to fast rope to the bridge, wearing white suits with reflective silver helmets. He closed his eyes and swore to himself.

The Elite Guard. We're in trouble.

CHAPTER FIFTY-SEVEN

"That jump ship better be close," Rust said to Vega as they reached the main entrance corridor of the old Quokex compound. A few minutes earlier, they had turned the wrong way in the maze of identical barren corridors, which wasted precious time and intensified Rust's frustration at this mission. It was supposed to be an easy pop-in and pop-out retrieval mission, and now, it was a gigantic mess. He consoled himself with the fact that he had the princess in custody.

It was obvious when they found the main entrance corridor from the increased lighting and the sounds of a firefight in the distance. This was not what Rust wanted to find. As they approached the main corridor, he could feel the draft of frigid air. Passing in front of him were groups of snarling, rifle-toting Bone Rattlers moving up and down the corridor.

Rust stopped at the intersection and gazed down the wide main corridor, which was easily three times as wide as the rest. At the far end was the massive metal door, which was wide open. A team of Bone Rattler warriors charged toward the door. Rust thought he saw Sckrahhg near the door giving orders. Snow was blowing in through the door, followed by red and green energy fire crashing into the walls and connecting with the occasional Bone Rattler. It shocked Rust to see so many fallen Bone Rattlers piled up in the doorway.

This was Rust's planned route to the bridge and his ride off this terrible planet. The jump ship planned to meet him outside that door in mere minutes. He shook his head angrily. This was no good. He didn't know what the battle on the chasm bridge looked like, or even who was assaulting the compound, but it was clear he wouldn't be walking out to the bridge to climb onto the jump ship to escape. This exit route was a no-go. If they even tried, it was likely he and Vega would be shot or killed before they could even get out the door. He was sick and tired of being shot today.

Need to adapt. Need a Plan B, Rust told himself as he straightened his mustache.

"How is she doing?" Rust asked Vega.

"She's almost awake. Starting to stir."

"We need to shift to Plan B."

"What's Plan B?"

"We're getting the information out of her here and now. I don't need the stupid princess. I just need the location of the crash."

Vega, still holding the princess on his shoulder, nodded in agreement.

Rust continued. "Worst case, I'll extract the information from her, and we'll send the location to the Hammurabi and then we fight to the death and die honorably for the cause. This is bigger than either of us, Rick."

Vega stopped nodding in agreement and raised an eyebrow. "I understand that, but to be honest, I'm not really a fan of how Plan B might end. I'd prefer to get off this planet alive."

Rust slapped Vega on the back of the head. "I don't pay you to comment on the plans or to complain. Your job is to get the job done, no matter what the job is. If the job includes dying for the cause, you better die for the cause. Got it?"

"Roger, boss."

Rust stared at him in fury for a moment. Hearing a noise behind him, he turned and saw Sckrahhg coming his way with several warriors behind him, so he stepped out in front of him and put his hand up like a crossing guard. Sckrahhg stopped.

"Arthur Rust, you are still alive?" Sckrahhg snarled.

"I'm not that easy to kill, General. I've been in the back, wasting time trying to find my princess that you lost."

"Good for you. Get out of my way."

"You have caused me a lot of trouble, Sckrahhg, and you are going to help me escape. You owe me that much."

"I owe you nothing," he snarled. "You have your package. Now get out of my way."

Sckrahhg pushed Rust aside like a child.

Rust grabbed his massive, hairy biceps. "Not so fast, General Sckrahhg."

Sckrahhg glared at him with murderous eyes through the skull helmet, fangs bared. These brainless animals wouldn't intimidate Rust. He wouldn't hesitate to drop Sckrahhg if it came to that. But he needed Sckrahhg for a bit longer. "Is there another way out of this compound? A back door? Alternate exit? Because of you, I can't go that way." Rust pointed toward the large door.

Sckrahhg replied with an equal dose of disdain for Rust, "I have no time for you. Maybe you are the reason they are here. Did you double-cross me?"

"We don't have time for a petty argument. Is there a back exit or not?"

The Bone Rattler General considered Rust and his options for a moment and then replied, "Yes. Backside of our headquarters room. Behind the back wall." Sckrahhg then ripped his arm free and stalked off.

"See, Sckrahhg, you aren't so bad after all," Rust shouted at him. "I don't believe any of those bad things people say about you."

To Vega he asked, "Is she awake?"

"Almost, boss."

Rust pulled Vega and the princess back into the smaller corridor, and they set the princess down.

"Tie her up. Legs and arms. Then, wake her up."

While Vega pulled zip ties from his equipment belt and began working on securing the small Okutan, Rust watched the door anxiously. The firefight continued. Bone Rattlers were dying at a rapid pace. He had little time. Whoever was out there would breach the door soon and they'd be in serious trouble.

Rust turned back to see Princess Omo-Binrin waking up and then, out of the corner of his eye in the darkness down the corridor, he saw the huddled group of Okutans. They'd been following the whole time. *Perfect,* he thought to himself. *Just the bargaining chip I needed.* He shuffled a few painful steps their direction and pointed his rifle at them, and then pointed at the floor near where Princess Omo-Binrin was sitting. They didn't move, so he shot the ceiling above their head and pointed again more dramatically. This time they moved as a group toward him and huddled on the floor.

Princess Omo-Binrin was awake but groggy. She saw her people and tried to reach out, but her arms were bound.

"Keep an eye out," Rust instructed Vega, then squatted down in front of the diminutive blue-skinned princess. Her elegant gown was stained and torn. Her eyes were droopy as she recovered from the effects of the stun gun.

"Now, Princess, let's make this as easy as possible for everyone. I need you to tell me right now the location of the Noct ship crash site."

She said nothing, but looked up at him.

"You see, the Noct are not someone you want to upset. You think I am bad? You think these stupid hairy cows with guns are bad? You have no idea what you are messing with. And right now, you stand between them and what they want. You think they will just leave your people alone when you have the information they need? No. Not a chance. Don't be so stubborn that you put your people and your family in danger. The Noct will torture and kill every last Okutan until they get what they want."

She interrupted him, "You can't scare me. I will never tell you."

"Is that right?" he asked sarcastically. "We'll see. Where is the Noct ship crash site?"

Still no answer.

Rust pulled a pistol from his holster and pointed it at the closest Okutan, while still staring her in the eye. He saw her resolve diminish as he threatened her people.

"No, don't. Please don't. They've suffered enough." She tried to move and scoot toward them.

"Do not test me. I will kill all of them," he then raised his voice to a furious scream, "unless you tell me where you found the Noct spaceship!"

She stuttered a bit but didn't form any coherent words.

Rust, without taking his eyes from Omo-Binrin's, pulled the trigger of his laser pistol. The closest Okutan woman, one of Omo-Binrin's own attendants, died instantly by the point-blank shot. She tumbled over onto her face.

"No!" Her scream blended with the screaming Okutans, and she tried to kick Rust with her bound legs.

He pushed her small legs out of the way and said in a measured tone, "You will not win this battle, Princess. You will tell me what I want to know. Because I'm a nice guy, I will ask you again. Where is the crash site?" He shifted the pistol barrel toward the next Okutan.

"No, no, no. Don't. Please don't. I will tell you what you want to know."

Rust lowered the pistol and smiled wickedly. "Where?"

CHAPTER FIFTY-EIGHT

Mac shivered as he squatted on the forklift's flatbed. The metal was sucking the last bit of warmth from his body. He also felt the cold finger of dread run down his spine as he watched his team approach. DJ and the others were a welcome sight on the battlefield. They were hard to see in their charcoal gray environmental suits as they moved with precision. These operators, whom Mac trained himself, were competent, well equipped, and like brothers to him. The three others in white behind them were a concern, though. He didn't know what to expect from the Elite Guard.

DJ moved straight towards Mac, Sanchez, and Lou on the forklift, as Dozer stood on the bridge, squatting with his legs wide for a stable foundation, and fired the Dragon. He held it with two hands at hip level and released a barrage of devastating energy blasts toward the compound building. A black cable extended from the back of the bulky Dragon to a backpack-mounted energy driver, which was emanating a blue glow from the vents. The energy driver was steaming as snowflakes landed on the surface. The deep *kachoonk, kachoonk, kachoonk* of the Dragon's rapid fire resonated along the bridge and Mac could feel it in his bones. He loved that feeling.

DJ climbed onto the flatbed, close to Mac, and hit the button on the side of his helmet, opening his face shield. Sanchez stood and fired downrange.

DJ smiled at Mac, who was wet and shivering. "Hey, buddy," he said with a friendly grin.

"Funny meeting you here," Mac said.

"Cold?"

"A little."

"Who's your friend?" DJ asked, nodding toward Louella Taylor, who was firing her rifle around the side of the forklift cab.

Dozer's Dragon fire paused for a moment, and the night was almost calm. Then Dozer resumed the relentless barrage.

Cory, Bones, and Zhou took cover behind the forklift.

"Lou Taylor. She's a Navy pilot."

Mac tapped her on the shoulder, and she turned.

"Lou, this is DJ. He's one of our best and brightest," Mac said.

Lou, looking frozen and frantic with her hair and jumpsuit soaked, said, "Glad you could make it. Did you bring me a coat?"

"Unfortunately, I did not. It seems you are terrible at picking friends," DJ said, indicating Mac and Sanchez.

"You're telling me," she said, and turned back to shooting.

"Mac, listen, we need to take you into custody. Orders from Colonel Miller and Prime Ambo."

Mac nodded. "I know. Is that why the Guard is here?"

"Yeah, Prime Ambo forced us to bring them. Miller was very clear about my orders. You understand?"

"Yes. I understand. I'd expect nothing less."

Sanchez dropped back behind the cab, smiled at DJ, and stuck his fist out. DJ bumped with his own.

"DJ, why do you always try to do the cool guy thing and be fashionably late to the party?" Sanchez asked.

DJ laughed. "I guess I'm just not as desperate for attention as you are."

"That's, cold, man. Heartless," Sanchez said, then popped up to fire downrange.

The Elite Guard finally arrived at the forklift under the protection of Dozer's covering firing. Two of them knelt and fired back at the compound. The third, however, stood at the edge of the flatbed a meter away, and removed his helmet.

Mac recognized him right away as Captain Tom Scott. He was short, with a handsome and friendly face. His black hair was wavy, and his tan face was clean-shaven. He didn't look too friendly today, however.

In a loud and authoritative voice, he announced, "Major Malcolm Lambert, you and your accomplices are under arrest for insubordination, going absent without leave, violating the sovereign diplomatic nation of—"

Mac cut him off by putting his hands up with palms toward him. "We will peacefully turn ourselves over to Master Sergeant Jameson and accept the consequences of our actions. But not yet." Mac popped up onto his feet, looking down at Captain Scott. "I've got more work to do." Then Mac shouted to the team, "Cover me!"

There was no question about the Space Warfare Group's loyalties. They responded to Mac as their leader. As Mac climbed onto the forklift cab and slid down the slippery windshield to the bridge surface, Mac's men provided cover fire. Even Dozer shifted his position to clear the way for Mac as he ran toward the compound entrance.

Mac stepped along the frozen bridge surface in a combat crouch. He aimed his RAP laser stream at any Bone Rattler he could see standing. There were many dead, scattered in the bloody snow. He saw movement to his left and glanced over to see Sanchez sprinting past him, screaming like a wild man, firing a Bone Rattler rifle from his hip.

Dozer's Dragon fire, along with the team's rifle fire, pressed the Bone Rattlers back. They turned and retreated into the safety of the compound building.

Sanchez reached the building first and pressed his back up against the metal door to the left of the huge opening into the building. Mac crashed up against the metal door next to Sanchez, followed a second later by Bones and DJ.

Cory, Zhou, and Taylor came slower, followed by the Elite Guard soldiers. Mac watched them approach through the carnage of dead Bone Rattlers littering the bridge and compound entrance. Mac was grateful and somewhat surprised they hadn't suffered any casualties yet. The forklift was a lifesaver, and the Starhawk's arrival was a game changer. The Bone Rattlers were incapable of matching the Starhawk's firepower. It would feel unfair if the Bone Rattlers weren't so evil.

Dozer arrived last. He moved slower with the heavy weapon. Mac, without a comm connection, used hand signals to instruct the team about how they would enter the building.

PRINCESS OMO-BINRIN LOWERED her eyes and mumbled something to Rust, who was still squatting in front of her as she sat on the cold hard floor against the wall.

"What was that, Princess?" he asked. "I can't hear you."

She spoke louder. "Zeicury. We found the crashed Noct ship on Zeicury. Now, leave them alone. Let them be," she pleaded with him, locking her eyes on his.

Rust stood and paced for a moment. He looked over Vega's shoulder at the compound entrance door. The firefight continued, and looked like it was intensifying.

He returned to the princess sitting on the floor and looked down at her, chuckling. He rubbed his forehead with the back of the hand holding the pistol. Through his laughing, he said, "Princess, do you think I am that stupid? Oh, man! Who do you take me for? This isn't my first rodeo!" He suddenly stopped laughing, and muttered, "We've already searched and eliminated Zeicury."

Rust raised his arm, pointing the pistol at the huddle of Okutans. He paused for a moment to let the drama of the moment settle in. Then, he pulled the trigger and killed another Okutan woman.

The Okutans screamed again, wailing from the trauma.

Princess Omo-Binrin screamed and cried, dropping her chin to her chest. She sobbed heavily.

"Why are you testing me?" Rust yelled. He sounded psychotic. Truthfully, he felt a bit psychotic. Time was running out. He needed the answers before the raiding party entered the building. "The bodies will continue to pile up until you tell me the truth." He was not going to die on this arctic planet.

He raised the pistol again, zeroing in on a new Okutan, and Princess Omo-Binrin put her bound hands up toward Rust.

"Please stop." Her voice was much quieter, and she looked broken. "I'm sorry. I'll tell you the truth. Please don't hurt them."

This time, Rust did not lower the pistol, but took a step closer to the Okutan he was aiming at, putting the barrel of the pistol only centimeters from the head of one of the older Okutans. His eyes still never left Omo-Binrin.

"The truth is, we found it a few ootautin," she paused, thinking "How do you say it? Uh, about seven UPG months ago while investigating a new mining site on Ubbion 5. The Noct crash site is on Ubbion 5."

Rust looked at her for a long time. He calculated if she was telling the truth. Ubbion 5 didn't ring a bell for him. He'd never even heard of it. Holstering his pistol, he pulled the communicator from his pocket and sent a quick message to the Hammurabi.

Intel on a planet called Ubbion 5? Possible crash site.

Standby popped up on the small screen.

As he waited impatiently, Vega looked over at him and nodded toward the entrance. Vega wasn't holding his rifle against his chest anymore, but had it against his shoulder and pointed toward the skirmish at the entrance. Rust joined him to see Bone Rattlers retreating through the door into the compound.

"We're out of time," Vega said. "They are coming in."

The message from the Hammurabi finally came through. *Existence and location of Ubbion 5 confirmed. Uninhabited, but past activity noted by three Galactic Coalition Nations: Lucinians, Chuboneraths, and Okutans. Not in our search grid.*

Rust responded quickly. *Could it be the location of the crash site?*

The response came immediately, *Affirmative. No disqualifying features. Location is different than our theory, but analysis confirms possibility.*

Rust closed his eyes and thought for a moment. *Do I trust her?* The deafening explosion and flash of light followed by a deep resonating *kachoonk, kachoonk* interrupted his thoughts.

His eyes popped open, and he darted the few steps to where Vega was. The Bone Rattlers were in disarray, and several human soldiers flowed in through the wide door with rifles behind a man with what he recognized as the X560 energy blaster. He'd personally tested that weapon before production and knew it was devastating.

"Time to roll," he said to Vega.

Vega began firing down the corridor toward the soldiers. Rust saw a tall black man wearing civilian clothes standing in the doorway. He wasn't wearing the standard environmental suits like the other soldiers. *Weird*. The man was looking his way, and while the distance between them was almost fifty meters, he could feel the man's eyes on him, and he felt more exposed than he liked. Then, without warning, the man broke into a sprint, coming his way, leaping over fallen Bone Rattlers. The man ran like a trained athlete.

"Come on!" Rust shouted, fired at the running man, and took off toward Sckrahhg's headquarters.

Vega ran toward the princess and started to pick her up.

"No, leave her!" Rust yelled, and Vega obeyed. He ran across the corridor intersection toward Rust and was hit in the shoulder by a well-aimed shot. Rust watched in slow motion as Vega spun around, slammed against the corridor wall, and slumped to the ground. The black man was closing in fast, firing his weapon, and charging fiercely.

Vega yelled to Rust, "Go! I'll hold them off!" He tried to raise his rifle but was hit again in the chest. His arm dropped and his head slumped.

Rust turned and ran as fast as he could on his injured leg, toward Sckrahhg's headquarters.

CHAPTER FIFTY-NINE

Outside Quokex Compound, Moments earlier…

Dozer slid to a stop and pressed his body against the metal door of the building with the rest of the team. DJ and Sanchez kept cover fire directed at the opening as the rest of them pressed their bodies against the cold metal of the door. Mac bumped Taylor's shoulder. She was standing next to him and shivering a lot now. Her jumpsuit and hair were soaked, and she held the Bone Rattler rifle she'd picked up along the way in a ready position, but Mac could see the end of the stubby barrel shaking. She wasn't doing well.

Bones stood shoulder-to-shoulder next to Mac, on his other side. He turned to Bones and asked, "Bones, check her vitals for me."

"Yessir," he responded and shifted over to scan Taylor with his E-Gear helmet. He also scanned Sanchez and Mac. "She's close to hyperthermic. You all are, but she is the worst," he said.

Mac hoped inside the compound was warmer, to prevent the hypothermia from taking over. *Time to move.* Mac got DJ and Sanchez's attention and then gave the signal to Bones, Zhou, and Dozer to breach the compound entrance.

In a synchronized and well-practiced maneuver, Zhou and Bones pulled grenades from their equipment belts, pressed the activate buttons with their thumbs, and tossed them through the wide doorway into the compound. After tossing the grenades, they pulled back and a second later, an explosion of light and booming concussive force made the ground shudder and the metal door shake violently. To finish off the breach maneuver, Dozer rotated out, away from the door to stand in front of the opening. He raised the Dragon and began firing the powerful weapon while sweeping it from left to right.

Once Dozer cleared enough of the Bone Rattlers from the entrance, he stepped out of the way, making room for DJ, Sanchez, and Bones to enter. They moved in with slow and steady footsteps, their rifles pressed tightly against their shoulders. They entered as a tight group and fanned out as they crossed into the building, with eyes gazing down their barrels and firing at any enemy movement.

Mac and Lou followed behind the team with Cory. Captain Scott and his Elite Guard wisely remained back for a beat.

As they stepped from the cold dark night into the lighted corridor of the compound, the warm, dry air Mac was hoping for greeted him. He wouldn't call it cozy, but coming in from the snow was a welcomed change. Mac nudged Taylor toward the opposite wall behind Dozer and signaled for her to stay with him. She nodded and jogged over to Dozer's position against the wall. She had to step over several fallen Bone Rattlers.

Mac asked Cory to keep an eye on Taylor, then drifted in the other direction. The firefight was coming to a quick conclusion. He scanned the space and assessed the situation. Sanchez and DJ had the last active Bone Rattler pressed up against the wall and were wrestling his weapon away from him. Then, a close-range shot to the chest killed him and he dropped to the floor.

Zhou and Bones were checking the fallen Bone Rattlers scattered around the floor by nudging them with their feet. They kicked weapons out of reach to protect the team from a surprise attack by anyone playing dead.

Then Mac's eyes caught movement down the corridor. It was not a Bone Rattler. He couldn't believe he was seeing a human. A tall dark-haired man stood at the end of the corridor pointing a rifle at him. Mac cocked his head and squinted.

Who is that?

Another man appeared, shorter but there was no question in Mac's mind, this guy was a trained operator. Both men looked like elite soldiers. Even from the distance, he could see both men were fit and well-equipped. This second man, with wavy dark hair and a huge mustache and pointed goatee, stood like a tested leader. Mac knew guys like this. Whoever this guy was, Mac was sure he'd been marinated in decades of grizzly warfare.

The man locked eyes with Mac. An unspoken message passed between them. This man was who he was after. He knew this was the man responsible for ambushing the Okutan Royal Vessel. He now knew this man was ultimately responsible for the death of Sam. This was his ultimate target.

Up to that moment, Mac had been operating in battlefield professionalism, focusing only on the mission. He'd compartmentalized everything else. For those few minutes, assaulting the compound distracted him from the pain of losing Sam. But seeing this man was like throwing gasoline on the smoldering coals of grief, and the flames of fury engulfed him.

The man must have sensed Mac's intentions because his posture changed. Without hesitation, Mac took off in a sprint toward him.

The man raised his rifle and fired before running off to Mac's left. His shot went wide, missing Mac as he ran. The larger dark-haired man darted out of sight and then returned, trying to run across the corridor intersection with the mustached man. Mac fired his RAP and hit him in the shoulder, which spun him around. He slammed against the wall and slid into a sitting position.

Mac pushed his frozen legs and body toward the men. He pressed the button on the RAP's grip to change the weapon from kill to stun. He wouldn't let them escape the easy way by dying. The tall man tried to raise his rifle with one hand toward Mac, but Mac was too fast. He fired, much closer now, and hit the man sitting against the wall in the chest. The man slumped unconscious and dropped the rifle.

When he reached the corridor intersection and kicked the unconscious man's rifle away, Mac was surprised for a second time as he noticed the group of Okutans huddled on the floor to his right in the crossing corridor. Looking left, he saw the mustached man dart down another corridor. He appeared to be limping.

"Freeze!" Mac yelled, but the man disappeared.

Sanchez, Lou, and DJ arrived at his side. He glanced at them. The Elite Guard were on their heels. He saw Cory and Dozer remain on guard at the front entrance.

Mac jogged backward down the hall toward the fleeing man and gave orders to the team, "Lou and DJ, take care of the princess. Captain Scott, arrest this man for galactic crimes," Mac said, pointing at the large unconscious man sitting against the wall. "Bones, Zhou, stay frosty. Set up a perimeter. Sanchez, on me."

"I thought you'd never ask, Major Mac," Sanchez replied with a wide smile. He looked soaked, but seemed to be enjoying himself.

Mac turned and ran down the hall with Sanchez at his side. As they turned the corner, they found several doors and crossing corridors. It was like a maze. A frustrating maze. They checked doors and peeked down the side paths but decided to follow the trail of wetness left from the Bone Rattlers passing back and forth from the snowstorm. The track of dampness stood out as the obvious path to follow because bloody footprints went in the same direction. It was a gamble, but the best option.

When Sanchez and Mac came to the last corner and carefully peeked around, they found double doors and two Bone Rattler guards who were alert and ready for their arrival. Mac and Sanchez were rewarded with rifle fire aimed at their heads. Concrete dust filled the air as they ducked back behind the corner for cover.

"Whoa," Sanchez said as he grinned at Mac. "This looks like the place. Did you bring our invitations?"

"Nope. Did you bring our flash bang grenades?"

"Negatory."

"I'll take the one on the right, you the left."

"Negatory," Sanchez said again.

"You have a better idea?" Mac asked as more blaster fire slammed into the corner near their heads and against the opposite wall.

"Yes, this," Sanchez said, and reached around the corner with the RAP and sprayed the Bone Rattlers with a continuous stream of green laser fire for several seconds, while hiding behind the corner, until the Bone Rattlers' defensive blaster fire ended. Mac heard two heavy thuds.

Sanchez, proud of himself, lifted the RAP's short barrel toward his lips and blew smoke off the barrel.

"Nicely done. I'll add that maneuver to our next training course."

"Only if you called it the *Great Sanchezio Maneuver*."

"Deal. Come on."

Mac shuffled around the corner, RAP at the ready, and saw the downed guards and a long squiggly burn mark along the walls from the *Great Sanchezio* in action.

The double doors were open a little, and he peeked in but didn't see Mr. Moustache or any Bone Rattlers. The room was dark as well.

"Why's it always gotta be the dark, creepy room?" Sanchez whispered.

"Bad guys love dark, creepy places," Mac whispered back.

He looked to Sanchez, who nodded that he was ready. Mac eased the heavy door open enough to pass through. Its hinges let out a groan and squealed softly. He paused a beat, then continued into the dark room.

Sanchez focused on the left, while Mac took the right. They found a large bone chair in the center of the room. It was like a throne. The room smelled terrible. Off to the right was a series of computers and communication equipment, with small lamps providing the only illumination. He didn't see any Bone Rattlers or humans.

After a tense moment of scanning the room, Mac felt like they were in the wrong place. But then, he heard metal scraping against concrete. Then something heavy crashed, followed by the distinctive bang and screech of a stuck and seldom-used metal door being opened. The sounds echoed through the large room. It came from the back of the room, where he saw a door leading to another room. Mac gave a silent signal to Sanchez, and they moved toward the sound.

Arthur Rust put all his weight on his good leg and leaned against the wall while Sckrahhg and another Bone Rattler cleared old metal cabinets and equipment to make access to the door. As they pushed over the cabinets and tossed old chairs out of the way, Rust received a message. He checked the small screen of his communicator.

Approaching compound bridge. 2 min.

He replied quickly. *Plan change. EXFIL on east slope behind the compound.*

Roger. Rerouting without delay.

Sckrahhg wrestled the heavy door for a moment, then it screeched open, making more noise than Rust preferred. A gust of cold air and snow blew into the room.

"Could you make a little more noise, Sckrahhg? Why don't you just call the UPG and tell them exactly where I am?" Rust shook his head in frustration. He glanced behind him, seeing no one. "Come on, come on, get it open."

"Arthur Rust, you are a bad human. You are lucky I don't kill you now and eat your flesh," Sckrahhg growled.

"In your dreams, you hairy idiot," Rust replied and stepped through the door into the frosty night. Sckrahhg followed. The door led toward a small landing pad extending out from the steep mountainside. Like the chasm bridge, small yellow lights on the handrail illuminated the landing pad. More powerful lights also shined from the building's exterior wall. The door was cut into the mountain and lined on both sides by tall concrete retaining walls, like a tunnel with no ceiling. The snow was several inches thick and falling fast. Rust and Sckrahhg shuffled through the snow toward the landing pad, which seemed to hover in midair over the eastside canyon.

CHAPTER SIXTY

Mac and Sanchez followed the noise coming from the next room. They entered and found the dark room was large and filled with organized stacks of storage, standing taller than themselves. In the darkness, it looked like the cube-shaped stacks included crates and old furniture. Scattered haphazardly on the floor to their right were a few chairs, metal cabinets, and crates. Mac felt an icy breeze, drawing his eyes to the metal door standing open on his right. The door was at the end of a narrow section of the room. Snow and dim light spilled in through the opening.

They had little time, so they quickly turned that direction and serpentined silently through the scattered debris toward the door. When they were a few meters from the door, an enormous shadow crawled along the floor and onto the wall, followed by a Bone Rattler who ducked his head to enter the door designed for humans. In the silence, they could hear the soft clanking of the bones as he moved.

This Bone Rattler was unprepared. He carried his rifle pointed toward the floor. Mac and Sanchez fired their weapons at the same time, getting the jump on him. But they weren't quick enough. The Bone Rattler yelled something in his monstrous native language before crashing to the floor.

Behind them, two Bone Rattlers entered the room howling and more prepared than their compatriot, lying dead on the floor.

Sanchez looked at Mac and said, "Go get that guy, Major Mac. I'll hold these guys off." Sanchez tore off at full speed, leaping over a cabinet and matching the Bone Rattlers with his own primal scream.

Mac turned and passed through the door. The cold air shocked his wet, tired body. He pressed the thoughts of his bodily discomfort out of his mind. He found himself in a roofless tunnel where the concrete walls on either side of him sloped downward to the ground level, following the slope of the mountainside. Leading from the door were footprints that disturbed the deep snow, heading towards a circular landing pad. The landing pad was only partly visible beyond the tunnel. It was eerily quiet. Mac didn't see anyone. He walked forward, cautiously scanning to the left and right.

There he was.

He stood on the left side of the landing pad.

Mac stepped forward and yelled, "Freeze! Do not move!" He pointed his weapon at the man.

The mustached man turned and looked at Mac. He didn't reach for a weapon or say anything. He just winked at Mac.

"Don't move. I won't hesitate to take you down."

He said nothing. With no wind, the big snowflakes floated down between them to join their uncountable brethren on the ground. Mac didn't like this man's lack of response. He was wearing two laser pistols in leg holsters.

"Who do you work for?"

Nothing.

Mac stepped forward.

"Why are you with the Bone Rattlers?"

Nothing.

"Why did you capture the princess?"

Nothing. The man just stared at him.

Mac approached, weapon pointing at him.

"You are under arrest. Put your hands behind your head."

The man didn't move a muscle.

"Do it!"

In the distance, he heard the unmistakable buzzing whir of a small spacecraft. He looked over his shoulder and saw the blinding lights on the bottom of the craft. It was right on top of him and coming down quickly. Mac burst into a run toward the man, but it was no good. It was too late. He couldn't get there in time. The man moved unhurried toward the small shoe-shaped spacecraft. It was all black, with no markings at all. It hovered close to the ground, blowing away the snow on the surface.

"No!" Mac yelled as he ran. He fired on the move but missed. So he stopped, planted his feet, and aimed across the short distance. The RAP was still set to stun and the easy shot was true this time, hitting the man who didn't seem to care one bit. The stun burst smashed into the man and his lights went out. He stumbled and fell toward the small spacecraft. Mac watched in horror as a black-clad figure hopped out of the ship's door and picked up the unconscious mustached man under the arms to drag him into the spacecraft.

"No! Stop!" Mac yelled again. His brain told him to fire at this new man, but before the neural signal completed its transmission to his body, a freight train hit him.

Mac was unprepared for whatever hit him. Knocked off his feet, his body hit the ground hard on his right shoulder, and his head bounced off the ground. Seeing stars and trying to catch his breath, he watched the mustached man being dragged through the small ship's door. Snow was being blown into his face and he was being pressed to the ground by the heavy, snarling beast. He tried to fire toward the ship, but it was useless. His aim was way off, and the Bone Rattler hammered his arm with a massive fist until he dropped the RAP, which slid several meters away in the snow.

The ship's door closed, and it lifted from the landing pad, disappearing into the darkness, and leaving Mac alone with only the vicious Bone Rattler intent on killing him.

The monster growled, "Dark human, you will die now."

Mac fought back, trying to break free, but it was useless. He wriggled and twisted until he got a look at the monster. It was Sckrahhg, the Bone Rattler general.

Sckrahhg shifted and released Mac's arm so he could pound on Mac's face. With his arm free, Mac took the opening and fired his elbow several times into Sckrahhg's throat. He fought back with every ounce of energy he had left. He hit as fast and violently as humanly possible, knowing he had to get the upper hand immediately, or Sckrahhg would, in fact, kill him. Mac's mind flashed through a photo reel of Sckrahhg, killing him, eating him, and polishing his bones for his armor. This vision intensified Mac's will to fight.

After the third piston-like elbow to the face, Sckrahhg's bone helmet broke and fell off. He rewarded Mac with a couple of meaty hammer fist blows to the jaw and shoulder. He tried to tuck his head and block the punches, but every blow from the beast was earth-shaking. Mac was exponentially over-matched in strength.

Sckrahhg stopped punching and tried a new tactic of wrapping his massive, clawed hand around Mac's throat. He could feel the claws digging into his skin. If he didn't change the momentum fast, Sckrahhg would kill him.

Can't. Let. Him. Win.

Mac bucked his body and tried to kick and release his legs. Sckrahhg didn't move much but leaned a little closer to Mac.

Perfect.

As the big leathery face of his attacker leaned closer, distracted by enjoying choking Mac to death, Mac jabbed his left arm out, like a piston. He kept his fingers extended and aimed at the Bone Rattler's eye. He connected and felt his fingers smash into the soft eyeball and press deeply into the eye socket.

The pain caused Sckrahhg to bellow and release Mac's throat to cover his own eye with both hands. Mac choked and gasped as he took in a deep breath. Blood oozed between Sckrahhg's fingers, coating the golden fur on the back of his hands. Mac pulled himself out from under Sckrahhg as he leaned back in pain.

He scrambled out of his attacker's reach and climbed to his feet.

Sckrahhg was on his knees and let go of his face now. Mac moved fast and aggressive before Sckrahhg could get to his feet.

Mac grabbed the back of Sckrahhg's neck and launched a knee into the face of the monster. Then, releasing the neck, he adjusted his footing and spun his body on the ball of his left foot while throwing his extended right leg in a roundhouse kick that connected against Sckrahhg's temple.

These three power blows to Sckrahhg's head did serious damage. Sckrahhg staggered and looked like he was seeing stars. This combination of attacks would kill a man, but he merely dazed the Bone Rattler.

To Mac's dismay, Sckrahhg shook his head and kept coming with a guttural roar. From his kneeling position, Sckrahhg launched his body toward Mac, who tried to jump out of reach, but Sckrahhg's arms were too long, and he snatched Mac's ankle.

Mac lost his balance and fell to the ground. He tried crawling away, but Sckrahhg pulled him by the leg. He had his ankle in an unbreakable vice grip.

No, get out, Mac thought frantically.

He tried kicking himself loose, but Sckrahhg was unrelenting. Mac kicked the top of Sckrahhg's head several times with all his strength but couldn't break free. Sckrahhg pulled him close, horrifying Mac to see Sckrahhg's barred fangs coming down onto his left arm.

It was as if time slowed nearly to a stop. He watched it all like an out-of-body experience. Sckrahhg's long saliva-covered fangs clamped onto his upper arm, breaking through the thin material of his shirt, and sunk deep into his flesh. Blood poured out of the wounds created by the sharp fangs. Mac saw himself scream, as the combined pain of piercing fangs and bone-crushing pressure of the monster's jaws ratcheted down on his arm.

Mac had experienced many injuries over his years as a soldier and special operator. He was accustomed to pain. This, however, was a category of pain he'd never experienced before. It was cruel and unusual. In the moment, his mind and body became paralyzed. He couldn't get his mind to engage with the situation. He felt like he wasn't part of the body lying in the snow. His body, now paralyzed by the all-consuming pain, redlined on the limits of what the human body could handle. Sckrahhg ground his fangs into the bone and gnawed on Mac's arm like it was a turkey drumstick.

Mac screamed in pain. He fought for mental clarity. He fought for consciousness. He fought for the will to fight. Forcing his head to move, he looked for his RAP. It was right there. He extended his arm out, but it was beyond his reach. He then punched Sckrahhg in the ribs, but it had no effect, as his strength was waning.

An image of Sanchez's grinning face on the Trek'et ship, as he handed Mac one of the power riveters, popped in his mind. He then saw Lou's face as she smiled and held the riveter high after killing the Bone Rattler.

Yes, the rivet gun. Pressing his good arm toward his chest, he reached for his own riveter tucked into his chest rig. He pressed his right hand in and got his fingers wrapped around the handgrip. He pulled it out and pressed the metal barrel of the riveter against Sckrahhg's head.

"Chew on this!"

Mac pulled the trigger five times, imbedding five long rivet bolts into Sckrahhg's brain. Sckrahhg died instantly, like someone pulled the plug. His jaws stopped grinding on his upper arm, and his massive furry body went limp in the snow next to Mac, his fangs still buried in Mac's arm.

The searing pain was unreal. Mac laid there for a moment, eyes wide, breathing through the pain for a moment. He tried to regain his strength before prying Sckrahhg's dead jaws open to release his arm. Every little movement created more pain. His arm and shoulder were on fire.

He jammed the barrel of the riveter between the jaws and used it to pry open Sckrahhg's mouth. Once he had enough room, he lifted and pulled his arm free. He screamed in pain again, flopped onto his back, and decided not to look at his mangled arm.

He laid there on his back, with arms spread out wide. His left arm was bleeding profusely, hanging on by tattered ligaments. His right hand held the riveter. He stared up at the thousands of snowflakes above him, falling gently to the ground. He felt the cold wetness of flakes on his forehead and cheeks. In the distance, he thought he heard someone calling his name. He tried to respond but only mumbled. Then, everything went gray, then to black as he lost consciousness.

CHAPTER SIXTY-ONE

When Mac's consciousness returned, the first thing he noticed was the searing fire in his left arm. He winced and kept his eyes closed for a moment as the world came back into focus. He heard voices talking above him.

"Mac, can you hear me?" It was Lou's voice. He felt her touch the side of his head. Her hands were warm. He also felt a set of stronger, and less gentle, hands checking his body for injuries.

"Give him the pain blocker, and we'll try to wrap this arm."

"Can the Starhawk land in here? Or do we need to get the gurney and carry him out the front?"

As Mac entered the conscious world again and listened to the voices of people he trusted and depended on, he had a second of peace. But then the pain came crashing in. Every second he lay there on the cold ground, his body heat seeped out of him. His left arm throbbed with searing pain, followed by the emotional pain returning.

Mac blinked a few times and opened his eyes. There was more moisture in his eyes than he wanted to admit. The faces of Lou and DJ greeted him as they squatted above him. Lou, even with her brown hair disheveled and drenched, somehow still managed to look pretty. Next to her, DJ looked craggy and rough as always, with his face covered in black stubble and a cigar poking out of the side of his mouth. The night was still dark, and the soft snowflakes were still falling from the sky.

"You're back," Taylor said joyfully.

Mac groaned out, "How could I not, with the smell of that terrible cigar? I'm surprised it didn't kill me."

"He's fine, everyone. Don't worry, he's just fine," DJ announced and stood, but continued to look down at Mac. "I'm going to get the Starhawk in here. Mac, just relax. We'll take good care of you."

"Did you track the jump ship?" Mac said weakly.

"What?" DJ asked.

"The ship…the ship that the mustached man got on. Did you track it?" Mac was struggling to get all the words out.

"What ship? We didn't know about any ship."

Mac closed his eyes. "So, he's gone?"

"Yeah, he's nowhere to be found." DJ paused for a moment and pulled the cigar from his mouth. "Listen Mac, this is all a mess, but we got the-"

Mac's eyes opened again, and he interrupted. "What about the other guy? The guy from inside?"

"Yeah, we've got him. He's awake and locked down in the Starhawk."

"Good." Mac visualized the interrogation that would lead to the identity and location of the mustached man. "DJ, we need to get an interrogation started right away. We'll be able to get the identity and location of the mustached man."

DJ interrupted, "Mac, listen, man, you are in no condition to be doing any interrogation."

"I have to." Mac tried to sit up.

Next to Mac, Liang Zhou, who was working on his arm and preparing to administer the pain blocker and pushed him back down. Taylor pressed a firm hand against Mac's chest.

"Whoa, hold on, sir," Zhou said.

"Mac, no, you need to just lie there," Taylor added.

With a stronger voice, Mac said, "That man is the one behind all of this, and he is responsible for killing Sam. We can't lose him by wasting time."

"I understand, Mac, really, I do. We all want to find the dirtbags behind this, especially for Sam. And, trust me, we will. But right now, you must relax and let us take care of you, or you will lose that arm."

Zhou added, in his gentle voice, "Sir, this injury could kill you if we don't act fast. Please, let me take care of this."

Mac nodded his head, and relaxed against the ground.

DJ continued, quieter this time, "And don't forget you are out of the game, and you still need to deal with Captain Scott. So, just lie there, relax, and trust us."

Mac nodded again, unable to form words.

Zhou finished cleaning up his arm and administering the pain blocker. "Alright, sir, in a moment you'll start feeling better."

"I hope you mean not feeling anything at all, Z," Mac said with a grimace.

"Pretty much, if I did my job right."

"Thanks, Z." Mac turned his head and looked at Lou, who was still on her knees and leaning over Mac to look him in the face. "Lou, are you OK? No injuries?"

"Yes, I'm fine. Just a little cold. Don't worry about me," she said.

"You fought well. I'm impressed. And you look pretty good for someone who just raided an enemy compound," Mac said.

She laughed and said, "Well, you look like death warmed over."

"Thanks, I appreciate the honesty." He laughed a bit, then noticed for the first time that her hands were bound at the wrists with handcuffs.

"What the? Why?" He tried to sit up again.

"Mac, no, no, no, no." She pressed her bound hands against his chest to keep him from moving again. "You must stay down. I'm fine."

"Sir, please don't move until I get this wound stabilized," Zhou said.

Mac dropped his head to the ground again in frustration.

Behind Taylor, another person came into view, wearing all white. He moved to where Mac could see him, and Taylor leaned back out of the way.

Captain Tom Scott stood above him, silver helmet tucked under his arm.

Before Captain Scott could say anything, Mac blurted out, "Where's Sanchez? You better not have done anything to him."

Captain Scott pointed toward the building behind Mac and said, "He's fine, but in our custody."

From behind him, he heard Sanchez say, "Hey, Major Mac, I'm back here. They've got me in cuffs. And your lady, Lou, too. Can you believe these guys? We save the princess and kill the Bone Rattlers, and this is the thanks we get. It's like they are jealous of how good we are. Don't worry, though. He's just on some kinda power trip. And he's a tool. Don't listen to anything Captain Tool says."

Captain Scott shook his head in annoyance and Mac knew for sure that while he was unconscious, Sanchez had gone *full Sanchez, maybe even full Sanchezio,* on Captain Scott when arrested. That made him happy. It made him smile just thinking about how absurd Sanchez must have been. Or maybe it was the pain blocker working.

"Sanchez, I'm glad you are alright," Mac called out. "But seriously, Lou is not my lady."

"Sure, bro. Whatever you say." Sanchez chuckled.

Next to him, Lou quietly said, "Would that be such a bad thing?"

He looked her in the eyes. She was still kneeling beside him. *Would that be a bad thing?* He thought. *Is that even a thing?* "No, that sounds like a good thing," he replied quietly.

In an annoyed voice, Captain Scott said, "OK, everyone. Are we done with the family reunion?"

"Captain Scott, I voluntarily turn myself over to your custody."

In the background, he heard Sanchez say, "Captain Tool."

"Thank you, Major. That is the right decision. We'll forgo the handcuffs for now because of your arm injury. You'll all be taken to the *McDaniels* in our custody, then to MedBay immediately. But once we get to Terra Libertas, you'll be transferred to the medical facility at Spaceport Soriano. You will remain in our custody and under guard until you are well enough to attend the preliminary hearing regarding the charges against you."

"Understood. Where is the princess? Is she safe?" Mac asked the group.

DJ stepped over again and, through the cigar poking out of his mouth, said, "She's fine. Tough little lady. She and the other Okutans are on the Starhawk with the others and Captain Scott's team."

"Captain Tool," Sanchez reminded everyone.

"Listen up, everyone. The ship will be here in six mikes. Z, I've got Dozer bringing the gurney out. He'll help you get Mac on the ship and settled."

After a few minutes, the Starhawk approached, shining its bright lights on the landing pad. The pilot cut the powerful rocket engines, which reduced the noise, but it was still a lot of spaceship for a small area. The ship came in close and hovered above the landing pad, using the small landing thrust engines. It came down and settled on the surface close to the edge of the landing pad that extended out from the mountain slope.

The back access ramp lowered to the ground and Dozer was the first to exit, pushing the hover gurney. Captain Scott's team came out and collected Sanchez and Taylor. Dozer, Z, and DJ lifted Mac onto the narrow floating platform. Mac's weight made the gurney dip and wobble a bit before stabilizing. Zhou did an admirable job bandaging Mac's arm and securing it to his abdomen. The pain was mild now, and he felt sleepy. His mind was getting foggy. They put a foil blanket over him and locked him on the gurney with two belts. Then they guided him up the ramp and into the dim and mercifully warm passenger cabin.

Zhou maneuvered Mac and the gurney into the tiny closet-sized room that served as a mobile MedBay, and locked the gurney in place for the brief trip back to the *McDaniels*.

Zhou took off his helmet. His black hair was cut short on his scalp. He looked so young. His black stubble was patchy and thin on his chestnut skin. "Sir, I'm so glad you are alive. This is a severe injury, but I'm sure the docs down at Soriano will take good care of you."

"Thank you, Z, you did a great job as usual."

"Listen, sir, I'm sorry about what's going to happen. I'm sorry about Sam."

Mac reached out with his good hand and squeezed Zhou's arm. "I'll be OK. I made some poor decisions and I'm not going to run from that, roger?"

"Roger," he replied and nodded.

Mac raised his fist and Zhou bumped it with his own and left the tiny room.

After Zhou left, DJ greeted Mac with Princess Omo-Binrin Oba.

"Mac, someone wanted to say thank you."

The princess was short, dainty, and delicate. Her fancy dress looked trashed, but she still exuded a royal bearing. A blanket hung over her shoulders. He noticed, like Jagoon, her blue skin was translucent, making her muscles, ligaments, and veins under the skin faintly visible.

"Mac, is it?" She looked from Mac to DJ, unsure. She spoke her accented words with a strong voice.

DJ said, "Uh, yes, ma'am. Major Malcom Lambert of the Interplanetary Army. But we just call him Mac."

"Major Malcolm Lambert, I am forever in your debt. Thank you for risking your life to save us."

"You are welcome," Mac said. "I'm sorry we didn't find you sooner and save more of your people. Princess, I wanted you to know that I spent some time with Jagoon Ina before he died. He was an honorable and valiant warrior."

"You met him? You found him alive?" This revelation surprised her.

"He was. We found him on your ship and brought him back to ours. He had a message from your kidnappers, which is how we found you. Sadly, and I'm so sorry to tell you, they killed him and one of our men in an ambush."

"I too am sorry. Jagoon was my personal protector since I was a small child. I loved him like a second father. There are many stories I could tell."

"I would love to hear those stories someday, Princess."

"Yes, we shall do that someday. Again, thank you." She smiled and touched his forehead with her small, warm hand. "I don't know all of what you are facing, Major, but I promise you, our king, who is my father of course, and I will petition the entire Unite Planetary Government to treat you with leniency."

"That is very kind of you," Mac said.

"I wish you the best," she said.

Before she could turn to leave, Mac said, "Your Highness, did you know those men? The big guy or the man with the mustache?"

"No. I don't know who they are. But he said he wanted the information I carry."

"About the Noct?" Mac's eyelids were feeling heavy, and he had trouble keeping them open.

The princess' almond-shaped eyes widened.

"How do you know that name?"

"I had a conversation with someone who told me that was why you were coming to meet with our president." Mac struggled to get the words out. He was fading fast.

"Yes, that is true. And, yes, that is what he wanted from me."

Mac shook his head and opened his eyes wide and said, "Did he give you his name?"

"No, he did not."

"I'm not surprised."

"There is much we must figure out, Major. We will launch a full investigation into these matters immediately. But you, my friend, need to rest and get better. Thank you again."

"Yes, Your Highness, there is much to figure out."

After she left, DJ leaned in close. "You need to get some rest. We'll be checking on you frequently. Sounds like once the Starhawk is aboard the *McDaniels*, we'll be back to T-Lib in about six hours." He used their nickname for Terra Libertas. "And Mac, Colonel Miller is a raging volcano ready to blow. You should probably take as many pain pills as you can and be numb or unconscious when you see him. Even being dead would be a better option."

Mac laughed at DJ's warning. He knew he was returning to a firestorm. But, for now, he would rest. He was so tired. He felt groggy, andis mind was swimming. "Just gotta embrace the suck, DJ."

"Ain't that the truth? By the way, I'm pretty sure Z dropped some sleepy juice in with your pain meds," DJ said, speaking of a medical sleep aid.

"I figured he must have. I'm having a hard time keeping my eyes open, and the world is spinning in circles."

"Good, don't fight it."

DJ squeezed his good shoulder and left. As the door was closing behind him, Mac closed his eyes and he could hear Sanchez in the passenger cabin say, "Hey, Captain Tool, why don't you come sit next to me?"

EPILOGUE

Interplanetary Navy Spaceport Soriano
New London City, Terra Libertas

Mac's eyes slowly opened. His eyelids were sticky, and the light to his left was glaring. He tried to look around, but it was too much. His mind felt as sticky as his eyes. His mouth was sticky as well, dried out, making it hard to swallow. He didn't know where he was. Closing his eyes again, he tried to organize the messy strands of thought.

He remembered being barely aware of arriving at the *McDaniels'* MedBay. He drifted in and out of consciousness the entire time he was moved from the Starhawk to the small medical facility. A couple of visions of Dr. Cornell stabilizing his arm popped into his mind.

The *McDaniels'* medical staff kept him comfortable, which meant mostly unconscious, throughout the flight to Terra Libertas. When they arrived in orbit, the medical team moved Mac to the waiting ambulance transport ship that flew him to the patient unloading area at Spaceport Soriano's massive military hospital. He was mostly unaware of the brief trip and transfer to the very capable hospital nurses and surgeons. An Elite Guard soldier remained with him the entire time.

Mac's memory of the journey was vague at best. He remembered the guard's presence and a few seconds of warm sunshine on his face as they moved him into the hospital. He also remembered the face of a Lucinian surgeon who spoke to him as he was being prepped for surgery. He didn't remember anything the doctor said, but he remembered being surprised to see a Lucinian in a Navy hospital, let alone working as a Navy surgeon. The memory of the Lucinian surgeon was vivid for Mac because as he opened his eyes again, stretching them wide, he saw the same surgeon standing before him.

"Hello, Major Lambert. I am Dr. Nhamjee. How are you feeling?" the Lucinian asked. It spoke with a snake like hissing tone. As with all Lucinians, Mac couldn't tell if the pale yellow humanoid was a male or female. He also couldn't tell how old the creature was. He had limited exposure to the Lucinians, but since they were a partner in the Galactic Coalition, he was familiar enough with them as a species. They were known as a peaceful people, gifted in science and engineering.

Lucinians have six dark eyes above a thin mouth with jaws structured to open horizontally, rather than the way human jaws open vertically. Being so close to a Lucinian was a little disconcerting for Mac, especially with all the medications on board. The surgeon wore a white medical coat, buttoned high around its thin neck. The pale yellow skin of the creature was hairless and wrinkle-free. Its skin looked thick and smooth. Its other worldly face somehow presented a friendly and inquisitive expression.

Mac tried to speak, but ended up coughing. He cleared his throat and managed to get out, "Well, Doc, I'm pretty groggy and my arm hurts."

Dr. Nhamjee stepped closer, moving as if floating above the surface. It raised Mac's bed to an incline position.

He watched in amazement while two of the Lucinian's black eyes looked at the vital signs on the screen beside the bed, and two other eyes looked at his arm, and the third pair of eyes looked at him. Each pair of eyes seemed to move and transmit information to the brain independently. Mac closed his two eyes. He was feeling a little queasy all the sudden. It was a lot for him to absorb in his post-surgery state.

The Lucinian reached out and touched Mac's injured arm with its spidery eight-fingered hands. Mac opened his eyes again and watched as the long wispy fingers moved across the silver surface of his arm. "Can you feel that?" Dr. Nhamjee asked.

His new arm, it seemed. Mac realized now that he'd lost his arm, and they had replaced it with a mechanical prosthetic. A million thoughts wanted to barge their way into the front position of his mind, but the drugs just kept him numb.

"Major Lambert, can you feel me touching your arm?" The doctor asked again.

"Yes, I can."

"Major, I need to explain what we found and how we helped you. There are two important situations you are dealing with. First, I am sorry to report, I could not save your arm. I tried, but the damage was too extensive. It was medically necessary for me to amputate your arm below the shoulder. But the good news is I did fit you with this permanent prosthetic."

Mac looked at the arm again and watched the Lucinian's spidery fingers moving along his arm. It looked metallic. It looked robotic. There were no exposed struts or gears, but it looked sort of like a normal human arm and hand with silver metallic skin. It surprised him that he could feel the doctor touching this new arm.

"The second issue is less obvious. It seems the animal that bit you also gave you a raging bacterial infection. I've given you antibiotics, and you'll continue them for some time, as well as receiving daily treatment in the bio-chamber."

Mac nodded. As he thought about it—and he had to really concentrate—he realized he felt numb about losing the arm and being fitted with a new robotic replacement. Maybe it was the drugs. Or maybe he just didn't care anymore. The infection didn't matter to him, either.

"You will be physically weak for a while and may experience other discomfort until we can fully rid your system of the bacteria. It will be a slow recovery, but I am confident you will recover fully," Dr. Nhamjee hissed.

The doctor waited for Mac to reply, but he remained silent.

"Can you wiggle your fingers?"

He tried and, surprisingly, could wiggle the new silver fingers.

"How about making a fist?"

He could also make a fist.

"Fantastic. That is enough for now. The arm looks like it is communicating well. Take it slow. You may have some strange feedback and confused neurotransmissions for several days as well. But I'm confident that soon you won't know the difference."

"Except for the fact it looks like a robot arm," he said sarcastically. *Maybe I'm not as emotionally numb as I thought.*

"Well, yes, of course, that is true," Dr. Nhamjee said solemnly.

"Is this silver metal the only option these days, Doc?"

"No, Major, there are many options that look indistinguishable from your body. But, unfortunately for you, this is the best model paid for by the Navy, and is what they instructed me to use."

"Of course," Mac said and turned away from the six black eyes toward the ceiling.

"I will check on you later today. Just rest. The nurses will take good care of you. I expect only a couple of weeks here in the hospital for you, with some rehabilitation and training, and then we'll release you. Your arm will bond quickly, but the infection will extend your stay. You'll be back in action before you know it."

If only that were true. He kept that thought to himself. "Thank you, Dr. Nhamjee."

"You are welcome," Dr. Nhamjee said and left the room.

The dull pain was manageable, but he felt weak. He tried to flex his muscles, and he didn't feel right at all. His brief conversation with the doctor had exhausted him, and after a few minutes, he slipped back to sleep.

He was awakened sometime later, with the stern face of Colonel

Miller standing at the foot of the bed. Miller was calling his name. Mac tried to sit up a little. He rubbed his eyes and then tried to raise his non-robotic right hand to salute. "Sir," he mumbled. He dropped his exhausted arm.

Miller looked like he always did, standing tall, buttoned up, and rigid in his dress uniform. Prime Ambassador Kumar accompanied him, looking short and angry. He wore a tan professional suit with no collar, buttoned in the back, leaving the front smooth and seamless. He saw the usual entourage in the hallway, outside his room.

"At ease, Major," Colonel Miller barked from the foot of the bed.

Both men were angry. They stood for a moment, saying nothing. Mac wondered if they were trying to make him as uncomfortable as possible. He wanted, needed really, to talk to Miller. Kumar's presence, however, complicated things. He'd have to be careful with what he said.

"Major Lambert, you have not only disappointed me greatly, but you have committed several galactic crimes," Colonel Miller said.

Kumar jumped in, moving closer to the bed. His voice was high and squeaky with anger. He jabbed his small, manicured finger toward Mac. "And not only did you attack a diplomat and torture my personal assistant, but you have also managed to ruin our hard-fought diplomatic efforts. It will take years to repair the damage you've done. You have disgraced the United Planetary Government."

Staring at Kumar with a deadpan expression, Mac replied with as much insubordination as he could muster, "I found and saved Princess Omo-Binrin, though."

Kumar, flustered, threw up his hands and left the room. Mac watched through the window of his room as Kumar and his guards disappeared into the hospital.

Miller stepped closer. "Yes, Major, we are glad to have the princess back, but her rescue is no excuse for you to go AWOL and become a vigilante. This was unacceptable behavior. I expected more from you." Miller was still Miller, but there was a hint of care in his voice.

Mac remained silent. He knew Miller was right. Mac had no excusable justification for his actions.

Miller waited a moment, then continued, "You will remain in custody and under guard until you are strong enough for your court-martial. We're keeping you sequestered. No visitors. No outside contact."

That one hurt, but he kept quiet. What Mac needed most was to see his team and to know they were all OK. He bottled up the disappointment and asked, "What about Sanchez and Taylor?"

Miller added, "They face the same fate. They are not injured or fighting an infection like you, so they will face court-martial this week."

That one hurt as well. They had willingly joined him, but it still hurt knowing they would lose their job and possibly end up in prison for his bad choices.

Since Kumar was gone, Mac jumped into the actual issue. "Colonel, what about the mustached man who escaped?"

"The team has briefed me. We don't know who that man is or where he has gone."

"But, sir, we must interrogate the other guy and find out. There is a mole or a conspirator within our ranks. What about the Noct?"

"At this point, Major, none of this is your concern. You removed yourself from the investigation by your choices. All you can do now is get healthy and focus on your trial. We will handle the investigation."

"But sir," he said, but questioning if he could trust Miller. Mac's hands were tied. He didn't know who he could trust. He wanted to tell Miller of his concerns about Sperry and especially Kumar, but kept it to himself.

Miller put his hands up. "We will investigate this further, but you are out. You chose this path, now you must live with the consequences. I will see you at the court-martial."

"Roger that, Colonel."

Mac laid his head against the pillow and stared up at the ceiling as Colonel Miller left the room. A guard remained outside the door of his room, but he was more alone than he'd ever been.

IN THE SAME HOSPITAL, several floors above where Mac lay sleeping, the tenth-floor elevator door opened and Arthur Rust stepped out. He wore a set of light blue scrubs, just like the other surgeons at the hospital. A small blue cap contained his wavy salt and pepper hair, and he wore a surgical mask over his face, hiding his handlebar mustache. He also wore gloves to avoid leaving fingerprints anywhere.

He turned to the right and strode purposefully down the hall like he was supposed to be there. Pleased he didn't see many people on this floor, he made a turn down a corridor with a series of private rooms.

A guard stood against the wall at the door Rust was looking for. The guard was young and wore the standard gray Interplanetary Army basic uniform. A rifle was slung over his left shoulder, with a pistol in a belt holster.

As he approached, the guard gave him a cursory examination, but the surgeon's disguise fooled him."Good afternoon," Rust said in a friendly tone. "Just a quick check on our patient."

The soldier grunted and waved him in.

Rust opened the door, walked in, and closed the door behind him. Lying in the hospital bed was Rick Vega. He was shirtless, with a large gauze wrap covering his chest and shoulder. Vega didn't react when Rust came into the room. He just laid there with his eyes closed. His wrists were handcuffed to the bed rail.

Rust came close and squeezed his arm. After a second, Vega opened his eyes. Then, after a moment, he recognized his guest, and his eyes widened.

"Arthur. Ah, what are you doing here?" he murmured. "How'd you get in here?"

"Listen, Rick," Rust said through his mask. "I'm sorry it had to be this way."

"What? What do you mean?"

Rust pressed the tip of a small handheld injection gun, with a glass vial attached, against Vega's neck and pressed the trigger. It clicked, and the glass vial's yellow liquid flowed into his bloodstream. Rust then covered Vega's mouth as he squirmed in fear. It only took a moment, however, and Rick Vega was dead.

Rust looked at Vega's dead body with disappointment. Vega was a good soldier, but he knew the stakes. Ending his brief memorial for his former sidekick, he tossed the injector into the garbage.

Rust opened the door and poked his head out. "Excuse me," he said to the soldier. "Can you help me for a second?"

The guard considered this for a moment and looked up and down the hall. "I'm not supposed to move."

"Sure, I understand that. But you'll be closer to this criminal. Just really quick."

The soldier shrugged, and came through the door. Rust held it open just enough so he could walk into the room, then closed it behind him. Rust moved with blinding speed, catching the apathetic soldier unprepared. He wrapped his muscular arms around his head and neck from behind and snapped his spine with a violent jerk. The soldier fell, but Rust caught his dead body. He dragged him over to the chair beside the bed and dropped his body into it.

Rust quickly left the room, closing the door again, and headed back to the elevator. As he passed the nurse's station and stepped into the empty elevator, he heard one nurse say, "Hey, room 10-20 is flat lined. Didn't you see that?"

As the elevator door was closing, he heard several other urgent voices and saw people rushing toward Vega's room.

Rust pulled the communicator from the pocket of his scrubs and typed out a small message.

My job is done. Do you need assistance?

He waited for the response.

No help needed. Finishing the job now.

ALDO SPERRY SAT up in his bed, still feeling sore, but the best he'd felt since the incident with the Trek'et ambassador. He sipped warm tea from a hospital cup and read the news on a handheld tablet screen.

He was surprised when the door opened and it wasn't his nurse checking on him, but his boss, Prime Ambassador Kumar, who entered alone. Kumar closed the door behind him and came close, wearing his stylish tan executive suit. He was smiling.

"Prime Ambassador. I am surprised to see you, but I'm glad you are here. I wanted to talk to you about—"

Kumar pressed his finger to his lips and shushed him.

"Sir, I…ah, what is that?"

Kumar pulled an injector gun from his suit pocket. The vial on the end contained yellow liquid.

"Aldo, I am very disappointed with your sloppiness," Kumar said. The smile was gone. The friendly demeanor morphed into an evil look Sperry had only seen a couple of times before. His voice was scratchy and sounded angry. "This will keep you quiet."

Kumar pressed the injector to Sperry's neck and pumped the chemicals into his veins, watching with satisfaction as the life drained from his body.

Kumar put the injector back in his pocket, planning to dispose of it later, and closed Sperry's open, lifeless eyes. He laid the tablet on his chest, making it look like he was napping. He then left the room.

As he closed the door and began walking down the hall, the two elite guards followed.

"Well, that was fast, sir," one guard said.

Kumar shrugged. "He was napping. I didn't want to wake him. He needs his rest."

Kumar pulled the communicator from the pocket of his suit and typed out a quick message.

Done.

The End…*for now*

Mac, Sanchez, and the team return soon in
Space Warfare Group Book 2: Shrouded in Darkness

Get it now at www.charleshack.com
or Amazon

And, if you enjoyed this book, would you please leave a star rating or review on Amazon and Goodreads?
Reviews help authors immensely!

Thank you,
Charles Hack

GLOSSARY

AFTS: Armored Fighting Tactical Suits
ALTrans: Auto Language Translator device
ASAF: Army Stryker Assault Force (Army special forces group)
Battlecruiser McDaniels: UPG Interplanetary Navy flagship
Coorlicht: Galactic Coalition planet of the peaceful Fraeklyns
CWGTOS: Cross Worlds Galactic Trade Organization Standards.
D-BICS: Galactic Coalition digital broadcast identifiers and credentials
E-Gear: Tactical environmental space suits
Elite Guard: UPG presidential and executive protection service
EP-17: Energy pulse rifle used by the Space Warfare Group
Epsilon District: A region of space within the Galactic Coalition
Exfil: Exfiltration
Fish Heads: Nickname for the Kraize
Fraeklyns: Peaceful Galactic Coalition alien race
Frag: Fragmentation grenade
FTL: Faster than light speed
Gaext: Alien race within the Galactic Coalition
Galactic Coalition: Coalition of over 40 alien species in partnership with UPG
Galactic Common: The official language of the Galactic Coalition

GC Neutral: Galactic Coalition common language
Honzoilian: Alien race within the Galactic Coalition
IA: UPG Interplanetary Army
IN: UPG Interplanetary Navy
INDAS: UPG Interplanetary Navy Department of Alien Science
Kraize: Alien race at war with the UPG
MCSAS: Marine Corps Special Action Squad
MedBay: Medical facility onboard the Battlecruiser McDaniels
Mikes: Minutes
MIL-SIG: IA Military Science and Investigation Group
M2-V: Space Warfare Group standard projectile pistol
ODVs: Overhead display and vision enhancement visors
Okutans: New Galactic Coalition member species
OPTEMPO: Operational Tempo, or tempo and frequency of operations
PTV: Personal Transportation Vehicles (inexpensive government issued vehicles)
QRF: Quick reaction force
RAP: Continuous fire energy pulse submachine gun
Regulated Zone: Galactic Coalition boarder region
SAP: Surface Access Pod
SCOUT: Surveillance Communication Observation Utility Tracking android service dog.
Sigma District: A region of space within the Galactic Coalition
SMART Ship: Space Maintenance, Recovery, and Transport Ship
SSRs: Single Soldier Rations
Starhawk: Military assault spacecraft used exclusively by the SWG
Strykers: Army Stryker Assault Force (ASAF)
SWG: Space Warfare Group
Terra Divinus: UPG colonial planet
Terra Fortuna: UPG colonial planet
Terra Honoris: UPG colonial planet
Terra Libertas: UPG colonial planet and location of UPG capital
Terra Magna: UPG colonial planet
Terra Placidus: UPG colonial planet

Terra Vita: UPG colonial planet
Theta District: A region of space within the Galactic Coalition
Tertollony: Alien race within the Galactic Coalition
Trek'et: Alien race within the Galactic Coalition
Triple-I (III): UPG Department of Interplanetary Intelligence and Investigation
UPG: United Planetary Government consisting of ten developed planets
X560 Dragon: Heavy energy weapon with backpack power module
#.# EG: Gravity levels compared to Earth

ABOUT THE AUTHOR

Charles Hack is the author of the *Space Warfare Group* space thriller novels. After writing for over twenty years, his first published novel is *Into the Darkness*. He studied electrical engineering in college and is still a licensed professional engineer with over twenty years of experience before retiring and entering full time Christian ministry. He currently serves as a pastor in his hometown and has a master's degree in systematic theology. Writing is one of his passions along with reading, woodworking, and coffee. Charles is married with two children and three noisy dogs. They live on a small ranch, known as the *Ranchini,* in the Great Basin of Northern Nevada.

Check out my website:

www.charleshack.com

Follow me on social media:

facebook.com/CharlesHackBooks

instagram.com/charleshackbooks

x.com/charles__hack

GET A FREE SWG BOOK

If you like free books, I invite you to join my email list to gain access to my free short story series called **Mission Brief**. When you sign up, you will be directed to a page for the 3-part box set of the **Mission Brief** short stories. The eBook version is ONLY available to email subscribers. And it's Free! So, go sign up!

You can join on my website: www. charleshack.com.

CHARLES HACK

NIGHT TERROR

A SPACE WARFARE GROUP NOVELLA: BOOK 0.5

CHARLES HACK

SHROUDED IN DARKNESS

SPACE WARFARE GROUP BOOK 2

Made in the USA
Las Vegas, NV
26 November 2024